DOZENS BURNED NATIONWIDE–CAUSE UNKNOWN

One Doctor Calls It "a New Black Death"

Beneath the headline was a photo: a dark, twisted shape like those in the photos Hadrian Farr had shown him. He sucked in a breath between his teeth, then scanned down the article.

Researchers have yet to discover the cause for the self-immolations that have been reported throughout the Midwest in the last six weeks. Some have labeled it a wave of copycat suicides, but in none of the deaths has a fuel or other flammable agent been identified. According to witnesses, many victims have shown symptoms of unusual behavior and high fever shortly before—

The article broke off, continued on an inside page. Travis dug into the pocket of his jeans, but his hand came up with only a scant collection of pennies. Not that it mattered. He didn't need to read any more; he knew now where he had to go.

Maybe this really was like the Black Death. Maybe it was a disease—a disease transmitted by touch.

THE KEEP
OF
FIRE

BOOK TWO OF
THE LAST RUNE

MARK ANTHONY

BANTAM BOOKS
NEW YORK TORONTO LONDON SYDNEY AUCKLAND

This edition contains the complete text of the original
trade paper edition.
NOT ONE WORD HAS BEEN OMITTED.

THE KEEP OF FIRE
A Bantam Spectra Book

PUBLISHING HISTORY
Bantam Spectra trade paper edition published
December 1999
Bantam Spectra paperback edition / December 2000

SPECTRA and the portrayal of a boxed "s" are trademarks of
Bantam Books, a division of Random House, Inc.

ISBN 0-553-57932-0

Published simultaneously in the United States and Canada

Bantam Books are published by Bantam Books, a division of
Random House, Inc. Its trademark, consisting of the words
"Bantam Books" and the portrayal of a rooster, is Registered
in U.S. Patent and Trademark Office and in other countries.
Marca Registrada. Bantam Books, 1540 Broadway, New York,
New York 10036.

PRINTED IN THE UNITED STATES OF AMERICA

OPM   10 9 8 7 6 5 4 3 2 1

For Bert Covert—
who has been a Companion on
many wondrous quests

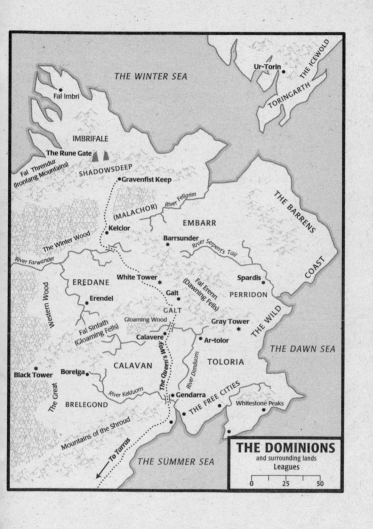

THE WINTER SEA

Ur-Torin

THE ICEWOLD

TORINGARTH

Fal Imbri

IMBRIFALE

The Rune Gate

Fal Threndur
(Ironfang Mountains)

SHADOWSDEEP

Gravenfist Keep

River Fellgrim

(MALACHOR)

Kelcior

EMBARR

THE BARRENS

Barrsunder

River Serpent's Tail

The Winter Wood

River Farwander

Spardis

White Tower

EREDANE

Erendel

Galt

Fal Erenn
(Dawning Fells)

PERRIDON

GALT

THE WILD COAST

Western Wood

Fal Sinfath
(Gloaming Fells)

Gloaming Wood

Gray Tower

THE DAWN SEA

Calavere

Ar-tolor

Black Tower

Borelga

CALAVAN

TOLORIA

The Queen's Way

River Dimduorn

River Keldurn

Gendarra

The Great

BRELEGOND

THE FREE CITIES

Whitestone Peaks

Mountains of the Shroud

To Tarras

THE SUMMER SEA

THE DOMINIONS
and surrounding lands
Leagues

0   25   50

"Beware—it will consume you."

PART ONE

CASTLE CITY

1.

The burnt wind blew out of nowhere, scorching the mountains to their bones.

Dry weeds rattled in the ditches along the empty two-lane highway, all life baked out of them before they could really begin to grow. April had sublimated under the indifferent sun, May along with it, and in June the high-country valley was as brown as in the waning of September. Summer had smothered spring in her crib; the green child would not come again that year.

A man stepped out of the haze of grit and heat, like a dark flake of ash from the rippling air above a fire. The dust devil tugged once at the black shreds of cloth that draped the man's wasted body, then danced away behind him. He staggered forward.

"Where are you, Jakabar?"

The words were the croak of a vulture, and his blistered lips bled as he spoke them. He lifted his head and peered at the wavering horizon with obsidian eyes—orbs without irises, without whites. He lifted a withered hand to shade the craggy desert of his face.

Something stirred in the coruscating air ahead. "Jakabar?"

The shape gathered its outlines behind the distant silver membrane that spanned the road, then punched through and hurtled toward the man.

The beast approached with hateful speed, growing larger with each fluttering of his heart, until it filled his vision and a roar deafened him. Sunlight glared off armored crimson hide, and the thing clung low to the ground, as if ready to pounce. Its eyes flashed twice, and it let out a keening wail that pierced his skull and rooted him in place. He abandoned motion, waiting to feel the beast's jaws close around him, to feel bones pop and flesh part.

Acrid wind ripped at him, and stones pelted his skin. The hollow grasses bent down, slaves before a terrible emperor, then rose as the world fell still. The man craned his neck to look behind him, but the creature already grew small and distant as it sped away.

He turned his gaze forward and forgot the beast. Again the fever rose within him, cauterizing thought and memory, burning away everything he was. He could envision the flames dancing along his papery skin. Soon. After all this time, it would be soon now.

He started to move once more but met resistance from the ground. He strained, then lifted a foot. Black strings of tar stretched from the sole of his scuffed boot to the pit where it had sunk into the surface of the road. He tugged his other boot free and lurched forward. He did not know what strange land he had found himself in. All he knew was that he had to find Jakabar.

"Beware," he whispered. "It will consume you."

The man staggered down the mountain highway, leaving a trail of footsteps melted into the asphalt behind him.

2.

Now that he was back, it was almost as if he had never left.

"It's coming," Travis Wilder whispered as he stepped out the door of the Mine Shaft Saloon.

He leaned over the boardwalk railing and turned his face westward, up Elk Street, toward the pyramid of rock that stood sentinel above the little mountain town.

Castle Peak. Or what he thought of as Castle Peak, for over the years the mountain had borne many names. In the 1880s, the silver miners had called it Ladyspur's Peak, in honor of a favorite whore. According to local legend, when a gunslinger out of Cripple Creek failed to pay his bill, Ladyspur shot him dead in a fair gunfight in the middle of Elk Street. She died herself from cholera not long after, and she was buried how she had lived and worked: with spurs on her high-heeled boots.

Before that, on maps drawn in St. Louis—fanciful documents meant to lure dreamers across the tall-grassed prairies—it was named Argo Mountain, although the only gold ever found on Castle Peak was the warm light of sunrise or sunset.

For a few years prior to the gold rush of 1859, the name Mount Jeffrey had hung over the mountain, a name it had shared with a minor member of the Long Expedition of 1820—a lieutenant who one afternoon climbed to the summit with a bottle of whiskey. By the time Lieutenant Schuyler P. Jeffrey died of septicemia in a Washington, D.C., tenement five years later, his name had tumbled off the mountain. Although the empty whiskey bottle he had cast down was still there.

The Ute Indians, who from forested ridges had watched Long's party stroll through the valley, had had their own name for the mountain: Clouded Brow, for the wreath of mist that often girded the summit. However, if the people who dwelled here before the Utes had called the crag anything, then it had passed with them. And before that . . . no names.

One mountain. Many names. But eventually the peak and the town had both come to wear the name of Mr. Simon Castle—who made his fortune in publishing back East and who came west with a dream of constructing a grand new kingdom. He built the Silver Palace Hotel and the Castle City Opera House, then returned to Philadelphia eight years later, after his wife perished of tuberculosis and his sandstone mansion outside of town was struck by lightning and burned to the ground.

Castle Peak. The name fit for now, at least until a new name came along. And after that, when once again there were no people here and the valley dreamed alone, then it would be simply the mountain once more.

Travis gripped the railing. Behind wire-rimmed spectacles he pressed pale eyes shut as he pictured it: high up the slope the first aspens quickening, leaves whispering silver-green secrets, then moments later the low thrumming as the canyon cleared its throat and the lodgepole pines circled in a graceful tarantella. It was coming.

On any world, Travis could always tell when the wind was about to blow.

"I knew you'd come back," Max said that white January day when Travis stepped into the Mine Shaft, still clad in the travel-worn clothes of another world.

It had been morning, and the saloon had been quiet and empty save for the two men.

"I knew it, Travis, even though . . . even though

Jace said you died with Jack in the fire. I kept everything going for you—the bar, the mortgage, the books. . . ."

Max's words got lost somewhere in his chest then, but that was all right.

"It looks wonderful, Max," Travis said as he hugged his friend. "It all looks wonderful."

And that was how Travis had come home.

The days that followed were strange and fragile. In some ways he felt as out of place as he had on Eldh, traveling in the company of Falken Blackhand. Things like indoor plumbing and electric lights and pickup trucks all had an exotic sheen. But just as he had on Eldh, he knew he would get accustomed to them. All he needed was a little time.

Unlike the inquisitive bard, no one in Castle City asked Travis for his story—where he had been for more than two months and why he had come back. Then again, people in Castle City didn't usually ask a lot of questions. It didn't really matter where you had been, only that you were here.

Jacine Windom came the closest to prodding Travis for information, and even the deputy's questions, while sharp as the creases steamed into her khaki trousers, were narrowly directed.

"Were you at the Magician's Attic the night of the fire?" Jace asked one afternoon at the saloon, straight-backed on her barstool, notepad and pencil in hand.

"I was," Travis answered.

"Do you know what caused the fire?"

"Jack was struggling with an intruder. I was outside the antique shop—Jack told me to run. When I turned around, the place was in flames."

"Did you get a good look at the intruder before you fled?"

"No. No, I didn't."

It hadn't been until later that he came face-to-face with them. In the White Tower of the Runebinders he had looked into alien eyes and seen death. But he didn't tell Jace that.

Travis waited for more questions, but Jace flipped her notepad shut and stood up from the barstool.

"I think that's enough, Travis. I'll call you if Sheriff Dominguez needs anything else." The deputy started for the door.

"Did you find him?" Travis looked up and met Jace's brown eyes. "Did you find Jack?"

The deputy pressed her lips shut at that, then gave one stiff nod. "There's a stone for him in Castle Heights Cemetery."

"I'll go see it, Jace. Thanks."

The deputy headed for the door, although not before glancing back at Max. The look the two of them exchanged told Travis he had been right about one thing: Jacine had roped her stallion. Max was wearing Wranglers now.

But maybe it wasn't such a bad thing to remake yourself for another. Sometimes Travis thought he might like to have the chance, although he could never really picture what he'd become, or for whom he'd change. Or did it even matter? Maybe it was just the act of changing itself that was important.

After his conversation with Jace, the days had started to come easier. Travis's cabin outside of town had been rented to someone else, so Travis had taken up residence in the empty space above the Mine Shaft. The old apartment was narrow and drafty, and the kitchen consisted of a hot plate and a sink, but it would do for now. Travis needed less than he used to; he had gotten used to traveling light.

Max had parked Travis's battered green pickup truck behind the saloon, and one day Travis got brave enough to try to start it. He turned the key in the ignition, then laughed as the engine roared to life.

Since then he had lost himself in the day-to-day affairs of the Mine Shaft. Moira Larson's book club met at the saloon every week—stuffy novels of class oppression traded for the sharp and vital wit of Evelyn Waugh. The dude ranch cowboys had progressed from single malt scotch to martinis. And Molly Nakamura still patiently taught saloon patrons to fold crisp sheets into origami chameleons and monkeys, and still always stroked with gentle fingers their mutant paper creations.

All in all, it was good and easy to sink back into his old life. And yet . . .

From time to time, as he wiped down the bar, or swept the floor, or gathered up empty beer glasses, Travis would find himself gazing out the window, toward the rocky slopes of Castle Peak, and thinking of the wind that blew down from the mountain. Thinking of traveling.

That journey is over, Travis. You're here now, where you belong.

He opened his eyes and drew in a breath. Electric wires hissed overhead. Litter danced along the cracked surface of Elk Street, choreographed into glittering auguries. Yes, it was coming.

He turned his face to meet the approaching wind, ready to feel its crisp embrace, to sense the possibilities it bore on its wings. The witchgrass along the boardwalk trembled. Newsprint manta rays levitated off the ground. Tourists reached up to clutch brightly logoed hats—

—then lowered their hands and continued on.

A single hot gust lurched down Elk Street, then died in a limp puff. The wires ceased their music. The witchgrass fell still. The newspaper rays settled back to the pavement.

Sweat trickled down Travis's brow, and the parched air drank it, leaving a crust of salt on his skin. There was no fresh awakening, no sense of endless possibility. Only the sun baking cement and wood and dirt until everything smelled like old, dry bones.

He didn't remember it ever being this hot. The sky was too hard, the valley too dull.

Travis reached up and fingered the piece of polished bone that hung from a leather string around his neck. The bone's surface was incised with three parallel lines. He traced them with a thumb. Yes, it was almost like he had never left. Except he *had* left. And nothing would ever really be the same.

Travis sighed, let go of the talisman, and walked back into the saloon.

3.

The cool air inside the Mine Shaft was a balm to Travis's skin. He stepped behind the bar, reached into the chiller, and brought out a bottle of root beer. He pressed it against his cheek, wincing at the frigid touch, then let out a breath and shut his eyes.

"You know, Travis, most people find it easier to drink if they take the cap off the bottle first."

"People can be so boring sometimes."

There was a snort of laughter. Travis opened his eyes to see Max lift a rack of glasses onto the bar.

"You're weird, Travis."

"That's a relief. For a minute I thought I might be losing my touch."

Max rolled his eyes and started unloading glasses.

Travis crossed his arms, leaned back, and watched his employee work. Max had done a good job keeping the saloon humming while Travis had been away. Better than good. And while Max clearly took pride in this fact, he had not hesitated in returning control of the operation back to Travis that wintry day in January.

Travis had been glad to take on the mantle of saloon proprietor again. Like everything about his old life, it felt warm and comfortable. And, like everything, it seemed different since his return. For more than two months the saloon had belonged to Max, no matter what the mortgage papers said.

Travis reached into a drawer, pulled out a folded piece of paper, set it on the bar, and pushed it over the knife-scarred wood toward Max.

Max stared at the paper, then looked up. "What's this?"

"See for yourself."

The erstwhile accountant picked up the paper, a frown written across his face. "You haven't been doing the saloon's books again, have you, Travis? I finally just managed to get them in decent . . ." He clamped his jaw and shot Travis a hangdog look.

Travis laughed. "No, Max. I haven't been doing the books. I haven't even found where you've hidden the ledger yet. Besides, that's your job in this partnership."

Max blinked. "Partnership?"

"Not if you don't sign that deed." Travis held out a pen. "Go on."

Max hesitated, then accepted the pen. He unfolded the deed like it was an old treasure map, then set the paper on the bar and in a deliberate hand committed his name to the bottom, alongside Travis's. He folded the deed and held it out.

"Thank you."

Travis took the paper and slipped it into the drawer, then regarded Max with a solemn expression. "You deserve it, Max. The Mine Shaft is yours as much as mine."

Max nodded, then a smile split his face. "So does this mean some of the phone calls to the saloon will be for *me* now?"

Travis rested a hand on his friend's shoulder. "I know you're excited, Max, but try not to be goofy."

Before Max could reply, Travis headed for the back

room, whistling a cheerful tune. Just because Max was his partner now didn't mean Travis had to stop tormenting him.

That afternoon, Travis left the Mine Shaft and headed to McKay's General Store to pick up a pair of hinges for the saloon's squeaky rear door. On his way back he stopped by the Mosquito Café—where one quick coffee turned into three leisurely cappuccinos as various locals wandered in and bought Travis a cup.

As soon as he left the air-conditioned sanctuary of the café, Travis wished he had ordered those cappuccinos on ice. The sun sank toward the rampart of Castle Peak, ruddy and bloated, as if too heavy to hang in the sky a moment more. Heat rose in sheets from Elk Street, bright and jittery as Travis's caffeine-enhanced nerves. He mopped the sweat from his forehead with a stiff handkerchief.

When Travis reached the Mine Shaft, he noticed a Harley-Davidson parked next to Max's rusting Volvo. A Celtic cross was painted on the side of the bike's jet-black gas tank, and a bunch of wind-worn feathers and carved bone beads dangled from one of the handle grips. The motorcycle seemed familiar somehow, but he couldn't place where or when he had seen it. Travis pushed through the front door into the welcome dimness of the saloon.

The place had started to fill up while he was gone. The Daughters of the Frontier had shown up for their biweekly meeting, clad in their usual red-fringed jumpsuits, their blue cotton-candy hair melting from the heat. Two of them played pool against a pair of handsome, clean-shaven young men—from Denver by their Doc Martens, casual shirts, and the astonished looks on their faces. That was what they got for challenging the Daughters of the Frontier. No one in Castle City was foolish enough to shoot stick with those sharks.

Over by the jukebox, Davis and Mitchell Burke-
Favor two-stepped to the tragic croonings of Patsy
Cline. As always, the two men were clad in matching
geometric cowboy shirts and spotless Wranglers. At
least once a week the pair drove in from their ranch
south of Castle City for a night on the town. They
moved with the brisk, effortless unison that had won
them back-to-back two-step championships in San
Francisco a dozen years ago, their wind-worn faces as
rugged and serene as the high-country plain.

Travis paused on his way to the bar, watching the
two men dance, and a sigh escaped him. He had
moved through life mostly alone. Would he ever be
that in-step with another person? He didn't know.
Sometimes he hoped so. Then again, when it came to
dancing, Travis had always had two left feet.

A yelp tore his attention away from the men. He
glanced up, then winced. Max was trying to shake up
a round of martinis for the dude ranch cowboys. One
of them frowned behind his well-groomed mustache
as a renegade pearl onion catapulted off an olive spear
and bounced around the rim of his freshly steamed
black Stetson. Travis moved to rescue Max.

Minutes later the cowboys had their drinks and
were off to their table to play dominoes.

Max slung a bar towel over his shoulder. "Thanks,
Travis. I owe you one."

"I know." Travis reached under the bar, pulled out
the martini recipe book, and handed it to Max. "And
you can start paying me back by reading—"

Travis froze as a knight, a lady, and a wildman
stepped through the door of the Mine Shaft Saloon.

"Travis?"

Max's voice seemed to come from down a long
tunnel. Travis could only watch as the trio threaded
its way among the tables.

This can't be happening. They can't be here.

The lady walked with chin high, clad despite the

heat in a confining gown of green velvet. The gown's bodice cinched her breasts up into a horizontal shelf, and the two orbs of flesh were pink from too much sun. The knight was short but powerful-looking. Sweat sheened his somber face, and Travis was certain that, if touched, the man's chain-mail shirt would be hot against his fingers. The wildman scuttled behind the knight and lady, his hunched form draped in rank furs and his hair caked with blue mud. The trio headed directly for Travis. Did they know, then?

But they can't know. They're not even supposed to be here. They should be a world away.

The three reached the bar. Travis couldn't move. The knight rested a hand on the hilt of his sword and spoke.

"I need a Coors, a glass of the house chardonnay, and . . ." The knight glanced back at the wildman. "What did you say you wanted?"

"Make it a Guinness," the wildman said.

The lady frowned. "How can you drink that stuff, Ted? It's noxious."

The wildman grinned, his teeth white and straight in his dirty face. "Don't knock it until you try it."

Travis stared, his mind flailing. Only then did he notice the mobile phone clipped to the knight's belt, the Day-Glo fanny pack around the lady's waist, and the shoes on the wildman's feet: nylon strap sandals with rubber soles.

Of course—he remembered the tents and stalls he had seen going up east of town the other day. It was June. The Medieval Festival had started up again for the year. Most nights, a group of workers from the festival would show up at the saloon near sundown to have a drink after a sweaty day of work.

Max touched his arm. "Is something wrong, Travis?"

He hadn't responded, and the knight was frowning.

"No, Max. Everything's just fine."

He moved to get the drinks, and the knight smiled and threw a twenty on the bar.

"Damn, it's hot out there," he said.

The wildman glanced at the lady's fiery breasts and grinned. "Looks like you've got a bad case of war chest, Sarah."

She adjusted her bodice and winced. "I know. Thanks to Alan forgetting the sunscreen."

"Sorry," the knight mumbled, and the three walked away with their glasses.

Travis watched them go, then noticed Max gazing at him. Max cocked his head but didn't say anything, and eventually he turned around to swab out a keg.

Travis glanced down at the buckskin boots that poked out of his jeans: the boots Lady Aryn had had made for him. They were one of his few reminders of Eldh, along with the carved piece of bone—the rune of hope—he wore around his neck, and the silver half-coin Brother Cy had given him, which had brought him back to Earth, and which he always kept in his left-hand pocket.

Travis shut his eyes and saw high battlements above stone-walled fields. Sometimes he burned to tell someone about where he had really traveled during those two months. But how could he? The only person in Castle City who could have understood was gone.

I miss you, Jack.

He opened his eyes and moved to rinse a tray of glasses in the bar sink.

On reflex, Travis looked up. It was hard to tell exactly what was being advertised. Scenes flashed by, showing smiling people engaged in various activities—boating on a lake, going for a walk, cooking dinner. No matter the scene, a bright crescent moon hung in the sky above or outside a window, casting a silvery radiance on whatever the oh-so-happy people were doing.

The commercial faded to black, and a corporate logo appeared: a crescent moon merging into a stylized capital *D*.

"Duratek," came the voice-over in a soothing, masculine tone. "Worlds of possibility, close to home."

Travis frowned. What was that supposed to mean? He pointed to the TV. "Would you shut that thing off, Max? Turn on the radio instead."

Max killed the TV with the remote, then flicked on an antique AM receiver. A second later the phone rang, and Max lunged for it before Travis could move an inch.

"The Mine Shaft," Max said. He paused, then shot Travis a smug little smile. "No, but I'm the co-owner, so I'm sure I can help you out. . . ." He turned his back and kept on talking.

Travis groaned. Now that Max was his partner, there would be no living with him.

He bent back over his work. Music drifted from the radio behind him: ancient sounds soaring above a new electronic drone. The song was all over the airwaves, a tonic for ears tired of angsty alterna-rock. Travis smiled at the seamless blend of old and new. Maybe two different centuries could meet after all. Like two different worlds.

A tingling danced across the back of his neck. On instinct he looked up.

She watched Travis with smoke-green eyes that sparkled above high cheekbones. He set down the glass in his hand, and the woman smiled from her barstool perch. She had close-cropped hair that was dark and fiery at the same time, and she wore a black-leather jacket, jeans, and biker boots. He could just make out the edge of a tattoo coiled around her collarbone—a serpent twisted into the shape of a figure eight, swallowing its tail.

"Deirdre? Deirdre Falling Hawk?"

"My gentle warrior," she said.

Then she leaned across the bar and kissed him, stunning him like a buck caught in the white-hot beam of a hunter's flashlight.

4.

Travis had met her three years ago.

It was in the dwindling days of July, when the frantic buzz of fresh-born insects had matured to a lazier drone, and clouds rolled across the blue-quartz sky every afternoon, filling the valley with thunder. She wandered through the saloon's door one evening with the sound of copper wind chimes. Her hair had been long then, like a wave of midnight water, but she wore the same leather jacket, the same square-toed biker boots, and she carried the same wooden case over her shoulder.

She said her name was Deirdre Falling Hawk, and she was a bard.

For the last month she had worked the big Medieval Festival down the highway, she explained. Now that the festival had closed down for the season, she had come to Castle City, hoping to find a little work before she moved on.

"The mountains give me songs," she said. "I always hate to leave them."

All Travis knew was that, when she played a melody on the burnished mandolin she took from her case, he had never heard anything so beautiful. He had cleared the boxes from a platform by the player piano that had once served as a vaudeville stage and on it set a chair. For the next two weeks, Deirdre

Falling Hawk sat on the tiny stage each night and played her mandolin. She was of both Irish and Native-American descent, and she blended both traditions in her simple, haunting music. After that first night, word spread, and locals packed the bar each evening to hear her play a repertoire that included thirteenth-century madrigals, Celtic ballads, and Plains Indian myths recited in her chantlike voice.

Travis never saw much of Deirdre during the days; the bard proved as fleeting as her music. But a few times she stopped her Harley as she passed him while cruising down Elk Street.

"Hop on, my gentle warrior," she would say.

My gentle warrior. That was what she always called him, after he told her the story of the antique spectacles he wore and how once they had belonged to the gunfighter Tyler Caine.

He would climb onto the back of her bike, and they would go roaring up the canyon, leaning deep into the curves. Finally, one night, they sat and talked after the saloon had closed, drinking whiskey and trading two-bit dreams. In a silent moment, Travis almost reached out a hand to stroke her hair. Almost. His hand faltered, then made a clumsy reach for his glass instead.

Afterward he was never sure why he hadn't done it, why he hadn't let his fingers tangle themselves in the softness of her hair, why he hadn't drawn her close, kissed her, and made love to her on a blanket thrown over the sawdust-strewn floor. But love was a kind of power, wasn't it? And power, as he knew well, was a dangerous thing.

The next night, after Deirdre had played her set at the saloon, he heard the roar of her motorcycle echoing down Elk Street. He never saw her again.

Until now.

Travis regarded her from across the bar. "I should have known that was your hog out there."

"Actually, it's new. I picked it up in Cody last summer." Her lips curved into a wicked smile. "I won it in a poker game against a Hell's Angel out of L.A."

Travis narrowed his eyes. "Remind me never to let you talk me into a hand of five card stud."

"Don't worry, Travis—I'd let you win. Once or twice, anyway."

He glanced at the wooden case slung over her shoulder. "Have you come to play, Deirdre?"

"Maybe. It depends on the going rate."

Travis punched a key on the saloon's antique cash register, then lifted the drawer to scrape up what was left of petty cash. He counted it out on the bar.

"How does fifty-two dollars and seventeen cents sound?"

Deirdre stood, scooped up the money, and shoved it into a pocket. "It sounds like you just booked yourself an act, Travis." She turned and sauntered to the small stage by the piano, moving with the litheness of a deer.

At the same moment Max set down the phone, although it was clear he hadn't been talking to anyone for minutes. "So, is she a good friend of yours?"

Travis poured two mugs of steaming coffee. "Not really."

"Of course," Max said. "That kiss was a dead giveaway. In New York, that's how complete strangers always greet each other."

"I didn't say she was a stranger."

Max's drooping mustache framed a toothy smile. "Make up your mind, pardner."

He considered telling Max that people in the West didn't really say *pardner* but as usual decided against it. The knowledge would devastate him. Travis carried the mugs over to Deirdre, set them on the player piano, and straddled the bench.

"It's good to see you, you know," he said.

She raised a dark eyebrow. "Is it?"

Once again Travis thought of that night, when he had wanted to touch her and hadn't. "Yes, it is. I always . . . I always wished that . . ." That what? But he wasn't really sure.

A smile twisted her lips. "I learned a long time ago not to regret my choices."

She took her mandolin out of its case and began tuning it with deft fingers. It was a sleek thing, crafted of dark wood and glowing with a patina of long use.

"So who's the lucky girl who finally got you, anyway?" Deirdre said.

He shook his head. She cast a sly glance at Mitchell and Davis Burke-Favor, who sat at a table across the saloon, heads bowed close, their square shoulders touching.

"All right, then who's the lucky guy?"

He laughed, then shook his head again. Her smile dimmed to a knowing expression.

"So you're going it alone, then?"

He shrugged. "Didn't you say not to regret your choices?"

"And is it a choice?"

Travis rubbed his right hand. He didn't know how to answer that one. Finally, he gestured to the mandolin. "You know, I had a friend who would have loved looking at this. He was an antique dealer. Jack was always telling me that the best way to understand the here and now was to look at it through the eyes of a distant time or place."

Deirdre strummed a mellow chord. "History is important to both my mother's and my father's peoples. This mandolin belonged to my mother's grandfather. He brought it with him from Ireland. Every time I play it, I think of him, and how brave he was to cross an ocean to a land he had never seen before." Her fingers plucked out a wistful melody. "Your friend Jack sounds like a wise man."

Travis was never ready for the hard lump that wedged itself in his throat. "Yes, he was. He gave me these. Remember?"

"The gunfighter's spectacles." Deirdre gave a playful smile, and her music drifted into a mournful dirge.

Travis laughed. He could still picture the day Jack had given him the spectacles. He had been rummaging through a box in the Magician's Attic, helping his old friend clean out the cellar, when he came across them—bent, tarnished, the lenses cracked. He had shown them to Jack.

So that's where those were hiding. Well, it's good that you found them, Travis. I believe they belong to you.

It was an odd thing to say, but Jack said plenty of odd things, so Travis had shrugged and accepted the spectacles.

Deirdre regarded him over her mandolin. "You know, it's interesting that those are the eyes through which you choose to look at the world."

"You think so? I guess I always thought it would be sort of fun to be the bad guy." He curled his lip into a mean snarl and gave Deirdre his best steel-eyed look. "This here's a holdup, ma'am."

"Fearsome," she said, green eyes dancing. "But I'm serious, Travis. Why a gunfighter's glasses? Why not a sheriff's, or a ranger's?"

Travis scratched the red-gold stubble on his chin. "I don't know. I suppose I'm just not really the hero type."

"Oh?"

"It's true. Even when I was a kid, I never identified with the heroes in fairy tales. I always secretly wanted the monsters to eat them." He smiled his nastiest smile. "Now the troll under the bridge—*that* was me."

Deirdre gave him a sharp look. "That sounds like your shadow self talking."

"My shadow self?"

"Your dark side, your doppelgänger, your manitou—whatever you want to call it." She picked up her coffee mug and warmed her hands around it. "Maybe, deep down, there's a part of you that knows you really could be a gunslinger."

Travis looked down at his hands. He couldn't see it, but he could feel it all the same—Jack's mark, the rune of runes—prickling beneath the skin of his palm. "No, I could never do what they did."

"Be careful, Travis. The human spirit is a great, deep ocean. Each of us has the ability to do things we don't care to think about. And that's fine. But if you try to deny that that ability exists, it can have a way of making itself manifest without your consent."

"I don't understand."

"Then put it this way. A hundred years ago, there wasn't much difference between the sheriff and the gunslinger. Each made his living with a revolver. The only difference was that one used a gun, while a gun used the other."

Travis stared. Deirdre couldn't possibly understand what it was like—how it felt to have power flow through you, and out of you, destroying another.

"I'm sorry, Travis. I didn't mean to lecture you. Besides, our shadow selves aren't always bad. Sometimes monsters can be heroes, too. Look at *Beauty and the Beast.*"

He lifted his head and gave her a crooked smile. "Don't go trying to spoil my fun."

· She took a sip of coffee, but the mug couldn't quite hide her grin.

Travis stood. "I should get back to my customers."

Deirdre tilted her head. "*Your* customers? You mean you own the saloon now?"

"Ever since Andy Connell died a few years ago."

"Well, then I had better try to drum up some business for you." Deirdre picked up her mandolin and brushed the strings. "Thanks for the gig, Travis. You're a good monster."

He laughed aloud. "Oh, I wouldn't go that far."

Her only response was an enigmatic smile that haunted him all the way back to the bar.

5.

Word must have spread that Deirdre Falling Hawk was back at the Mine Shaft, for by sundown the saloon was jammed with people who had come from all over the valley to listen to her music. Travis watched Deirdre from behind the bar. He thought of another bard he had known, in a place far from here, and he smiled at the memories, although it was a sad expression as well. Not a day went by that he didn't think of Falken, Melia, Grace, and all the people he had known on Eldh.

Except that wasn't true, was it? Because lately there had been days when, distracted by the business of the saloon, he didn't think of Eldh at all. Would he forget it altogether someday? Or convince himself that it had all been the anguished hallucinations of a man who had lost his best friend—the compelling and realistic but entirely deranged construction of one who had wandered for two months in a haze of grief, trying to make some sort of sense of what never made any sense?

The warm sounds of Deirdre's mandolin ended in a surge of applause. Travis gazed at the cluttered saloon and shook his head. It wasn't that you couldn't come home again. It was just that home was never quite the same as when you left it. How could Dorothy have ever stood the stark black-and-white drabness of Kansas again after dancing down the Technicolor roads of Oz? Except he did love his home, drabness and all.

He smiled again, and this time there was genuine mirth to it. Max stepped out of the back room, overloaded with two racks of beer glasses. Travis took one of the racks. As he did, the strumming of the mandolin rose again on the air along with, a moment later, the wine-rich sound of Deirdre's voice:

> We live our lives a circle,
> And wander where we can.
> Then after fire and wonder,
> We end where we began.
>
> I have traveled southward,
> And in the south I wept.
> Then I journeyed northward,
> And laughter there I kept.
>
> Then for a time I lingered,
> In eastern lands of light,
> Until I moved on westward,
> Alone in shadowed night.
>
> I was born of springtime,
> In summer I grew strong.
> But autumn dimmed my eyes,
> To sleep the winter long.
>
> We live our lives a circle,
> And wander where we can.
> Then after fire and wonder,
> We end where we began.

Travis dropped the rack of glasses on the bar; several broke. The applause of the crowd was cut short as people turned around to look for the source of the noise. Travis stared, a gauze of paralysis woven around him by the music.

How could she know that song?

Across the saloon, a shadow touched Deirdre's forehead. She had noticed him. The bard stood, unslung her mandolin, then threaded her way through the chairs and tables. The sound of conversation welled forth, and someone put a quarter in the jukebox. A woman asked Travis for a beer, but he couldn't connect his thoughts with his hands. Fortunately, Max was there, and he didn't seem to see Travis's stunned expression as he moved in to help the customer.

Deirdre reached the bar.

"Where did you learn that?" he said in a hoarse voice.

She regarded him with almond eyes. "What's wrong, Travis?"

He gripped the edge of the bar. "That song. Where did you learn it?"

"It was a couple of years ago. I learned it from a bard."

The floor turned to liquid beneath Travis. Falken? Did she know Falken Blackhand? But that was impossible.

Impossible like traveling to other worlds? Impossible like magic?

He licked his lips. "A bard?"

"That's right. I met him at the big Renaissance Festival up in Minnesota last year. We were . . . that is, I . . ." Color touched her cheekbones like Indian paintbrush.

Travis winced. She didn't know Falken. She had learned the song from an ex-boyfriend, and Travis had embarrassed her by making her talk about it. How the ex-boyfriend had learned the song, who could say? But the connection between Eldh and Earth had worked in two directions. Why couldn't a song have crossed as easily as a person? And once on Earth, there was nothing to stop it from being traded among singers.

Deirdre's fingers crept across the bar to touch his. "Travis, something's wrong. Will you tell me what it is?"

He opened his mouth, knowing he had to tell her something, but unsure what he was going to say.

Whatever it was, the words were cut short as the saloon's door banged open. He jerked his head up, along with a dozen of the saloon's patrons.

At first Travis thought the man was from the Medieval Festival, like the three who had come in earlier. He was clad in a heavy black robe, as if posing as some sort of monk. Except the garment was dusty and tattered, and the more Travis looked at it, the less it looked like the robe of a monk and the more it looked the robe of a judge. Or an executioner.

The man in black lurched into the crowded saloon, and now Travis wasn't certain he was from the Medieval Festival after all. His hands were curled into claws, and his face was scarred and pitted like the wind-scoured surface of a stone. His blistered lips moved in fretful rhythm, as if he chanted something to himself. He stumbled against a table. People leaped to their feet and scrambled back. Max was already moving to intercept him. Travis hurried after.

The man reached a hand toward a passing woman. He rasped several words—they might have been, *Where is he?*—then the woman let out a stifled scream and twisted away.

Travis swore. He considered calling Deputy Windom, but now he was closer to the man than he was to the phone. Half the people in the saloon had stopped their conversations to turn and gape. Travis swiped at his damp forehead—it was stifling in here.

Max had reached the stranger now, and he held out a hand to steady the other. The man in the black robe hissed, recoiling like a serpent before Max could touch him.

Max drew his hand back. "I'm sorry, I—"

"Where is he?" The man's voice was tinged with a metallic accent. "Where is Jakabar?"

Max frowned beneath his mustache. "Who?"

"I must find Jakabar." The stranger's hands fluttered to his robe like wounded birds, scrabbled against the cloth, tore it. "Where is Jakabar of the Gray Stone?"

Travis stopped in mid-step. *What?*

Max scratched his head. "Do you mean Jack Graystone?"

Travis tried to speak, but when he drew in a breath it scorched his lungs. He saw others around him dab at glistening cheeks and pluck at shirts gone wet.

"I'm afraid Jack passed away last fall," Max said.

"How?" The man's voice was both whisper and shriek. "How did he go? Tell me!"

"It was a fire. At the antique shop."

The man pressed his eyes shut, his expression at once rapt and afflicted. "Ah, yes. Fire. In the end, fire shall take us all. . . ."

He opened his eyes and it was only then Travis saw that the man's eyes had no whites. They were black—completely and utterly black, like two hard orbs of onyx.

Someone bumped hard against Travis's shoulder. People jostled against each other. Some were trying to leave the saloon.

"Listen, mister," Max said in a soothing voice, "I need you to turn around and—"

"You!"

The man's cry was like a gunshot. People scattered, then started shoving for the door. A knot formed in front of Travis, and he was pushed back. Then the knot untangled itself, and he looked up. The man pointed at him with an accusing finger, his impossible black eyes locked on Travis.

"You are the one who drew me to this place. You are Jakabar's heir!"

Travis clenched his right hand, and it burned like he had grabbed a fistful of hot lead. The man lurched toward him, a marionette controlled by a drunken puppeteer.

Max reached out to grab the man. "Hey, you stay away from—"

There was a sizzling sound, and the stench of burnt meat. Max howled and yanked his hand back. He clutched his wrist, his face a mask of agony.

A few last stragglers dashed past—the saloon was deserted now—and the man in black stood less than an arm's length away. A gray wisp rose from his robe and curled into the air. It was smoke. The man's robe was smoldering.

"Travis," a soft voice said behind him. "Travis, take a step back."

Deirdre. He could see her out of the corner of his eye. Travis wanted to listen to her, but the man's black gaze stabbed him, fixing him to the spot.

"The key," the man said.

Travis shook his head. His brain was roasting in his skull. "I don't . . . I don't understand."

Peace crept across the man's cracked face. "Yes, it is you to whom I must give the key."

"Now, Travis," Deirdre said. "Get back."

Max slumped against a wall, still holding his wrist, his expression hazed by pain.

Movement was futile. The heat welded Travis, fused bone and muscle. Somehow he forced his jaw to work. "Who . . . who are you?"

The man smiled, sharp as a knife wound, and reached out a hand. Travis watched smoke rise from the dark fabric of his sleeve.

"Beware—it will consume you."

"Travis!"

Deirdre's shout broke through the fatal heat. He heaved himself back, clattered against a table, then looked up to see the man in black go rigid. He raised twisted arms, threw his head back, and shrieked.

"Kelephon! Jakabar! Help me!"

Then the man in the black robe burst into flame.

6.

Sunlight crept into the valley as Castle County Sheriff's Deputy Jacine Fidelia Windom drove the coroner's van up the hill south of town to the Castle Heights Cemetery.

The sun had just crested the eastern escarpment of Signal Ridge, but the sky had been blue for hours—a trick the mountains always played on the dawn. Jace rolled down the van's window, and dry wind rushed into the vehicle. The morning was already hot. By noon it would be another scorcher. That concerned the deputy.

Not that the heat bothered her. Despite the oppressive weather, Jace hadn't traded her crisp khaki trousers, shirt, and tie for lighter attire. She wasn't afraid of sweat. But there were others on whom the heat wasn't so easy. Ranchers and their livestock. The frail and elderly. If this heat wave kept up, she would be making more trips up this hill.

Jace checked the black box on the seat beside her to be sure it wasn't wandering when she hit the curves. Taking a John Doe's ashes to the cemetery for interment wasn't part of her job description, but Kyle Evans, the Castle County coroner, was at that moment in New Jersey burying his mother, so it fell to Jace to see to it this stranger made it to his own last rest. Not that Jace minded. *To protect and to serve.*

That was the oath she had sworn to Sheriff Dominguez on her twenty-fifth birthday two years ago. And as far as Jace was concerned, anything that helped someone else was part of her job description.

The deputy guided the van around a switchback, her eyes locked on the road behind green, wire-rimmed Ray-Bans. She took all the curves at exactly the speed posted on the yellow road signs, and she steered the van with precise movements of her small, strong hands. She did so because that was the right way to drive a vehicle. There was one right way to do everything in this world, and that was the way Jace did it.

Although every day in her work she encountered people who broke the law, Jace never understood them. Some screamed and cursed at her as she wrote them a ticket or handcuffed them, shouting that the laws oppressed them, while others wept and sobbed that the laws weren't fair. But Jace knew they were wrong. A world without rules was a world without meaning. Laws didn't limit. Instead they made things like happiness, comfort, and beauty possible. Artists painted using principles of color, hue, and perspective. Music was based on mathematics. The laws of physics kept humans from flying off the planet and into space.

The deputy was seldom troubled by dreams, but one that came to her from time to time chilled her to the core. She would dream she was in a tiny boat, tossed on a great sea that was neither light nor dark, liquid nor solid. Then a wave would come, tearing apart the boat. She would try to swim to safety, except it was impossible to determine which way was up. Jace would wake gasping and for an hour would stare into the night, looking at the hard, distinct outlines of bed and walls and floor before she could shut her eyes and return to sleep again.

A world of order Jace understood, but the world she glimpsed in her dream, the great sea of chaos . . .

All she could think was that that must have been the world her father had glimpsed the day she came home from fifth grade and found him hanging from a rafter in the garage.

The road turned to gravel. Jace adjusted her speed to compensate, then guided the vehicle around the last few twists. She came to a halt in the dirt parking lot, scooped up the box of ashes, and stepped out of the van.

There wasn't much to the Castle Heights Cemetery these days. Not that there ever really had been. Throughout the last 130 years, most people in Castle County had their loved ones transported to the more fashionable and expensive cemeteries of Denver when it was time for the long sleep. Weeds tangled over anonymous graves, their wooden markers long turned to splinters, and wild raspberry gathered over other mounds like thorny shrouds. Elsewhere gravestones were planted in the ground at odd angles, as if at any moment the entire place might slide down the slope to the valley bottom for its own final burial.

Jace glanced down at the box tucked into the crook of her arm. This was not how she liked cases to end up—without even a name to put on a marker. But there had been nothing left of the man to run an ID on, not even his teeth. Just a few splinters of burnt bone and a heap of ash. Jace had checked a description of the man, given to her by Travis Wilder, against a database of missing persons, but to no avail. She would keep checking, but doubted she would find an answer.

How he had immolated himself was another mystery. The fire had been so hot, there had been no need for cremation. Yet the man had not set the Mine Shaft ablaze with him. The only damage was a black mark on the floor and the smell of smoke. And Max Bayfield's hand.

Max had said that he touched the man before the fire started, but Jace was sure that was a mistake. Max understood how numbers worked, but the workings of the world were sometimes beyond him. That was fine—that was Jace's job. And she knew people didn't catch fire or get their hands burned for no reason. Probably the man had doused himself with some caustic chemical and had ignited himself where a large crowd would see.

But why? Jace didn't know. The only thing she did know was that you could never truly know the heart of another.

He had to know she would be the one to find him, Maude. I know it's awful to say, but I'm your sister, and it's the truth. She always puts her bike in the garage when she comes home from school. Never leaves it out for the rain. Such a good girl, that Jacine. He had to know. Bless the poor little thing. . . .

A gust of wind kicked up a cloud of sun-baked dust. Jace tucked a stray lock of her short brown hair behind an ear and scanned the cemetery. Where was the undertaker? Dale Stocker, who had managed Castle Heights for the last twenty years, had passed away that spring. But there had been a replacement, hadn't there?

"Hello?"

The wind snatched her voice away. Jace pushed through the iron gate. There was a rise in the middle of the cemetery. He might be on the other side, where he wouldn't have heard the van approaching.

The deputy made her way past forgotten graves. Many of the headstones were too wind-worn to read. But there were some she could still make out, their shallow carvings made sharp again by the shadows of morning. She passed by the graves of failed prospectors, Depression-era mothers, and young men sent back in boxes from Normandy. Then she saw a grave that made her pause. She crouched and parted a tuft of weeds to reveal the words scrawled on the cracked sandstone marker:

NATHANIEL LUKE FARQUHAR
1853–1882
A good Man. A good Father.
"God will forgive you."

Jace frowned at the stone, her mission forgotten. What did it matter if God forgave him? What about the people he had left behind? Had they forgiven him? If he was really such a good man, a good father, how had he gotten himself killed at the age of twenty-nine? A good man would have been careful, would have stayed around to watch his children grow up. He wouldn't have been stuck here in the ground. Jace started to stand, hesitated, then reached out to touch the sun-warmed sandstone.

"Can I help you, ma'am?" a raspy voice said behind her.

Jace pulled her hand back, stood, and turned around all in one smooth motion. It took conscious effort to keep from moving her hand to the butt of the revolver at her hip.

The man before her was tall—far taller than the deputy, who had reached her full five feet two at the age of twelve. Despite the heat he was dressed in a long, shabby suit of black wool that looked as if it had been salvaged from a coffin. His shirt had yellowed like ivory, along with his teeth.

"Well, now," the gravedigger said, a grin splitting his gaunt face, his voice at once slick and rusty, "I see you are a woman of the law." He leaned on the shovel whose handle he gripped in large, bony hands.

Jace opened her mouth to answer but could only manage a nod. There was something strange about the man. Usually she could size up another inside of five seconds, but the figure before her defied easy definition.

The man pushed up the brim of his black hat, swiped with a dingy handkerchief at his knobby brow, then settled the hat back down as he nodded toward the grave marker behind her. "Did you know him, then?"

Jace found her voice. "Sir, that man's been dead for well over a century."

The gravedigger shrugged, as if this fact were not important.

Furrows dug themselves into Jace's forehead. She had never seen the gravedigger around town before. When had he arrived in Castle City? Then again, even Dale had liked to keep to himself. Undertakers were a lonely lot—or maybe they just preferred the company of the dead.

Jace held out the box. "Sir, I have a burden here I need to discharge."

The gravedigger gripped his shovel and laughed: a deep, terrible sound. "Well, now, you've just said a mouthful, Deputy."

"I'm sorry?"

"No, don't be sorry." Dust swirled off the shoulders of his suit, and he gazed at the horizon. "We all have our burdens to discharge." His dark gaze turned toward her. "Don't we, Deputy?"

Jace bit her lip, uncertain what to say. She didn't like this man. There was no order to his words, no reason. She held out the box of ashes. He planted the shovel in the ground and took the box from her, enfolding it in long fingers. Sadness touched his craggy face.

"He has traveled long, this one," the man whispered. "Rest is welcome now. But even a welcome end is not without sorrow."

Jace itched to leave. Sweat trickled down her sides.

But she had to be sure she had done all she needed to do. "You've got it under control, then?"

The gravedigger looked up from the box, as if surprised she was still there, then gave a slow nod. "Do not fear. I'll watch over him now, daughter."

Jace went rigid. Words echoed in her mind, and the cemetery faded to white around her.

God will watch over him now, Jacine.

Why wasn't He watching over him before, Reverend Henley? Why didn't He protect him?

That isn't the way it works, Jacine. Sometimes bad things happen, even to those who are good.

That's not fair. It doesn't make any sense.

His ways don't always make sense to us.

But it's not right.

Jacine, you cannot question His—

The words were drowned out by a clattering sound. The whiteness vanished, replaced by dull browns and hard blue: earth and sky. The cemetery snapped back into focus.

Jace looked around, but the man was gone. Except how could that be? She had been distracted only for a moment. She looked down, and she saw the source of the noise that had jarred her back to the present: The shovel had fallen to the ground. Next to the shovel was a square of freshly turned earth, clear of weeds, the iron-rich soil red as blood. Planted beside the patch of earth was a small granite marker, its surface incised with a single, sharp word she could not comprehend:

MINDROTH

Jace sucked in a breath. This was impossible. The sun hadn't moved in the sky; only a moment had passed. Yet she had no doubt that, were she to pick up the shovel and dig through the soil, she would find the black box of ashes. Sickness rose in her throat, as it did when she dreamed of the roiling sea.

The deputy cast one more look at the fresh grave, then hurried back to the van, shivering despite the heat.

7.

Everything had changed again.

There had been no bells this time, but there had been a man in black, just like before, and once again nothing in Travis's life would ever be the same.

"Travis?"

He looked up at the sound of the quiet voice. Deirdre stood on the other side of the bar, her expression concerned. Travis felt something damp against his hand. He glanced down and saw that he clutched a wet rag. He must have been wiping down the bar, only somewhere in the course of the task he had stopped. How long had he been standing there, just staring?

Beware—it will consume you.

He tried to force the rasping words out of his head, but he couldn't. What did they mean? The words were a warning of some kind, but a warning about what? And why had the burnt man given it to Travis?

You are the one. It is you who drew me to this place.

He clenched his right hand around the cloth, afraid he knew the answer, and water oozed onto the bar.

Deirdre reached out and brushed the back of his hand. He shuddered and let go of the rag.

"We're almost ready to open, Travis. We just need to get a little more air moving in here. Is there an extra fan we could use? I thought we could put it in the north window."

Travis nodded, although he wasn't sure there was a point to opening the saloon. He doubted any of his customers would come back. No matter how hard he scrubbed, no matter how much air he blew through the place, he would never get rid of the black splotch on the floor or the acrid stench—not completely. Then there were the pits melted into the asphalt surface of Elk Street, leading up to the saloon: pits shaped just like footprints. They would always be there, reminders of the burnt man. Once you were marked, Travis knew, you could never forget.

However, he didn't tell Deirdre what he thought. She had been an amazing help these last three days, an unexpected source of light in the midst of this darkness.

"There's a fan up in the rafters in the storeroom," he said. "I'll get it."

He came back with the fan a few minutes later, a bit grimier for the effort, and found Deirdre arranging chairs and wiping down tables. The saloon's door stood open, but no customers had come through, only hot air and dust. Travis put the fan in the window and turned it on, but it only seemed to blow the grit around.

"Don't you have to be at the Medieval Festival?" he said as he helped Deirdre pull a table away from the wall.

She grabbed a chair in each hand and swung them into place. "Just on the weekends."

"Are you sure? It's not like I paid you enough to do all this. I don't want you to miss out on making some money."

She dusted off her hands. "With this heat, there isn't much at the festival to miss. People with sunstroke aren't the best tippers." Her voice grew quiet. "Besides, it's not me you need to worry about."

Deirdre glanced at a corner, and Travis followed her gaze. So someone had come to the saloon after all.

Travis sighed, then approached the small table in the corner.

"Max, you should be home. What are you doing here?"

Max grinned his hound-dog grin. "I wasn't sure you could handle the place on your own, Travis. So I thought I'd come down and make sure everything was all right." His expression tightened into a grimace, and he gripped his right wrist. The hand was mummified in white bandages.

"Max . . ."

"It's all right, Travis. Really." Max unclenched his fingers from his wrist. "I just . . . I just didn't want to be home by myself."

Travis drew in a breath, then nodded. It was when Travis was alone that he heard the burnt man's words most clearly. But the pain written across his partner's usually cheerful face troubled him. Somehow, Max's hand had been badly burned when he touched the man in black. By the time they got him to the Castle County clinic his entire palm had blistered. Now sweat sheened Max's face, but despite the heat he was shivering. He was feverish—he needed to rest.

Or was there something else that might help Max? An idea came to Travis, along with a memory. He saw Melia, huddled in a blanket outside the heap of rubble that had been the White Tower of the Runebinders. Falken had made a brew for Melia, and Travis remembered how it had eased her shivering.

He glanced at Deirdre. "I'll be back in a minute. I have . . . I have to get something."

Deirdre met his gaze, then nodded. Max only stared into space.

Travis headed for the back room, then bounded up a steep staircase to his apartment above the saloon. The long, narrow room was stuffy; heat radiated from the pressed-tin ceiling. Travis moved to a scuffed bureau, leaned against it, and shoved it away from the wall. He stuck a finger into a knothole in one of the wall's rough-cut pine boards, then with a tug pulled free a section of the board. Beyond was a dark space.

Travis reached into the cubbyhole and pulled out a tightly wrapped bundle. He rose, set the bundle on the tarnished brass bed, and unrolled it. Inside were a pair of mud-stained breeches, a green tunic patched in half a dozen places, a silvery cloak, and a stiletto with a single crimson gem set into its hilt. Travis brushed his fingers across the road-worn garments. It seemed a lifetime ago he had worn them, although it was only months.

He reached into the pocket of his tunic and drew out a handful of leaves. They were dry and brittle now, and a darker green than the day he had plucked them in the cool shadows of a Tarrasian Way Circle, but even as they broke, a sweet, sharp fragrance rose from the leaves. On the road to Calavere he had picked these for makeshift toothbrushes. He had another use in mind for them now.

Travis kept two of the leaves, slipped the others back into the pocket of his tunic, rolled up the bundle, and returned it to its hiding place. Then he headed downstairs.

Deirdre sat on a stool, strumming a quiet song on her mandolin. Max still slumped at a nearby table, his eyes half-closed, although whether it was music or pain that was causing him to drift wasn't clear. Travis headed for the bar, crumbled the leaves into a coffee mug, and filled it with hot water.

Deirdre looked up as she played. "Isn't it a little warm out for tea?"

"It's not tea. Not exactly, anyway."

He let the leaves steep for a minute, then carried the mug to his partner.

"Hey, Max. I've got something for you to drink."

Max blinked, then his eyes focused on Travis. He grinned, but it was a weak expression.

"Dr. Sullivan said I'm not supposed to have alcohol. But I suppose I could make an exception for a single malt."

"It's not Lagavulin, Max. Now go on—drink it."

With slow movements, Max accepted the mug and brought it to his lips. He took a tentative sip, glanced up with an expression of surprise, then drank the rest. He set down the cup. As he did, a trace of color crept into his cheeks, and his shivering eased.

Max wiped his mustache with his unbandaged hand. "Thanks, Travis. I feel . . . better."

Travis nodded and picked up the mug, some of the tightness gone from his stomach. Max was still hurt, but at least his eyes had lost their too-bright glaze.

"What was that, Travis?" a soft voice said behind him.

Travis turned around. He hadn't noticed when her music had stopped.

"Just some herbs," he said.

Deirdre picked up the cup and held it under her nose. "I know a little about herbal medicine—my great-grandfather was a shaman—but I don't recognize this leaf." She looked up. "What do you call it?"

"It's—" He had to bite his tongue to keep from saying *alasai*. What would he tell Deirdre if she asked what language the word was from? "It's called green scepter, I think."

"Where did it come from?"

"I got it through Jack Graystone."

Deirdre studied him, then shrugged and set down the cup. Travis let out a breath between his teeth.

"I'll go make sure the kegs are full," he said.

It was edging toward evening when Sheriff's Deputy Jace Windom stepped into the saloon.

As the day wore on, contrary to what Travis had expected, a number of locals and regulars had wandered through the door of the Mine Shaft—although the place was still only half as full as on a typical night. However, Travis was grateful for everyone who had decided to come, and he would have given them all free drinks, except no one would let him.

Jace tipped her hat as she reached the bar. "Evening, Travis. I just thought I'd stop by and see how business was doing."

Her gaze flickered to a figure hunched in the corner, and Travis knew the real reason she had come to the saloon. When would Jace and Max decide to tell him what he already knew? He didn't understand why they hid their feelings for each other. But secrets were strange things, and the reasons people kept them stranger yet.

Travis poured the deputy a cup of hot coffee. "Did you learn anything yet, Jace?"

The deputy took a deep swig of coffee, then shook her head. "No one was able to positively ID the stranger. And there wasn't much left for the forensics lab to work on. This is a mystery we might never solve." She set down the mug. "But if it helps to know, my guess is that he was under the influence of an illegal substance when he came in here. LSD. Heroin. Electria."

Travis topped off her coffee. "Electria?"

Jace nodded. "A new designer drug. It started showing up on the coasts about a year ago, and it's been working its way in ever since. Gives the user a feeling of extreme euphoria. The reports say it can also induce a sense of invulnerability. Whatever the John Doe doused himself in, my bet is he didn't think it would really hurt him."

Travis shuddered, and shrill words echoed in his mind.

In the end, fire shall take us all. . . .

No, the deputy was wrong. The man had known he would burn. Besides, a drug couldn't explain the melted footsteps.

Travis took a bottle of water from the chiller and

slid it toward Jace. "Would you take this to Max? The doctor says he's supposed to keep his fluids up."

Jace took the bottle and headed toward the corner of the saloon. Travis followed her with his eyes, then his gaze dropped down to the dark splotch on the floor.

"The Immolated Man."

Travis looked up at Deirdre. She was wearing only a white tank top with her black jeans, but her skin still glowed from the heat. The tattoo above her collarbone glistened like jade: a serpent eating its own tail.

"What do you mean?" he said.

She met his eyes. "It's an archetype, one that shows up in many different myths and cultures. The Immolated Man. The Burned God. The Sacrificed King. Again and again myths tell about a man or woman or god who is consumed in fire."

Sickness rose in his throat, but Travis forced it down. "Why? Why does that story get told so many times?"

"I don't know for certain. It's about transformation, I think. It's like the Phoenix or Shiva or the Christ." Deirdre brushed a finger across the serpent tattoo. "You have to die to become something new."

Travis's gaze drifted back to the scorch mark. "But become what?"

"That's up to you. In the end, we must each choose what we become."

With that, Deirdre picked up her mandolin and returned to the small stage to fill the saloon with music.

Travis sighed, then grabbed a tray and started rounding up used beer glasses. He halted as movement through the open door caught his eye. Outside, a vehicle drove slowly past the saloon: a black sport utility with tinted windows. A logo was emblazoned on the side of the vehicle—a crescent moon that merged into a capital letter *D*. Travis read the words that followed it:

DURATEK. WORLDS OF POSSIBILITY, CLOSE TO HOME.

He recalled the commercial with all the smiling people, the one that didn't seem to be selling anything, and once again he frowned at the odd slogan. He had always looked forward to the sense of possibility that the wind brought. But sometimes possibilities could be frightening things.

The vehicle rolled up Elk Street and out of sight, and Travis went back to collecting empty glasses.

8.

Deirdre Falling Hawk stepped out of the Silver Palace Hotel, her black biker boots beating a war-drum tattoo against the planks of the boardwalk.

It was almost time.

She slung her black-leather jacket over her shoulder and surveyed the empty expanse of Elk Street. It was early, and the sky was a dull steel bowl. However, already the coolness of dawn was beginning to lessen. Right now she was comfortable in her white tank top and black jeans. In an hour, no more than two, she would be sweating.

Deirdre slipped a hand into her pocket and felt the small square of paper she had found last night, tucked into her hotel message box. There was a need for swiftness. All the same, she took a moment to lean against the boardwalk railing and greet the day. Too often in the hurry and action of their lives people forgot to halt for a minute and say a prayer, or contemplate a great question, or simply look at the world. But no matter how urgent things became, she always remembered to stop and steal a moment for herself. As far as Deirdre was concerned, the world could do with a little more ceremony.

She gazed forward and let herself *be.* Henna had drawn the fire from deep in her close-cropped black hair, and her one concession to makeup was a line of kohl that outlined her smoky jade eyes. A cross dangled from one ear, and an ankh from the other. Against the hollow of her throat rested a yellowed bear claw that her great-grandfather had given her the day he died.

Bear will give you strength, little one. Do not forget him when you are alone and afraid.

She brushed the claw with a finger and smiled. The blood of three Indian tribes ran in her veins, and she could trace her lineage to the legendary hero Cuchulain—or at least so her Irish grandmother had claimed. But she wasn't just where she had come from. She was where she was, and where she was going. And she had a new tribe now.

Deirdre stepped into the street; her Harley was parked around the corner. It was nice to be able to leave the bike out without having to worry about it. Not like Paris or Athens. Definitely not like London. She straddled her hog, then started it and wheeled down the street in one seamless sequence. A helmet would have been a good idea; she usually wore one. But not here, not today. Today she needed to feel the wind tangle its fingers through her hair. Lovers were fine, and their caresses sweet, but the wind would never abandon you.

Square false fronts flashed by, then the town was gone, and it was only two-lane and mountains before her. As she rode, Deirdre let the last few years drift through her mind. She had been on many journeys since she last set foot in Castle City, and she had seen many wonders. She had prowled through catacombs beneath the Tower of London. She had meditated in the stony company of Notre Dame's gargoyles. She had climbed the jungle pyramids of Tikal, had stood small and humble beneath the dome of the Hagia Sophia, and had gazed into deathless eyes in silent Egyptian tombs.

Yet, despite all the sights she had witnessed, nothing filled her with awe like the Colorado mountains. Theirs was no human beauty, limited and ephemeral, carved by mortal and imperfect hands. The mountains were great and ancient, and they did not need people. All the same, they were generous with their wonder. No sight she had encountered in all her travels gave her songs like the mountains did. It was good to be back, if only for a short while.

Deirdre cruised down a flat stretch of blacktop. Up ahead, a rusty speck grew rapidly into a car—a faded Volvo with crumpled bumpers. Inside, the shadow of a driver hunched over the steering wheel. By the time Deirdre recognized both vehicle and driver, they had flashed by. She glanced over her shoulder. Behind her, the Volvo slowed, then turned off the highway and headed down a dirt road. The car disappeared behind an outcrop, leaving only a plume of dust to rise like smoke into the dull morning sky.

Where was Max Bayfield going at such an early hour? He should have been home resting. These last days his burnt hand had seemed only to get worse, not better. Deirdre hoped Travis's partner was all right; pain could make people do strange things. She almost considered going after him, but she had other duties that beckoned her.

She turned her gaze forward just in time to lean into a sharp curve. The valley floor fell away, and the highway bore her up into a twisting canyon. Last night she had told Travis not to expect her at the saloon that day, that she was going to the Medieval Festival. And maybe she would go there later, so her words would not become lies and, like cursed arrows, fly back to strike her. But it was not to the festival that she was going now.

The canyon opened up, and the two lanes of asphalt funneled into a narrow bridge. Deirdre veered onto a pull-off and brought the Harley to a halt. Years ago, this had been her favored place to find a moment of solitude. She hoped it would grant her the same now.

She drew something out of the Harley's saddlebag, then walked to the edge of the pull-off and gazed down a slope of tumbled boulders. In her memory, Granite Creek rushed over those rocks in a hurry to reach the ocean. Now a trickle oozed between the boulders, and mosquitoes clouded the air over pools of standing water. All the same, there was beauty in the slender aspens that clung to the sides of the creek bed. She glanced up, made sure she had good exposure to the southeastern sky, then lifted the object in her hand—a slim phone—and flipped it on.

Deirdre touched one button and held the phone to her ear. Three seconds later, a voice from another part of the world answered.

"I've made contact," she said.

The voice spoke several careful words. A thrill coursed through her, and she gave a slow nod.

"Yes, I suppose it would be. A Class One encounter. If you're right."

Now the voice was sharper.

Deirdre winced, then licked her lips and forced her voice to remain even. "That's what I'm here to confirm."

A question. She ran a hand through her short hair. High above, a hawk wheeled against the sky.

"No, I haven't verified anything. Not yet. But there was something—a medicinal herb. He used it to make an analgesic tea for his business partner. I know a fair amount about herb lore, but this was not a plant I recognized." She nodded. "Yes, I saved some of the leaves from the cup. I've already couriered the specimen to the London Charterhouse for testing. It should arrive today."

She listened for a few seconds more—the plan had not changed. The voice started to conclude.

"Wait," she said. "There's something more. There was . . . there was an incident at his place of business. Spontaneous combustion. Four days ago. There was no ID for the victim, but it was a textbook example. I think it might be related to the others."

She listened, then nodded. "Yes, it is. But I'll have opportunity for more observation. I helped him reopen the saloon after the incident, and he expects me to check back."

Another question, and this time it was Deirdre's voice that contained a note of annoyance.

"No, I haven't forgotten the Third Desideratum, or the Vow for that matter. I've been watching, or doing what an old friend would do, and that's it."

A few more words from the phone. They were not conciliatory. She forced herself to breathe.

"If you think that's wise."

There was a click, and the connection was closed. Deirdre pressed a button and lowered the phone. So it had begun. There was no turning back now. She could only hope she was doing the right thing.

But it is right, you know it, Deirdre. You knew it when you swore the Vow in London. To Watch—To Believe—To Wait. This is how it has to be.

Deirdre sighed. If she hurried, she could still be at the gates of the Medieval Festival when they opened and save herself from being a liar. She turned to head for the motorcycle—

—and stopped in mid-stride.

"Hello," the girl said.

The child's voice was high and clear, silver against china. Deirdre blinked, mouth open. The girl before her appeared to be eight or nine years old, her dark hair pulled back from the pale cherub's cameo of her face. She wore an old-fashioned dress of black wool and equally old-fashioned buttoned shoes.

Deirdre glanced up. Her Harley was the only vehicle in sight. But how had the girl gotten here? How had she approached across ten yards of gravel without making a sound? And what did she want?

"To watch," the girl said. "To believe. To wait."

Deirdre sucked in a breath. But the girl had only overheard her conversation, that was all. Deirdre must have spoken the words aloud.

"Are you lost?" she said.

"No," the girl replied in her lisping voice. "Are you?"

Instinct prickled the back of Deirdre's neck. Stories echoed in her mind, told beside a fire by her great-grandfather—spirits that haunted stones, shadows that spoke from trees. The sun had crested the canyon rim, but twilight still clung to the girl's dress.

"I don't understand," Deirdre said.

Purple eyes bored into her. "Seek them as you journey."

Deirdre found herself crouching down to meet the girl's eyes. "What do you mean? Seek what?"

"Fire and wonder," the girl whispered.

A shrill cry pierced the air, and Deirdre looked up. The hawk had wheeled lower on red-tinged wings, and Deirdre gazed into small, bright eyes. The hawk rose on a column of air, dwindled into blue sky, and vanished.

Deirdre looked back down, but she already knew the girl would be gone. That much her great-grandfather's stories had taught her.

9.

The sun broke like a blister against the sharp summit of Castle Peak, and crimson flowed down into the valley. The day was almost gone. Its death would bring only relief.

A few locals and fewer tourists passed Travis as he walked down Elk Street. Castle City should have been bustling this time of year, but the usual flood of vacationers had dried to a trickle under the summer glare as steadily as Granite Creek. Travis hadn't bothered to open the Mine Shaft yet. There was no sense in rushing. Those few customers who did come wouldn't show up until after sunset, when the valley cooled—at least a bit. He would wait until then.

Nor were Max and Deirdre at the saloon. Last night, Deirdre had told him she would be playing at the Medieval Festival that day, and all afternoon he had imagined red-faced Denverites buying hot pewter dragons and gnawing greasy turkey legs under the fierce high-altitude sun. It seemed less a recipe for entertainment than a prescription for sunstroke. He hoped the bard was having some luck.

As for Max—Travis had stopped by his place on the way into town, but Max's apartment had been dim and silent, and the Volvo gone. For some reason, Travis had gotten out of his truck to peer through the apartment's front window. The curtains had been drawn, but through a crack he had glimpsed a clutter of crumpled clothes, newspapers, and dirty dishes. At first he was sure he had looked into the wrong apartment—in his experience, Max's neatness bordered on pathological—then he checked the number. He hadn't made a mistake.

On his way back to his pickup, something shiny

had caught Travis's eye, tangled in a web of dry weeds. It was a piece of glossy paper, from a brochure maybe, although Travis could make out only fragments of hyperreal images, so that it was impossible to tell what it was selling. He had shrugged, then shoved the paper into his pocket and climbed back into his truck.

Travis had hoped he would find Max once he got to the Mine Shaft, but his partner hadn't been at the saloon either. Now, as he walked, a sick feeling rose in his throat. He clenched his jaw and swallowed it.

Of course Max is all right. It's just a burn, Travis, that's all. And it's no mystery that his place is a mess—I'm sure it's harder to be obsessive-compulsive with just one hand.

Travis angled across Elk Street, toward McKay's General Store. In his back pocket were the door hinges he had bought four—was it really only four?—days ago. He needed to return the hinges, to exchange them for new ones. They didn't fit.

As he stepped onto the boardwalk, Travis noticed a black sport utility parked outside of McKay's. He paused. It might have been the same vehicle he had seen driving past the saloon the other day. Or it might have been different but identical. It was impossible to tell. The glossy jet paint was without dent or blemish, and the tinted windows were as impenetrable as midnight. The crescent moon logo on the side door glowed scarlet in the fiery light of sunset.

A dude ranch cowboy jostled past Travis, and he blinked, realizing he had been staring. He mumbled an apology, then headed through the creaking side door into the familiar clutter of McKay's General Store.

McKay's had opened its doors in the 1870s and hadn't closed them since, barring holidays and the Great Depression. Ian McKay, son of the original owner, had sold the store in the forties, but about ten years ago his granddaughter, Onica McKay, returned to Castle City on a genealogical research trip, got caught by the spell of the valley, and bought the store her great-grandfather had built.

The store hadn't changed much over the years. The gigantic discount warehouses had invaded other mountain towns, leaving McKay's pressed-tin ceiling and plate-glass front window intact. The high shelves were just as crowded with merchandise as they had been in the waning days of the silver rush—although now they were more likely to hold garlic presses and cans of Indian curry than pickaxes and bottles of mercury.

Travis breathed in dusty, spicy air and smiled at the smell of history. At least there were some things he could still count on. He wandered back to the hardware section, found a new pair of hinges, and headed toward the front of the store.

The high, chiming sound of bells drifted on the air.

Shock crystallized Travis. Once before he had heard silvery music like that in Castle City. Once before, when everything had begun to—

"Thank you for coming to McKay's," a chantlike voice drifted from up ahead.

A man with a plastic shopping bag appeared from around a corner, smiled at Travis, then headed for the side entrance of the store. Travis stepped around the corner and saw the source of the sound.

The antique brass cash register that had dominated the front counter of McKay's for time out of mind was gone. In its place lurked a low, aerodynamic shape molded from black plastic. Again the chiming shimmered on the air, and Travis knew it was not bells. Instead the sound had that hard, perfect clarity that could come only from an electronic chip.

Another customer—a young woman—waited at the counter. Waunita Lost Owl stood on the other side. Her black-and-white hair was woven into a thick braid, and she wore jeans and a geometric-patterned shirt. A pair of thick-lensed glasses perched in front of her serene brown eyes.

At first Travis thought Waunita was ringing up the young woman's purchases, but then he wasn't so certain. Waunita touched each item lightly, then when she was done she touched the black unit on the counter. A pale luminescence frosted the sculpted features of her face, and again the chime sounded on the air.

"Seventeen-thirty-two," Waunita said.

So she had been totaling the items after all.

The young woman held out a credit card. Waunita took it and passed it over the wedge-shaped unit without touching it. Another chime. Waunita handed the card back, placed the goods in a shiny plastic sack, and nodded as the young woman stepped away.

"Do you need help, Travis?"

He shook his head—he had been staring again. He hurried to the counter and set the hinges down.

"Hello, Waunita. I need to exchange these."

She nodded and touched the hinges—no, that wasn't right. Instead she carefully touched the metallic price sticker attached to each one.

Travis frowned as she worked. "What happened to the old cash register?"

"This is better."

For the first time he noticed that she wore what looked like a black wrist brace, made of nylon and Velcro. On the back of the brace was a small black box. Waunita touched the main unit on the counter. It chimed, and at the same time a small LED on the wrist brace flashed.

His frown deepened.

"It uses my body as a wire," she said.

"What do you mean?"

"When I touch things, this remembers." She brushed the box attached to the wrist brace, then she gestured to the unit on the counter. "And when I touch this, it listens through my body and hears what things I touched. Then it adds them up."

Understanding crept into Travis's mind. He remembered sitting at the saloon with Max on a slow night a few months ago, watching the Wonder Channel on the TV behind the bar. The show had been about new technologies. One had involved a device that could use the human body to transmit data instead of a network cable. Personal area networks—PANs—that was what the monotonous voice of the narrator had called them. But the prototypes had been large and clunky. They had looked like something from a junior high school science fair compared to the slim, elegant device Waunita wore.

"They do good things," Waunita said.

He shook his head. "What do you mean, Waunita? Who did this for the store?"

She reached under the counter, pulled out a brochure, and handed it to him.

"Maybe they can help you, too, Travis."

He glanced down at the brochure and almost laughed. Maybe he should have been surprised to see the crescent moon and capital *D*, but he wasn't. Duratek. So this was what they did—this was one of the possibilities they advertised.

"Mrs. McKay was worried," Waunita said. "But now she is full of hope all the time. She says things have not been this good in many years. She is paying me more."

Travis gazed out the front window. Desiccated scraps of litter blew down Elk Street like dirty tumbleweeds in the gloom. No, Waunita was wrong. Things were not good—they were not good at all. Who were these people? What did they know about real possibilities? He glanced down at the crescent moon on the brochure. Once before he had seen a symbol all over town right before things had changed.

Travis crumpled the brochure, shoved it into his pocket, and turned to walk from the store.

"Travis? You forgot your hinges."

He barely noticed as Waunita pushed the slick plastic sack into his hand, then he stepped out the front door and walked into hot, gritty twilight. He glanced in both directions, looking for the black vehicle, ready to confront these people, to ask them who they were to come here and change things.

The street was empty, the vehicle was gone. Travis sighed and headed back to open up the saloon.

10.

Max called the Mine Shaft at a quarter to midnight.

Behind the bar, Travis fumbled with the handset. "Max? Max, is that you?"

A digital hiss phased into words. "—course it's me, Travis." The voice sounded thin and metallic, as if Max spoke from down a long steel tube.

Travis turned his back to block out the low din of conversation. To his amazement, people had been waiting outside the Mine Shaft when he returned from McKay's. Now the saloon was over half-full. People were kind sometimes. Too kind. He had thrown a rug over the scorch mark on the floor, but he could still smell the stench of fire.

"Max, I—" He lowered his voice. "I was a little worried when I didn't hear from you today."

"Travis, you worry when one of the Daughters of the Frontier breaks a press-on nail opening a beer."

He couldn't help a small laugh. It was genuine Max, all right, even if the voice was a poor silicon facsimile. "Where are you? I . . . are you at home?"

A surge of static, then, "—feel great, Travis. Better every day. Really, I mean it."

Travis knew he should take Max's word for it. But it was hard not to remember the feverish light in Max's eyes when Travis had last seen him. He licked dry lips. "Have you seen Deputy Windom lately?"

A faint buzzing, and silence.

"Max? Are you—?"

"Yes. Yes, I saw—"

Max's voice was cut off by another sound: a whine so piercing Travis had to jerk the phone away for fear his skull would shatter.

"Max? Max, are you there? What was that?"

Static coalesced into a faint voice. "I've got to go, Travis."

"Wait—are you coming to the saloon tomorrow?"

"Maybe. I'm not sure. But I'll see you soon, Travis. Promise."

Travis clutched the phone, as if holding it more tightly would keep his friend on the line. "Max, just tell me—"

This time the hiss was replaced by the monotonous drone of a dial tone. Travis hung up the phone.

It was only when Molly Nakamura asked him for a refill on her chai that he realized he had been staring at the phone. He mixed a cup of the fragrant tea and pushed it toward her. She gave a solemn nod, then returned to the table where she was giving an impromptu origami lesson.

Travis turned to unload a tray of dirty glasses. Something on the bar caught his eye. He picked it up and cupped it in his hand. Crisp paper wings stretched from its black body, and its sharp beak curved downward. Although he was sweating, a shudder coursed through him.

It was a gift, Travis. Molly couldn't have known. On this world, it's just a bird. . . .

He set the origami raven back on the bar. Maybe she would think he hadn't seen it.

Two hours later, the last of the cowboys stumbled

out the door of the saloon. Travis turned chairs up on tables and swept the floor. He wished Deirdre was there. Not to help with the work, but to keep him company, and maybe play a soft song on her mandolin. He finished the rest of his work in silence.

It was late. Time to lock the door, head upstairs, make a try at sleeping. Travis grabbed the keys from the hook behind the bar, then paused. He let his gaze wander over the saloon. It all should have been warm and familiar. Instead it was like looking at a foreign landscape. Nothing was right anymore. The heat, the town, Max. What had happened to Castle City?

What happened to you, Travis?

He wasn't certain if the voice in his mind was his own, or if it was the *other* voice, the one that told him things, the one that sounded like Jack. But that voice hadn't spoken to him since his return to Earth. Whatever its source, there was truth in the voice's words.

Maybe Castle City hasn't changed, Travis. Maybe you have.

All the same, something *was* wrong. Travis wasn't sure what it was, but it had something to do with the weather, and the man in black, and the crescent moon logo. But how did it all fit together?

He shook his head. Once before he had wondered where he was going to get answers to his impossible questions. But this time there was no old-fashioned revival tent glowing in the night before him.

Maybe they can help you, too. . . .

Or did he have someplace to go for answers after all? He dug into the pocket of his jeans and pulled out the crumpled brochure. The crescent moon glowed in the illumination of the neon bar lights. Duratek. What could they do for him? What changes might they bring to his life? He hesitated, then opened the brochure.

New shock flowed through him, as if his own body had become the wire. A mosaic of brilliant images met his eyes, depicting laughing people and too-real landscapes. He shoved his hand back in his pocket and dug deeper. This time he came out with a small scrap of paper, the one he had found outside Max's apartment. He didn't need to place it atop the brochure to know it matched, but he did all the same.

"What are you doing, Max?" he whispered. "What are you doing?"

Travis folded the brochure and scrap, paused, then picked up the origami raven—no one had taken it from its perch on the bar—pressed it flat, and folded it inside the brochure. He shoved the bundle of paper back into his pocket, scooped up the keys, and headed for the door.

Afterward, Travis was never sure what made him stop as he pushed the key into the dead bolt, what made him turn the knob, open the front door of the saloon, and step out into darkness. Sometimes fate drew one onward. Sometimes danger did as well.

The onyx vehicle merged seamlessly with the night. Only the cool sheen of starlight against glossy paint betrayed its presence. He could just make out the pale curve of a crescent moon, far too low to be in the sky.

Travis stepped to the edge of the boardwalk. There was the solid chunk of a car door shutting, then the grinding of shoes on gravel. The man stepped out of the shadows into the pool of light in front of the saloon.

"I've been waiting for a chance to talk to you," the man said.

Travis gripped the rail of the boardwalk. It wasn't so much surprise he felt as dread. "Who are you?"

The man smiled, but the expression was secret, as if only for himself. He was short and handsome: blond hair and goatee shorn close, shoulders solid beneath a dark silk shirt, hips slim in black jeans. His eyes were blue behind wire-rimmed glasses that were a mirror of Travis's own.

"Worlds of possibility," the man said. "Close to home."

Travis shook his head. "But what does it mean? What are you selling?"

"Everything. Haven't you seen our commercials?" His laugh was wonderful—low and inviting. "But of course you have. They're sort of hard to miss. Thank our marketing department for that. Whatever people want, whatever people need, whatever they're too afraid to dream of—that's what we sell."

"Possibility," Travis murmured.

"Worlds of possibility." The man paused. "But then, you know all about other worlds, don't you, Mr. Wilder?"

The night was perfectly still. Sweat seeped down Travis's sides. What had he been expecting the other to say?

The man stepped away from his vehicle and moved toward the boardwalk. His blue eyes were earnest behind his glasses.

"Do you know what it means, Mr. Wilder? Do you understand the implications of what you've discovered? What it means for this world, what it means for all of us?"

Travis's mouth was filled with dust. It was hard to form the words, and when he did they were utterly hollow. "I don't know what you're talking about."

This time the man's smile edged into a smirk. "On the contrary, you understand better than anyone, Mr. Wilder. You've seen for yourself what another world has to offer."

"What do you mean?"

The man moved closer. "You really can't see it, can you? That's ironic. You've been there, but you don't get it." He shrugged. "Consider it this way. What do you think the Vikings thought when their dragon ships landed on the desolate shores of Greenland? What did Christopher Columbus think when he realized that the jumble of islands he had found weren't anywhere near India? What do you think was going through the minds of the men and women who sailed across a vast ocean to settle at Jamestown?"

Travis could only stare.

The man spread his hands wide. "A new world, Mr. Wilder. That's what I'm talking about. The whole history of mankind can be measured as long intervals of meaningless static punctuated by the discovery of new worlds. These days most people believe there are no more worlds to find, at least not without climbing into a spaceship for a few hundred years." He brought his hands together. "But you and I both know that isn't true."

"Leave me alone," Travis said.

The man had reached the edge of the boardwalk. "Please, Mr. Wilder. I'm not your enemy. Far from it. Haven't you wanted to meet someone who could understand what you've been through? Someone whom you could tell everything?"

Yes. Yes, more than anything. But this man hadn't been there. He could never have understood.

Travis let go of the railing. "I said leave me alone."

The man sighed. "All right, Mr. Wilder. I can see you're not ready to hear what I have to say. But let me give you some advice. I know you don't trust me. And I'm sure you know people whom you think you *can* trust." He cocked his head. "But you can never really know another, Mr. Wilder. Not truly, not what burning secrets they keep deep in their hearts. Everyone is seeking something. At least I've told you what I want."

Travis could not breathe. Despite the darkness the heat was suffocating. What was the man talking about? But the other only nodded, then turned toward his vehicle. Without thinking, Travis raised an arm.

"Wait—"

The rest of his words were cut off as the roar of an engine tore apart the night.

Travis jerked his head up in time to see a white-hot beam pierce the darkness. He shielded his eyes with a hand, and when he lowered it again he saw a motorcycle skid to a halt in front of the boardwalk. The rider flipped up the visor of a black helmet. Smoke-green eyes flashed.

"Get on, Travis!"

He stood frozen, then shock became motion, and he jumped down to the street.

The blond man laughed over the growl of the engine. "And here is one who seeks even now!"

Travis hurried to Deirdre. "What's he talking about?"

"Don't listen to him, Travis." Her words were hard behind the face guard of her helmet.

Travis glanced at the man. The other's hands were on his hips, his expression grave now.

"Remember what I told you, Mr. Wilder."

Travis looked back at Deirdre. "What's going on?"

"Come with me, Travis. Come with me if you want to understand."

For a heartbeat movement was impossible. Travis could feel the man's eyes bore into him along with Deirdre's.

You can never really know another. . . .

Then he climbed onto the back of the motorcycle. He barely had time to circle his arms around Deirdre's waist before she cranked the throttle. The Harley screamed forward like a Chinese dragon, and everything vanished in its dark wake.

11.

Deirdre cut the Harley's engine, and the motorcycle coasted to a stop. Silence descended over the night like a curtain of hot black velvet. Travis brushed wind-tangled hair from his eyes and saw, looming in the murk, the graceful facade of the Castle City Opera House.

These days the opera house was abandoned, but at its zenith its stage had played home to some of the finest tenors and sopranos of Europe, and it was said that once President McKinley himself had viewed a Parisian burlesque show there. Even in decay, there was an air of elegance about the opera house. Greek Revival columns glowed in the cast-off shine of a streetlight.

For what seemed an hour he had clung to Deirdre while the motorcycle sped down empty roads, but at some point they must have turned around, for they had come to a halt at the end of Elk Street, no more than half a mile from the saloon. He let go of Deirdre and stumbled off the Harley. It felt as if the world were still moving beneath him. Then again, maybe it was.

Deirdre stepped off the bike and removed her helmet in one fluid motion. She shook out her short black hair, then turned her eyes on Travis.

"Are you all right?"

It was the first thing she had said since the moment she shouted for him to get on the bike. He opened his mouth, but he could find no words to answer. Travis wasn't even sure he knew what *all right* was anymore. Deirdre turned and gazed into the night. He was suddenly certain that she knew far more about what was happening than he did.

Travis looked up at the ghostly opera house. "Why here?"

"There's someone you need to meet."

With that, Deirdre headed up the sweeping marble staircase to the entrance of the opera house. Travis hesitated. Once, at the weird revival show, Brother Cy had told him that he always had a choice. Now he wasn't so certain that was true. He hurried after Deirdre.

Travis caught up to her as she paused before the door. "It's locked," he said. "This place hasn't been used in—"

He halted as she pulled a device from her pocket. It was shaped like a river pebble, but molded of plastic. She touched a small button. There was a click, and one of the double doors swung open an inch. She slipped the device back into her pocket and pushed through the doorway. Travis took a breath, then followed her into darkness beyond.

They moved through dimness, then came to the edge of a vast space. Across an ocean of shabby seats was a stage lit by a single spotlight.

Deirdre leaned against an ornate railing. She did not shout, but her voice rang out across the old theater. "They found him."

Travis glanced at her. Who was she speaking to? Then a voice drifted through the proscenium arch, carried by the acoustics of the opera house.

"The Philosophers will not be pleased."

Deirdre tightened her grip on the railing. "Damn the Philosophers."

Now laughter floated on the air. "Speak carefully, Deirdre Falling Hawk. The Philosophers have many ears. You've always had a tendency to forget that fact."

A figure stepped from the shadowy wings of the stage, into the spotlight.

"Welcome, Travis Wilder," the man said.

Travis shook his head, and a sick feeling oozed into his stomach. Who were all these strangers who seemed to know him so well? He glanced at Deirdre, but her eyes were dark and distant, fixed on the stage. At that moment she might as well have been a stranger to him, too.

"What do you want?" Travis said, surprised at the way his trembling voice rose on the air of the opera house.

"To help," the man onstage said.

Travis sighed. He noticed that the other had not said, *To help you.*

Deirdre touched his arm. "Come on, Travis."

She led the way down to the stage, and he followed.

By the time they reached the bottom, the man sat on the edge of the orchestra pit. He looked to be Travis's age, early thirties, or perhaps just a little older given the flecks of gray in his curly black hair. He wore rumpled chinos and a white linen shirt rolled up to the elbows. Stubble shadowed his square jaw, and his nose was aquiline above sensual lips. He looked like a movie star from some forties film noir: handsome, disheveled, possibly dangerous. On the stage next to him was a manila envelope.

"Who are you?" Travis said.

The man held out a hand. "My name is Farr. Hadrian Farr."

Travis didn't accept the gesture. That wasn't what he had meant.

The man—Farr—seemed in no way rebuffed. His hand moved to the manila envelope, as if this was what he had been reaching for all along.

Travis tried again. "What do you want?"

The man smiled. His teeth were crooked. It was a charming expression. "We seek things," he said. "Unusual things. Wonderful things."

Travis drew in a sharp breath.

Everyone is seeking something. . . .

He breathed out, wanting to ask more, but he didn't know where to begin.

Farr pulled something from the envelope and held it out. "Do you know this woman, Mr. Wilder?"

Travis's hand shook as he accepted the photograph, as if somehow he already knew what he would see. The woman in the photo was desperate and regal. She ran down the steps of a building, her hand to her throat, staring forward with stunning green-gold eyes. In that instant, he understood.

Travis looked up and met Farr's gaze. "You're Seekers, aren't you?" He turned toward Deirdre. "Both of you."

Farr raised an eyebrow, and Deirdre's mouth dropped open. Travis allowed himself a humorless smile. It was good to know that he could spring a few surprises of his own.

"Don't look at me," Deirdre said when Farr glanced her way. "I didn't tell him."

Farr nodded. "We need to remember that Mr. Wilder might well know much more than we imagine."

Deirdre reached out, as if to touch Travis, then pulled her hand back. "How did you . . . ?"

He smiled and brushed a finger across the photo. "It was Grace. Grace Beckett. She told me about the Seekers." He glanced up. "And about you, Hadrian Farr."

Farr's expression was intent. "So you are acquainted with Dr. Grace Beckett."

Now Travis did laugh. He thought of all he and Grace had been through, all they had done, all they had survived. "You might say that."

He handed the photo back to Farr. Shadows pressed around them like silent actors.

Travis looked at Deirdre. "I suppose this means you didn't really come to the Mine Shaft to play music."

Her smile was small and private. "In a way, I did. That time I sang at the saloon, three years ago, is more special to me than you can know. I suppose part of me was hoping I could feel a glimmer of that magic again. And maybe I have. But you're right. There's another reason why I came to Castle City."

"The Immolated Man," Travis whispered.

Farr slipped the photo back into the envelope. "You're right, Deirdre. He is indeed perceptive."

Deirdre met Farr's eyes. "Do you want to tell him? Or should I?"

"I think I can manage."

Travis pushed the gunslinger's spectacles higher on his nose. "Tell me what?"

Farr slid from the edge of the stage to stand. He was several inches shorter than Travis, but somehow Travis felt like the smaller one. There was an air of quiet power about Farr. In some ways he reminded Travis of Falken Blackhand.

"To tell you why we've been searching for you, Mr. Wilder."

12.

It was only when Deirdre caught his arm and led him to the front row of seats that Travis realized his knees were shaking. As he sat, a dusty exhalation rose from the cushion. He looked up at the two Seekers. Deirdre's eyes were concerned. Farr's expression was more difficult to fathom.

Farr pulled a slim silver case from the pocket of his chinos, took out a cigarette, then cocked his head toward Travis. "Do you mind if I smoke?"

"I don't tell other people how to live their lives."

Farr nodded. "That's good advice, Mr. Wilder. I'll do my best to heed it." He lit the cigarette, and spicy smoke coiled to the catwalks above. "But allow me to tell you this. There is one who approached you tonight. He didn't tell you his name, nor is it important. It's whom he represents that matters. And I say this not in an attempt to control you, but in an effort to save you, Mr. Wilder. *Do not talk to them.*"

The force of Farr's words struck Travis by surprise, pushing him back into the seat. "Duratek," he said.

Deirdre crouched down beside Travis. "Yes, the man at the saloon was from Duratek Corporation. They've been—"

Farr raised a hand. "Not yet, Deirdre. There are some things we must tell Mr. Wilder first."

Deirdre stood and gave a curt nod.

Farr leaned against the stage. "It's true that we're interested in the man in the black robe who came to the saloon. We've been investigating cases like this for some time. However, we investigate many things, and it was not because of him that we came to Castle City."

"But what happened to him?" Travis said, his voice a croak. "How did he . . . ?"

Farr picked up the envelope and pulled out more photos. He handed them to Travis. Although he did not want to, Travis forced himself to look. Images met his eyes: dark husks twisted into horrible poses. He recalled a television special he had seen about Pompeii. Thousands had been buried by the scalding ash of Vesuvius. Nineteen centuries later, archaeologists had poured plaster into the hollows where their bodies had been burned away. Those casts reminded Travis of the shapes in the photos, each one a perfect effigy of the final moment of pain, before the fire consumed them.

Farr held out a hand, and Travis gratefully surrendered the photos.

"What's happening to them?" he said.

Farr drew on his cigarette. "That's a question we

very much want to answer. There have been incidents of spontaneous combustion recorded for centuries, but the current cases are different in subtle ways.
Our tests show that the spot temperatures reached
are far higher than in previous cases. Even so, with
almost all victims, the body is not consumed by the
heat. Instead, we've recorded distinct changes in mor-
phology, organic chemical composition, and even
DNA structure. The man who entered your establish-
ment is one of the few exceptions, as his immolation
was complete. In virtually all other cases, it is not as
if the victim is being burned so much as . . .
changed."

Travis glanced up at Deirdre, his gray eyes wide
behind his spectacles. "It's just like what you told
me, the story about the Immolated Man. But you said
that was only a myth."

Deirdre gave a wry smile. "*Only a myth* is an oxy-
moron, Travis. Myths have the power to reveal truths
about our lives in ways our senses can't. In some
ways, myths are *more* real than the world we see, not
less."

Farr crushed out his cigarette in a rusted sardine
tin. "Over the last several months, there has been an
epidemic of these new cases of spontaneous combustion. Some in our organization believe they might be
related to the current heat wave on this continent.
Some have . . . other ideas. Regardless, right now
the outbreak is largely unknown to the public. But
that might soon change."

"Why?" Travis said, not sure he wanted to know.

Farr's expression was grim. "Just last week I
watched a man in a Kansas City hospital burning,
even as the doctors there tried to save him. His case
was atypical in that, for several hours after the immolation, he survived."

Travis pressed his eyes shut. No, he had not

wanted to know this. He forced his eyes back open. "What . . . what did he . . . ?"

"What did he become?" Farr shook his head. "I'm not certain. However, the hospital's tests will certainly reveal what our own studies have. It is only a matter of time before this story is more widely known. But to answer your question: Toward the end, before he ceased, his flesh was the color and texture of basalt, and when a nurse attempted to give him an injection, witnesses say that he touched her, and she caught on fire. She's in an intensive care unit at the moment. The doctors doubt she will survive."

Travis swallowed hot bile. "So what does this have to do with me?"

"Nothing, or so we thought," Farr said. "We did not think these incidents were related to your case. And they still might not be. But one thing I have learned over the years is to seek connection in coincidence."

Something was wrong—something beyond the Seekers, beyond the immolations. "But if you didn't come to Castle City because of the burnt people, why did you come?"

Farr glanced at Deirdre. "I think you might do a better job here."

Deirdre perched on the corner of the seat next to Travis. "You say you've spoken to Dr. Beckett. That means you know what happened to her last fall at Denver Memorial Hospital, when—"

"—when she killed one ironheart, and Hadrian helped her escape another at the Denver police station." He knew it was wrong to enjoy the surprised looks on their faces, but he did all the same.

Deirdre gave a slow nod. "I imagine Grace told you the Seekers were interested in her experiences. After the incident at the police station, we tried to regain contact with her, but we failed. The car we had given her was found abandoned just outside Castle City. In the time since we've tried to discover where she went next."

"It's a world called Eldh," Travis said quietly.

He could see both Deirdre and Farr tense as they exchanged looks. Deirdre started to lift a hand. Farr gave a slight shake of his head, and she nodded.

"Here," Farr said as he took another photo from the envelope. "I want you to look at something else."

Travis took the photo, afraid he would see more images of shriveled bodies. Instead it was a view looking west down Elk Street, in tones of sepia rather than Kodacolor. The muddy street was crowded with horses and wagons. Men in rumpled wool suits stood in groups, and women walked by in dark, heavy dresses.

"This photo was taken here in Castle City in 1897," Deirdre said. "I found it in the archives at the county library."

Travis squinted. "What am I supposed to be looking at?"

"Here," Farr said, pointing to a figure in the lower left corner of the old photo. "This man."

The photo was blurry at the edges, but Travis could still make out an elderly, dignified gentleman in a dark jacket and waistcoat. His white beard was neatly trimmed, but his hair flew about his head, and he gazed forward with piercing eyes.

It felt as if someone had slipped a needle into Travis's heart. He looked up. "But that's . . . that's Jack."

"Yes," Farr said. "We've been searching for your friend Jack Graystone for some time now, Mr. Wilder."

Travis clutched the photo. "You're too late."

Deirdre met his eyes. "I'm so sorry, Travis."

Silence settled over the opera house.

"I'd like a cup of coffee," Farr said. "Would anyone care to join me?"

Minutes later they stood on the stage. Travis gripped a Styrofoam cup in his hands, filled from a thermos that Farr had produced. Travis had thought the stage to be empty, but he saw now it was just an illusion conjured by the spotlight. A table stood at the back, cluttered with folders, laptop computers, and pieces of electronic equipment whose purposes he couldn't guess.

Travis took a sip from his cup. It burned his tongue, but he didn't care. "What's going on, Deirdre? What is all of this?"

She glanced at Farr. "What can I tell him?"

"Whatever you need to tell him. Just remember the Nine and the One."

Deirdre's expression was thoughtful, then she nodded and looked up. "It was the autumn after I left Castle City that I first heard of the Seekers." She paced as she talked, her black biker boots beating against the stage. "I traveled to Ireland, looking for some inspiration for my music, and after that I spent some time tramping around England, Wales, and Scotland. For a week I played at a pub in Edinburgh. That was where I first met Hadrian. We talked after my set one night, and he said some amazing things about . . . possibilities. Possibilities I've wondered about myself." She smiled. "A week later, he took me to the Seekers' Charterhouse in London."

"I was lucky to find you," Farr said. "The Seekers were lucky."

Deirdre's eyes grew distant. "I've always known there are many worlds besides our own, worlds that can sometimes draw near to this one. It's a belief both my parents gave me." Her gaze focused again on Travis. "I knew the moment I met them that I belonged with the Seekers."

"So you look for other worlds," Travis said.

It was Farr who answered him. "As I said, Mr. Wilder, we seek many things. But to answer your question—yes, for five centuries the Seekers have sought out, cataloged, and studied evidence of worlds other than this Earth.''

Deirdre gave a wry smile. "It's not quite as glamorous as it sounds. After I joined, I found out that most of what the Seekers do consists of reading boring old papers and entering records into a computer."

Farr glanced at her. "However, it was in doing just such *boring* work that you found the key to a case that had hit a dead end over a century ago."

Deirdre picked up a folder. "This file concerns a man the Seekers know as James Sarsin. We don't know what his real name is, as he's had many. However, he went by the name of Sarsin when the Seekers first became aware of him. He was a bookseller in London at the time. This was early in the reign of Queen Elizabeth." Deirdre glanced up from the folder. "By the way, that's Queen Elizabeth *One.* All of this occurred in the year 1564, but it was clear even then that the man who called himself Sarsin had been living in and around London for nearly two centuries."

Travis shook his head. "But that's—" He cut the sentence short. *Impossible* was a meaningless word. Anything was possible. Hadn't he learned that well enough?

Deirdre pulled several papers from the folder. "These are copies of the deeds for Mr. Sarsin's London bookshop, dating from 1532 to 1851. If you look at them, you'll see that, every fifty years or so, the proprietor of the Queen's Shelf died, and the business was bequeathed to another individual."

Travis flipped through the pages. Reading was always hard, and the ornate script complicated the task, but his work with runes helped him concentrate and decipher the signatures: *Oliver Sarsin, Jacques Gris-Pierre, Louis Gris-Pierre.* He looked up. "What's so unusual about this?"

"Not much—that is, until you take a look at this." Deirdre pulled another sheet from the file. "All of these deeds were drawn up in the days of inkwells and quill pens. Occasionally, the person signing the deed smudged the document, leaving a fingerprint. This shows a comparison of prints lifted from deeds signed in the years 1592, 1651, and 1799."

Travis glanced at the sheet. He was no expert on the subject, but even he could see that the magnified sections of the three prints bore the same pattern of whorls. "So you're telling me that this man lived in London for over three centuries, every once in a while pretending to die and leaving his business to himself so the neighbors wouldn't get too suspicious?"

Deirdre's dark eyes sparkled. "You make it sound so mundane."

"The Seekers suspected that there might be something otherworldly to Mr. Sarsin's nature," Farr said. "So over the centuries we have observed him, hoping to learn more."

"Didn't they ever consider just asking him?"

Farr set down his coffee. "Seekers tried to approach Mr. Sarsin on several occasions. However, he refused to speak to them. It was clear he was aware of us and our curiosity, and he had no intention of cooperating. Then, shortly after 1880, the Queen's Shelf burned to the ground. Mr. Sarsin vanished, and the case was closed. That is, until Deirdre came along."

She shrugged. "It was chance, really. I was archiving old folders, scanning evidence into the computer system in London. One of the pieces was a letter—the last bit of information about James Sarsin that the Seekers retrieved. It was addressed to an acquaintance in London, but there was no return address, and no way to know from where the letter had been sent."

Deirdre searched through the folder, then pulled out a crisp, yellowed sheet. She read in a low voice.

I fear, my friend, that I cannot impart where I am currently, but let me say that I have found my way quite by accident into the most glorious valley. The native people call the great, rugged mountain that rises to the west *Clouded Brow,* but to my eyes, as I am certain you can quite understand, it looks rather more like a castle. I shan't be surprised if I soon decide to make a home for myself here.

Travis went rigid. "Clouded Brow? But that's the Ute name for Castle Peak."

"Yes," Deirdre said. "It is."

At last Travis understood. "It was Jack. He was James Sarsin. That's why you came to Castle City, isn't it?"

"You saw the photo," Deirdre said. "Jack Graystone lived in Castle City for more than a century, and he didn't age a day. I think you know the answer as well as we do."

"Would you like to sit down, Mr. Wilder?" Farr gestured to a chair by the table.

Travis nodded and sank into the chair. He gripped his right hand. He knew that Jack was—had been—a wizard from Eldh, but would he ever really understand who Jack was? And what Jack had done to him?

Deirdre laid her hand on his shoulder. "Are you all right?"

Travis shook with silent laughter. Why were people always asking him that just after they'd pulled the rug out from under him?

Farr sat on the edge of the table. "Once we knew of Jack Graystone, we suspected it was not chance that Grace Beckett came to Castle City just prior to her disappearance. Deirdre knew that you were friends with Graystone. And, as we began investigating, we learned that you yourself had vanished the same night as Dr. Beckett. So I think you can understand why we wished to speak to you."

Travis only stared at the folder on the table.

"You are an amazing man, Mr. Wilder," Farr said, his brown eyes intent. "You realize that, don't you? James Sarsin and Grace Beckett are two of the Seekers' most important cases. Both are without doubt otherworldly travelers. And you are connected to both. In fact, I would hazard that you are an otherworldly traveler yourself."

"Why?" Travis said. "Why do you care so much about other worlds?"

Farr's voice was low. "What is life without new discoveries, new knowledge, new experiences? We are scholars, Mr. Wilder. What motivation do we need beyond wonder itself?"

Travis ran a hand over the folder, certain the other he had met that night would be very interested to see it, would pay dearly for the information within. He looked up. "What about them? What about the others?"

"Duratek." Deirdre spoke the word like a curse.

"We are not the only ones who seek other worlds," Farr said. "But we seek them for very different reasons. As I said, we are scholars and academics, interested in knowledge for knowledge's sake."

Travis licked his lips. "What about Duratek? What do they want?"

Deirdre clenched her hand into a fist. "To use. To consume. To rape."

"What do you mean?"

Farr leaned close. "Think about it, Mr. Wilder. An entire new world of resources, completely unspoiled, with an indigenous population whose technology is centuries behind our own. We're talking about a whole new Third World. Only on that world, there are no laws, no regulations, no international social organizations that must be considered and obeyed. There is only raw wealth, ready for the taking by whomever finds it first."

Travis stared at Farr, then beyond. He saw the silvery *valsindar* of the Winter Wood cut down to the bare ground. He saw the rugged highlands of Galt gashed by open mines, pitted with smoking holes. He saw the nine towers of Calavere crumbled by the force of a wrecking ball. New fear filled him, not for himself, but for Eldh and all who dwelled on it. They had saved the Dominions from the Pale King. Would it now fall to a new kind of master?

"No," Travis said. "No, that can't happen."

"Then help us," Farr said.

Deirdre touched his hand. "Please, Travis."

He looked down at the folder, opened it, and ran his fingers through the old papers—Jack's papers. He didn't want to be this important. It was being thrust on him as surely as the power Jack had given him. All the same, Brother Cy was right. You couldn't choose what happened to you in life. But you could choose what you would do with it.

"All right, I'll—"

He halted as something caught his eye. A corner of paper stuck out from the folder. Travis could only make out a few of the words written on it, but they caused him to pull the paper from the stack. It was a poem—no, a song. The words were written in a spidery hand, but they were so familiar he had no trouble making out the first lines:

> *We live our lives a circle,*
> *And wander where we can. . . .*

He set down the paper and looked up. He could only imagine the expression on his face, for both Deirdre and Farr took a step back.

Deirdre shook her head. "Travis, what is it?"

He spoke the words in a quiet voice. "You used me."

Farr shot Deirdre a concerned look. She opened her mouth and struggled for words.

Travis stood. "The song. 'Fire and Wonder.' You said you learned it from a singer in Minnesota. But that's not true." He slapped the folder with a hand. "You learned it here, in Jack's papers. You played it in the saloon just to see if I would react."

Deirdre's face was stricken. "I'm sorry, Travis. I didn't mean to manipulate you. But I had to know if you recognized the song. There wasn't any other way."

She reached for him, but he pulled back. *You can never really know another. . . .*

"Yes there was," he said. "You always have a choice. You could have asked me."

She moved toward him, and he took another step back.

"Please, Travis. Don't go." There was fear in her dark eyes, but whether for him or herself he couldn't tell.

Farr had not moved. "There is a great discovery to be made, Mr. Wilder. And it *will* be made. You cannot hide what you have learned forever. Help us make this discovery for the right reasons, not the wrong ones."

Anger turned Travis's blood to fire. Who were they to ask such a thing? This wasn't some peculiar artifact they wanted to dig up. It was a *world:* a world with living, breathing people. Putting it under a magnifying glass, pinning it like a specimen to cardboard—how was that any better than grinding it all into metal and plastic?

"No," he said. "You don't understand. I won't let you use me to get there. Not you—not anyone."

Before either could answer him, Travis turned and ran through the darkened opera house and into the night.

13.

"We have to go after him."

Deirdre grabbed her helmet and pulled fingerless leather gloves from inside.

Hadrian raised an eyebrow. "You're so certain, then, you know entirely the nature of what we've found here?"

Deirdre jerked on the gloves. "No, we don't know, but that doesn't matter now. Travis could be in danger. There's no telling what Duratek might do if they got him."

Hadrian crossed his arms, and his lips twisted in an ironic smile. "I'm not so certain, at the moment, he thinks any more of us than he does of them."

"Then I'm going to change that." She raised the helmet to put it on.

"Very well. I'll contact the Seekers and let them know that you've decided Desideratum Three is no longer necessary. I'm sure they'll be happy to strike it from the Book."

Deirdre winced and lowered the helmet.

Hadrian stepped toward her. *"A Seeker watches but does not interfere.* You've already broken that rule once by coming between Mr. Wilder and Duratek. Do you really want to compound the infraction? In the past, the Philosophers have tended toward mercy with those who violate the Desiderata once and demonstrate sufficient remorse. However, they don't have a reputation for indulging repeat offenders."

Deirdre gritted her teeth. "Fine. Then I'll go after Travis as a friend, not a Seeker."

Hadrian laughed. "And now you're forgetting the Vow."

Deirdre stared at him, then her shoulders slumped. *"A Seeker's duty is first to the Seekers."*

"So you remember it after all."

She set down the helmet, and molten anger faded away, replaced by a cold amalgam of dread, sorrow, and resignation. At that moment she hated Hadrian. But it was only because he was right. She had not sworn the Vow lightly that day three years ago, beneath the sprawling sixteenth-century manor just outside of London. The Seekers were her life now. And although they sometimes seemed exasperatingly restrictive, the Vow and the Nine Desiderata had been created to protect both agents of the Seekers as well as their subjects. It was just that sometimes situations were more complicated than had ever been anticipated by the ancient rules—first set down in the Book five centuries ago by the medieval society of alchemists known as the Philosophers.

Deirdre leaned against the stage. "So we just let him go, then?"

"For now, yes. The Desiderata are clear on this. We cannot force Mr. Wilder to speak with us. We can only observe. That's because the Seekers must see what individuals with otherworldly connections do of their own free will—without being influenced by our activities, which might contaminate any knowledge we gain from them. In the meantime, remember our motto. *To Watch—To Believe—To Wait.*"

"But wait for what?"

Hadrian was silent. Then, "For the danger you fear to become real, so that even the Philosophers must see it."

Deirdre stood up straight. *Of course. That's how he*

did it—that's how he made contact with Grace Beckett but didn't bring down the wrath of the Philosophers.

"The Ninth Desideratum," she said aloud.

Hadrian's crooked grin flashed in the gloom. "Very good. You're thinking now." He moved to the table, drew out the photo of Dr. Grace Beckett, and ran a thumb over it. "The Ninth Desideratum. *Above all else, a Seeker must let no other being come to harm.*"

He set down the photo, turned, and fixed his dark gaze on Deirdre.

"It's the Ninth that keeps us human. The Ninth that pricks our arrogance and keeps us from using the knowledge we gain to play games with fate." He gestured to the electronic surveillance equipment on the table. "We observe, we catalog, we study. It's all very proper, even antiseptic. But the moment another sentient being's existence is imperiled, all Desiderata are meaningless save the Ninth."

Deirdre ran a hand through her hair. It was good, but not good enough. She wanted to act *now*. "So how long do we have to wait?"

"If you're right, Deirdre, not long. Not long at all."

Deirdre studied her associate. From the beginning she had suspected there was more to Hadrian Farr than she could see on the surface, and at that moment she was certain of it. One did not rise through the ranks of the Seekers as he had done without good cause. Rumors told that Farr had found evidence of an otherworldly portal—only recently closed—inside a Mayan pyramid in the Yucatán. This, in combination with his Class One encounter with Grace Beckett, had caused some to whisper that he was being groomed to become a Philosopher.

Of course, no one Deirdre had met in the Seekers knew for certain exactly who the Philosophers were, or if any of them had once worked as Seeker agents before becoming part of the organization's secret governing circle. Although all orders ultimately came from the Philosophers—by letter, or more recently by electronic means—after three years in the Seekers Deirdre had yet to see or speak with one. Unless she had done so unknowingly, for there were those in the Seekers who held that the Philosophers walked disguised among them.

She moved to the table. Hadrian was flipping through the pages of a small, leather-bound journal. It was from the Sarsin file. The Seekers had recovered it over a century ago, from the remains of the Queen's Shelf in London. Those pages not darkened by fire were still illegible, for the symbols written upon them, although runelike in appearance, were similar to no current or historical system of writing. No system known on Earth, at least.

Hadrian ran a finger over a half-obscured line drawing. The drawing depicted a sword, the flat of its blade incised with the strange runes. There was one connection they had not told Travis about—another link between Grace Beckett and the man known as both James Sarsin and Jack Graystone.

She picked up the photo of Grace Beckett and touched the image of the subject's necklace. It was a trapezoidal piece of metal. Deirdre could not see them in this picture, but she had studied digitally enhanced enlargements, and she knew that the symbols on Dr. Beckett's necklace corresponded exactly to those in a portion of the journal drawing. That the pendant was a fragment of the sword depicted in the sketch was not the question. How Grace Beckett had come by the necklace—and without any known contact with Jack Graystone—was.

Deirdre sighed. "What does it mean?"

It was a rhetorical question. She didn't expect Hadrian to answer, but he did all the same.

"It means we don't know," Hadrian said without

looking up. "It means for all our observations, for all our centuries of studies and analyses, we are as children when it comes to understanding the mysteries before us."

"But children learn, Hadrian. We can learn. We'll watch Travis." She clenched a fist. "And we'll get to him before Duratek."

"Perhaps. But what of those who might get to him before that?"

Deirdre frowned, lowering her hand. "Who do you mean?"

Hadrian shut the journal and said nothing.

14.

The sky was burning.

Travis sat on the crumbled remains of a wall—its bricks darkened with smoke and cracked by heat— and watched the dawn trickle into the valley. He craned his stiff neck and gazed at the ruins around him: the slumped remnants of a stone chimney, the scorched plane of a plaster wall, pieces of furniture scattered on the ground, as charred and tortured as anything dug up from the ash beds of Pompeii.

What had made him come to the wreckage of the Magician's Attic? It wasn't until first light transmuted the sky from slate to steel that he had even realized this was where his feet had led him after he fled the opera house. But maybe it made some sort of sense. In a way, this was where the fires had all begun.

Where is Jakabar of the Gray Stone?

Travis heard the desiccated hiss again, as if the man in black had just whispered it in his ear. Jakabar of the Gray Stone—Jack Graystone. It was Jack. It had to be. Who else would the man in black have been searching for? If Travis still had any doubts, then the evidence Deirdre and Farr had shown him last night had erased them.

Travis gripped his right hand and stared at the remnants of the antique shop. Anger flared in his heart, as hot and bright as the sun.

"It's not fair, Jack," he whispered. "It's not fair, leaving me the way you did. Now I'm stuck with everything you abandoned, and I don't understand it. I'm not even close. People are looking for you, and it's me they're finding instead, and I don't know what to do. You got off easy."

The sun peered over the shoulder of Castle Peak. Travis lifted his head, stared into the hot eye, and willed himself to burn as Jack had burned.

Something dark eclipsed the sun, and a cool shadow fell across his face. At first he could not see, then his eyes adjusted, and his gaze discerned the two figures who stood before him. He pushed up his spectacles, then slipped from the wall.

The woman and the girl wore dresses black as cinders, and their faces were pale as the moon in day. The child's hair was dark—as if the stuff of night still clung to her—but the woman's hair caught the dawn light and spun it into copper. Travis drew in a breath of wonder. But this too made sense. They had been here the last time everything had changed.

"Samanda," he whispered.

The girl regarded him with wise purple eyes. "We have been looking for you," she said in a lisping voice.

Despite the strangeness of the moment, Travis's lips curled in a bitter smile. "You're not the only ones."

The woman groped with a hand, then clutched the girl's shoulder. "Is it him, then? Does he stand before us?"

"Yes, Sister Mirrim," the child said. "He does indeed."

Travis glanced up, and only then did he see the strip of gauze that had been bound across the woman's face, concealing her eyes. He looked back at the girl. "What happened to her?"

"She gazed into the fire, to see what lay within."

Travis shook his head. "She's blind, then?"

Now it was Child Samanda who smiled, the pink bud of her mouth turning upward in a knowing curve. "Fear not for Sister Mirrim. She has other vision, other eyes."

It felt as if Travis stood on a carousel, the world slowly spinning around him. "I don't understand."

The girl held out a hand. A black shape rested on her small palm: a raven folded of crisp paper.

Travis staggered back and caught himself against the wall. This couldn't be happening, not again.

"I see it," Sister Mirrim whispered. "The birds of night have fallen, their wings have been burned. New dark ones come, and all the land shrivels under their touch." Her hands curled into claws at her sides, and her voice rose into a shrill chant. "The Dead One who was forgotten walks again. He has locked the heart of fire in his prison, and—no! It must not be! He holds a flaming sword in his hand. He will cut a wound in the sky, to grasp the stars, and all the world will drown in a rain of blood!"

Travis stared at Sister Mirrim, and wet horror filled his lungs. Red tears streamed from the bandage that covered her eyes and ran down her cheeks.

"You must go," the girl said.

Travis tore his gaze from Sister Mirrim and looked down at the child. The paper raven was gone. Her small hand held only ashes, and even as he watched the wind blew these away.

"But where?" His mouth was a desert, his voice a croak. "Where am I supposed to go?"

Wise purple eyes glinted. Her voice was a faint whisper, as if she were already fading. "You must die to be transformed."

He held out a hand. "No, wait—"

Light struck Travis's face, blinding him. He turned from the glare of the sun. It was only a second, maybe two, but by the time he turned back the fire-baked ground where both child and woman had stood was empty.

Laughter bubbled in his throat, but he knew it would be a mad sound, and he swallowed it back down. It was easy for them, easy for the ones who went away. But what about him? What about the ones who stayed behind? What were they supposed to do? Then he thought of Sister Mirrim's eyes, and he knew that it wasn't easy for any of them.

Travis stepped away from the broken wall, then halted. He still didn't know where to go. If Child Samanda's words had held an answer, then he could not grasp it. He considered going back to the saloon, then forced himself to forget the idea. Duratek knew to find him there. And so did Deirdre and the Seekers. He turned his back toward Castle City and started walking across an empty field. Maybe it didn't matter where he went, just so they didn't find him.

He reached the highway that led out of town and kept on going. Sometimes the act of walking was purpose enough. Then something caught his eye.

Travis approached the dented newspaper box that rested beside the road, next to a row of mailboxes. He squatted down and, through the scratched plastic panel, read the headline:

DOZENS BURNED NATIONWIDE—CAUSE UNKNOWN
One Doctor Calls It "a New Black Death"

Beneath the headline was a photo: a dark, twisted shape like those in the photos Hadrian Farr had shown him. He sucked in a breath between his teeth, then scanned down the article.

Researchers have yet to discover the cause for the self-immolations that have been reported throughout the Midwest in the last six weeks. Some have labeled it a wave of copycat suicides, but in none of the deaths has a fuel or other flammable agent been identified. According to witnesses, many victims have shown symptoms of unusual behavior and high fever shortly before—

The article broke off, continued on an inside page. The column below held only a small story about the increasing use of Electria among young people, compared to other drugs. Travis dug into the pocket of his jeans, but his hand came up with only a scant collection of pennies. Not that it mattered. He didn't need to read any more; he knew now where he had to go. Maybe this really was like the Black Death. Maybe it was a disease—a disease transmitted by touch.

He shoved the coins back into his pocket, lurched to his feet, and glanced at the horizon. "Hang on, Max," he whispered. "You've got to hang on."

Travis thought about getting his truck, but it was still parked at the saloon. It would be quicker to walk to Max's place than to go back and retrieve the vehicle. He scrambled over a slumped wire fence and headed across the empty field south of the road. Minutes later he crested a rise and saw the Castle City railyard ahead. The road to Max's apartment was just on the other side.

He skidded down a gravel slope to the flats around the railyard. A hundred years ago, trains had passed through Castle City three times a week, carrying people, dry goods, tools, and coal. However, the last train had rolled out of this place two decades ago. Now the railyard was a silent place: a cemetery where dreams of wealth had died, and boxcars lay strewn about like the corpses no one had bothered to bury.

Travis picked his way over rusted tracks, passed the caved-in remains of the old station house, and crossed to the farside of the railyard. From here it was just over a mile to Max's place.

He came up short against a twelve-foot chain-link fence.

Travis stared at the fence, not comprehending. Then he remembered. They had raised this fence a few years ago. A boy playing in one of the boxcars had shut the door, locking himself in. They hadn't found his body for weeks.

Travis took a step back and looked up. The fence was topped with coils of razor wire. Rust tinged its edges, but it looked like blood, and he knew the wire would still slice through skin like butter. The only way out was to return the way he had come, then circle around the yard. Except that would take him farther out of his way than heading back to town and his truck.

He gripped the chain link, but he didn't bother tugging on it. There was nothing to do but go back and hope he hadn't wasted too much time. Besides, maybe he was wrong. Maybe all Max had gotten when he touched the man in black was the burn on his hand. At that moment Max was probably in his apartment, resting like he was supposed to be, and he would laugh when Travis knocked on his door.

Or maybe Travis would look through the window of Max's apartment again, only this time he would see a picture like the one in the paper. He shook his head, forced the image from his mind, and turned away from the fence.

"Hello, Travis."

Travis spun and stared back through the fence, jaw open. The man stood where, a moment ago, there had been only dead weeds and empty air. Then Travis saw the curve of black metal just protruding from behind a boxcar. But how had the man known to come to the railyard?

"Look in your pocket," the other said.

The man was still clad all in black, and, with his neatly trimmed goatee and shorn blond hair, he looked ready for a New York art opening. But shadows touched the pale skin beneath his eyes, and stubble darkened his cheeks. This night had taken its toll on him as well.

"Your pocket, Travis. I can see the question on your face. Go on—you'll find the answer there."

Travis hesitated, then slipped a hand into the pocket of his jeans. He pulled out the same few pennies he had at the newspaper box. "I don't understand."

The man smiled—a compelling expression. Travis had always envied men like him: short, compact, brightly handsome. Sometimes it felt ridiculous to be tall.

"That one," the other said. "The Denver 1966. Look at it—bring it in close."

Travis held up the coin. At first he saw nothing unusual. Then he noticed it was thicker than the other pennies, and a seam ran along the edge. He worked a thumbnail into the seam. The penny split in half. Inside the thin, copper shell a silicon chip shone like a diamond in the morning light.

Travis looked up, eyes wide. "But you were never close enough."

"To plant it on you? No, I wasn't. But a customer in your saloon would have been, don't you think? In fact, I bet you'd probably never even notice if she slipped it into your pocket while you delivered a round of drinks to her table."

Travis shook his head. It didn't make sense—everyone at the saloon last night had been a local.

"It's like I said, Travis." The man spread his hands. "You can never really know another."

So that was the answer. Someone else he knew had used him. Travis turned and heaved the transmitter deep into the railyard. There was a *ping*, then silence. He turned back, and his words edged into a sneer.

"So what took you so long to find me?"

"The mountains have a strange effect on radio signals, especially after dark. We couldn't pick you up until sunrise. Then we came as quickly as we could."

Now Travis grinned—it was not an expression of humor—and rattled the fence. "It looks like something got in your way."

The man shrugged, his expression sheepish. "We try to account for everything we can. This mission took several months of planning. But even we can't predict all factors. I'm afraid our map of Castle City was somewhat out of date."

Travis's grin faded. "I'll be gone by the time you drive around, you know."

"What makes you think I don't have wire cutters in the car?"

"You would have used them already if you had."

The man laughed. "Very good, Travis. You're a smart man. A fascinating man." He gripped the chain link, his blue eyes bright behind his glasses. "I so want to speak to you. Do you know that, Travis? Do you have any idea how much I want to listen to you, to hear about everything you've done, every place you've gone, all the sights you've seen?"

"Why?" Travis said. "So you can know which mountain range to start mining first?"

"Is that what the Seekers told you I wanted?"

"Isn't it?"

His knuckles whitened as he gripped the fence. "The Seekers are as blind as they are arrogant. They think they're so open-minded, but they're not." He let go of the fence, took a breath. "Listen, Travis. The

Seekers say they're scholars, and they are, but they're the worst kind. They're not trying to learn and understand. They already think they have everything figured out. All they want are a few specimens they can stick in a case to prove it."

"How do you know so much about the Seekers?"

He fixed his eyes on Travis. "Because I was one once."

Travis opened his mouth, but he had no response.

"It comes down to this," the other said. "The Seekers think they have ownership of any new world that's discovered—that only the elite should be able to see it, study it, catalog it. Duratek is different. That's why I joined. We think that a new world should belong to everybody, not just a few academics in their high towers. We want to give this world to everyone."

"You want to exploit, you mean. To sell it."

"Words, Travis. Those are just words. And the Seekers' words at that, I'd guess."

Travis took a step back from the fence.

"Listen," the man said, his voice hushed with urgency. "I know I don't have much time with you. So let me just say one last thing. Two worlds are drawing near, ours and another. You know that better than anyone. That connection is going to be made—you can't stop it. But what you *can* do is help us manage it, control it, to make it happen the right way, not the wrong way."

Travis hesitated. "What do you mean?"

The other shook his head. "What are you asking? Are we going to harvest its resources, mine its ground, farm its soil? Is that the question? If so, the answer's yes. I'm not going to lie to you, Travis, I've told you that. This isn't some park we're talking about. We're not going to put a fence around it, not like this." He brushed a hand across the chain link. "But the exchange doesn't have to be one-sided.

Think of the things we have to offer. Jobs. Technology. Medicine. This isn't the first time we've discovered new worlds, Travis. But this can be the first time we do it right. Except we need your help." He stepped back from the fence. "It's your choice."

Travis didn't move. The wind moaned around the abandoned boxcars. Wasn't that what this place had been once? A jumping-off point to a new world of prosperity? They had pushed out the Indians, killed off the buffalo, and pulled the guts from the mountains looking for wealth to cart to the world back East. Now the silver and gold were gone, but the mountains still bore the open, oozing wounds. Yes, he did have a choice. He always had a choice.

"No." Travis's voice was hard. "No, I won't help you. What you want to do is wrong. No matter how hard you try to make it right, it's still wrong. There's no price you can pay to balance what you want to take."

The other's eyes were regretful behind his glasses. "I'm sorry to hear you say that, Travis. You see, now that I've met you, I had hoped that we could be friends. But, it doesn't matter. With or without your help, we'll get what we want. We always do. Because we're on the side of right, the side of history." He lifted a hand, almost like a salute. "Good luck, Travis. But you can't stop us."

Travis hissed the words between clenched teeth. "If you really want to find a new world, then go to hell."

He turned before the other could reply, picked his way across the railyard, and waited until the fence was out of sight before he broke into a dead run.

15.

Travis skulked inside the hot shadows of an alley on the eastern end of Elk Street. He almost laughed at himself. Was this what it felt like to be an outlaw? Or a fugitive on the run? Except he wasn't the one who intended to do wrong.

Beyond the mouth of the alley, the air danced and shimmered above the weathered asphalt. Afternoon had draped its stifling golden gauze over the valley, binding the sun in the sky. It seemed like this day would never find an end. But one way or another, it had to.

From his shirt pocket, Travis pulled a crumpled paper. He had finally made it to Max's place around midday, after hours of picking his way through town, doing his best to make sure no one saw him. It was an indication of his fear of being seen that he did something he had not attempted since his return to Earth. Travis spoke a rune.

It was *Alth,* the rune of shadows. As always, his right hand tingled when he spoke the rune, and a rushing noise filled his ears. But the sound was distant and hollow, and it ended too quickly. The air seemed to dim a shade around him, but that was all. However, even this minor result had left him weak and shaking from effort. Clearly his power here was but a fraction of what it was on Eldh.

He supposed he should have been relieved—he had never wanted this in the first place. In the end, power could only harm. But he had to admit, his abilities as a runelord might have come in handy right now.

Whether the weakly spoken rune was enough, or whether any eyes had noticed his progress, Travis couldn't say, but he had made it to Max's apartment without getting accosted. However, before he even reached the door, he knew his partner wasn't there. He forced himself to peer through the window, dreading what he might see, but this time the curtains were closed. A sigh of relief escaped him, then he swore at himself. Max was fine, he had to be.

Travis turned to go, and it was only then that he noticed the paper tucked next to the doorknob. For the dozenth time, there in the alley, Travis unfolded the sheet torn from a yellow legal pad and read the words printed in Max's neat, ambidextrous handwriting:

> Travis,
> Since you're reading this, it means I was right and you did stop by. Sorry I keep missing you. I'm going to be out all day again—doctors and all that—but meet me at the saloon at sundown. I'll help you open things up.
>
> Max

Travis grinned—like a corpse in the desert grinned as the heat and dry shrank the flesh from its skull. *Meet me at the saloon at sundown.* It sounded like a line from a late-night Western: some sort of apocalyptic showdown at the You-Name-It Corral. But it was just a note, and Max couldn't have known what had happened to Travis in the last less-than-a-day. Max had been sick, only now he was getting better, and he was just trying to get back to work.

But maybe, in a way, it would be like a showdown. After all, *they* would be watching the saloon, waiting for him. Duratek and the Seekers. Travis folded the note and slipped it back into his pocket.

He jerked his head up at the sound of an engine. A dark vehicle cruised down Elk Street. He tensed to run, although he didn't know where he would run to. The vehicle rolled past: a navy blue pickup. He sighed, then clutched a hand to his gut. It was hard to tell where dread ended and hunger began. He hadn't eaten all day. And he was tired of hiding in shadows.

Travis made a decision. Maybe it was stupid, maybe he would get himself caught, but it was still three hours to sunset, and he couldn't stay in this place any longer. Besides, all that mattered was finding out that Max was all right. If they caught him, he still wouldn't help, he still wouldn't tell them anything about Grace or Eldh.

And you think they don't have ways of making people talk, Travis? In the end they get what they want. That's what he said, and you know it's true.

But no, he couldn't believe that. If he had thought that way on Eldh, the Pale King would have frozen all of the Dominions in ice by now. Then again, the Pale King hadn't had slick television ads, personal area networks, and microchip transmitters. How could magic compete with power like that?

Travis stepped from the alley and glanced in both directions. Elk Street was deserted. The afternoon swelter had driven people indoors—into the dimness, at least, if not the cool. He moved along the boardwalk as quickly as he could without looking like he was running. The Mosquito Café was only a block away. He stuck his hands in his pockets and crunched his broad shoulders in, expecting at any second to hear the squeal of tires, the *chunk* of a car door, and the sound of an angry voice shouting his name. He counted the remaining steps to the Mosquito Café and ducked inside.

The comforting din of conversation and clanking dishes rolled over him, and Travis's fear receded. In some ways, this was safer than hiding. At least he knew these people.

Or did he? Here and there someone nodded or lifted a hand in greeting. Travis started to wave back, then hesitated. These people were his neighbors, his customers. But did he really know any of them? Last night, one he had thought he knew had slipped Duratek's transmitter into his pocket. Maybe she was here now.

"Just yourself, hon?"

Travis blinked. Delores Meeker cocked her head to look at him, chomping on a piece of gum, a menu in her hand. He gave a jerky nod, then followed her toward the back of the café. They were halfway there when he saw Deputy Jace Windom seated at the café's counter. He hesitated, then reached out and touched her arm.

Jace snapped around on the stool, hand on the revolver at her hip. Her eyes were flat and hard. Travis took a startled step back. Jace blinked, and her gaze softened to warm brown.

"Travis—I didn't see you there."

"I'm sorry, Jace. I didn't mean . . . I didn't mean to startle you."

The deputy rose from her stool. Her brown Smokey-the-Bear hat sat next to a mostly uneaten blue plate special. There was something odd about the deputy. Usually she was sharp and precise in the way she moved, in the things she said. Today she seemed slower, that edge dulled.

Delores snapped her gum. "Travis, hon, did you need to ask the deputy something?"

"I'll be just a second," he said.

Delores nodded. "I'll put your menu at the booth back there. Just sit down when you're ready."

Travis managed a smile, and Delores moved away. He turned back to the deputy, and the smile faded.

"What is it, Travis? Is something wrong?"

He swallowed, then forced the question to sound casual. "I was just . . . I was just wondering if you'd seen Max today."

It was subtle but noticeable: Jace stiffened, and the focus of her gaze moved past Travis. "I'm afraid I haven't spoken to Mr. Bayfield in the last seventy-two hours. You're his business partner, Travis. I'm sure you know more about his condition than I do. Besides, I'm a law officer, not a doctor. There's nothing I can do for him."

Travis winced at the harshness in her voice, then realized it wasn't for him or for Max. He glanced down and saw the newspaper next to her plate. With a pen, she had circled the photo of the half-charred corpse.

"It doesn't make a lot of sense, does it, Jace?"

"Nothing makes much sense these days," she murmured.

Travis searched for a reply. There were so many things he wanted to tell her, but he couldn't find the words. "If I see Max, I'll tell him you were thinking of him, Jace."

She nodded without meeting his eyes, then turned back to her cold plate of food. Travis headed to his booth, sank into a slick vinyl seat, and lifted the menu Delores had left for him—more to hide than to decide what to order.

After all that had happened, he thought eating would be difficult, but it was the opposite: The mundane task of putting food into his body was reassuring and familiar. No matter what happened to you, no matter where you went, you still had to eat. Delores brought him meat loaf, mashed potatoes, vegetables, rolls, and apple pie. Travis ate them all.

A shadow hovered over him.

"Travis?"

He pushed back the pie plate. "That's enough, Delores. Really. Just leave the check and—"

She sat in the opposite side of the booth and folded her hands on the spangled Formica.

A lump of fear slid into Travis's stomach, and he wished he hadn't eaten so much. He flicked his eyes from side to side, but no one in the café so much as glanced in his direction. But then, why should they? Everyone in Castle City knew that Travis Wilder and Deirdre Falling Hawk were friends.

"I'm glad I found you, Travis."

"I bet you must get a lot of extra credit points for cornering an otherworldly traveler. I'm sure Farr will give you an A."

Color touched Deirdre's high cheekbones, but she did not flinch. "I probably deserve that. You're right—sometimes scholars can get too caught up in their studies and forget that their subjects are people, too. But that's not what I meant. I'm glad they . . . I'm glad you're all right, Travis." Her hand edged toward his across the Formica. "I've been afraid for you."

He pulled his hand back. "I can take care of myself," he said, but the words were hollow. At that moment he felt as alone as he had those first days on Eldh, traveling through the forlorn silence of the Winter Wood and away from the world he had always known.

Deirdre shook her head. "I want to believe that, Travis. And I know you're smart, and that you have a strong spirit. But you don't know what you're dealing with. You can't."

Travis looked down and ran his thumb across the palm of his right hand. "But maybe I do, Deirdre." He looked up. "Maybe I know better than any of you."

She pressed her lips together, her smoky jade eyes serious. "Please, Travis. You've got to listen to me."

Her voice was low, touched by a quaver he hadn't expected. Maybe she really was afraid for him. He let her eyes draw him in.

Deirdre leaned forward, her voice an urgent whisper. "We blew it, Travis. I blew it. I know I did. I should have trusted you with the truth. But you've got to understand. Duratek will talk to you if they think talking will get them what they want. But they'll do whatever it takes to get the information they need. For their book-balancers, one human life is a small price to pay for an entire new world."

She reached into a nylon pouch slung over her shoulder, drew out a plane ticket, and pushed it across the table.

"This is a ticket to London. Parked in front of the café is a white sedan. Go out, get inside, and the driver will take you to Denver International Airport. She'll see that you make it to the plane. When you get to London, Hadrian Farr will be there to meet you. He'll take you to the London Charterhouse, and we'll all talk again there."

Travis stared at the ticket. "Why?"

"It's not safe for you here, Travis. In London the Seekers can help protect you. You can stay at the Charterhouse as long as you like—and you can leave anytime you want to, I swear it. We won't keep you, not like they would." She shook her head. "I know it's hard to understand. But just come to London, get away from them, and give yourself time to think."

Travis reached out a hand and brushed the corner of the ticket. It would be so easy. He could get away from here, away from the hot, dusty streets of Castle City, and go to London—cool, moist, ancient London. Would it be so bad? After all, the Seekers had helped Grace escape the ironhearts. Travis drew in a breath, then started to pick up the ticket.

Deirdre licked her lips. "There's more, Travis, things we haven't had the chance to tell you yet. About Jack Graystone, and about the immolations. If you come, we can show you what we've found, things Duratek would never give you."

He looked up at her, his gray eyes narrowing behind his spectacles. So there was more Deirdre hadn't trusted him with. He let go of the ticket. What else had the Seekers neglected to tell him? What other information would they dispense in precise doses calculated to make him behave exactly the way they wanted? There was a Travis once who would have let himself be used like this. But he had left that Travis behind on Eldh, in the frozen wastes of Shadowsdeep.

He grinned, a feral expression. "So, is that *your* shadow self, Deirdre? The one that can lie?"

Her eyes went wide, and her jaw worked as she searched for words. "Travis, I had to—"

"No." His voice was quiet but hard. "We choose what we become. That's what you told me. So why should I trust you and not Duratek? They didn't lie to me, Deirdre. You did."

Her face was pale. "Travis, you can't go to them."

"I'm not going to anybody." He rose from the booth.

Deirdre leaped to her feet and reached for him. "Travis, wait. You can't just go. You have to share what you've learned. You have to tell us."

He turned and stared at her. "Why?"

She took a deep breath, then nodded and spoke with calm conviction. "Before you go, answer one thing for me. Just one thing. If you were hiking in the mountains, and you stumbled upon a fabulous Spanish treasure—a chest filled with wonders, lost for centuries—who would you call? A museum dedicated to studying and preserving precious objects? Or a company that would take the gold and melt it all down? Tell me—what would you do?"

Travis met her eyes. "I'd take a shovel, and I'd bury it."

Her mouth opened, but no words came out.

"Good-bye, Deirdre," he said and walked away.

He was almost to the rear exit of the café when he saw Deirdre start moving toward him. Except at that moment Delores Meeker ran after her, waving the check for Travis's food. Deirdre kept going, but Jace Windom stepped in her path, and Delores caught up. The last image Travis saw was Deirdre digging in her pockets, scrambling for money. She shot one last look in his direction: desperate, imploring.

Travis turned and stepped into the fiery light outside.

16.

The sun was still two handspans above the shoulder of Castle Peak, but Travis couldn't wait any longer.

For the last hour he had hidden amid the heaps of junk behind Castle City's old assay office. Kneeling in the dirt, he had passed the time fidgeting with a corroded brass scale he had picked from one of the piles. Once prospectors had used the scale to weigh out their dreams in sacks of gold dust. Now he could not get the arms to swing. Rocks, glass, metal: Nothing tipped the old scale anymore. Everything he had once thought to be solid and real was without weight, without effect. There was nothing left for the device but to melt it down.

He cast the scale back into the dirt, then stood and brushed off his hands. It was time to step into his own crucible.

It wasn't far to the Mine Shaft. He kept to an alley that ran parallel to Elk Street, moving between trash bins, empty crates, and the remains of cars that had rolled off assembly lines when Hitler was still that peculiar little man in Germany. Several times, between buildings, he glimpsed the street beyond, but the few vehicles that drove past were neither black nor white. Then he was there.

Travis climbed the cement steps to the back door of the saloon and put his hand on the knob. He hesitated. It was too early, Max wasn't there yet, the door would be locked.

He turned his hand, and the door swung open.

Dimness beyond, like a cave. Travis stepped inside and shut the door, leaving the last pieces of the day outside.

He stopped and waited for his eyes to adjust. One by one, shapes appeared from shadows: cardboard boxes, empty kegs, a stack of chairs, the hulking form of the saloon's old cast-iron boiler. Travis made his way past the clutter, slipped through a door, and stepped into the main room of the Mine Shaft.

It was a little brighter in here—daylight squeezed through small windows—and Travis saw him at once. Max sat at a table, hunched over something, his back to Travis, his long hair unbound and tangled. A low sound rose and fell on the air. Like muttering. Or like a chant.

Travis moved among the empty chairs, his boots of Eldhish buckskin making no sound against the floor. He came to a stop in front of Max's table, but his partner still bent over the scarred wood, sorting, counting.

"What are they, Max?"

The words were barely a whisper, but they shattered the silence. Max looked up with wild eyes; his matted hair fell back from his face. Travis had prepared himself for the worst, but he took a step back all the same.

"Oh, Max. . . ."

Max's eyes wavered, racking into and out of focus, then locked into place. "Travis?"

The word was the croak of a man lost in a desert, and Max looked the part. His flesh was dark and had sunk close to his bones, and his lips were cracked and oozing. His clothes were disheveled, and a yellow crust caked the bandage that wrapped his right hand. However, no odor rose from him—save for a dry smell, like dirt baked by sun. On the table were a medicine bottle, a plastic bag, and two piles of pills.

The pills were glossy and purple, each marked with a white lightning bolt.

Travis stared at the pills. "Max, what are you doing?"

Max grinned, a terrible caricature of his usual mirth. "You know me, Travis . . . always counting."

Max scooped the pills into the bottle. One of them rolled from the table and bounced across the floor. With shocking speed, Max threw himself from his chair, scrambled on hands and knees, then grabbed the pill with his shaking left hand and brought it greedily to his mouth. He swallowed it dry, then pressed his eyes shut. A few heartbeats limped by, then his trembling eased, and his thin shoulders slumped in a sigh.

When Max opened his eyes again, they were as clear as a hurricane's. "All better now," he said with a laugh.

Travis shuddered at the sound.

Max started to use the table to pull himself up. Travis reached out a hand to help him.

"No! Don't touch me!"

It was the snarl of an animal in pain. Travis leaped back and clutched his hand to his chest. Max staggered to his feet. His eyes were brighter now, burning with feverish light.

A moan escaped Travis. "What's happening to you, Max?"

The expression on Max's face flickered somewhere between wonder and fear. But then, maybe there was little distance between the two. "I don't know, Travis. It's like I'm getting clearer. Clearer and lighter all the time. Everything I always thought was real or important seems so dim to me now. The town, the saloon, the people. I can hardly make them out. But other things . . . they're so bright, so sharp, that I wonder how I didn't ever see them before."

"What things, Max? What things do you mean?"

But Max only smiled and shook his head.

Travis's gaze moved to the bottle of pills on the table. "What are they, Max? Did the doctor give them to you?" But there was no prescription label on the bottle, and before Max could answer the question, Travis knew the answer. He had never seen pills like them before, but what else could the little lightning bolt signify? "It's Electria, isn't it?"

Max picked up the bottle. He held it in the crook of his right elbow. The bony fingers of his left hand fumbled with the lid, then snapped it on.

"I don't know how they knew, Travis. I'd almost forgotten myself. Sure, I used stuff in New York. Then again, I was a senior accountant at one of the top advertising agencies in the city. Things moved so fast, it was almost company policy." He laughed, and it sounded like the old Max. "If you weren't using, they'd send you to the company doctor to get your prescription. But that was ages ago. I left that all behind when I . . . when I came here."

Travis took a step nearer his friend. "Who, Max? Who gave them to you?"

Max didn't look up from the bottle. "They knew me, Travis. They knew all about me, but I didn't know who they were. Sure, I'd seen the commercials. But I never knew what they were advertising. I don't think . . . I don't think it could have been this."

A jolt ran through Travis, like one of those little lightning bolts. The word was more reflex than statement. "Duratek."

Max shoved the bottle into the pocket of his jeans. "I didn't want to. I didn't want to take them. But my hand—nothing else made the pain go away, nothing the doctor gave me, and this . . . this made it stop. At least for a little while." He hung his head, his voice a rasp. "Forgive me, Travis."

Travis tried to blink the stinging from his eyes. He

started to reach out, then remembered and pulled his hand back. "It's all right, Max. It's all right. The pain would make anyone do it. And they're just pills. We'll get you off of them."

Max lifted his gaze. "No, Travis. Not Electria. That's not what I want your forgiveness for."

"Then for what, Max?"

"For what I'm about to do."

A shrill whine pierced the air of the saloon. Travis went rigid. He had heard that sound once before, the last time he had talked to Max on the phone.

Max reached down and unclipped a small object from his belt. A pager. He gazed at the glowing screen, nodded, set the pager on the table, and looked up.

"They're coming."

Invisible hands reached out of the dimness to clutch Travis's throat, strangling him. He stumbled back from the table, sending chairs clattering. Max stood stiff, his expression calm with a kind of sorrowful resignation. Travis fought for air. It was so hard to breathe; the heat was going to suffocate him. A trap. It was a trap.

"How long?" His voice was a croak. "How long do I have?"

Max cradled his wounded hand. His tangled hair hid his face. "Three minutes. Four at the most. They were supposed to be here before you, waiting, but you were early. I guess they hadn't counted on that. I guess they thought you'd stay away until the last minute."

Travis's lips pulled back from his teeth in a rictus grin, and he thought of the fence in the old railyard. "Even they make mistakes."

Max nodded. "But not many."

Travis's grin faded. He clenched his hands into fists, but the gesture was formed of anguish not anger. First Jack had hidden things from him. Then Deirdre.

Now Max had betrayed him—good, kind, goofy Max. What was going on? Was everyone hiding some truth that, like a poisoned sword unsheathed, could only wound when it was finally revealed?

Then again, you know all about hiding things, don't you, Travis Wilder?

He forced his hands to unclench, forced his eyes to meet Max's.

"I'm sorry, Travis." Max's blistered lips barely moved as he whispered. "I'm so sorry. I never told you how . . . how bad it was. I wasn't sure I was going to be able to keep going. When they first came, when they first gave it to me, I thought they were a godsend. The Electria, it . . . it was like . . ." He shook his head. "You can't understand. It was like life, like hope. Then they told me they couldn't give me any more. Not for free, not unless I did something for them." His body was trembling now. "Not unless I wrote you that note."

Travis knew he should run, knew he should get out of here, but he couldn't move. Max reached out thin, shaking arms in what seemed a gesture of supplication. Then he snatched them back and hugged them close to his hunched body, as if they were something precious, or something dangerous.

Travis's anger melted away, replaced by—what? Not fear, not pity. And not just sorrow. Understanding, then. And what a terrible thing that could be. A tremor passed through Max. Travis could feel the heat radiating from him in waves.

Max licked his lips with a swollen tongue. "I'm burning, aren't I, Travis? Like the people I saw in the newspaper this morning. Like the man who came into the saloon, the man in the black robe."

No, Travis started to say, then he swallowed the word. "We'll do something, Max. We'll figure something out. The truck's outside. I'll drive you to

Denver. We'll go to a hospital, and we'll get you taken care of, all right? Let's just get out of here, and—"

The sound of a car door shutting drifted through the window along with the bloody light of sunset. For a few moments, as Travis had spoken, hope had shone in Max's brown eyes. Now they grew hard and dull.

"You're too late, Travis."

Travis shook his head. "No, I won't believe that."

The sound of another car door shutting. So there was more than one of them. He glanced around, searching for the best route of escape.

"Which way, Max? Which way are they coming?"

Max stared into space, a statue.

"Which way?"

Max blinked under the force of Travis's words. "The front," he said, gasping. "I was supposed to have locked the back."

"But you didn't. Good, Max. That was good. It means we have a chance. Come on."

He started toward the back room, and he would have tugged Max after him, but he didn't dare. Not yet. Not until they were sure how this disease of fire was transmitted. However, after a few seconds, Max lurched behind him. Faint but distinct, Travis heard the sound of feet on the boardwalk out front. He stumbled into the dimness of the storeroom. Max followed. Travis shut the door, then groped into the gloom until he found a shovel. He placed the shovel across the door and wedged the ends behind pipes that ran on either side.

"It's no use," Max said. "That won't hold them."

"It doesn't have to," Travis said, turning around. "We just need it to—" His words ended in a sharp intake of breath.

"What is it, Travis?"

"I can . . . I can see you, Max."

Max lifted his left hand and gazed at it. It was dim, but in the darkened room it was obvious: a deep red nimbus emanated from Max's skin. He was glowing. No, he was *radiating.*

Max shook his head. "What's happening to me?"

Travis opened his mouth, but he had no answer, and at that moment a crash sounded from the other side of the door. There were a few seconds of silence, then came the muffled sound of talking. Travis made out at least three distinct voices.

He looked back at Max. Now, at last, fear won out over all other emotions. "They're here."

Max lowered his hand. Then he gave a small nod. "Of course—I see it now. I see what's happening, and it all makes sense. I know what I'm supposed to do."

"What are you talking about?"

Max moved. In the dimness it was hard to see what he was doing, but Travis could follow the crimson outline of his body. Max stooped, rummaged in a corner, then stood again, an object in his left hand. Then he turned, and a stray fragment of light caught a sharp edge. It was an axe.

"Max—no!"

It was too late. Max lifted the axe and swung.

Travis ducked, but the axe went wide of his head. There was a bright clang of metal on metal, then a hiss like a serpent's dying breath. The axe clattered to the floor, and Max sagged against a wall, drained by effort. Travis struggled to grasp what had happened. Then he caught the sweet, rotten scent.

It was the pipe that ran to the old boiler. Max had broken it. The room was filling with natural gas.

Footsteps sounded on the other side of the storeroom door. The noise of the axe had alerted them. The door moved inward a fraction, then it met the shovel and stopped.

"Max?"

"Go, Travis."

"Max, what are you doing?"

A thud sounded against the door. The shovel rattled against the pipes, but it held.

"You've got to go." Max's voice was quiet and measured, as if he had found some strange sort of peace. "Thank you for everything you've done for me, Travis."

"Max!" Travis was frantic now. His heart clawed at his throat. Once before a friend had told him to run. He couldn't abandon another. Not again.

A second blow struck the storeroom door. The handle of the shovel cracked.

"Now, Travis. While there's still time. Open the door to the alley."

The scent of the gas was cloying now. Travis staggered, dizzy from lack of oxygen. In seconds it would asphyxiate them. They had to get out of there—both of them. He stumbled forward, and his hands found the doorknob. Just inches away, on the other side, was breathable air. But Max wasn't behind him. He looked over his shoulder.

A third blow struck the storeroom door. The shovel splintered, and the door burst inward. In the opening stood a compact man with a blond goatee and glasses just like Travis's own. The man dusted his hands together and smiled. Behind him were two shadowy forms.

"Now, Travis!"

Max stretched his left hand toward the broken gas pipe, palm turned up. The Duratek agent turned toward the motion, and his smile altered into a frown. Max pressed his eyes shut, then opened them, an expression like ecstasy twisting his face. That was when Travis saw it: A crimson blossom of flame unfurled on Max's outstretched hand.

The blond man's eyes went wide. Travis turned, jerked open the door, and dived through. Behind him came the rich, mirthful sound of Max's laughter.

Then the world expanded into fire.

17.

Red clouds hung in the sky as Travis climbed the last few feet of the road that wound up the hill south of town. He knew it wasn't possible. It should have taken him at least an hour to walk to this place from the burning destruction of the Mine Shaft. But somehow it had seemed to take no time at all—somehow it was still sunset. Then again, maybe it would always be sunset now: the day forever dying in flames.

As he walked, he stuck his hands beneath his armpits. It lessened the sting a little, and it slowed the bleeding. When he had dived out the back door of the saloon, he had sailed over the steps and fallen six feet to the alley, landing on his outstretched hands. Bits of gravel and pulverized glass had ground into his palms, lodging beneath the skin. The wounds hurt. But not that much, not so much he couldn't bear it, and the drop was the only thing that had saved him.

For several seconds after he had fallen, he lay there as splinters of burning wood and scraps of hot metal rained down on him. Although he didn't remember the percussion—it had all seemed to unfold in perfect silence—his ears shrieked with the aftereffects of one. Then, quickly, the heat had become too much. He lurched to his feet, stumbled down the alley, and turned to gaze at the inferno that a minute ago had been his life, his livelihood, and his home.

It was several seconds before he could take it all in, before the scene in front of him had made any kind of sense. Most of the rear half of the Mine Shaft was gone. Only the cement block of the steps that had led up to the back door was intact; it was this that had protected Travis from the blast.

A second explosion had shaken the ground then.

Glass shattered, and a gout of flame shot into the sky, merging with the crimson sky. Flames embraced the buildings to either side of the Mine Shaft; they would go as well. However, the force of the second explosion seemed to have extinguished part of the fire, and at that moment the sirens had sounded over the roar.

Travis had known that he should stay, that he should talk to them, should tell them that Max Bayfield was dead, along with three people whose names he did not know.

Yet what did it matter? What could he say that might possibly make a difference? Max was beyond help now. And Duratek would take care of their own: He had no doubt of that.

The wail of the sirens had grown louder, and a shard of fear had pierced the numbness that encapsulated him. What if Duratek *was* on its way there? What if he stayed to talk to the fire marshal, to the sheriff, and *they* showed up? Max had bought Travis's escape with his life. What was that worth if Travis just walked into their waiting arms?

Thank you for everything you've done for me, Travis.

Everything Travis had done *to* him. Wasn't that what Max should have said? Travis had killed Max as surely as the man in black. As surely as Duratek had. But now his pain was over.

With a groan, the roof of the Mine Shaft had slumped in, weaving a funeral shroud of sparks. Travis's eyes stung from smoke and loss, but his scorched tear glands could produce no soothing moisture.

"I'm sorry, Max," he whispered.

Then, for the second—and last—time in his life, he had turned to run from the place where a friend had died.

As the scarlet curtain of sunset still hung in the western sky, Travis reached the top of the hill. He turned to look back the way he had come. The valley splayed out below him like a map. He let his eyes move from point to point. From the center of the valley rose a column of black smoke: the Mine Shaft, or what was left of it. His gaze moved south, to a cluster of brown buildings where Max had lived. Now northwest, up the pencil-thin line of the railroad tracks, to the scattering of tiny rectangles he knew to be boxcars. Then finally across the black serpent of the highway, to a smudge on the edge of town. The remains of the Magician's Attic. Jack Graystone's antique shop. Where all of this had begun.

Except that wasn't true. His gaze moved eastward, but the sight he looked for—fields stretching to the flat and hazy horizon, an old farmhouse washed of color by years of rain and sorrow—was beyond the reach of his eyes. Yet it was there, somewhere, beyond the ruddy slopes of Signal Ridge, across the sundering sea of the plains. That was where his journey had really begun.

Now his gaze traced its way back: antique shop, railyard, Max's place, the Mine Shaft, here. For a moment Travis wondered what he was doing. Then he knew that he had just said good-bye.

Where am I supposed to go?

That was the question he had asked Child Samanda when she and Sister Mirrim had appeared to him. As he ran from the saloon, her murmured answer had come to him once again.

You must die to be transformed.

In that moment, he had known where he had to go.

Travis opened a rusted iron gate, stepped through, and shut it behind him. Then he moved down a gravel path, deeper into Castle Heights Cemetery. The wind moaned a low hymn as it passed among weathered headstones. Travis made his way among the old and nameless graves. It did not take long to find what he was seeking.

The man stood near the center of the cemetery, on a low hump of rocks and weeds, as if he needed a better view than the hill alone could grant. He was tall and straight as a fence post, clad in a black suit. A long hand held his broad-brimmed hat against the tug of the wind, and his craggy face was turned toward the far distance—not the fiery horizon of the west, but the deepening line of the east, and the coming of night.

Travis made his way across the cemetery, but the other did not move, as if he did not see, or did not care, or already knew and was patiently waiting. Then Travis was there.

"Who are you?" he said.

Brother Cy did not turn his gaze from the east, but a grin sliced across his cadaverous visage. "Well, it's good to see you again, too, son."

Travis winced. Strange how a voice so low and sweet could smite so sharply. He circled around the mound, until he stood before the preacher. "Tell me."

Silence. Then, "We are the forgotten ones, son. But we have not forgotten ourselves. Is that not enough?"

Travis thought about this. *No*, he started to answer, but then he stopped. Perhaps it was enough after all. He knew about Jack, he knew about the Seekers, and he knew about Duratek. But knowledge had gained him nothing in all this. Maybe it was time to give mystery a chance.

"Why are you here?" he asked, because a question was all he could think of.

Brother Cy's lank black suit coat flapped in the day's dying breath. Cinders of twilight drifted from the sky.

"Two worlds draw near. When one burns, so then does the other."

"I don't understand," Travis said, even though he thought maybe he did. *A New Black Death*, the paper had called it. But few diseases really sprang forth anew. They almost always came from somewhere else.

"Eldh needs you, son. They're calling for you even now. Can't you hear?"

Travis clenched his bleeding hands into fists, but it wasn't anger he felt, only weariness. "I don't care. All I want to do is look out for myself for a change. I don't want to save the world."

Now Brother Cy did move: He threw his head back, stretched his gangly arms wide, and laughed. His face screwed up into a homely, comical mask, and his Adam's apple protruded so sharply it looked as if it would burst from his neck. Travis stared at the grotesque sight. At last the preacher's mirth faded. He sagged weakly, as if exhausted.

Travis squinted at him. "What's so funny?"

Brother Cy wiped tears from his eyes. "Why, it's a joke, son. You made a great joke."

Travis only shook his head.

"But don't you see?" Brother Cy clapped big hands together. "Save the world, save yourself. What's the difference, son? What's the difference?"

But Travis didn't see. He wished he could laugh like the preacher did, but it felt as if his heart had burned up, and all that remained were ashes. "There's nothing left for me here," he said.

Brother Cy nodded, his expression solemn now, and one of profound understanding. "Then it's time to go."

He gestured to the plot of earth beside him. There were two graves on it. The first looked freshly filled. Beside it was a granite marker carved with a single word:

MINDROTH

Was the word a name? Travis wasn't sure. His gaze moved to the other grave.

This one was open still, a rectangle six feet deep, a shovel stuck into the pile of dirt beside it, waiting. At first he thought there was no headstone by this grave, then he blinked and saw there was. He read the sharp words carved upon it:

TRAVIS RALPH WILDER
"In death do we begin."

Travis started to laugh, but the sound was strangled somewhere in his throat before it could escape. Yes, of course. Die and be transformed. But into what? He gazed at the preacher, then nodded. He would find out soon enough.

"Take your boots off, son."

Travis hesitated. Didn't gunfighters always want to die with their boots on?

"Now, son. There's not much time."

Travis glanced up. Only a few wisps of red laced the sky. The remainder was purple hardening to slate. He bent and pulled off his boots.

"The rest, son. All of it. Naked are we born, and naked must we go."

Travis unbuttoned his shirt and let it fall to the ground. He shrugged out of his T-shirt, his singed jeans, his socks and briefs—everything but the bone talisman that hung around his neck. Then he stood naked before the preacher. The parched wind threw dust on him like a gritty baptism.

Brother Cy bent, picked up the boots, and tossed them into the open grave. Then, from nowhere, a bundle of cloth appeared in his hands, and this too he heaved into the open hole. Finally, he reached into the pocket of Travis's fallen jeans, pulled something out, and pressed it into Travis's hand. It was small and hard: a half circle of silver.

"You'll be wanting this," the preacher said.

Despite the heat, Travis shivered. "I'm afraid."

Brother Cy gave a knowing nod. "As are we all, son. As are we all."

The last tinge of red slipped from the sky. Overhead, the first stars appeared, diamonds in the veil of night.

"Now, son, while there is yet time."

Travis turned and gazed at the yawning hole in the ground. He swallowed, then crouched down on the edge and lowered himself into the grave. It was deeper than he had thought, and darker and hotter. He lay down on the floor and curled up like a small child. Time to sleep.

From above came a final whisper. "Ashes to ashes, dust to dust. . . ."

Then Travis felt the first shovelfuls of dirt pour down on him. Only it wasn't dirt.

It was rain. Sweet, cool, quenching rain.

PART TWO

THE
RED
STAR

18.

Grace clung to her horse's saddle as the castle receded in the distance behind her.

The morning air was moist with the green scent of life, and the sun was a balm on her cheeks. Before her, the land rose and fell in gold-and-emerald waves, marching south toward the heart of Calavan. It was a glorious day for riding—just as yesterday had been, and the day before that. Summer had come at last, and it was impossible to imagine it would ever leave.

Of course, Grace still remembered the gnawing chill that had radiated from Calavere's stones only a handful of months ago, and the clattering of her teeth when she rose each morning and went to bed each night. Then, one afternoon early in Erenndath—which by her calculations was akin to March—she had looked out the window to see patches of brown amid the usual fields of white. By the next evening the snow was gone, and the world had become one gigantic puddle.

At the Feast of Quickening, it had been warm enough to hold the required revel in the upper bailey, and the scent of flowers had drifted from the castle's garden to sweeten the air. Yet spring had been as brief as it had been mild. It was summer in her brilliant crown who ruled in this Dominion now.

And King Boreas, of course.

Grace leaned forward in the silver-trimmed saddle. The palfrey—slender, long-legged, and blond as new honey—was only two years old that spring and required little urging. She sprang forward in a gallop, splashed across a shallow stream, and raced up the long slope of a knoll. Grace shut her eyes and cast her mind outward. Yes, if she concentrated, she could *feel* the land rushing past; the imprints of plants and small, hidden animals flashed across her mind like bright snapshots.

She sighed, then opened her eyes and gave a pull on the reins. The palfrey slowed to a halt and tossed her head. Grace laughed—she laughed often these days, as if the action were natural for her, and she supposed just maybe it was. Lord Harfen, the king's marshal and keeper of his horses, had warned her that the young mare liked to run.

"All right, Shandis, that's enough for the moment," Grace murmured, stroking the palfrey's arched neck. The horse had been a springtime gift from King Boreas, and Grace had picked the name herself. It meant *sunberry*.

Shandis gave a delicate snort, as if to indicate she hardly required rest, but if Grace needed the excuse in order to take a break, then so be it. At least, that was how it sounded to Grace. However, as a scientist, she knew it was at best silly and at worst dangerous to personify nonhuman species. A two-year-old mare could no more grasp a concept like humor than she could grasp a baseball with her hoof.

Then again, science had nothing to do with the way Grace's heart had pounded that day in the stable when Lord Harfen had led the palfrey into the aisle, or the thrill that had coursed through her when Shandis had approached with halting steps to nuzzle her outstretched hand. Maybe thumbs weren't everything.

Low thunder approached, not in the cloudless sky, but up the hill behind Grace. She turned to see four riders—two women and two men—gallop up the grassy slope. They brought their mounts to a halt alongside hers.

Aryn pushed dark hair back from bright cheeks. Her blue riding gown was askew around her saddle. "Grace, what on Eldh possessed you to ride like that?" the young baroness asked. "You know shepherd's knot is hard to see before it blooms. How do you expect to find any when you're flying above it?"

The second woman nudged her mount closer. Her hair was long, coal black, and tightly curled, and her skin was the rich, dark color of *maddok*. The smile that played across her full lips was mysterious—as all of Lirith's expressions were. "Perhaps it was not shepherd's knot that Lady Grace was looking for."

Grace grinned at the slender, brown-eyed witch. "Perhaps," she said, trying for a bit of mystery herself.

Durge blew a breath through his drooping mustaches. The craggy-faced Embarran knight towered over the others on the back of his sooty charger, Blackalock. Despite the fair day, he was dressed in heavy garb of gray. "My lady," he said to Grace, "it is perilous for you to ride ahead like that. There is no telling what dangers you might encounter, even in sight of the king's castle."

"With all respect, my lord, I would hazard that Her Radiance has the ability to care for herself."

These good-natured words were spoken by the last member of the riding party, a knight by the name of Sir Garfethel. He was a powerful and broad-shouldered man—if not very tall—and while his beard was only a brown dusting on his cheeks, he sat straight on his charger and gripped the reins in capable-looking hands. All the same, Grace found it hard not to think of him as just Garf, the squire who had tripped after her through the muck of the bailey one day several months ago, and who had humbly begged her to sponsor him for knighthood.

Grace had been horrified at his words. She wasn't a duchess, no matter what Boreas or Aryn said. It would be utter fraud for her to knight a man. Like many squires, Garf was a second or third son who had right to neither land nor title and who was seeking a lord or lady who would grant him such in exchange for his allegiance. However, Grace had nothing to grant, and in no uncertain words she told him to leave her alone.

Garf followed her, of course. For the next two weeks, Grace found herself stumbling over him at every turn as he made a dogged effort to be of service. At last she advanced on him, and asked him flat out, "Why me, Garf?"

He had seemed genuinely surprised at this question. "What knight would not wish to pledge himself to the noblest and most beautiful lady in the Dominion?"

Grace had let out a groan. "And if I were really that, then I would have men falling at my feet to serve me."

"Do you mean like Sir Durge, my lady?" Garf had said with an innocence so perfect it could only be genuine.

That had shut Grace up.

The next day she spoke with King Boreas, and they worked out an arrangement. Garf had squired with Sir Belivar, one of the king's household knights, and Belivar recommended Garf for knighthood with such enthusiasm that Grace wondered if Belivar, who was getting on in years, wasn't just relieved to be discharged of his duty. As was typical, Boreas had a

number of lands at his disposal—fiefs left heirless or
seized from intractable lords—and he generously
granted Grace a small manor in western Calavan,
which she in turn granted to Garf.

They held the knighting on the first day of Vardath.

At dawn they gathered in the upper bailey. Barefoot and clad in a white shift, Garf knelt before Grace
while Boreas, Aryn, Durge, and Belivar stood behind.
At that moment he had looked so much like a boy
that Grace nearly lost her nerve. However, a nod from
Durge steadied her. She gripped the sword taken from
Boreas's armory, and while she feared she would fum-
ble the heavy weapon and lop his head off, she instead
tapped each of his shoulders with surgical precision.

"Rise, Sir Garfethel," she had said, and she might
have laughed at the absurdity of it. Except at that
moment the sun crested the wall of the castle, and as
he stood in its gold radiance Garf looked so proud and
noble that her mirth stopped short at the sudden
lump in her throat.

"Do not weep, my lady," he said, and she laughed,
wiping the tears from her cheeks. Why were her
knights always telling her that?

After that, Durge led a dappled charger stamping
and snorting into the bailey, and Garf promptly forgot
his new mistress while he fell in love with his horse.
Grace cast a grateful look at Durge. She had remembered the sword, but she had forgotten that a knight
required a warhorse.

Thank you, she had mouthed the words to him.

He had nodded, and while she could not quite
make out what he said beneath his mustaches, it
might have been, *I am ever at your service, my lady*.

Now Durge turned in his saddle to cast his somber
brown gaze on Garf. "You make light of danger, Sir
Garfethel. What if our mistress were to ride far ahead
of us and then come upon a nest of brigands?"

"Then I think they should find themselves put under a spell," Garf said. "And when we came upon our mistress, we would discover her waving a finger while the brigands danced in time around her with flowers in their hair."

Lirith clapped both hands to her mouth, and even Aryn—who laughed so seldom these days—smiled at Garf's words. However, Durge looked even less amused than usual. Grace knew she needed to say something. As far as she could tell, the primary duty of a noble mistress was damage control.

"I do thank you for your confidence, Sir Garfethel," she said. "But Sir Durge is right, of course. It was wrong of me to ride so far ahead."

"Although I would have liked to see the dancing brigands," Lirith said.

Grace glanced at her. Sometimes it was hard to diagnose whether Lirith was being earnest or making a jest. Maybe for her there was little difference between the two.

Lirith had arrived at Calavere not long after Queen Ivalaine's departure. This had been in late Durdath, and even though the world was still frozen, the various rulers who had journeyed to Calavere for the Council of Kings, and who had stayed on when it was renamed the Council of War, were returning to their own Dominions. Ivalaine was the last of the rulers to go, and Grace and Aryn ventured to the lower bailey, bundled in their fur-lined capes, to say good-bye.

The queen sat upon her white horse, as regal as the day Grace had first seen her riding up to the gates of Calavere—a day that seemed so long ago now. They bid farewell to the queen's advisor Tressa first, and the plump, red-haired witch climbed from her horse to encompass each of them in a motherly hug. Grace felt tears welling up, but they froze solid when she turned to speak to the queen. After all that had happened, she still did not know Ivalaine. The queen was as cool as the stars and every bit as impossible to reach.

"We will keep studying, Your Majesty," Aryn had said.

Ivalaine's ice-colored eyes had shone. "Yes, sisters," she said. "You will."

A week later, on the first day of Erenndath, Lirith rode up to the castle gates, accompanied by a pair of Tolorian knights. She asked to speak to Lady Grace and Lady Aryn even before begging King Boreas for hospitality.

"Greetings, sisters," Lirith had said to them in the castle's entry hall. "Queen Ivalaine bade me to make haste here from Ar-tolor. I have come to see to your studies."

Grace had thought the witch's words would fill her with dread. So far King Boreas had not discovered what she and Aryn were doing; so far they had not done permanent harm to themselves with what they had learned. So far. Instead, at Lirith's words, a flood of relief had washed through her.

You want to learn more, don't you, Grace? No matter how dangerous it is, no matter how inevitable it gets that Boreas will find out what you're doing and have your head lopped off. You'll do anything to feel more, won't you?

But she had not needed to answer the question then, and she did not now.

Garf guided his charger to the crest of the knoll. He shaded his eyes and gazed out over the undulating landscape.

"What is it you search for, Sir Garfethel?" Durge asked. "The campfire smoke of cutthroats? Signs of wild boar? Bogs where our horses might founder?"

"A place to have dinner," the young knight said.

Grace smiled. Garf's concerns were always a bit more practical than Durge's.

They all sat straight on their horses and scanned

the distance, looking for a dell or hollow that would offer protection from the wind and water for the horses.

Aryn gasped.

Grace turned toward the baroness, to ask her if she had caught sight of a good stopping place, but Aryn was not looking at the green-gold hills. She was looking at Grace.

"What is it?" Grace said, startled.

"The land," Aryn murmured. "It's the same color as your eyes, Grace."

Lirith nodded. "So it is."

Grace opened her mouth, but she didn't know what to say.

Garf laughed. "Why, if her eyes are the same color as the land, then she must be the queen of this fair place." He bowed in his saddle. "All hail the Queen of Summer!"

It was a poor jest. Grace shook her head and started to protest. However, her words faltered as a second sun appeared in the sky. It streaked above them, casting impossible shadows in all directions. The five jerked their heads up in time to see the white-hot bolt vanish into the north.

Durge was the first of them to find his tongue. "A firedrake."

Only as the knight spoke did Grace realize what it was she had witnessed. A shooting star. Except she hadn't known it was possible to see a meteor in broad daylight.

"I've never seen a firedrake so bright," Aryn said.

Lirith still cast her face to the sky. "It was beautiful."

"Let it be our good omen, then," Garf said with a grin. "We will certainly find a good spot for a picnic."

Durge gave the young knight a solemn look. "If you wish, Sir Garfethel."

For the first time in many months, Grace shivered.

But that was foolish. "Let's go," she said. "I may not be a queen, but I am hungry."

Together they rode down the slope and cantered deeper into summer.

19.

Not surprisingly, it was Garf who found the perfect place to rest and eat.

The other four brought their horses to a halt beside the young knight's charger at the base of a hill so perfectly conical in shape that Grace doubted it was natural. There were many such mounds and tors scattering the verdant fields of Calavan, raised by the barbarians who had dwelled in these lands before the Dominions were founded, before the emperors of Tarras had come to plant their golden banners here. Or perhaps the hills had been made by some nameless people long before that—the same people who had raised the circle of standing stones that stood north of the castle.

Grace surveyed the spot Garf had picked for them. The ground sloped gently to a brook, its banks shaded by willow and green rushes. The chaotic song of water chimed on the air, and Grace swallowed, suddenly thirsty. For all she knew the water in the brook would be muddy and brackish, but it sounded *cool.*

Grace waited for Durge to dismount and assist her. It wasn't that she felt it was his duty to serve her; it was just that getting off a horse while wearing a gown without falling face first into the turf was a trick she hadn't consistently mastered. All in all, she would have preferred a pair of Lycra biking tights with ample rear padding, but one had to make do with what one had, and she was a good rider, even before she had had much practice.

Too bad you can't control people as well as you do horses, Grace.

She winced at the thought. But the voice in her head was hollow now, the words bitter but empty. Grace still had difficulty interacting with people— whole, conscious people. She knew she always would. But she had learned that she didn't have to be perfect to have friends. When others cared about you, they seemed to develop an amazing ability to accept all of your flaws wholesale. You could break a body into each of its components: organs, fluids, bones. But in the end, Grace was beginning to think, people were a package deal.

Grace swung one leg over the saddle, trying to keep it from getting tangled in yards of violet linen, and let Durge catch her in hard, powerful arms and ease her to the ground. She smiled her thanks at him. Kyrene had been right about one thing: Men did have their uses.

Her smile faded as she thought of Kyrene. Some- times, when she turned a corner in the castle, Grace still expected to come upon a green-eyed lady clad in a revealing gown, a sly smile on her coral lips. How- ever, if the past was a shadow, its touch was fleeting, like a cloud over the sun soon gone.

Durge moved to help Lirith dismount, and Grace glanced back at Aryn. Garf was helping her off of her horse—a white mare—and if the young knight's hand lingered a moment more than was strictly necessary around Aryn's slender waist, the baroness seemed not to notice. He stepped away and bowed, but she had already turned her back to him.

"Well done, Sir Garfethel," Lirith said, turning around and spreading her arms, as if she were drink- ing the warmth and life of the dell.

And perhaps she is at that.

Grace gazed at the Tolorian witch, and Lirith smiled back. What the smile meant was a mystery, but it wasn't coy, not like Kyrene's expressions had been. Instead it was secret and inviting.

Lirith started toward the banks of the brook, as lithe as a deer even in her russet riding gown, and the two knights followed, carrying a pair of saddlebags between them.

Grace hung back, letting them get ahead, but Aryn stayed with her, as if she knew Grace wanted to talk.

"Can we trust her?" Aryn asked before Grace could.

"I don't know, Aryn. Can we trust any of the Witches?" It wasn't the first time they had discussed this topic. "Sometimes I'm not sure we can even trust ourselves."

"I can trust myself," Aryn said.

Grace stopped short to stare at her friend. The words had been quiet and hard. She searched Aryn's face, looking for pride or anger or sorrow—anything, any emotion that might give her a clue as to how to respond. But as usual the baroness's lovely face was pale and impassive.

"She flaunts her secrets," Aryn went on. The baroness hugged her left arm around the bodice of her gown. The right arm—slender and withered—was hidden as always beneath a fold of cloth. "Lirith, I mean. Sometimes I think she likes baffling us. Those smiles of hers—she must do it on purpose."

Grace thought for a moment. "No, I don't think so. Lirith isn't like Kyrene was. She has secrets, yes, and they're locked away. But I think it's up to us to find the key. I think that's what she's trying to tell us."

"Maybe," Aryn said, but her smooth forehead creased in a frown.

Grace studied her friend, but whatever was wrong was beyond her ability to diagnose. Something had happened to Aryn, something amid all the dark and remarkable events of last Midwinter's Eve, but what it was Grace didn't know, and the baroness had never spoken of it in the months since.

But then, mysteries were not Lirith's sole purview. *We all have our secrets, don't we, Grace?*

She sighed and began walking again, with Aryn following alongside her.

Despite Lirith's enigmas, their lessons with her had progressed well—if slowly. To their surprise and delight, Lirith had not begun with such mundane tasks as weaving or gathering herbs as Ivalaine had done. Instead, the day after she arrived at the castle, their first lesson had been to spin a web along the Weirding. Grace had reveled in the experience, listening to the smoky chant of Lirith's voice, imagining the silver-green threads of the Weirding running through her fingers like the threads of the loom as she spun them into a shimmering gauze of power. Then Lirith laughed, and it all had fallen apart. Grace had blinked and opened her eyes to see Aryn looking as stunned as she must have.

The next day they attempted the same exercise. And the next day, and the next, until it was no longer a joy to touch the Weirding, but rather an act of drudgery she could barely force herself to attempt. Grace would work for hours spinning a web—eyes clamped shut, jaw clenched, head throbbing—then Lirith would merely tap her shoulder and the strands of magic would unravel, slipping through her clutching fingers.

"Try again," Lirith would say, and the exercise would begin anew.

As tedious as the lessons were, neither Grace nor Aryn was ever late for one. Sometimes Grace wondered if King Boreas already knew what they were doing. The pretenses for Lirith's visit had been weak at best. She had delivered a spoken message from the queen and had asked Boreas if she might stay on in

Calavere to visit with a cousin. Boreas had granted her request. However, just who this cousin was, and why Lirith was never seen in his company, were questions that had yet to be answered.

And there was something more, something else about Lirith's arrival at the castle that had always bothered Grace these last months. Then, in a flash as bright and unexpected as the firedrake, she had it.

She gripped Aryn's arm.

"What is it, Grace?"

"Remember how Lirith arrived at Calavere just a week after Ivalaine left?"

The baroness looked puzzled. "It's only a week's journey to Ar-tolor."

"Yes. And that means Lirith would have had to set out from Ar-tolor at the exact same time Ivalaine left Calavere."

Aryn lifted her left hand in protest. "That doesn't make sense. Lirith said she had spoken to Ivalaine, and that the queen bade her to come here."

Grace met Aryn's gaze. "Exactly."

Aryn's blue eyes went wide. Yes, she understood.

"It's like us, Grace," the young woman murmured. "Like the way we spoke on . . . like the way we spoke that time."

Grace nodded. Except neither she nor Aryn had been able to speak to the other across the Weirding since Midwinter's Eve. At best each had heard only the barest whisper, and even that might have been imagination. Somehow the urgency of that moment had granted them a power that now eluded them. And they had not mentioned it to Lirith for fear, like so many things, it was something they were forbidden to try on their own.

"Come on," Grace said. "I think that's one mystery answered at least."

And a new one opened. Was this something Lirith

would ever teach them? But there was only one way to learn. They started toward the brook, following the others.

20.

The afternoon was wearing on toward nightfall. Even in summer, days could not last forever. The five of them would have to ride back to the castle soon. The guards would be watching for them—waiting to shut the gates against the dark.

The guards could wait a while longer.

Grace let her eyelids droop. She sat on a blanket, drowsing in the late-day warmth as she listened to the drone of insects. The air was like gold wine: She drank it in, tasting cool water and sun-warmed grass, then breathed out in a soft exhalation. She wasn't certain what it was, but there was something about this moment—a peace, perhaps, or a power—that made her want to live it just a little longer.

"Night approaches, my lady," a rumbling voice said beside her. "I imagine predators will be roaming the land soon—those that prowl on four feet and two."

Grace did not open her eyes. "Hush, Durge."

There was a low grunt, but no other reply.

She remained still, listening and feeling. However, both moment and magic were gone. The sun dipped behind a line of trees, and the air cooled from gold to green-gray as the insects ceased their toneless song. Grace sighed and looked up. Durge was on his feet, scanning the distance with deep-set brown eyes.

"Any sign of them?" she asked.

"No," the knight said. "I fear they might have fallen into a—"

A hole? A gorge? An improbable though convenient pit of poisonous adders? Grace didn't get to find out what it was Durge feared, because at that moment three figures appeared atop a low ridge some distance away. One of the figures—the broadest but not the tallest, which meant it was Garf—waved to them. So the day really was over then. A feeling of sadness filled Grace, so sudden and strange that she almost gasped. But that was silly; Durge was good enough at finding things to worry about without her helping him. She gained her feet as the others started down the ridge.

As the trio approached, Grace saw that the basket slung over Garf's shoulder was filled with bunches of green and purple. So Lirith was right. The shepherd's knot was beginning to bloom after all. That boded well for their simples. Garf grinned and hefted the basket high, showing off. She laughed and waved. Behind her, Durge muttered something she did not quite catch.

She turned to regard the dark-haired knight. It had been interesting to see how Durge's reactions to her studies differed from Garf's. While the steadfast Embarran would never have questioned her—or Aryn or Lirith, for that matter—it was clear from his manner that he did not entirely understand or care for what Grace was doing with her spare time. When it came time for her lessons with Lirith, he usually made himself scarce. Were most men uncomfortable with the idea of witches?

But Durge's response isn't the same as Boreas's, is it, Grace? You've seen how the king acts at the mere mention of the word witch. *He just about needs a full rabies series.*

Grace knew Boreas's reaction was more instinctual than angry. As far as she could tell, the relationship between the Witches and the Cult of Vathris was much like that between cats and dogs, only not so cordial. However, Durge did not follow the mysteries of the warrior cult—or those of any cult. His mind was given more to logic than religion, occupied by his late-night studies of chemicals and compounds. Grace imagined he simply thought the Witches silly, their craft a matter of love potions and empty rhymes, not a true science.

Of course, Grace was a scientist herself, but she doubted Durge understood that. On this world medicine was women's work, itself at best a half step from the workings of hags and witches.

Then there was Garf. The young knight seemed to regard Grace and Aryn's studies with an amused curiosity. *As it pleases my lady*, Garf was fond of saying when she made a request, be it large or small. Grace supposed if she told Garf they needed a basket of a given herb in order to fly around the castle's towers, he would grin and ask how much. And if the three of them really took off into the sky, he would no doubt clap his hands and laugh at the sight. Garf seemed to take it for granted that Grace could work magic. Would she ever feel the same way?

She hoped not.

"He is a fine man," Durge said.

Grace glanced at the knight, but he did not meet her gaze.

"I have heard that Boreas is to choose a husband for Lady Aryn this autumn," Durge went on, his voice gruff. "I hope it will be a man such as Sir Garfethel."

So Grace was not the only one who had noticed. The others were close now, picking their way across the stones of the brook, although Grace could not yet hear their voices. Even now, while he remained a polite distance from both Lirith and Aryn, Garf's body was turned just slightly in Aryn's direction, his head bowed toward hers. A beatific smile hovered on his lips, and his eyes shone.

Grace gave a wry smile. "Something tells me I'm

no longer the noblest and most beautiful lady in the Dominion."

"My lady?"

She shook her head. "It's nothing, Durge. Tell me, does the king know?"

Durge shrugged stooped shoulders. "I cannot say, my lady. The mind of King Boreas is a foreign land to me."

"Then maybe I had better bring it to his attention."

Aryn was laughing now, pressing her hand to her stomach. Grace could hear the sound of her mirth, as clear as the music of the brook, although she could not hear what Garf had said to bring it on. It didn't matter. Grace resolved to speak to Boreas tomorrow. Someone who could bring joy into the baroness's life would be a blessing, and Grace knew Boreas would agree.

A thought occurred to her. "What about you, Durge? When will you look for a wife?"

Even as Grace spoke the words she regretted them. A grimace crossed the knight's face, and he turned away.

"Old men do not marry," he said.

Grace searched for a reply, but as usual words that healed were far harder to come by than those that wounded. Then the moment was lost as the others reached them. Garf unslung the basket of herbs from his shoulder, his face a mask of pain as he let it fall to the ground.

Grace's medical instincts replaced all other concerns. "Is something wrong, Sir Garfethel?"

"I believe that's Sir Ox, my lady," Garf said with a bow. "It was not a noble knight but a beast of burden the good ladies required today."

Now he grinned: He was not in pain, it had been a joke. Grace forced herself to take a breath. It was amazing how such small things could throw her off still.

"Perhaps one day, Sir Garfethel," Lirith said with perfect seriousness, "you can instruct the rest of us in the subtle but intriguing distinction between oxen and knights."

Garf let out a booming guffaw, and Lirith's eyes sparkled like the sky at night.

"It grows late," Durge said. "We should be going."

Garf stifled his mirth. "I'll get the horses."

Grace smiled fondly at both of her knights. She might be only a counterfeit duchess, but her good fortune in having these men as her retainers was genuine.

Durge helped Grace mount Shandis, then turned to assist Lirith. However, the Tolorian woman sat astride her horse already, gown neatly arranged. It might not have been magic, but it was a trick Grace wanted to learn all the same. She struggled with her own gown in a vain effort to keep from sitting on a hard knot of fabric and tried not to hate Lirith too much.

Garf, in turn, helped Aryn onto her white mare.

"Thank you," the baroness murmured.

"As it pleases my lady."

The baroness bowed her head, but not before Grace glimpsed the smile that touched her lips.

As they rode north across the land, long shadows stretched to their right. They crested a rise, and Grace saw Calavere atop its hill. She guessed it to be about a league away, but that was mostly because she had yet to gain a good sense of any of the measures of this world, and in her mind any distance over a mile and less than ten was *about a league.*

They lost sight of the castle as they descended into a gulch. Granite outcrops rose over their heads, and the air grew cool and purple. The floor of the valley was thick with vegetation. Grace suspected a botanist from Denver would have found the trees and shrubs fascinatingly deviant, but to her they looked a lot like pine and scrub oak. They reached the bottom of the gulch and headed up the other side.

Grace heard the sound the same moment Durge raised a hand, bringing the party to a halt. They sat still on their horses, listening. Then Grace heard it again: a low, rhythmic sound she could not place. Durge glanced at Garf, and the young knight's hand moved to the hilt of the sword at his hip. Grace swallowed, startled by the hard look on Garf's face. For all his good humor, at twenty-two years of age he was a man of war.

The sound drifted again on the moist air, although it was difficult to tell from which direction it came. Aryn cast a look at Grace, her blue eyes concerned. Lirith's own eyes were closed, as if she were listening for something. Grace opened her mouth to ask a question, but a look from Durge made her clamp it shut again. Maybe the Embarran's fear of brigands was not so impossible after all.

Durge dismounted from Blackalock. Grace watched as he took three steps forward along the path. Then the bushes to his left exploded, and a black ball of fury burst forth.

It was upon Durge before Grace even realized what it was. The horses whinnied and leaped back. The bear reached out huge paws to engulf Durge. The knight curled up and fell to the ground. Aryn let out a muffled cry of terror.

"No!" Grace shouted, but she wasn't certain if her lips really formed the word. She reached out a hand, but Durge was impossibly far away. Out of the corner of her eye she saw Garf leap from the back of his warhorse and draw his sword. Then there was another dark flash of movement.

For a horrified second Grace thought it was a second bear. Then the beast let out a trumpeting cry, and she realized it was Blackalock, Durge's charger. Eyes wild, the horse reared onto its hind legs, then brought sharp hooves down on the bear's humped back. The bear snarled and scrambled around, but Blackalock had already galloped away. Grace knew that chargers were trained for battle, but she had not understood what that meant until now. Shandis trembled beneath her and would have bolted but for Grace's death grip on the reins. Aryn was struggling with her own mount—although Lirith's horse stood stock-still, the witch's hand pressed against its neck.

Durge staggered to his feet. He reached over his shoulder and drew his Embarran greatsword from the harness strapped to his back. Blood streamed down his face, but he stood straight, and his motions were quick and deliberate. Grace understood; when he fell it was not because he was severely wounded, but rather as a defense mechanism. Bears wouldn't attack creatures they thought were already dead—wasn't that how it worked?

Except there was something wrong with this animal. Wild bears were supposed to be afraid of people, but this creature opened its maw, exposing gigantic teeth as it roared. It started after Blackalock, then abruptly turned to face Durge. That was when Grace saw the bare patches in its pelt. Over large parts of the bear's body the thick fur had been scorched away, and the skin beneath was blistered and oozing. So it was injured, burned in a brush fire, perhaps. And there was no telling what an injured animal would do.

No more than ten seconds had passed since the bear had burst from the underbrush. It took a lumbering step toward Durge. The Embarran backed away. Garf approached cautiously from behind the bear, sword raised, face grim.

Whether it smelled or heard the younger knight

was impossible to say. The bear spun around, hackles raised, and roared at Garf. Grace could see past its monstrous teeth into the deep pit of its throat. Garf lifted his sword.

"No, Sir Garfethel!" Durge shouted. "Don't move!"

Durge's words came too late. Garf thrust with his blade. The sword sank deep into the bear's chest—so deep it seemed the animal should have died instantly—but the bear did not fall. It let out a horrible shriek, then lunged forward, ripping the sword out of Garf's hand. Garf stared as the bear fastened its jaws on his shoulder.

Then the young knight screamed.

The world ceased to move except for the bear and Garf. The bear shook its massive head, and Garf fluttered limply, like one of the little string men Grace sometimes saw the village children playing with. The bear tossed him to the ground, placed a paw on his stomach, and almost casually tore at his flesh. His screaming stopped.

Just when she thought it would drive her mad, the moment shattered. Durge rushed forward and with both hands plunged his greatsword into the bear's back. A cold part of Grace appreciated the surgical precision of the blow. Yes—between two ribs, angled toward the midline, past the lung. She could see the moment the tip pierced the bear's heart. The creature's entire body went limp, and it rolled onto the ground. The bear gave one heaving breath. Red foam bubbled around both of the blades embedded in its body. Then came the stillness of death.

"My lady . . ."

The words were not shouted, but they caught Grace's attention all the same. She tore her eyes from the carcass of the bear. Durge knelt beside a crumpled, bloody form. He looked up at Grace.

"My lady, I think you had best come here."

21.

Everything had changed; the idyllic ride through summer had vanished. Durge started to reach toward Garf, then pulled his hand back. Grace understood. There was nothing the knight or his sword could do. This was her battle now.

She slipped from Shandis's back—the motion was easy, as if she had known how to do it all along—and approached the two knights, one kneeling, one lying on the ground. She was aware of Lirith following after her, and of Aryn sitting atop her mare: rigid, staring forward, her face as white as surgical gauze. Then Grace reached the two men.

Fear clamped her heart like a pair of cold, steel forceps, but only for a second. If Garf was to have a chance, then he could mean nothing to her. He was just another nameless victim pulled from a wrecked car or an overturned bus and wheeled on a gurney into Denver Memorial Hospital's Emergency Department. She would put him back together, then head for the Residents' Lounge to have a cup of bad coffee and watch Elizabeth Montgomery's antics in a rerun of *Bewitched* on the blurry television. She crouched beside the patient, and the metallic scent of his blood filled her skull, triggering a chain reaction of instincts.

"Get me four units of O-neg. *Stat.*"

"My lady?" Durge said, his brown eyes confused.

She shook her head. Of course. This wasn't the ED. This was a wooded valley three miles from a medieval castle on another world from Earth. But it didn't matter. It was what she and the doctors, nurses, and PAs did that mattered, not the walls, not the trauma rooms, not the name of the place.

"My lady, I don't think he's breathing."

Grace bent over the patient. She was aware of a great deal of blood, and of wounds to the right shoulder as well as the chest and abdomen. However, she did not focus on these things.

ABC. Airway, breathing, circulation.

She had repeated the words so many times during her internship and residency that they might as well have been cut into her brain with a scalpel. What she did in these first few minutes would affect everything that came after—whether the patient lived or died, whether he would be whole or paralyzed, whether he would be himself when he woke up or a brain-damaged vegetable.

Grace moved through the prescribed steps. She stabilized his head between her knees, tilted his head back, and forced his jaw open. She slipped a finger into his mouth, past his pharynx, into the trachea. Just before the larynx her fingers encountered a soft, wet mass. His airway was obstructed with a plug of blood and mucus. That wasn't good—it meant injury to his lungs—but she couldn't think of that, not until its time. She freed the plug and heard the rasp as air flowed into him—he was breathing again.

Next step. She pressed her ear against his chest and listened. There were no breath sounds on the right. Her suspicion was correct; the right lung had been punctured and had collapsed. She needed a chest tube, but she didn't have the tools. Maybe in the castle she could fashion something, but not here, not now. Fortunately, the breath sounds on the left were good. One lung was working. That would have to be enough until they got him back to the castle.

Grace turned her attention to the source of the blood. Third step: Breathing did no good if there was no blood in his arteries to carry oxygen. She had to stop the bleeding. Now.

She pulled aside his shredded tunic and examined

his chest. He drew in a labored breath, and crimson foam bubbled from a puncture wound. Air was seeping between two ribs: That was the source of the collapsed lung. Otherwise, the wounds to his chest and stomach appeared superficial.

"Give me your hand." She looked up at Durge when he did not respond. "Your hand!"

The knight blinked and held his hand out. She grabbed it, took his index finger, and stuck it into the puncture. The little boy and the dike. It wasn't exactly elegant, but the bubbling stopped.

"Keep your finger there."

Grace knew her voice was hard, but it had to be. The others had to follow her orders without question. Durge nodded, holding his arm stiffly so he could keep the wound plugged.

Grace turned her attention to the right arm. Barely a minute had elapsed since she had reached the patient, but as she worked instinct had told her that she had to hurry, that the arm would be the worst. Damn her instincts for always being right.

But maybe it's not just instinct, Grace. Maybe it's more than that. Remember what Ivalaine said. What you did in the ED wasn't so different from what witches do. . . .

There was no time for that thought. She concentrated on her patient.

It was bad. The arm had been completely dislocated from the shoulder joint. She could see the white ball of the proximal humerus, and the surrounding muscle had been torn to shreds. The arm was attached to the shoulder by only a thin thread of skin and tendon. Blood pumped from the torn end of the subclavian artery and soaked into the bed of pine needles.

"Sister, his lips are blue," Lirith spoke in a soft voice. "And his fingernails. I have seen such in drowned men, but he yet breathes."

He is drowning, Grace wanted to say. *He's drowning in his own blood, and what little oxygen he's managing to take in is pouring out of his shoulder and into the ground.* But Grace didn't have time to teach a lesson about the consequences of a collapsed lung to a medieval witch, or to explain the meaning of words like *cyanotic* and *hypotension*. She grabbed the severed artery between two fingers and pinched it shut.

"We have to stop the bleeding," she said. "It's the loss of blood that's making him blue."

Lirith met her eyes. "What do you want me to do, sister?"

"Hold this."

She brought Lirith's hand to the wound and guided her fingers, until the witch had the torn artery firmly in her own grip. Grace leaned back and considered options. There was no hope of reattachment in these conditions. Even with an ice chest for the severed limb and a waiting helicopter it would be difficult. Here there was no question. The patient would lose his arm. Grace could accept that. Life was always better than death; that was what Leon Arlington had taught her. But the patient would not lose his life. That she could not accept. Amputation, then. Stop the bleeding, and get him back to the castle.

"Aryn!" she called out. "Bring me the saddlebag from my horse."

There was no response. Grace looked up. Aryn still sat on her mount, her gaze fixed forward and distant, her left hand white as it clenched the reins. No—no one could do this to her, not now. She needed everyone.

Aryn! Do it now!

Grace had meant to shout, but somehow it was not her mouth that formed the words. The baroness blinked and stared at Grace. Then she climbed from her horse, grabbed Grace's saddlebag, and ran toward them.

Grace turned back to see Lirith watching her, the witch's dark eyes intent. Lirith nodded, but she said nothing. Whatever had happened, she had noticed it. Grace didn't know if that was good or bad. It didn't matter. She had other things to worry about.

Aryn knelt beside the patient. As she did, Grace grabbed his left wrist for a pulse check. Rapid and faint. His heart was working too quickly, trying to make up for the lack of blood and oxygen by beating faster. Grace didn't need a clock to feel the seconds draining away along with his blood.

"Aryn—the knife."

The baroness pulled a small knife out of the saddle-bag—the very same knife Aryn had given to Grace what seemed a lifetime ago. It wasn't a scalpel, but it was sharp. Grace took the knife and, with precise strokes, finished amputating the arm. She was dimly aware of the horrified gazes of the others—Aryn clutched her own withered right arm—but Grace kept her attention focused on the wound.

"Needle and thread."

Aryn pawed through the bag and came out with the embroidery Grace had been working on. She still hadn't gotten any better at the noble lady's art, but she was glad she had carried it with her. The tools were inadequate for the job, but Grace made up for the lack with skill. She stitched shut the worst bleeders and closed a flap of skin over the stump of his arm. Then she turned to the puncture wound and sutured it shut. Infection was going to be a problem, but that was something to deal with later.

Lirith and Aryn had torn a blanket to strips, and Lirith had rubbed some of the strips with pine sap. That was good—it would be sterile. Grace took the makeshift bandages. By the time she looked up, Durge had already cut two saplings for a litter. He had tied another blanket between the poles and was even then lashing them to Blackalock's saddle.

Grace made a quick inventory of the patient. His color was better, and his breathing was regular if still labored. However, even at that moment he was slipping into shock. They had to get Garf back to the castle.

Garf. She had thought of him not as a stranger, but as someone she knew. However, maybe it was a good sign. Maybe it meant he was going to make it.

Durge led Blackalock closer, positioning the litter alongside Garf. On Grace's count they lifted him onto the vehicle, then they used more strips of blanket to lash him into place.

Grace glanced at Durge. "Ride as fast as you can without jolting him too much."

The Embarran nodded. "I will do my—"

"Grace! He's not breathing anymore!"

It was Aryn. Grace snapped her head around. The baroness knelt beside Garf, her eyes wide.

Grace crouched beside the young knight. Aryn was right. His body was rigid. She groped for his pulse, but she couldn't find it.

"What's happening?" Lirith said.

Grace shook her head. She didn't know. Damn it, she needed a heart monitor.

Or was there another way?

Before she could think about it further, she shut her eyes and reached out to touch the Weirding. She gasped, and for a second the rich web of life almost entangled her. She forced herself to gain control, to pick Garf's thread out from those belonging to people, horses, trees. Then she had it: so thin and weak it seemed like a strand of gossamer in her imagined hands. She followed it down to his body.

"Yes, sister," a voice whispered. Lirith. "Yes, use the Touch. Ivalaine was right. It is your gift."

Grace hesitated. But hadn't she done this a hundred times before in the ED? Perhaps not consciously, but all the same she had used this power—*her* power—to assess what was wrong with others in a way no monitoring device could. She gathered her will, then forced herself to reach down into his chest.

His heart fluttered against her phantom hand like a wounded bird trapped in a cage.

Grace's eyes flew open. "He's fibrillating! I need point-five milligrams of epi, IV push!"

Lirith regarded her with unreadable eyes. "I do not know these words you speak, sister."

Grace shook her head. She had discovered the problem, but what use was that to her? There was no crash cart, no adrenaline. His heart was beating madly in a last desperate attempt at life, and in a few seconds it would fail.

"My lady, can you not . . . do something?" Durge made a small motion with his hands.

Grace glanced at him, and only then did she realize what he was asking of her. Her jaw opened.

Lirith met her eyes. "Spin the web around him, sister. You have the power like neither Aryn nor I."

"Please, Grace," Aryn said. "Please, you have to try."

No, she was a doctor and a scientist. She had used her power to probe, yes, to understand and diagnose. But that was all. The rest was medicine. It had to be.

"I can't," she whispered.

Lirith spoke in a soft voice. "Then he will die, sister."

Grace licked her lips, then held shaking hands toward Garf and laid them on his chest. She was afraid she wouldn't be able to do it again, but even as she closed her eyes she saw the shimmering web. Except now he was connected to it by the barest thread, and even as she touched it the strand began to unravel. She fought to hold it together, but it was too fragile. The thread slipped through her fingers. There was no more time. . . .

In her mind Grace almost laughed. Of course—once she saw it, it was so clear. She had simply to connect his thread to her own. Let her own life become a link between him and the great web that could sustain him until they reached the castle. She reached out a ghostly hand and touched the silver-gold thread she knew to be her own.

"Yes!" Lirith's triumphant whisper seemed to come from all directions. "That's it, sister!"

Grace brought Garf's thread toward her own—

—and froze.

Terror filled her. There was a darkness in the web of the Weirding, a terrible black blot, and only after she recoiled from it did Grace realize that her own thread led directly to it. The blot had been hidden, but when she had pulled on her thread the thing had been revealed.

The blot heaved upward, taking on shape: a long, rambling building with windows like soulless eyes. Pale hands stretched out of the darkness, reaching for her. Grace shrank from them. The calls of owls sounded in her ears. Now the words that spoke in her mind belonged to another witch and another time.

Much of who you are lies behind a door, and I cannot see past it. However, you must know that you cannot lock away part of who you are without locking away part of your magic. If ever you want to discover that power, you will have to unlock that door. . . .

No. She couldn't do it. She couldn't let the shadow escape. If she set it free, then it would surely consume her.

She let go of her own thread. The door shut. The blot vanished.

"Grace!"

The cry was faint, as if it came from very far away.

Grace hardly heard it. She clutched for Garf, but the remaining wisp of his thread unraveled, and the shining web became a gray shroud in her hands.

22.

They reached the high gates of Calavere with the last red light of day.

Grace and Aryn rode at the fore of the party with Lirith just behind. Next to the dark-skinned witch, on a gray charger, rode Sir Meridar, another of the king's knights. He was a quiet man about Grace's age, with gentle eyes set deep in a face ravaged by pox. Meridar had tied the reins of the dappled charger to his saddle, and the riderless horse followed after the gray. At the rear of the party came Durge and Blackalock with their grim, blanket-wrapped burden trailing behind.

None of them had spoken, not since they had left the purple valley. It had taken no more than half an hour to ride back to Calavere, but it might as well have been an eternity. Tears streaked Aryn's face as she wept openly, and even Lirith looked shaken. Durge's face was etched with hard lines. In a way Grace envied them. Maybe it would have been better if she could have felt something—anything besides this hollowness. But then there was an advantage to numbness. Wasn't that the purpose of anesthesia? To feel no pain.

They might still have been there in the valley had Sir Meridar not found them. Grace had attempted resuscitation. She had showed Lirith how to tilt Garf's head back, how to make a good seal around his mouth with her own, how to fill his lungs with air. Then Grace had worked his chest—endlessly, brutally, long after it was useless, long after she had heard ribs crack. Still she had not stopped, even when Aryn, sobbing, begged her to, even when Durge laid strong hands on her shoulders and tried to pull her back.

She halted only when the thunder of hoofbeats echoed off granite. Moments later Meridar rode into the valley. From the back of his charger he took in the body of the bear, then the figure lying in front of Grace. Had word of what had happened somehow gotten back to the castle? Then he spoke to her, and she had realized that was impossible.

"Lady Grace, you have grave circumstances to concern you. From what has met my eyes, this is a dire and sorrowful thing that has befallen your party. However, I bring a summons from King Boreas, and even now, with what has happened, it must be obeyed with all good speed."

Meridar's eyes were compassionate, but there was a sharpness to his words—an edge not meant to hurt, but to cut through the dullness, to remind her that even now she had noble duties. Grace leaned back, let her hands slip from Garf's chest, and stared at the ravaged body that a short time ago had been whole and strong. Sometimes no power was enough.

Except you did have the power, Grace. You did, you saw it, and you were afraid. . . .

The words sounded in her mind again as the riders passed between the castle's guard towers and through the raised portcullis. She saw again—felt again—the shadowy blot upon the Weirding; then she pressed her eyes shut and forced the image away. They rode through an archway into the castle's upper bailey. The last color drained from the stone walls, and the world faded to monochrome.

Meridar dismounted before the stable, then reached a hand up toward Grace. "The king awaits you, Your Radiance."

She opened her mouth, then glanced at Durge.

"I will see to him, my lady," he said softly.

She nodded, then accepted Meridar's hand and slid to the cobblestones. The knight started to lead her toward a door; then she halted to look back at Aryn. But Durge had already helped the young woman from her horse, and Lirith had wrapped an arm around her shoulders. Grace decided she had better worry about herself and concentrated on keeping upright as she followed Meridar into the dimness of the castle.

When they reached Boreas's chamber, the guard standing at the door stared as if they had startled him. Had he not been watching for their arrival? Then the man recovered, bowed to Grace, and opened the door. Grace stepped through, and only as the door swung shut behind her did she realize that Sir Meridar had not followed.

Boreas pushed himself up from the dragon-clawed chair that sat next to the hearth. The mastiff at his feet rose to its haunches and growled. The king glared at the dog, silencing its noise, and the beast skulked to a corner, but it did not take its black eyes off Grace.

"What has happened, my lady?" the king said in his thrumming baritone.

Grace blinked. How could he have heard that something had befallen the riding party? Sir Meridar had not come here before her. Then she followed his gaze, looked down at herself, and she understood the guard's startlement, the dog's growling, the king's strange look.

Her lavender riding gown was drenched in crimson, dark with Garf's blood, which was stiffening as it dried. Grace held out her hands, and they were caked with gore and dirt. She could only imagine the mask of her face. She met Boreas's steely eyes.

"Garf, Your Majesty. Sir Garfethel. I did everything in my power. But his heart stopped beating, and he died."

The words came easily to her lips. But then, she

had spoken them countless times to the wives, husbands, parents, and children in the hospital's waiting room. In the past the words had always held the conviction of truth. But did they now? Had she really done everything in her power?

Spin the web around him, sister. . . .

In clinical tones Grace recounted what had taken place. However, she did not speak of the Weirding, or of the web of magic she had tried and failed to weave.

She was startled to realize she had finished the story. Boreas leaned against the heavy table. His black hair and beard shone in the light of an oil lamp; a servant must have slipped into the room to light it, but she hadn't noticed.

"I saw the firedrake, as well, my lady. All in the castle did. And I thought it to be a harbinger of the news that reached me not an hour later. They say such a sign appears only when a king passes. But perhaps the tales are wrong. Perhaps it was for another." His deep chest heaved as he let out a breath. "Regardless, you tell a strange tale, my lady. Bears seldom venture down from the Gloaming Fells. And it is not like such a beast to come straight for a man."

The king had not invited her to sit, but all the same she sank into a horsehair chair near the door. *You'll get blood on it, Grace.* But it was either that or fall to the floor. Boreas looked at her but said nothing about her impertinence.

"It was wounded," Grace said. "Burned. I think it was mad with pain."

Boreas nodded. "It is good you and Lady Aryn are well. And the others."

Grace winced. Well? She was hardly well. But it didn't matter. In the ED she had learned to move without thought from the dead to the living. Finish that chart and start a fresh one. She had a new case now.

"Why did you summon me, Your Majesty?" However, even as she spoke the words she knew. *They say such a firedrake appears only when a king passes.*

Boreas met her gaze. "Perridon is dead."

"When?"

"A fortnight ago. King Persard died in his sleep."

Had she the ability, Grace would have laughed. *And how many nubile maidens were in the bed with him?* At least one, she was willing to bet. It was a fitting end to the spry old king. But the news troubled her. Grace clutched the arms of her chair, and her mind clicked and whirred. It was good to have something else to think of, something more distant and impersonal.

It seemed a lifetime since the white days of winter, since she had worked as Boreas's spy at the Council of Kings, since her friend and fellow Earther Travis Wilder had helped her uncover the murderous plottings of the Raven Cult, and since Travis had bound the Rune Gate, stopping the Pale King from riding forth to freeze the Dominions in everlasting ice.

For a month after their Midwinter's Day decision to band together, the rulers of the Dominions had labored at the council table to forge new treaties should the Pale King—or any other threat—ever face the Dominions again. Calavan, Toloria, Galt, Brelegond, Perridon, and Embarr: All pledged to aid any Dominion that was attacked by an outside force, and also to act as arbiter should there arise a dispute between any two Dominions.

While these were good steps, the council's greatest act had been the founding of the Order of Malachor.

Oddly, it was Grace who gave the council the idea for the order. But for her—at least until recently a citizen of the United States—the idea of a multinational force working together against a global threat seemed like standard operating procedure. It wasn't until she saw the stunned light of realization in the eyes of the monarchs that she realized, for a feudal society, just how revolutionary the idea was.

There was some debate, of course. Would each Dominion contribute an equal number of knights or a number based on size? How would the order be funded? From whom would these knights receive their commands? But in the end, the decision was unanimous.

"Peculiar times call for peculiar measures," King Sorrin, the gaunt ruler of Embarr, had said.

The greatest challenge facing the council seemed to be in naming the order, but fortunately Falken Blackhand helped in this. After an hour of squabbling among the rulers, the bard approached the table. He did not speak, but simply pointed with his black-gloved hand to an empty seat: Chair Malachor.

The monarchs fell silent, then one by one nodded. While it might have been mere myth, it was spoken that should ever a king of Malachor come again, he would be lord over all the Dominions. To name their new order after the lost kingdom was only fitting.

A few days later the council disbanded, and in the last frozen days of Durdath the rulers departed Calavere for their respective Dominions. Although his was the smallest Dominion, it was King Kylar of Galt who granted a modest castle on the southern marches of his Dominion to the Order of Malachor. However, who would lead the order had not been so easily decided as where it would be housed.

The council first offered leadership to Beltan, King Boreas's nephew and Grace's friend. The blond knight was growing stronger each day, healing from the terrible wound he had suffered on Midwinter's Eve when he had protected Travis from hordes of *feydrim* at the Rune Gate. Grace's heart had soared when she had heard this decision—then had sunk again when Beltan refused the honor.

"I will humbly serve the order," Beltan had said

before the council. He stood straight and tall, but Grace could see that the wound in his side still caused him pain. "However, it is not for one such as me to lead it."

Boreas's eyes sparked with rage, but he only nodded, and the council instead appointed Sir Vedarr to lead the Order of Malachor. Vedarr was a graying but still hale Embarran whose face was craggier than even Durge's. He was a competent knight, and Grace knew he would do a fine job. Yet his name did not cause the eyes of other men to light up, not like the name Beltan of Calavan. She wished her friend could see the effect he had on others: the way he could win a man's loyalty with just a look and a nod. However, his gaze was turned inward these days.

All knew that Beltan, bastard though he was, might have been king of Calavan after his father, Beldreas, was murdered. Instead he had vowed to find his father's killer—and had failed. It was Boreas, Beltan's uncle and Beldreas's younger brother, who had become king instead.

For a time during the winter, the air of sorrow around Beltan had receded somewhat. But not long after Travis Wilder returned to Earth, the knight's melancholy returned. Grace supposed he missed Travis; they all did. She sighed as Beltan walked stiffly from the council chamber. Some wounds were not so quickly healed as those of muscle and bone.

A fortnight later, Beltan had left Calavere to help Vedarr set up operations at the order's new keep. Vedarr had offered Beltan a position as captain, and this the blond knight had not refused. The first mission of the order was to stamp out the last vestiges of the Raven Cult. The cult had been a front for the workings of the Pale King, and most of its leaders had perished when Berash was defeated—the iron hearts their master had given them failing as he was locked in his icy Dominion of Imbrifale once again. However, there were pockets where the cult remained active and continued to practice bloody rites of human branding and mutilation.

Grace had feared for Beltan the day he readied himself to ride off with Vedarr and two dozen other knights. She stood in the upper bailey, watching with concern as Beltan saddled his roan charger. His wound had closed, but just barely, and it was an injury that should have killed him in the first place—only the magic of fairies had kept the thread of his life intact.

Her fears had not gone unnoticed. Lady Melia left her pale mare and approached across the bailey.

"Don't worry, dear," the amber-eyed woman said. "I'll watch over him."

Grace had smiled. Beltan was supposed to be Melia's knight protector, but Grace knew sometimes these things worked both ways.

Falken called to Melia then, and after giving Grace a warm and unexpected embrace the dark-haired lady returned to her horse. Falken and Melia were leaving Calavere as well, and for the first part of their journey they planned to ride with Beltan and the other knights. Where they were going after that Grace didn't know. Melia had only mentioned something about traveling to see an old friend.

In all, after the momentous happenings of Midwinter's Eve, things had gone startlingly well. Still, despite their progress, not all things gave occasion for joy. For after Midwinter's Eve there had been one other empty seat at the council table: Chair Eredane. Queen Eminda had died at the hands of Lord Logren, her high counselor and an ironheart. The first messengers to Eredane had passed into the Dominion with this news, but they had never returned. Now stories told that all travelers were stopped at the borders by grim knights and were forced to turn back.

That some struggle was going on within Eredane in the wake of Eminda's death was certain. However, who the players were and what the outcome would be was a dark cloud none could see through.

Now, sitting in her bloody dress in King Boreas's chamber, she turned her attention to yet another empty chair: Spardis, the seat of Perridon. It was curious that Boreas had summoned her and not another to consult about this issue. Then again, Lord Alerain, the king's seneschal and advisor, was dead—revealed as an ironheart himself and a traitor. Maybe she was all he had left.

But it's more than that, Grace. You know it is. When he first asked you to serve him it was because you were useful as a pawn. Now it's because you've earned his respect.

Grace studied Boreas. He paced now, as he always did when he was thinking, as if his muscular body could scarcely contain the energy within. A month ago, one of the castle's ladies-in-waiting had stunned Grace by asking her when she was to marry the king. Grace had had to clamp a hand to her mouth to stifle the mad laughter. She would have thought Boreas more likely to behead her than marry her, although on an objective level she could see that in some ways they would be a good match. Boreas was strong, but she had learned that she was just as strong. Maybe stronger in some ways.

All the same, Grace knew she would never be queen of Calavere. She did care for Boreas, but more as she might have cared for a father, had she ever had one. And she doubted he had need of her affections. Besides, Grace could never let herself be touched again, not like that. She had almost dared to let herself believe she could love Logren only to discover he was a monster with a heart of iron. That mistake had nearly cost her life and her soul. She would not make it again.

Boreas moved to the sideboard and poured two cups of wine. Grace cringed in her chair, belatedly realizing that she should have offered to serve the king. It was a lapse she could have been imprisoned for in this world. Instead Boreas handed her one of the cups, and she gratefully accepted it and drank its contents down. Maybe that was the real reason Boreas still asked for her counsel and company. He didn't have to be a king around her. He could be simply a man: flawed, temperamental, honest.

"You observed Persard during the council, my lady." Boreas gazed into his wine but did not drink it. "And you spoke with him a great deal—more than myself, really. What's more, I know you won the admiration of his counselor, Lord Sul."

Grace bit her lip. Poor Sul. She still remembered the day she and Durge had convinced the mousy little man to speak to them by pretending Durge was out for his blood and that only Grace had the power to make the knight see reason.

"Tell me, my lady. What do you think this news bodes for us?"

Grace forced herself to forget the events of the day, to forget her bloody dress, and consider the question. "It's not good, Your Majesty. The council's decision to work together is a great step forward. However, the ink on the treaties is hardly dry. Persard does have an heir, but he's only an infant, and his wife is little more herself. I heard she was fourteen when Persard married her two years ago."

"Seventy winters his younger," Boreas said with a snort that might have been disgust, admiration, or both.

Grace nodded. "So we have a child bride and an heir in diapers. Hardly the kind of situation in which you can count on a fragile new alliance to be upheld. If one of Persard's dukes or barons ever had schemes to take over the Dominion, he couldn't have asked for a wider door. But then, I've heard it said that schemes are as rare in Perridon as foggy days."

"My lady," Boreas said in a growling voice, "it is always foggy in the Dominion of Perridon."

"Well, then, I think you have your answer."

Boreas grunted. "So what do we do?"

Grace sighed. Sometimes making a diagnosis was so much easier than finding a cure. "I don't know. But Lord Sul spoke highly of Duke Falderan, who was keeping things running in Persard's absence. If he were to act as a regent to Persard's son until the boy reached ruling age, there might be a chance things would remain stable. As stable as they can in Perridon, at least."

A small part of Grace was amazed at her analysis. But then, she had always been a good student, and these last months had given her a crash course in feudal politics.

Boreas was silent, then he nodded. "Thank you, my lady. You may go."

Grace blinked, then rose to her feet. She was curious what Boreas intended to do, but it was not her place to ask. When the king dismissed you, you went. She moved to the door.

"And Lady Grace . . ."

She halted at the gruffly spoken words but did not look up.

"My lady, remember . . . it is the greatest honor of a knight to give himself in defense of his lord or lady."

Grace clenched the doorknob. *Fuck honor, Your Majesty,* she wanted to say. Instead she bit her lip, then stepped through the door into the corridor beyond.

23.

After her meeting with the king, Grace returned to her chamber to find Lirith waiting for her, along with a serving maid clad in dove gray. Next to the fire was a tub of steaming water. When Grace had asked where Aryn was, the dark-eyed witch informed her that Aryn was resting in her room, and that soon Grace would be doing the same.

Grace did not have the will to argue. Exhaustion enfolded her, as well as fresh horror at the day's events. She was too numb even to care as the serving maid untied the laces of her bloody gown and let the garment slip to the floor.

Lirith took the leather pouch that was usually attached to Grace's sash and set it on the mantle. Belatedly Grace realized that the silver half-coin Brother Cy had given her was inside the pouch. Without it she wouldn't be able to speak and interpret the language of this world. Except that wasn't entirely true, was it? After much practice she had gotten to the point where she could understand a good portion of the musical language the people here spoke, although she doubted she could have spoken two words of it herself. However, there was no need to talk right then, and it was easy enough to understand the murmured instructions she was given: *Take off your undergarments, climb into the tub, close your eyes.*

After the bath, when she was clothed again, the serving maid had brought a platter of food, and Lirith watched while Grace ate every bite of meat, bread, and dried fruit. When she finished, she climbed into bed and let Lirith pull up the covers like she was a small child. Grace closed her eyes, and when the witch kissed her brow it was comforting rather than strange. Grace felt the light leave the room as Lirith blew out the candle. Then the door opened and shut, and Grace was alone.

However, despite her exhaustion, sleep was elusive. At last Grace rose from the bed and stood before the window. It was after midnight, and there was no moon.

A spark of crimson caught her eye. The new red star that had appeared in the southern sky with the coming of summer had just risen over the castle's battlements. A month ago, when she first pointed out the star to Durge, he had frowned and had muttered something about "celestial orbs that shone where none should be."

Since then, from talking to others, Grace had discovered that no one in the castle had ever seen this star before. Perhaps it was a comet then, or a planet— one on an irregular orbit that brought it near this world only after long absence. Of course, these explanations implied that Eldh was a planet itself, in a solar system much like Earth's. Maybe it was even in the same galaxy, although Grace doubted that. Something told her it was more than mere physical distance that separated this world from Earth.

Grace gazed at the red star for a while more, then was surprised to find herself yawning. She turned from the window, climbed into bed, and shut her eyes. Sleep should have been impossible after all that had happened, but at last exhaustion won out, and she descended into slumber.

That night Grace had a dream.

She stood at the top of a mountain, on a pinnacle of rock, surrounded on all sides by swirling mist. Then the mist parted, and on another nearby peak, separated from her by an undulating sea of gray, was Travis Wilder. Excitement coursed through her at seeing her friend. She had thought he had returned to Earth, but here he was only a short distance away. His back was turned to her, so she called out to him, but the fog muffled her voice, filling her throat and lungs like wet cotton.

A light flashed overhead, and she looked up to see the firedrake she had seen earlier streak through the mist. Only then it ceased to move, and it wasn't the firedrake at all, but the new red star. Its light tinged the fog scarlet, and a note of alarm sounded in Grace's mind, although she wasn't certain why. All she knew was that she had to talk to Travis. She tried to call out again, but still he did not turn around. Then the red mist surged upward, engulfing him. Only it wasn't mist anymore, Grace saw as the tendrils licked up and coiled around her.

It was fire.

24.

Grace stepped through a vine-covered archway into the castle's garden.

"Hello?"

Her voice drifted among the trees; there was no one else in view. She moved down one of the stone paths, deeper into the tangle of living things.

It was almost Midsummer now, and the garden was a nave of emerald and gold. Grace breathed in warm air that tasted of honey, and for the first time in a week she felt the muscles of her neck unclench and her shoulders ease downward a notch. There was something peaceful and ancient about the garden. In a way it made Grace think of Gloaming Wood and the Little People. And indeed the garden was not unlike the impossible forest she and Travis had once glimpsed in the castle chamber occupied by Trifkin Mossberry and his troupe of actors.

Maybe Lirith was right. Maybe this was a good

place to come after all. Although there was no sign of the one Lirith had spoken of that morning.

There's someone I believe you should meet, sister. You'll find her in the garden, I think.

Seven days had passed since they had gone, at Grace's urging, for a summer ride. Seven days since she had felt the delicate thread of Garf's life slip through her fingers and melt away.

They had held a small service for the young knight in the circle of standing stones a few leagues from the castle. The last time Grace had stood among the megaliths had been to say good-bye to Travis before he returned to Earth. This time it had been a different sort of farewell. She knew Garf had followed the mysteries of Vathris Bullslayer, and that Boreas would hold a more secret rite to mark the knight's passing. So this ceremony had been just for her and Lirith, for Aryn and Durge. They had done nothing more formal than to hold hands, to speak fondly of Garf's good humor and sincerity, and to lay a wreath of flowers on the ground. It had been enough.

Perhaps the most shocking thing about death was that, in spite of it, life moved relentlessly onward. The sun rose every morning; the castle bustled with activity; Grace ate and slept. It all seemed so petty and stupid in the face of larger things, yet it was a comfort all the same.

In a way it was a sad realization, but Grace knew she would be all right. Being an utter wreck might almost have been more reassuring. It certainly would have been easier. But she knew—with that same certainty she felt when she knew a patient in the ED would survive—that she would go on.

Lirith would be fine as well, of that Grace had no doubt. Not that the Tolorian woman seemed untouched by Garf's death. On the contrary, of all of them she seemed to grasp on its most fundamental level what a loss his passing was to the web of life

that bound them all. But something told Grace that
Lirith had deep roots to draw upon and to hold her
steady.

As for Durge and Aryn, Grace was less certain of
their prognosis. No doubt Durge had witnessed many
men die in his years as a warrior, but she doubted it
was ever easy for the stalwart knight. The other evening she had seen him standing at a window, leaning
against the sill, hunched over. It was the first time
she ever remembered thinking that Durge looked old.
However, when she called to him, he had stood
straight at attention and asked in a crisp voice how she
might serve her.

*You can let yourself cry, Durge. You don't always
have to be a rock. Doctor's orders.* But as so often in
her life, she had not known how to speak the words
she really wanted to.

"Go see if Lady Aryn needs anything, Durge," she
had said instead, and he had given her a brisk nod
before turning to see to her request.

Unlike Durge, Aryn had wept with surprising and
worrisome frequency since the incident. Grace or
Lirith—or sometimes both of them—would hold the
baroness as sobs ripped themselves from her chest.
Had the young woman known about Garf's love for
her? Perhaps that was it, but there was something
about Aryn's grief that made Grace think it wasn't all
for the slain knight. Grace had heard weeping like
Aryn's before. She had been a girl at the Beckett-
Strange Home for Children, and she had heard it at
night sometimes, drifting on wings of dark through
silent rooms: the primal, wordless sounds of utter
despair.

Grace sighed. She would keep observing Aryn, but
she didn't know what else to do. In this case, whatever was truly wrong, she couldn't diagnose it without the patient's help.

The garden path wound on, and as Grace walked

her thoughts turned to Travis. These last days she had found herself thinking of her friend more often than usual. For some reason he weighed upon her mind almost more heavily than Garf did. Then again, given the dreams, perhaps it was not such a mystery.

Nearly every night now she had the queer dream of Travis standing atop the foggy mountain. It was always the same: calling in vain to him, then the red star, and the swirling mist that became fire.

Throughout her life, Grace's dreams had been murky and nonsensical: a series of badly edited foreign films made by drunken directors. This dream was different. Vivid, real. When she closed her eyes she could see the curling fog, the blazing star. But what did it mean?

It didn't mean anything, of course. Dreams were merely the synaptic equivalent of leftovers. Looking for meaning in one was about as useful as looking for a haiku in a bowl of alphabet soup. All the same, it was hard to shake the feeling that Travis was in trouble somehow. However, it was pointless to worry. Even if Travis were in danger, he was a world away now, and far beyond her ability to help. Besides, Grace had far nearer concerns.

Twice more over the last several days, Boreas had called her to his chamber to discuss the matter of Perridon—although as yet the king seemed not to have decided whether action was required, and if so what that action might be. Regardless, Grace had been glad to have a mundane problem to focus on, and she had helped the king by giving him what knowledge she could.

Her studies with Lirith were another matter. She would have thought that, after what had happened, Lirith would have suspended their lessons. And in Aryn's case this was so. But not for Grace. The evening after Garf's death, just as the moon was rising, Lirith had knocked on Grace's chamber door.

"There is comfort in work, sister," she had said in answer to Grace's astonished look. "And you have much to learn yet."

Grace had almost laughed. *That's the understatement of the century. Sister.* But she had let Lirith into the room and had shut the door behind her.

However, despite her efforts, in the time since that evening Grace had not been able to touch the Weirding once.

"You must concentrate, sister," Lirith would whisper. She always smelled of citrus and cloves. "Unshackle your mind from fear. Allow yourself to reach out, to feel the life around you, to bring it close."

Grace would try, but every time, just as she glimpsed the sparkling threads of magic around her, she would see the shadow that lurked in the heart of the web, and she knew that if she were to follow the thread of her own life it would lead right into the blot of darkness. A sound would split her mind, like a door shutting, and she would blink as the Weirding vanished.

"I can't," she finally said last night, trembling and gasping, sinking to her knees. "I can't do it anymore."

Lirith studied her, then left the room without a word. Grace thought the witch had given up on her at last. However, that morning she returned to Grace's chamber. And that was when Lirith told Grace to look for someone in the garden.

"Hello?" she called once more.

The word drifted through the vibrant tapestry of vines and branches. She had stepped through another gate into a smaller space walled on all sides by high hedges. The profusion of life there was even greater than what she had glimpsed so far—a dense and glorious cacophony of color that grew with abandon.

"Get out of here, you rascal!"

Grace jumped at the sound of the high-pitched voice. Where had it come from? She turned around, then blinked. A bush on the farside of the garden was moving. Its branches flailed about, as if it were angry, and leaves fluttered to the ground.

"I said get out!"

Grace hesitated. It was hard to know exactly what to do when one was shouted at by a bush. Once, while at a feast, she had seen a heap of pine boughs shake, then had glimpsed a small, green man within. That had been last winter, when the Little People were prowling the halls of Calavere. But there had been no sign of them since Midwinter's Eve. Was there a greenman in the castle again?

"Out!"

With this last word, the bush exploded in a cloud of leaves, and a figure stumbled from it. It wasn't a greenman.

She was old. Grace was a good judge from experience, and she assessed the woman's age at eighty years, although ninety was possible. She was twig-thin, but not hunched or osteoporotic. Her skin had the soft translucence of petals, and veins traced lines beneath. She wore a simple gray dress that was streaked with dirt, and leaves and bits of bark clung to her wispy white hair.

"I knew I'd get you," the woman said, blue eyes sparkling above smudged cheeks.

At last Grace understood: The woman had not been speaking to her, but rather to the thistly-looking weed she gripped in a gloved hand.

Grace stepped forward. "Hello," she said again.

The old woman dropped the weed. Grace winced—she should have known that speaking suddenly would startle the other. The old woman searched about with that unfocused look the elderly sometimes have when attempting to locate a sound or a voice. Then her blue eyes locked on Grace, and her expression sharpened at once.

The old woman smiled. "Well, now. Here is a lovely flower, sisters."

Grace winced again. She hardly thought of herself as a flower. And who was the woman speaking to? Grace didn't see anyone else in the garden.

"What is it, sweet? Have you found your tongue only to lose it?"

Grace shook her head. No one had ever called her *sweet* before. But she supposed it was better than *Your Radiance.* "I'm supposed to meet someone here. In the garden. Although I'm not sure who it is. Have you . . . ?"

"Have I seen anyone?" The old woman shook her head. "No, sweet. There's only me. And my sisters, of course."

A frown tightened Grace's forehead. The old woman had said it again. *Sisters.* Who was she referring to? Or perhaps she was senile.

Grace tried again. "If you see anyone who's looking for me, could you tell them I was here?"

The old woman nodded. "As you wish, sweet. Although, if you'd like, you could stay a while. If you don't know who you're looking for or where you might find him, aren't you as likely to find him here as elsewhere?"

Grace opened her mouth, but she had to admit there was a logic to it. Perhaps she would rest a bit, then head back to the castle to tell Lirith she had not found the one she was supposed to.

"You can sit there, sweet." The old woman pointed to a marble bench half-lost within a stand of poppies. "Don't mind while I work. One can't lower one's guard for a moment, or the rogue's thistle will creep in and steal the life from everything else." She bent down, scooped up the recalcitrant weed, and heaved it onto a small pile.

Grace sat on the bench. It was odd to rest while the old woman worked, but she wouldn't be much help.

Grace had a feeling she could steal the life from any given plant faster than rogue's thistle. She glanced down at her hands.

Maybe you're not much better with people, Grace.

Except she knew that wasn't true. Ivalaine was right; healing was Grace's gift. But then why hadn't she been able to heal when it mattered most? Why had she let the thread of Garf's life slip through her fingers?

"Is something amiss, sweet?"

Grace glanced up. The old woman was gazing at her, a curious expression on her wizened visage.

"No, I'm fine. Really." She struggled for something to say. "I'm Grace. What's your name?"

"My name is Naida, but most people call me the Herb Mother. You can call me whatever you wish."

Grace thought about this. "I'll call you Naida."

"If it pleases you, sweet." Naida bent beside a cloth bag, rummaged inside, then pulled out a clay bottle. "Would you like a drink?"

The day was getting hot. Grace accepted the bottle and lifted it to her lips. She had thought it would contain water, but instead it was cool, earthy wine. Naida took the bottle, drank, and returned it to the bag. A warmth permeated Grace, from both sun and wine. She let her eyes droop shut. This was a peaceful place.

"My poor sister," Naida said in a soft, sad voice. "You are so beautiful still, but inside you are dying."

Grace's eyes flew open. She fought for understanding. Did Naida know what had happened? But how? Grace searched for the old woman, then saw her standing under a tree. It looked something like an ash tree, although the leaves were tinged with gold not silver.

Grace stood and approached Naida. "What do you mean?"

Naida rested a hand on the tree's bark. "You cannot see it, sweet. But I can feel it there, like a darkness. I'm afraid she rots from within."

The tree: She was talking about the tree, not about Grace.

Naida sighed, then turned from the tree and held out her arms. "We must say good-bye to our dear friend, sisters. This season will be her last."

Grace frowned. "Excuse me, but you keep saying the word *sisters*. Who are you talking to?"

A smile deepened the wrinkles of Naida's face. "Why, I'm speaking to them, of course. They are all my sisters."

Finally Grace understood. The plants in the garden—it was to them that Naida spoke. Maybe the old woman was daft after all. But no, there was something about her—a calmness, a strength—that was familiar to Grace. She moved to the tree and laid her hand on its trunk, then shut her eyes. At first she was afraid, then she forced herself to reach out with her mind, into the tree.

Her eyes blinked open. She had seen it: a dark blot in the shimmering web of threads that wove around the tree. She clutched a hand to her stomach. Was that what was happening to her? Was she rotting from within like the tree?

Naida had been watching her, and now the old woman nodded. "The Touch runs strongly in you."

A breath of uncertainty filled Grace's chest. "Where did you come from?" she asked quietly.

"Why, I journeyed to Calavere with my queen, of course." She brushed a blossom with her fingers, and her gaze grew distant. "I can still remember the last time I stood within the borders of Calavan, although I was only twelve winters old. One day a nobleman I had never seen before rode up to my father's manor on a white horse. Behind him was a mare with no rider. It seemed so strange—I couldn't imagine why he had come. That night the nobleman dined with us. I remember thinking him to be terribly old, although he was only twenty-four. Twenty-four! And look at me now."

She held out her hands. Grace could see sunlight through them, the bones as frail and twisted as wisteria.

"The next morning I sat aback the mare, trailing behind the nobleman whose name I barely knew, and watched my family wave good-bye. I never saw them again. We rode to his manor in the duchy of Arthannon, and I lived there with him for many years, until he died and I went to be of service to my mistress, who was not yet queen at the time."

She gazed around the garden. "I always meant to return here. And before my queen rode for Ar-tolor, I begged of her that I might stay, and the king was kind enough to invite me in." She sighed. "There are no more journeys in me, save for one."

Grace wasn't certain at what point in the old woman's story she had finally grasped the truth she had been too blind, and too caught up in her own shadow, to see. "It was you," she said. "It was you that Lirith wanted me to find."

Naida shrugged. "Sister Lirith is ever full of peculiar ideas. But she is such a lovely thing. She should be married to a strong, handsome man. As should you, sweet." She gave Grace a sly wink. "A garden grows more beautiful if it is tilled more often."

Color bloomed on Grace's cheeks. "I don't . . . I don't think I'll ever be that close to another."

Naida scowled. "But what is it you fear? That if a man looks closely he will see you warts and wrinkles and all, and that he will turn away? Is that it, sweet?"

Grace stepped back. No, she didn't want to talk about this. There was no way Naida would understand why Grace could never be touched that way— not by a man, not by anyone.

"What sadness on your face! But you have aught to worry about. Not a precious thing like you."

Naida reached for her, but Grace pulled back and turned toward the dying tree. She folded her arms across her chest, as if to conceal her own black center. "Is there nothing that can be done to save it, then?"

Naida regarded her, then shook her head. "I fear not, sweet. Perhaps if we had known sooner. But the darkness inside has eaten at her too long."

Grace nodded. It was a harsh prognosis, but she had spoken ones just as bad a hundred times.

"Well," she said, turning to face Naida, "I guess Lirith sent me here to help you. So what can I do?"

Naida pressed her lips together, watching Grace, then she pointed to a patch of flowers. "The rogue's thistle is beginning to creep among the fairy's breath."

"I'll see to it," Grace said, and she turned to begin her task.

25.

That week, Grace returned to the garden each afternoon to visit with the Herb Mother.

Plants were not people. However, it turned out that gardening was not as alien to Grace as she had thought. Herbs and shrubs were still life—just a different sort of life from the kind she was used to working with. In the past her occasional houseplants had met with bad ends, but that was because she had always treated them as she did patients in the ED: Give them the prescribed treatment, and they should respond. As it turned out, plants were a bit trickier than that.

"You have to want them to grow," Naida said one afternoon.

Grace halted in her work. "Excuse me?"

Naida swiped a fluttering wisp of hair away from her face. "Well, you can't simply stick something in the ground, dump water on it, and expect it to perform wonders, now can you, sweet?"

Grace looked down at the clump of fairy's breath she had just transplanted. It leaned at an odd angle and already looked as if it was wilting. "Why not? It's just a plant, isn't it?"

The old woman shook her head. "Forgive her, sisters. She does not know what she speaks."

Grace looked around, suddenly glad plants couldn't move. If they had the power, she suspected they would be happy to coil their little green tendrils around her neck.

"Look here," Naida said, moving to the clump of fairy's breath Grace had been working on. "See how she tilts to one side? But she would rather grow straight up to the sun, would she not? And here she is nearly rising out of the ground when she would feel much better if her roots were tucked in securely, so that she might stand up tall. And how about a nice little well all around, to catch the rain when it falls that she might drink?" The old woman finished tamping down the soil around the flower. "Now, isn't that better?"

Grace had the feeling Naida was not talking to her. However, she nodded all the same. She reached out and touched the fairy's breath. "What are the properties of this one?"

"A tea will ease an upset stomach and bring sleep. A tincture of the root is good against rashes. That is its magic."

Grace studied the delicate white flower. "But it isn't magic. It's just chemicals—tannins, alkaloids, other secondary plant compounds. That's all."

Naida sighed. "If that is what you believe, Lady Grace, then that is all you will ever see in them."

Grace looked up and opened her mouth, but the Herb Mother had already turned her back to see to another flower.

That night, Grace went to Lirith's chamber in the west wing of the castle and asked the witch why she had sent Grace to see Naida.

"Your studies with the Weirding were not proceeding well," Lirith said without looking up from her embroidery. The evening song of insects drifted through the open window.

Grace folded her arms. "Naida hasn't taught me anything about the Weirding."

"The Herb Mother has ever been weak in the Touch."

A groan escaped Grace. "Then why did you send me to her?"

Lirith looked up. "Why do you think, sister?"

The air in the chamber was suddenly stifling. Grace lifted a hand to the bodice of her gown. Had Lirith seen the shadow in her, just as Naida had seen it in the dying tree?

Lirith bent back over her work. "Both Ivalaine and I studied with the Herb Mother during difficult times, as have many others. I do not think it will cause you harm."

So that was it. There was no great point to studying with Naida. It was merely a respite. A chance to rest away from the more challenging work with the Touch and the Weirding. Grace bade Lirith good night and left the room.

She proceeded to Aryn's chamber, but a serving maid informed Grace, in regretful tones, that the baroness was finally resting, and that King Boreas had given a strict command that nothing was to disturb her. Grace could not find fault with this order. No therapy had the power to heal as sleep did. But she would have liked to have seen Aryn all the same. Instead she returned to her chamber, alone.

The next day, Grace plunged into her work in the garden with the same intensity she had always shown in the ED. If this was what Lirith wanted her to study, then she would study it with all her ability. And if Naida noticed this new fervor, the old woman did not comment on it. Instead she showed Grace how to prune a branch so that more branches would grow, how to gather the seeds of the mistmallow, which could prevent pregnancy, and she listed the medicinal properties of a dozen other herbs.

As the sun sank over the castle wall, the two sat on the bench and drank from the flask Naida always kept full.

"How did you do it, Naida?"

Grace asked the question before she really decided to. The old woman raised a thin eyebrow. Grace was committed now.

"Ride away with a man you had never met before, I mean."

Naida clasped dirty, wrinkled hands in her lap. "I had to do it. The welfare of my family depended upon it. My bride-price was enough to keep them in bread for years to come."

"But weren't you afraid?"

This elicited a burst of laughter. "I was terrified! All the way to Toloria I threw up from the back of the horse. And I shall never forget our wedding night. Poor Ederell. He had to coax his bride out from under the marriage bed. But he was always a good man, kind with me from the first day we met, and in all the years I knew him he never raised his voice once." She pressed her eyes shut. "But it hurt. It hurt terribly, as kind as he was."

Grace looked down at the stem in her hand. It ended in a pale flower. Mistmallow. A sharp, metallic scent rose from it, and memories of the orphanage came to her, shocking as always in their clarity after all these years. She saw herself, nine years old, stepping into the dusty, slatted light of the shed behind the home. She heard again the low, animal moan, saw again Ellen Nickel hunched in the corner.

Ellen?

Go away, Grace.

Ellen, what are you doing?

I've got to get it out.

Get what out?

You wouldn't . . . you wouldn't understand.

I understand. It's something they put inside you.

Oh, Grace, it hurts. . . .

Only as she stepped closer had she seen the wire. And the blood. Grace had gotten rags to stanch the flow. It was the first time she had tried to save another's life. It was the first time she had failed. But not the last.

"Sweet one?"

Grace surfaced from the dark lake of memories. Naida had been a year younger than Ellen Nickel had been. In Colorado, had Ederell's deed ever been discovered, it would have been a crime. On this world it was a matter of bread.

"I don't think I could do it," she said.

Naida gripped Grace's hand in her own. Her touch was as warm and dry as soil in the sun. "Yes you could, sweet. You just have to decide to give yourself up for another—to sacrifice everything with abandon."

"But don't you lose yourself when you do that?"

Naida smiled. "Why no, sweet. That's when you find yourself."

That evening Grace wandered the castle's corridors, thinking about Naida's words. There was a beauty to them, and perhaps even a kind of truth. But after an hour the cool logic of Grace's mind found the fundamental flaw: What if there was nothing left inside to discover?

Only when she paused did she realize she stood before the door to Durge's chamber. She had not seen the knight in days. Of course, had she summoned him, he would have come to her in an instant. But sometimes one wanted a friend, not a servant. Grace lifted a hand.

Before she could knock, a muffled clatter—as of something shattering—came through the door. Instinct overrode decorum, and she opened the door and pushed through. He knelt on the floor, sweeping up shards of green glass with a handbroom. Smoke and the reek of sulfur clouded the air, stinging Grace's eyes.

"Durge, are you all right?"

He looked up. "My lady!"

"I'm sorry. I should have knocked. But I heard something break, and . . ."

He set down the broom and rose to his feet. "You need never apologize to me, my lady."

Grace did not know what she had done to deserve such forgiveness, but she was grateful for it all the same. As the smoke cleared, she saw that Durge's face was haggard, the lines around his mouth no longer just etched but chiseled. The wound he had received from the bear was now a thick scab on his forehead. She took a step farther into the room.

"Durge, is something wrong?"

"Yes, my lady. I mean, no." He gestured to his workbench. It was cluttered with vials and crucibles. "I fear I have not yet mastered the process I've been attempting, that's all."

He moved to the sideboard and ran a hand over a yellowed sheaf of vellum. Grace approached and, over the knight's stooped shoulder, peered at the manuscript. Despite the magic of the silver half-coin, the faded diagrams and scribblings made little sense to her, although in the center of the vellum she could discern a drawing of a man and woman.

No, Grace—look. They're wearing crowns.

Not a man and a woman, then, but a king and queen. Other than their crowns, the two figures were naked. They clasped hands, standing together inside an oval shape while flames coiled up around them. Symbols, smaller drawings, and spidery text were written all around the figures. Grace could not understand what it was all supposed to be, although the flames reminded her of the dreams she had been having.

"What does it mean?" she said.

"It is the Great Work, my lady." Durge pointed to the two figures. "Do you see? That which is male and combustible comes together with that which is female and liquid. Through fire they are wed, and their child is perfection given form."

Grace studied the ring drawn between the two figures. Then she understood. "It's gold. You're trying to make gold, aren't you?"

Durge shook his head. "No, my lady. I have many steps to master before I can attempt the Great Work myself. Right now I seek only to fix and whiten brimstone, which is one of the most basic steps along the path."

"Whiten brimstone?"

"Yes, my lady. See how it begins its existence?" He held up a rough, yellowish lump. "But when it is heated in the proper fashion, it becomes thus." Now he held up a vial of opalescent white powder. "Through fire, the brimstone's secret attributes are made manifest."

For some reason, the knight's words disturbed Grace. She gestured to the vial. "And did you make that, Durge?"

The knight rolled the vial in his hand, then set it down. "No. The brimstone turns black on first heating, as it should, but I cannot seem to move it then to white." He let out a sigh. "I fear I am not applying the heat evenly enough. I will have to try again, although I imagine I'm bound to fail."

The knight reached for a crucible, fumbled, then dropped it onto the workbench. He started to retrieve it, then staggered and leaned against the sideboard, head bowed.

Grace recognized the symptoms of sleep deprivation. How long had he been working on his experiments without rest? One day? Two? She touched his shoulder. "Durge, you should get some sleep. You can work on this again tomorrow."

He did not look up. "Tomorrow. Yes, I suppose I do have tomorrow."

She drew her hand back. "What do you mean?"

The voice he spoke in was soft, low, and profoundly weary. "I am old, my lady. Past my forty-fifth winter this year. It should have . . . it should have been me."

Grace could only stare, unable to speak the word in her mind. *What?*

He looked at her, his craggy face solemn. "Sir Garfethel was bright and young, my lady. He had much life ahead of him."

For so many years Grace had feared she had lost her heart, that it had been stolen from her as a child at the orphanage, but she knew once and for all this was not so, because at that moment she felt it break.

"As do you, Durge."

He nodded. "If you wish, my lady." Then he turned again to face the sideboard.

Grace watched his broad back and tried to understand. Something about Garf's death had affected Durge more than just the death of a fellow knight. But what was it?

If there was an answer to that question, it was beyond Grace's reach. She folded her arms over the bodice of her gown and watched him work.

"Will you ever do it? Make gold I mean."

He placed a lump of sulfur on a scale. "It takes a pure heart to perform the Great Work, my lady. As pure as the gold one would create."

Grace thought about this. "Durge, look at me."

The knight immediately obeyed her command, a fact which almost made her wince. She licked her lips and forced the next words out.

"I don't . . . I don't know if anyone's heart is pure." Her mouth twisted into a wry grimace. "In my experience, flesh is a whole lot softer than metal. And I don't know if you'll ever manage to turn lead into gold. But there's one thing I do know." She laid a hand on his arm. "You're a worthy man, Durge of Stonebreak."

Durge gazed at her, and now his eyes did not seem so much bleak as simply tired.

"I believe you are right, my lady," he said at last. "I will go to bed now."

He set down the pair of tongs he had been holding. Grace pressed her lips together and nodded. Then she turned, stepped through the door, and left the knight to his quest.

26.

That night she dreamed again of Travis.

Once more she stood on the pinnacle of stone. In the gloom she saw other sharp summits, islands in the ocean of mist. She turned carefully on her eyrie, searching, until she saw him.

As always he stood upon a needle of rock not far away, his back to her. Crimson flashed overhead. The firedrake. No—even as she looked up the firedrake halted and hung in the gray sky above her: the red star. If a meteor was a harbinger of royal death, then what might the star foretell?

Fear filled her. There wasn't much time. She reached a hand toward Travis and called to him, even though she knew it was futile, that the mist would encapsulate her words as she shouted them, that he would not hear her.

"Travis!"

This time he turned around.

It was Travis just as she had remembered him, wearing the same baggy green tunic, his sandy hair and beard still shaggy and wild. A thrill coursed through her. He had heard her! She started to call out again, to warn him that he was in terrible danger.

The words died on her tongue. The elation in her chest was replaced by damp fog.

Behind his wire-rimmed spectacles, Travis's eyes were completely black. There were no whites, no irises. Only empty, borderless pupils. Tendrils of mist circled around him. Except it wasn't mist, she saw now. It was smoke, and it was rising from his clothes.

He smiled at her. Then Grace screamed as the mist went red and fire leaped up to consume them both.

27.

Grace sat up in bed, pushed snarled hair from her face, then fumbled in the dark for the top of the ladder. She climbed down to the floor. Coals still glowed on the hearth, guiding her like red beacons. She took a splinter of wood from a jar, held the tip against a coal, then guarded the resulting flame with a curled hand until she transferred it to a candle on the room's table.

The borders of night retreated to the corners of the room. Grace sat in a chair, folded hands in her lap, and stared at the candle, letting the mundane light fill her vision. She was sweating—the heat of the dream still—but she shivered in her underclothes all the same. The image of Travis and his black eyes would not leave her mind.

It was just a dream, Grace. A bunch of synaptic vomit, that's all. Besides, even if Travis is in trouble, it's not as if he's anywhere you could reach him.

Logic dulled her fear. Travis was on Earth now. Of course, there were plenty of dangers there—drunken drivers, crashing jetliners, rapidly mutating jungle viruses with no vaccines—but at least they were familiar to her. And perhaps it was a good thing Travis was a world away. Because if he were on Eldh again, Grace suspected he might find himself in a far different kind of peril.

She still wasn't certain—not completely. It had been impossible, as always, to get definitive answers from either Ivalaine or Tressa while the two were here, and it was a topic Lirith had been flatly unwilling to discuss since her arrival. But all the evidence was there. Tressa had been both shocked and fascinated when he broke the rune of peace bound into the council table. *Runebreaker,* she had whispered. And Kyrene, well into her mad descent after being cast from Ivalaine's favor, had approached him. Clearly she had thought that casting him under her spell would win her favor again among the Witches. But why were the Witches interested in Travis Wilder?

Grace didn't know, but while Ivalaine was always an enigma, she had let one clue slip the day she had inquired about Grace's relationship with Travis.

Why do you wish to know, Your Majesty? Grace had dared to ask. *Do you think he might be the Runebreaker?*

The queen's ice-blue eyes had narrowed. *Where did you hear that word, sister?*

Tressa said it at the council.

After a long silence Ivalaine had spoken. *The one*

*called Runebreaker is a great evil, sister. And like all
evil this one can wear many masks, some ugly, some
fair. But if we are lucky his evil will not come to pass
as has been foretold. That is enough for you to know.*

It hadn't been much, but it had been enough
to confirm Grace's suspicions. Whoever this
Runebreaker was, he was a concern of the Witches,
and as a result they were interested in all who had the
power to break runes. Which, from what Falken had
told her, was a list of people that contained a single
name: Travis Wilder.

But Travis was hardly a great evil. Whatever the
queen said about masks, Travis had saved this world
on Midwinter's Eve, not harmed it.

Grace pushed herself up from the table and turned
to pour herself a cup of wine. Maybe it would calm
her enough so she could sleep again.

Self-medicating, are we, Doctor?

She ignored the thought, sloshed some wine into a
goblet, hesitated, then filled the vessel to the rim.
Regardless of what the Witches were up to, Travis
was far beyond their reach. She lifted the cup to
drink.

The goblet halted an inch from her lips. Outside
the window, just beneath the slender crescent of the
waning, almost-new moon, shone the red star. It
stared back at her from the night like a crimson eye. If
only there were a way to glimpse him—just for a second, just to make sure he wasn't in peril.

But there was a way, and she knew it.

*Don't be an idiot, Grace. The last time you tried it
you just about turned yourself into a vegetable. And
this time Ivalaine is not here to rescue stupid begin-
ner witches who get themselves into trouble.*

Even as she thought this, she set down the cup,
moved to the mantelpiece, and drew an object from
the leather pouch she placed there each night.

It glittered on her hand in the candlelight: the silver half-coin Brother Cy had given her back on Earth. Wherever he was, Travis had the other half.

She returned to the chair. Once before she had used the Touch to descry, not a living thing, but an object. It had been a knife, and the spell had taken her to the circle of stones south of the castle. There she had watched, bodiless, as Logren and Alerain plotted to murder one of the rulers at the Council of Kings. The experience had been remarkable, but she nearly had been lost in it, and she would have been had not Ivalaine called her back.

She gripped the half-coin in her hand and gazed into the heart of the candle's flame.

This is pointless. Travis is fine. You'll probably see him sleeping, or eating a bowl of cereal, or sitting on the toilet. Or more likely you'll see nothing at all. You haven't been able to Touch the Weirding once without it all falling apart, not since Garf died. What makes you think you can do this?

Except she knew she could, knew it was different, that touching the Weirding—the vibrant web of life that wove itself among all living things—was something beyond her just then. But this, an inanimate object, a thing of cold, hard, lifeless metal—this was something she could touch.

You should at least tell Lirith what you're doing.

But she did not rise from the chair. Instead, she shut her eyes, let the darkness fill her, and reached out with her mind to touch the half-coin. This time she felt it—almost like a tug, followed by a wet sensation of parting.

Then she was flying.

By the time she gathered her wits enough to look down, the ground was already far below: a textured canvas painted in blue tones of shadow. She glanced back—dimly noticing that this action required only a thought, not motion—and could just barely pick out

Calavere from the backdrop of stars. Only here and there did the spark of a torch flicker against the night. The town at the foot of the castle's hill was no brighter, and of the villages she knew dotted the landscape around the castle, Grace could see no trace. The darkness was complete. It was utterly unlike being in a jet above North America at night, when one could look out the window and see the cities like glittering jewels strung along the gleaming strands of the highways.

Except this was no airplane she rode in. Right now her body sat slumped in a chair in a room in Calavere while the rest of her sped toward a destination she did not know.

A broad, black serpent undulated below her, its curves catching the faint light of the moon: the River Darkwine. Grace thought back to her fireside geography lessons with Aryn. Didn't the Dimduorn flow east from Calavere to the marches of Toloria? Yes, she could still recall the charcoal map Aryn had drawn. Once it reached Toloria, the Dimduorn turned south, and a smaller river flowed into it. Just east of the confluence Aryn had placed a dot: Ar-tolor, the seat of Queen Ivalaine of Toloria.

Ar-tolor? Was that where she was going?

She forced her attention down, and even as she did she saw the great river curve sharply to her right. At the bend, nearly as Aryn had drawn it, a lesser river joined the Darkwine. Just beyond was a pale shape on a hill. Slender towers reached toward the sky and, unlike in Calavere, fires danced atop all seven of them. So the Witch Queen at least dared to defy the night.

Grace expected her descent to begin, but instead she seemed to move faster yet. Ar-tolor slipped past and was gone. Land flowed beneath her like dim water. Then jagged shapes heaved up before her, taking a ragged bite out of the starry sky. Mountains.

The air grew hot around her, until her whole being felt brittle and desiccated. In an instant it was no longer night; the sun burned in a sea of crimson clouds on the horizon. Dawn had come.

No, that wasn't right. The sun lay behind her, to the west. Before her, a full moon, pink as a shell, rose above the mountains. Not dawn then, but sunset.

The peaks were close now, and she began to drop. At the foot of the mountains, on a thrusting outcrop of stone, stood a tower. So this was her destination. But what was it?

The tower grew to fill her vision, and she saw that her first impression was wrong. The tower was not simply built upon the pinnacle of stone. Rather, the spire had been hewn from it. The base of the tower merged seamlessly with the outcrop, while the three-horned summit soared above. All of it—stone, tower, turret—was as gray as mist.

A gray tower. Where had she heard of a gray tower?

There was no time to think. The ground rushed up to meet her. She came to a halt atop the ridge that led from tower to mountains. Then, for the first time on her journey, she heard a sound other than the rushing of the wind.

"He has defiled the runestone," a deep voice, filled with anger, said. "The runestone, which is the heart of our tower and the source of all we are. His punishment has been decided."

There was a pause, then another voice—sadder, more hollow—answered. "Then let the judgment be carried out."

The gravity of the tower tugged at her, but somehow Grace turned around. They stood a dozen paces away, had she had feet with which to walk. A hundred men in robes as gray as the tower gathered in a semicircle. Two of them stood slightly ahead. One had black hair and a hard face crisscrossed with scars.

The other was white-haired and stooped, leaning on an intricately carved staff.

In front of the men, near Grace, was a standing stone, slender and about ten feet high. Its surface was incised with symbols she could not read. At the stone's base was a pile of wood and sticks. Only after a moment did Grace see that there was a man bound with ropes to the stone. His head hung down, but she could see that he had sand-colored hair and a short beard. Even as she watched, a pair of robed men stepped forward, bearing lit torches, and approached the standing stone. Who was the prisoner? And what had he done to deserve this sentence?

"Have you any words to speak before the end?" the white-haired man asked the prisoner.

"He's spoken enough lies already," the man with the cruel face sneered, but a look from the older man silenced him.

All were silent, then the bound man lifted his head. Had she a mouth, Grace would have screamed.

It was Travis.

Her mind flailed about. How was he here? And what was happening to him?

"I've only told you the truth, Oragien," Travis said in a quiet voice.

At these words, the old man pressed wrinkled eyes shut. The other one, the scarred man, made a sharp gesture with his hand. The two with the torches hesitated, then stepped forward and plunged the flaming brands into the pile of sticks. Smoke billowed up.

Travis turned his head away from the smoke, so that Grace could see his face. She feared his eyes would be black, as in the dream, but they were gray as his robe and frightened behind his spectacles. Then his eyes went wide.

"Grace!" he said in a hoarse whisper.

Shock crackled through her. She tried to speak his name, but she had no organ of sound. Had he seen her somehow? But that was impossible; she wasn't even there. Perhaps it was simply her name that he called at the end, out of terror and desperation.

The smoke was thicker. Flames crept up through the pile of sticks toward the hem of his gray robe. Travis turned his face forward again. No, he had not seen her. He clenched fingers into fists and shouted to the sky.

"Olrig's hand will save me!"

He was wrong. No godly hand descended from the clouds to pluck him from the fire. The flames rose higher.

This couldn't be happening. Grace reached for Travis, even though she knew it was no use, that she couldn't help him. Travis's body went rigid. He threw his head back, and a scream ripped itself from his lungs.

Then, just like in the dream, the flames leaped up to surround him. Grace was too close; the heat of the fire sucked at her. She struggled and somehow managed to turn around. There—stretching behind her into the distance was a faint, shimmering strand. The thread that bound her to her living body back in Calavere.

Her last conscious thought was to reach for the slender thread. Then Travis's scream merged with the voice of the fire, and everything went red.

28.

It was a pounding noise that woke her. At first Grace thought it was the beating of her heart, for it seemed to vibrate through her entire body. Then the sound came again, along with a muffled voice.

"Lady Grace! Are you in there?"

Slowly, her eyes opened. Crimson light flooded her

brain. Was it the fire then? No—she blinked and saw
it was not flame that poured through the window but
the light of dawn. It was morning, and she was still
alive.

"My lady, unbar the door!"

She lifted her head, then gasped at the sudden,
shocking jolt of pain that coursed through her stiff
muscles. What had happened? It felt as if her mind
had burned to ashes, but she forced herself to remember: the tower of gray stone, Travis, the flames. A new
kind of pain filled her. This had been no dream. She
could feel the hot metal of the half-coin clutched inside her right hand.

The pounding at the door ceased, and she thought
she heard faint words through the wood: *I'm going to
break it down.* With brittle motions, Grace rose from
the chair. She shuffled to the chamber's door, pulled
back the iron bar, and opened it.

She came face-to-face with a stout Embarran
shoulder. It would have struck her face and bloodied
her nose except that Durge was able to skid to a halt
at the last moment. Lirith stood just behind him, a
stunned expression on her face. Grace supposed she
looked like hell on a bad hair day.

Durge regained his composure, but his deep-set
eyes were concerned. "My lady, what has happened?"

She opened her mouth, but her throat was a desert.

Lirith breezed past Durge, all traces of surprise
gone from her serene visage. "Can you not see the
obvious, Sir Knight? She needs something to drink, of
course."

The witch laid a dusky hand on Grace's arm and
led her back to the chair. Looking chagrined, Durge
filled a cup from a decanter on the sideboard and
handed it to her. Grace accepted it in a trembling
hand. *Wine—it's not just for dinner anymore.*

She took a sip. The wine stung her throat, but she

gulped the rest of it down, then handed the cup back to Durge. Her shaking eased a degree. Now both knight and witch gazed at her with curious expressions.

"It's Travis Wilder," she said before either of them could speak. "He's on Eldh. And he's in danger."

She wanted to tell them everything then, but before she could say more Lirith clucked at her underclothes and gave Durge a pointed glance. The stalwart knight actually flushed, then turned his back while Lirith took Grace's gown from a chair and helped her into it.

Lirith's instincts were right, as always; as she dressed, Grace was able to gather her wits. By the time she sat in the chair again, this time holding a cup of steaming *maddok* brought by a servingwoman, she was able to speak in calm, precise words. Not that she didn't feel urgency: She did. But if she was right, there was still time to save Travis.

When she finished speaking Durge and Lirith regarded her—one with astonishment, the other with interest.

Lirith crossed slender arms over the bodice of her rust-colored gown. "What you did was foolish, sister. And it was forbidden. If Ivalaine were to discover what you have done, she might cast you from the Witches altogether. And with good cause. What you did endangered yourself, but it might also have placed me or Aryn in peril had one of us been forced to attempt to retrieve you."

Grace bit her lip at this chastisement. All the same, her dread receded a fraction. *If Ivalaine were to discover . . .* Grace had a feeling Lirith had chosen those words carefully. The witch did not intend to tell Ivalaine what had happened.

Grace gripped her cup. "Yes, Lirith," she said, and it was not difficult to find a contrite tone.

Durge stroked drooping mustaches. "Are you certain about the moon, my lady? It was full in your . . . your vision?"

"Yes. I saw it clearly. All of it. It was just like before, at the circle of standing stones. What I saw hasn't happened yet."

"But will it?"

Both Durge and Grace looked at Lirith.

The witch paced, a hand poised beneath her chin. "It is not so uncommon a thing to use an object as a focus for visions. Several sisters have the power. However, they usually see but fragments, and these of things past. I have heard about visions such as Grace describes—visions which illuminate what will be rather than cast shadows of what was. But the power is rare." Her eyes flickered toward Grace. "Quite rare."

Durge shifted from foot to foot, and Grace gripped the arms of the chair.

"But will it happen, Lirith?" she said. "That's what I have to know. Can what I saw be stopped?"

"Should it be stopped?"

The words were like a slap. Grace's jaw dropped.

Lirith spread her hands. "He can break runes, sister. What if he were the one?"

The one what? Grace wanted to ask. But she already knew. *Runebreaker.* The one whom the Witches feared even more than the warriors of the Cult of Vathris.

"The tower you saw can be only the Gray Tower of the Runespeakers," Lirith said. "And why would the Gray Men put one of their own to death unless they knew him to be a peril?"

Grace shook her head. "He's my friend, Lirith. And he saved everyone in Falengarth from the Pale King. Now will you answer my question or not?"

"Very well, sister. But the truth is, I don't know the answer to your question. Perhaps Ivalaine might.

Yet it seems to me that if you saw it, then it must be so. Else why would it have been revealed to you?"

No. Grace wouldn't accept that answer. If it hadn't happened yet, then there was still a chance to change it. How many times had someone been pronounced dead only to be brought back to life on her table in the ED?

She shut her eyes and thought. Unlike Earth's satellite, the moon of this world took precisely a month to wax, wane, and wax again. Today the moon was one day from new. Then fifteen more until it was full again. That gave her just over a fortnight. She counted in her mind. It was a week to Ar-tolor. And how far from there to the Gray Tower of the Runespeakers? She tried to remember the charcoal maps. Four more days? Five?

Grace opened her eyes and saw Durge gazing at her. His expression was odd. Somber, as always, but eager as well. "What are you thinking, my lady?"

Of course. He was a knight and a man of action. How long had he stayed at this castle, seeing to her small needs, attending her on her little rides into the countryside? How long had she expected such trifles to occupy him?

"I don't know," she said. "Not yet."

But she had an idea, and every moment it grew clearer.

Lirith glanced at Durge. "I fear in all of this we have forgotten about the king."

"What about the king?"

"He is the reason we came to your chamber, my lady," Durge said. "Boreas asked me to bring you to him."

Grace stood up and smoothed her gown. "Well, then I had better go."

Lirith gave her a concerned look. "Are you well enough, sister?"

Grace gave her a tight smile. A meeting with Boreas was the last thing she needed just then. But there was something she had to tell the king, and she might as well get it over with.

"I'll be fine," Grace lied.

Ten minutes later she stepped into the king's bedchamber. His need for her must have been urgent indeed for him to have summoned her there. She expected to be berated for her tardiness, but Boreas only grunted and waved for her to sit.

He sat at a table, poring over a sheaf of parchment, a scowl on his bearded face. His black hair was tousled from sleep, and he wore only tight-fitting knee pants and a loose white shirt open to expose a triangle of hard chest. He looked for all the world like what he was: a barefoot warrior who had just rolled out of bed.

As she watched, the king grabbed a quill pen, dunked the tip into an ink pot, and scribbled on the parchment. He regarded his handiwork, then set the pen down and looked up at Grace.

"Well, what is it, my lady?"

Grace did not try to hide her puzzlement. "You sent for me, Your Majesty."

He snapped his fingers. "That's right." His blue eyes sparked. "What took you so long?"

Grace groaned. She should have quit while she was ahead. Her only chance was to detour the conversation.

"What is that, Your Majesty?" She gestured to the parchment on the table.

"This," he said, folding the sheaf and sealing it with a blob of candle wax, "is a letter of endorsement."

"A letter of endorsement?"

"Didn't I just say that?"

Grace drew in a breath. It was going to be one of *those* conversations. She tried again, choosing her words like surgical instruments.

"What does the letter endorse, Your Majesty?"

"My new envoy to Perridon, of course."

"Envoy?" Grace bit her tongue, but she was too late to prevent the word from escaping.

Boreas glared at her. "My lady, you will fail miserably in Perridon if all you can do is state the obvious. All words spoken in Castle Spardis are vagaries mixed with half-truths wrapped in a gauze of subtle misdirection. And that's when you're talking to a servant about what you want for breakfast. I'm beginning to have second thoughts about sending you."

Grace clawed at the arms of the chair. "Sending me? Where?"

Boreas crossed his arms. She crunched down into her seat.

"To Perridon?" she said in a small voice.

"However did you guess, my lady?"

The air was suddenly unbreathable. He wanted her to be an envoy to a foreign nation? She could hardly ask a serving girl for a second cup of *maddok*, let alone make demands and negotiate treaties. "But . . ."

"But why you?" Boreas rose and paced to the window. "Because you're the best spy I've got, my lady."

A sigh escaped him at this utterance, and some of her dread was replaced by indignation. She wasn't *that* bad of a spy. After all, she had helped uncover the Raven Cult's plot to murder one of the rulers at the Council of Kings.

"And who am I to spy on, Your Majesty?"

"Everyone. I want you to watch and speak with every person who is scheming for the throne of Perridon—which, in Spardis, is a list that likely includes the kitchenwife and the stableboy. I need you to find out who is the most trustworthy of the lot—if there is such a person in that foggy dominion—and who is most likely to serve dutifully as a regent to the infant prince without seizing control of the Dominion himself. That's who we'll back if there's a struggle for the crown."

It was impossible. Grace had gotten better at dealing with people—whole people—these last months, but she had just learned to walk, and now Boreas was asking her to run up a mountain. This was utterly beyond her. She opened her mouth to tell him she couldn't possibly go—

—and an image flashed in her mind. She saw the map Aryn had drawn that day. There, in central Falengarth, was Calavan. Perridon lay to the east. And between the two . . .

Toloria. And the Gray Tower of the Runespeakers.

That was it. She wouldn't need to beg Boreas's permission to leave Calavere. And no doubt he would send knights to accompany her. That was good—she had no illusions about what could happen to a woman traveling alone in a medieval world.

The plan crystallized in her mind. It was perfect. Almost too perfect. Had she influenced the king somehow without trying? Had she made him want to send her east?

Now she was thinking like Kyrene. Not every one of her whims was a spell. Besides, it wasn't important. All that mattered was that she get to Travis before the moon was full. Grace looked up and met Boreas's blue eyes with her own of green and gold.

"I will be honored to serve you, Your Majesty."

29.

Evening drifted on soft gray wings through the castle. Outside the high windows, mourning doves sang of loss and sorrow. The day was dwindling. Her last in Calavere.

Grace walked down a corridor, although she had no idea where else to search. Earlier she had gone to Aryn's chamber to tell the baroness about what had happened, how she would be leaving for a time. However, the young woman had not been in her room. Nor had she been in the great hall, or the kitchens, or either of the baileys. For the last two hours Grace had looked everywhere in the castle she thought the baroness might be.

Finally, she had ended up in the little shrine in the north wing sacred to the mysteries of Yrsaia the Huntress. Aryn seemed to believe Grace did not know about the prayers the young woman sometimes spoke to Yrsaia, but Grace had overheard her whispers on more than one occasion. Why did Aryn think she had to keep her religion a secret?

She's afraid that if you knew the truth, you wouldn't feel the same about her.

Grace understood. After all, she had secrets of her own.

She stopped, sighed, and considered going to Boreas's chamber, to tell the king she was worried about Aryn. Maybe Boreas could send some of his guards to search for her. She turned to go.

A faint, rhythmic sound floated through an open doorway. Grace halted. Where had she heard that sound before? She listened a moment more, then she stepped through the doorway. Beyond was a spiral of stone steps. She started up the steps and after a few revolutions realized she was climbing into one of the smaller towers that flanked the main keep. The clacking ceased as she climbed, then came again moments later, louder than before.

Grace stepped from the staircase into a short hallway. At the end was a wooden door, slightly ajar. The sound was clear now. *Clack-clack. Thrum. Clack-clack. Thrum.* She approached, then stopped at the half-open door, finally recognizing the sound even as she saw its source.

So this is where she's been coming.

The circular room was empty except for a wooden loom and a chair in the center. For a time—she wasn't certain how long—Grace stood in the doorway, watching as Aryn worked the loom, using the small, folded hand at the end of her withered arm to help catch the shuttle as it passed through the warp. After seven passes, Aryn would stop, set down the shuttle, and with deliberate motions pick out the threads she had woven. Then she would lift the shuttle and begin again. That was why the sound had come and gone.

"Aryn?"

The shuttle clattered to the floor.

Grace rushed into the room and picked up the block of wood before Aryn could react. She straightened, then pressed the shuttle into the baroness's good hand.

"I didn't know you were there, Grace."

The words were listless, and Aryn didn't look up as she spoke. Grace pressed her lips together. She had stood by on enough psych evaluations in the ED to know that repetitive behavior and lack of eye contact were both troubling signs.

"Aryn, are you all right?" Grace cringed even as she spoke. Words were so damn worthless sometimes.

The young woman turned back to the loom. "I'm just weaving, Grace. Like Ivalaine said we should. I've got so much to learn still. Only I can't seem to get it right. The threads never make the picture I want. But I'll keep trying." She smiled, but the expression was as thin as a paper cut.

Grace sucked in a breath. This was worse than she had thought. She cursed herself for not having read the signs better. But it was broken bodies that she knew how to reassemble, not broken minds.

Aryn began weaving again, humming a dissonant song under her breath. Grace caught only a few words:

> *My love is coming in the spring,*
> *I'll weave a garland gold—*
> *And when he's buried in the fall,*
> *A shroud against the cold.*

Grace knelt beside Aryn's chair. It was going to be as crude as operating with a dull scalpel—she didn't have the training or the instincts for this kind of procedure—but she had to try. She might have been a flesh doctor, but she knew enough about psych to know it wasn't the weaving Aryn was trying to correct.

"Aryn," she said in a quiet but insistent voice. "Aryn, listen to me. Fixing the tapestry won't make it better. I know something happened to you. On Midwinter's Eve."

Aryn ceased motion. She stared forward, her body rigid.

You should leave her alone, Grace. You could drive her over the edge doing this.

But tomorrow she was leaving Calavere. This was her only chance to understand. "What is it, Aryn? What are you really trying to make better?"

Silence. Grace hesitated, then reached up and touched Aryn's shoulder.

An animal howl of pain filled the chamber, and Grace leaped to her feet. Aryn threw her head back, spine arching away from the chair, and her cry echoed off hard stone. At last her anguish phased into words.

"I killed him!"

At first Grace thought she meant Garf, then the baroness slumped forward, choking out words between sobs.

"Leothan. I killed him, Grace. I killed him with my magic. On Midwinter's Eve."

Grace shook her head, trying to comprehend. She had not thought of Leothan—the young lord who had once spurned Aryn's invitation to dance—in many months. However, she remembered vaguely that Leothan had been among the dead of Midwinter's Eve. She had assumed *feydrim* had killed him, as the monsters had a dozen other people that night.

Aryn's right arm writhed against the warp of the loom like the broken neck of a swan. Grace clenched her jaw; this was a pain she had little power to ease. All the same, she moved again to the baroness.

"Tell me, Aryn. Please."

The young woman nodded, then in a halting voice recounted a story that froze Grace's blood: how Leothan had coaxed Aryn into an antechamber, how he had forced himself on her, revealing himself for an ironheart, and finally how the rage had flowed out of Aryn, turning Leothan's brain to gruel.

By the time Aryn finished she was rocking back and forth in the chair. Grace gathered her into a clumsy embrace, holding the baroness's slight, shaking body against her own.

"It's all right, Aryn," she murmured. "You did what you had to, and it's over."

"No, Grace." Sobs like convulsions shuddered through the young woman. "You don't understand. I killed him."

"You had to protect yourself, Aryn."

"But was that the only way?"

Grace shook her head. "I don't understand."

"Healing is your gift, Grace. Ivalaine said so." The young woman clutched her withered hand. "But what if all I can do is harm? What if that's *my* gift?"

No. Aryn had been punished enough by others for something beyond her control. Grace would not let her torture herself. Her power made her evil no more than did a deformed arm. She pushed the baroness away.

"You use what power you have. Do you understand me, Aryn? You do what you have to in order to survive, and you use whatever ability you have to do it." She gripped Aryn's shoulders and squeezed. Hard. "Do you understand me?"

Aryn stared, her face smudged with tears. Then one last shudder passed through her, and her body relaxed. A light shone in her blue eyes.

"Yes, Grace," Aryn whispered. "Yes, I see. I must use what power I have. . . ."

Grace held her breath. There was something odd about the way the baroness spoke the words. She wasn't certain Aryn had really understood.

Yet after that Aryn's trembling eased, and she managed to stand on her own, to gather herself, and to walk with Grace back to her chamber. There they spoke long into the night, talking about all that had happened to them in the last months, and by the end Aryn was laughing—a genuine if fragile sound. Maybe Grace had gotten through to her. At least she hoped so. She was going to be journeying far from Calavere, and she didn't know when she would get back.

By the time Grace finally finished her good-bye, both of them were weeping, although this time the tears were the normal byproduct of good, plain sorrow. Then Grace returned to her own room, lay in her bed for a few dim hours, and rose long before the sun to ready herself for the journey.

30.

They set out at dawn the next day.

Grace let Durge help her onto Shandis's back. The palfrey pranced in a circle, eager to be gone. It seemed she knew this was more than just a morning jaunt into the countryside, but once more Grace was giving an animal too much credit.

Then again, for all you know, she can calculate pi to twenty decimal places.

Grace decided to stop worrying about personifying.

Durge swung himself up into Blackalock's saddle, his shirt of chain mail jingling. "Have you made all your preparations?" the Embarran asked the other two knights who, like him, sat astride tall warhorses.

"I believe I'm ready," Sir Meridar said, making a last check of the leather bags tied to his saddle.

Grace remembered Meridar. He was the knight who had come upon them in the valley after the attack by the bear. His eyes were kind in his pock-marked face.

The remaining knight, Sir Kalleth, gave a curt nod. "We should already have left by now. The day wastes."

Grace's frown was a mirror of Durge's. There was something about Kalleth she didn't like, although it was hard to pin down exactly what it was. He was a plain man, if powerfully built, with salt-and-pepper hair and unremarkable features, save for a broken and badly reset nose. Maybe it was the flatness of his eyes. Regardless, Grace wished Boreas had not ordered Kalleth to accompany her.

Both Meridar and Kalleth had pledged their swords to the new Order of Malachor. Accompanying Grace was to be their last duty for King Boreas before he released them from service. On their return from Perridon, the two knights planned to journey to the order's new fortress in Galt. Grace would have to remember to tell Meridar to say hello to Beltan for her. She missed the big blond knight, and she hoped he was doing well.

"The king has granted us his leave," Durge said. "There is nothing holding us."

Grace glanced around the bailey, but there was no sign of either Aryn or Lirith. But why should they have come? Grace had spoken with Aryn at length yesterday, and she had already bid Lirith farewell over breakfast that morning.

It's better not to draw out good-byes. You know that well enough, Grace.

Yet it was hard not to feel a pang of disappointment.

Durge looked at her. "Are you ready, my lady?"

Grace hesitated. There was one more she had wanted to say farewell to. However, yesterday, when she had ventured into the garden with the gold light of afternoon, she had found no sign of Naida. The little grotto where the Herb Mother usually worked was silent. As she turned to leave, Grace had seen that the tree in the corner had finally died. Its brown branches hung down, as if to touch the other plants in a final embrace. Grace had lifted a hand to her chest, then had turned and left the garden.

Now she glanced up at the flawless summer sky. It promised to be a hot day. She searched the blue dome, and although she could not see it, she knew it was there, sinking even then toward the horizon. The new moon.

She lowered her head and met Durge's gaze. "Let's go."

They rode through an archway into the lower bailey. Grace gazed at the stone walls within which she had lived most of the last eight months of her life.

When would she set foot in this place again? Then they passed through the castle gate and into the world beyond.

Once they reached the foot of the hill they broke into a brisk but far from rapid trot. Grace forced herself not to order the knights to ride faster. It was still two weeks until the full moon; they had more than enough time for the journey. Yet it was hard not to feel that what she had seen in the vision had already happened, that no matter how hard they rode they would be too late. She concentrated on riding, and by the time she remembered to look back Calavere was already lost to sight behind her.

They rode north from the castle to the old Tarrasian bridge over the Dimduorn, then before crossing turned east, ascending the grassy ridge that paralleled the south bank of the river.

"Why don't we just cross the Dimduorn here in Calavan?" Grace had asked Durge yesterday after studying a map of the Dominions with him. "It looks like we'll have to go five extra leagues to the south to cross the bridge on the border of Toloria."

"No, my lady," Durge had said. "We must keep to the south side of the Darkwine. There are too many tributaries to cross if we were to ride on the north bank, and all of them will be swollen with snowmelt this time of year."

Grace had nodded. But even five leagues seemed too great a sacrifice to speed.

They had ridden an hour in silence when Durge dropped back and brought Blackalock alongside Shandis. "We have not discussed Ar-tolor, my lady. Will we be begging the hospitality of the queen for a time?"

Grace opened her mouth to answer, but harsh words beat her.

"We ride straight to Perridon."

Grace jumped in her saddle. Kalleth's horse was

just a half length behind her own. She hadn't realized he had been following her so closely.

Durge's mustaches twitched. "Lady Grace is a close companion of the queen. What if Queen Ivalaine were to extend an invitation to stay?"

"Then Lady Grace will politely decline," Kalleth said, baring yellowed teeth in what was not a smile. "We will stop at Ar-tolor to beg permission of the queen before riding through her Dominion, as protocol demands. But then we will be on our way. We have our orders from King Boreas, and a holiday in Ar-tolor is not mentioned in them."

Kalleth jerked the reins of his charger—so hard the beast snorted and rolled its eyes—and the horse veered to the side and dropped back.

Grace glanced at Durge. The knight gave a somber nod but said nothing. It might prove difficult to convince the other two knights to go out of their way to the Gray Tower. Grace suspected that Meridar could be persuaded with effort. But Kalleth seemed about as malleable as a block of granite. All the same, that was exactly what Grace had to do.

And what will you do when you get to the Gray Tower, Grace? Just how do you intend to help Travis?

But she had over fifty leagues in which to figure that one out. She hunkered down in the saddle and kept her eyes on the horizon.

Grace had gone for a number of rides in the last months, and her equestrian skills had improved, but she had never ridden hard for an entire day, and by the time the sun threw their shadows out before them her whole body hurt. Just when she was fearing they would never stop, she saw the thin trails of smoke rising into the sky not far ahead.

"The village of Foxfair lies just beyond that rise," Durge said. "We will beg the hospitality of Gaddimer, the local lord, for the night."

Grace nodded, grateful they were close to the village and to rest. Although she wasn't certain that, when they did stop, she would actually be able to pry her fingers from the reins.

As they reached the base of the knoll that separated them from the village, the trail passed into a stand of trees. They were nearly through the stand to the other side when Kalleth hissed behind them.

"We are being followed."

Durge came to an immediate halt. He cocked his head, listening, then looked up and made two sharp motions with his hand. Meridar and Kalleth wheeled their horses around and plunged into the thicket to one side of the road.

"This way, my lady," Durge whispered.

He guided Blackalock into the undergrowth opposite of where the other knights had vanished. Grace and Shandis followed. She waited, watching the road through a screen of leaves. Then she caught the sound of hooves, and she held her breath.

The riders came into view. There were two of them. Both wore dark capes, the hoods pulled up to conceal their faces despite the warmth of the late-summer afternoon. A blade of fear stabbed at Grace. Raven cultists? No, the followers of the Raven had always worn robes, not capes. Highwaymen, then. Not so terrifying, but still dangerous.

The riders brought their horses to a halt. Their hooded heads turned from side to side, as if searching. Panic slithered up Grace's throat. Did the brigands know their prey was hidden among the trees? The two bowed their heads together. One seemed to speak something, and the other nodded. Then they nudged their horses, and Grace breathed a sigh of relief as the two cloaked riders started onward again.

Her sigh became a gasp as, with a crashing noise, a horse burst out of the undergrowth in an explosion of leaves. The two cloaked riders jerked their heads up, then fought to keep their own startled horses under control. Grinning, a naked sword in his hand, Kalleth thundered toward them aback his charger. The riders fumbled with their cloaks, as if trying to grab weapons concealed beneath, but they did not have time.

"Hold, Kalleth!" a voice roared beside Grace.

Blackalock surged forward, a dark blur, out of the trees and onto the path.

"I said hold!"

Durge's face was a deeply etched mask of fury. At the last moment Kalleth changed the direction of his blow, and the sword passed its mark, missing one of the riders by a scant inch.

The knight cast a venomous look at Durge. "What is the reason for this?"

Durge did not answer. Instead he rode forward, grabbed the hood of the nearest rider, and jerked it back.

Grace sucked in a sharp breath. *Of course. You should have recognized the horses.* She nudged Shandis forward, reaching the path at the same time as Meridar.

All looked at Aryn as she blinked wide blue eyes against the light of the westering sun. Her face was pale, and she lifted her left hand to the throat that nearly had been sliced through by Kalleth's blade. The other rider reached up dark, slender hands and pushed back the concealing hood. Grace was shocked again. It was Lirith. What were the two doing here?

Kalleth shoved his sword into its scabbard. "This is a foolish game you've played, my ladies. And it might well have cost you your lives."

"Thanks to your swiftness, Sir Kalleth," Durge said in a hard voice.

Kalleth frowned at him, but the Embarran did not look in the knight's direction.

Grace shook her head, struggling for words. "Aryn, Lirith—what are you doing here?"

Aryn's fear vanished, replaced by a brilliant smile. "We were following you, Grace. We're coming with you."

Grace was stunned anew. Yesterday Aryn had been weeping and distraught over what she had done on Midwinter's Eve. Now she was more cheerful than Grace had seen her in months. Lirith's gaze fell on Grace, and Grace stared back. That Aryn had done this was almost comprehensible given her age, but that Lirith had agreed was impossible to believe.

"Forgive us," the dark-eyed woman said. "But we did not want you to go without sisterly companionship to . . . your destination."

Meridar glanced at Durge, his eyes filled with mirth rather than anger. "And what are we to do with these bandits?"

"It is too late to do anything tonight," Durge said. "We will ride to Foxfair and hope Lord Gaddimer has room enough to keep us all. No doubt King Boreas sent another of his knights after Lady Aryn and Lady Lirith when he discovered their absence. They can wait for him at Gaddimer's manor until he arrives."

"But he won't arrive," Aryn said. Her eyes shone. "By the time Boreas finds out we're gone, we'll be days ahead, and not even the king's fastest chargers will be able to catch us."

The knights stared at Aryn, and she smiled. The expression was slightly smug. Lirith cast a shocked look at the baroness, and dread pooled in Grace's stomach. Now she understood. Lirith had ridden with Aryn only to keep watch over her, believing Boreas's men would come upon them before they got too far from the castle. But Aryn had done something—some spell—to conceal their absence. Only what? From the look on Lirith's face, even she did not know.

Durge shifted in his saddle. "If Boreas has not sent a man, then one of us will have to return to Calavere tomorrow with the ladies."

Kalleth spat on the ground. "And which of us will that be, Sir Durge?"

The Embarran grumbled under his mustaches. Grace didn't need to hear his words to understand. His plan wasn't going to work. The knights all had their orders to ride to Perridon. None would be willing to go back.

It was Meridar who offered the solution. "Let the ladies ride with us, then. It is hardly dangerous while we are here within the king's borders. And let us not leave them to stay at some crude village, but rather take them to Ar-tolor, where they can stay with Lirith's queen until such time Boreas sees fit to send for them."

It was a good plan. Grace knew Durge had to agree, then was surprised to find him looking to her. Of course. It wasn't the knight's decision. *You're the duchess, Grace.*

She swallowed the mad laughter that bubbled up in her throat. "We'll do as Sir Meridar says."

Durge nodded. Meridar appeared relieved, and while Kalleth did not look altogether pleased, he did not disagree. Aryn laughed, and Grace turned to meet Lirith's dark eyes. The witch nodded. They would speak about the baroness later.

"Night comes," Durge said. "We had best hurry on to Foxfair."

The Embarran led the way, and the ladies came behind, followed by Meridar and Kalleth. Grace glanced at Aryn and Lirith as they rode. Despite the rashness of what they had done, she was glad for their company. Durge was a stout and true companion, but he was a man. It would be good to have other women along on the journey. Other witches.

But just how had Aryn arranged their unseen escape?

Grace nudged Shandis alongside the baroness's palfrey. "What did you do, Aryn?" she whispered.

The young woman shrugged. "I only did what you said, Grace."

"What do you mean, what I said?"

"If you have power, use it."

Before Grace could say anything more, Aryn smiled and nudged her horse into a trot.

31.

The traveling party rode east through the Dominion of Calavan, never straying more than a half league from the southern bank of the Dimduorn as they went.

Grace could not help marveling as they cantered across the gently undulating landscape. In the time she had lived on this world, she had hardly ventured outside the castle walls, and then only for short jaunts into the well-tilled countryside a few furlongs from Calavere. There, nearly always surrounded by crowds of dirty, foul-smelling people, she had been able to believe that Falengarth was a populous land, filled with similar keeps and towns. She was wrong. As far as Grace could tell from her vantage atop Shandis's back, this world was just about empty.

It was not so noticeable in the beginning. On that first day out they came upon villages with predictable regularity—one every two miles. Foxfair, where they stayed that first night, was typical of the others: a stone manor house about as big as the average subdivision tract home on Earth—although built to stand for centuries rather than decades—with a stable, a common green supporting a few sorry-looking cows, a well, a shrine to the lord's favored mystery cult, and about two dozen hovels of thatch, wood, mud, and stone scattered among rock-walled fields that were each about a quarter acre in size, and a third of which were lying fallow.

It was hard to believe this was the basis for the economic system that supported the entire Dominion. Then, as they rode on, Grace realized there wasn't that much Dominion to support.

They set out from Foxfair at dawn after saying farewell to Lord Gaddimer and his wife—a kindly and diminutive couple who possessed deeply lined, good-natured faces as well as a trio of large, handsome sons. The oldest of the sons, all of nineteen, was helping his father run the manor, while the others, once they were a year or two older, would head for Calavere or the castle of one of Boreas's barons to become squires and, hopefully in time, knights.

As they rode that second day, the size and frequency of villages decreased rapidly. It was only that evening, when they stopped at the first village they had seen in hours, that Grace understood the reason. Once again they begged the hospitality of the local lord: a younger, unmarried man named Unreth who was more reserved than Gaddimer but no less welcoming. When Unreth's ancient housemaid brought an extra blanket to the damp bedchamber Grace and the other women were to share, the maid begged for news of Calavere.

"Do you know Elthrinde of Orsel?" the old woman asked Grace in a wavering voice. "She is my cousin, you see. She went to Calavere to work in the king's kitchen."

Aryn and Lirith shook their heads. Grace thought, then realized she did in fact know the name. She sighed and laid her hand over the old woman's. Why was it so much easier when she had grim news?

"I did know Elthrinde," she said. "Although not well, I'm afraid. A few months ago her granddaughter asked me to see to her. I'm a . . . I'm a healer. I did everything I could. But I'm afraid Elthrinde was worn-out, and she died."

The old woman considered Grace's words, then nodded. "Was she still beautiful? Elthrinde was so beautiful when she left for the king's castle."

Grace pictured the crone—toothless, arthritic, scarred by scrofula—who had struggled for breath on the flea-infested bed in the town beneath Calavere. "Yes, she was still beautiful. When did you see her last?"

The maid blinked in watery surprise. "Why, when she left Orsel, of course. I remember it clearly. It was the year we both reached our sixteenth winter."

After the old woman left, Grace stared at the folded wool blanket. From further discussion she had learned that the maid had never journeyed to Calavere to see her cousin, even though it was a ride of only two days, and a walk of perhaps four. But then, shouldn't she have known this would be the case?

Remember your world history class, Grace. In medieval times, on Earth, people hardly ever traveled more than ten miles from the place they were born.

She supposed it was the same on Eldh. Only the nobility seemed to travel about with some frequency. It was a hard concept to grasp—at least for someone who was used to hopping into a car or a plane and zipping across a continent. Miles might have shrunk on Earth, but here on Eldh the leagues were still vast and forbidding.

They set out at dawn again the next morning, and after Orsel vanished from sight they did not see another village all that day, and the farms they passed looked practically abandoned.

Grace had hoped she would have a chance to speak with Lirith as they traveled—about Aryn and what had happened when the two left Calavere—but by that third day she knew it was not going to be easy.

As they rode, Aryn was never far from either Grace or Lirith. Nor, in any of the cramped manor houses at which they stayed at night, had there been a place she could talk to Lirith without Aryn overhearing. Grace's questions would have to wait.

By that third day, Grace was already growing weary of traveling. Her riding gown was hot and uncomfortable, bunching up around her as she rode, and it collected dust in every fold of cloth, so that by the end of the day she was covered with grime and had to spend half an hour just shaking herself out. Her muscles hurt constantly, and her jaw felt as if she'd spent the last three days chewing a piece of vulcanized rubber.

Aryn, in contrast, seemed to enjoy the journey immensely. She smiled aback her palfrey as they rode, and when they stopped to rest, while Grace plopped down on a stone and concentrated on simply not moving, the baroness hunted around, gathering herbs, flowers, and leaves. At night she would spread them on a kerchief and discuss their names and properties with Lirith. She laughed often, and the sound was as bright as silver.

It was clear early on that Sir Meridar was enthralled by Aryn. He hardly bothered to hide his grin as he watched her, and the baroness often asked him to do small tasks for her, which he performed eagerly, and when he did she cast smiles at him which Grace thought bordered on cruel. For even were the kindly knight's pockmarked face not too homely for the baroness, his station was without doubt too low.

Lirith seemed to notice this behavior as well, and the witch would frown when Aryn asked Meridar to bring her water or pluck a leaf from a high branch for her. Sir Kalleth frowned as well, but this was the only expression of which he seemed capable. And if Durge noticed, he said nothing about it.

Grace did her best not to worry about Aryn. The

fact was, the young woman seemed fine, and Grace knew she shouldn't argue with results. It didn't matter how the patient got better, just that she did. Besides, Grace had other matters to worry about, and with each league they consumed her mind more and more. Would she and Durge be able to convince Meridar and Kalleth to ride to the Gray Tower? If so, would they reach it in time? And once there, how would she help Travis?

The sun was sinking on the third day of their journey when Grace noticed a line of smoke rising into the sky not far ahead.

"There must be a village on the other side of that down," Kalleth shouted above the horses.

Durge pulled on Blackalock's reins and dropped back. "That would be Tarafel," the Embarran said. "I was hoping we had not passed it by. If I recall correctly, there is not another village for some leagues."

Grace breathed a sigh of relief. She did not often know Durge to be mistaken.

Aryn shaded her eyes. "I do not see the smoke," she said. "Where is it?"

Meridar brought his charger close to Aryn's horse. "There, my lady," he said, leaning toward her and pointing.

The baroness nodded, then turned to smile at the knight.

Grace ground her teeth but said nothing. She didn't need to glance at Lirith to know the witch was looking at her.

"Let's go," she said.

The riders ascended the low ridge. The shrubs covering it were thicker than they had appeared from a distance, and by the time they reached the top the sun was heavy and low behind them, spilling red light across the land. They pushed through the last tangled wall, then came to a halt.

At first Grace thought the shadow cast by the

down was playing tricks on her. Everything was black. Then she understood. The smoke was too dark to be from cookfires. And there was too much of it.

Aryn clapped a hand to her mouth, and Lirith sighed, her eyes deep with sorrow.

"By Vathris," Meridar said. "What happened?"

Durge shook his head. The village was gone.

At least most of it. Grace could make out the square lines of stone foundations, cracked and scorched, and here and there the remnants of a wall or chimney still stood. But that was all. The village of Tarafel had burned to the ground.

"Wildmen." Kalleth spat the word. "They must have ridden down from the mountains and done this."

"I do not think so," Durge said. "There is not a place to cross the Dimduorn for many leagues."

Kalleth glared at the Embarran but did not disagree.

"I don't understand," Grace said. "The fires are almost all out. It must have been some time since this happened. Why didn't we hear about it in Orsel?"

But even as she asked the question she knew the answer. In all likelihood they were the first people from outside Tarafel to come to the village in a week. But if invaders had not destroyed the settlement, what had? Grace couldn't believe that fire could sweep through the village so easily—even houses that stood at a distance from others had burned.

For the first time in days Aryn was not smiling, and her voice sounded like that of a small girl. "But where are we to sleep?"

Grace almost laughed. No doubt this no longer seemed like such a grand adventure.

Durge squinted at the horizon. "There is a farm near that stand of trees, on the farside of the village. It looks as if it is unharmed."

There was little discussion given the lack of

choices. The six rode down the slope and in silence skirted around the remains of the village. At one point, lying in their path, was a form that should have been charred beyond recognition but was not. The arms were thrown above the head, as if in a final gesture of supplication. Or terror. Aryn gasped and hung her head. Grace forced herself to look ahead as they rode on.

It was dusk by the time they reached the farm. At first Grace thought it must be deserted. Heavy wood shutters covered the windows, and there was no light beneath the door. Then she noticed the smoke oozing from the daub-and-wattle chimney. She glanced at Durge. He nodded, nudged Blackalock's flanks, and rode up to the farmhouse while the others waited at a distance.

Grace watched as Durge dismounted and knocked on the door. He knocked again, then a third time, and looked ready to knock the rickety plank in when the door opened a crack. She could not see who stood on the other side, but the knight took a step back. Why? Was he startled? She watched Durge speak for a few moments more, then the door shut. He climbed onto his sooty charger and pounded back toward the others.

What is it? Grace started to ask as he thundered to a halt, but the knight spoke first.

"Plague," he said, his weathered face grim.

The others cast startled looks at the knight. Grace rolled the word over in her mind. *Plague.* Was that the reason for the destruction of the village? She had heard that, during the time of the Black Death in Europe, entire villages had been torched to prevent the spread of bubonic plague.

Grace nudged Shandis forward. "How many in the house are ill?"

"Just one from what I could gather," Durge said.

"An old woman answered the door. It's her husband that's sick."

"What are the symptoms?"

"I don't know. All she said was that he's burning up."

That wasn't good enough. Fever was a symptom of countless pathogens, and plague was too generic a word to be helpful. There could be a dozen different pandemic diseases on this world, all as bad as bubonic plague—or worse. There was only one way to find out what she was dealing with.

Before Durge could reach out to grab Shandis's reins, Grace urged the palfrey into a gallop.

"Grace!" She heard the shout behind her, although she didn't know if it was Aryn or Lirith. She caught a dark blur out of the corner of her eye and knew Durge was riding after her. He would be too late. She reined Shandis to a stop in front of the farmhouse and moved to the door.

Durge was faster than she had thought. Clods of dirt struck her as Blackalock skidded to a halt two paces away. Durge leaped from the saddle, chain mail ringing, and laid a hand on her arm.

"My lady, this is madness. You cannot go in there."

A strange sensation welled up in Grace's chest as she gazed at Durge's hand on her arm. It was not anger. It was too icy for that, too distant. The only way she could understand the feeling was to give words to it.

How dare you touch our person!

She did not speak them, but her look must have communicated the words all the same. The knight snatched his hand back, his expression one of astonishment. Grace turned and pushed through the door. It was dim inside. The air was sharp with smoke and rank with the wet scent of illness.

"My lady," a voice rasped, "you must not enter here."

Grace searched, then picked out the form of the woman outlined by the sputtering light of a fire. She huddled beside a crude cot, barefoot and wearing rags. Something on the bed writhed and moaned.

For the first time, a shard of uncertainty pierced her doctor's confidence. Grace ignored it. This wasn't just duty. It was need. Dimly she was aware of Durge standing in the open doorway, the hem of his cloak pressed over his mouth and nose.

"It's all right." Grace's voice wavered. She cleared her throat and spoke again. "I'm a healer."

The woman pawed at her matted hair. Despite Durge's description she was not much older than Grace. Just worn and battered by life on this world.

"You cannot help him," the woman said. "You cannot help any of them now. It's too late. Too late."

"Let me see," Grace said.

She approached the bed. The moans grew louder, the stench of smoke thicker. The figure coiled and uncoiled beneath a filthy blanket. Grace stared, oddly reminded of a moth wriggling inside its cocoon, undergoing metamorphosis, its body dissolving and reforming. It seemed wondrous, but it had to be agony as well. She reached for the blanket.

"No, my lady!" the woman hissed. "Do not touch him!"

Grace hesitated, then glanced at the other. "Why? Is that how it's transmitted?" But it was a stupid question. The woman couldn't understand the concept of disease vectors.

"It's the Burning Plague, my lady. He'll be like the others soon. He'll join them when the others come again."

"Others? How many others have this plague?"

The woman made a limp gesture toward the door. "All of them. It took all of them. It will take you, too, if you don't go. I'm the only one left. Me and Yaren. Oh, Yaren!"

The woman hugged thin arms around scabby knees and rocked back and forth on the floor, sobbing now as Grace stared. There was something wrong about this. The woman's words didn't make sense. If the plague took the others, how could they come again? She steeled her will, reached for the blanket, and pulled it back.

Grace clasped a hand to her mouth but could not stifle her gasp. The man on the bed was only vaguely human. His skin was blistered and oozed yellow fluid, as if every inch of his body had been severely burned. The gas of decay that rose from him was so thick Grace's head swam for lack of oxygen. In places his burned skin had peeled off his body in strips, and that had exposed not naked muscle but something else: something that looked as hard, smooth, and black as polished obsidian.

"What's happening to him?" Grace whispered, struggling for comprehension.

The man opened his eyes. One was beautiful and blue in the bubbled ruin of his face. The other was completely black—without white, without iris.

A shriek split the air of the hovel. The woman leaped to her feet, her face wild with terror. "*Krondrim!*" she screamed. "The Burnt Ones!"

She hurtled away from the bed and nearly knocked down Durge as she pushed past him, through the door, and into gray twilight beyond. The knight gazed at Grace with wide eyes. She tried to swallow, but her mouth was a desert. She forced herself to turn back around.

The man on the bed was still and quiet now. He watched her with his perfect blue eye. Then, impossibly, his ragged lips moved. Dark fluid dribbled down his chin. Despite her revulsion, Grace bent close to hear his words. As she did, she could feel the heat radiating from him.

"Kill me," he whispered.

Grace shuddered. His blue eye flickered toward the fireplace. Grace followed it, then saw the sharp iron poker that leaned against the stones. She glanced back at him and opened her mouth, but she could not speak.

"Please." The words were as dry as ashes. "While you still can. Kill me."

Grace started to shake her head. She couldn't do it. It was against everything she was, everything she stood for as a doctor. She started to rise. Then she saw a wisp of smoke coil up from the blanket that covered his body. It was burning.

He'll be like the others soon. . . .

His one human eye locked on her face. An ocean of terror flooded the blue orb, while the other was as flat and empty as space. There was only one treatment left for him.

"Please. . . ."

Grace clenched her teeth, then reached for the poker.

32.

It grew warmer as they journeyed east.

Shortly after dawn the heat began to creep from the moist, sun-warmed ground until Grace could see it hanging on the air like gold mist, throbbing in time to the drone of insects. Evaporative cooling was impossible, given the humidity, but her sweat glands did not know this and continued to produce great, useless floods of salt water, until her eyes stung and her riding gown was heavy and sodden.

The dampness was the result of their proximity to

the river, Grace knew, as well as the density of the vegetation; eastern Calavan was far more wild and overgrown than the heart of the Dominion, which had been tilled for centuries. Here, slender conifers stretched skyward even as entangling vines throttled them and pulled them back to the forest floor. In all, Grace had not been in a place so rank with life since medical school in North Carolina. There all objects had had the uncanny power to mold instantaneously. She kept checking her dress for the first blotchy, tell-tale signs.

Last night, the travelers had ridden in silence from the farmhouse near the ruins of Tarafel. Grace spoke to no one of what she had done inside, and Durge had not seen her actions. However, she knew she would never forget the weight of the iron poker in her hand, or the resistance she had met when she pressed the tip against the man's obsidian flesh and found it far too hard to penetrate. Then a glint of sapphire had caught her eye, and she had known there was only one soft place left on his body.

His scream was short, dry, and horrible. Durge rushed to her, but by then the blanket was on fire, and flames licked up the tinder-dry walls of the hovel. The two burst out the front door, and by the time they reached the others the entire farmhouse was an inferno. What had become of Yaren's wife they did not know. The others saw her stumble out of the farmhouse moments before Grace and Durge, then run in the opposite direction, disappearing into trees and gloom.

Darkness fell, and the six spent a miserable night huddled inside the only structure in sight still standing—a rickety shed that, in its most recent incarnation, had housed chickens. They did not sleep, and they set out again at first light, only too glad to be away from the place.

The sun was just rising when they discovered what

had become of Yaren's wife. It was Durge who found her body, crumpled in a shallow stream at the bottom of a ravine. Evidently she had not seen the edge in the dark as she fled. Or had she seen it after all? Grace remembered the woman's terrified scream and shuddered. Kalleth and Meridar dismounted and scrambled into the ravine. The knights pulled her body onto the bank and covered it with a cairn of stones. Then the party continued on its way.

As they rode through the heat that day, Grace tried to comprehend what had happened. What sort of disease was this Burning Plague? Was the agent virus or bacillus? Was it airborne or transmitted by fluid? However, she knew these were useless questions, that this was no disease like she had ever dealt with at Denver Memorial. Despite his grotesque appearance, Yaren hadn't been dying. All her instincts as a healer told her that. But if medicine couldn't offer an answer, perhaps biology still could. A caterpillar could undergo metamorphosis inside its cocoon—why not a man?

But if that's the case, then what was he becoming?

Even as she asked herself the question, an answer followed.

Krondrim. The Burnt Ones.

She could still hear the woman's shriek. But what did it mean? She asked the others if they had ever heard these words, but no one had. Only one thing was for certain. Whatever these *krondrim* were, Yaren's wife had been afraid of them enough to run into the dark and, whether intentionally or not, fling her body off a cliff. As they rode, Grace tried not to think of what else the woman had said.

. . . *when the others come again* . . .

She still had her mission—and Travis—to concern her.

That night they camped in a hollow beneath a stand of trees, for they had not seen a village all day, and Durge said they would be fortunate to reach another by the end of the next. They ate a meager meal, less for lack of foodstuffs than for lack of will to build a fire, then the women made beds on the ground while the knights took turns standing watch some distance away.

Grace lay atop her blanket on the lumpy ground, eyes open long into the still, hot night, watching as meteors shot across the sky. She had never seen so many falling stars in her life. For a time she played a game, counting her heartbeats after seeing a meteor. However, she never got to more than eight or ten before another bright needle of light pierced the black veil above. The last thing she remembered was the new, red star rising above a ragged line of treetops, casting its own crimson gauze upon the world.

She woke to damp, gray light, clammy and shivering. At first she feared fever and clamped a hand to her forehead, but her temp was not elevated. It was a combination of sunburn and the chilly predawn dew, that was all. She climbed stiff and aching from her makeshift bed to find Lirith and the knights already awake, then moved to rouse Aryn from a sound sleep. After displaying a temporary horror at the burnt village, the young baroness had grown cheerful again yesterday. Even the prospect of camping in the open had not daunted her.

As the group broke bread, Grace mentioned the meteor shower. "Is it usual for there to be so many shooting stars in Lirdath?" she asked Durge.

It was Kalleth who answered. "No," the knight said in a sharp voice, "it is not."

The lump of bread Grace had been chewing stuck in her throat. She glanced up and, although it was dim against the horizon, could just make out a crimson spark sinking in the sky. Was the red star connected to the meteors?

And what about the Burning Plague, Grace? Is that related to the star as well?

She dismissed the question. Coincidence was not causation, and right now she had no evidence that suggested the Burning Plague was related to anything. For all she knew it was an isolated incident, and not a pandemic at all. She packed the breakfast things while the others broke camp, and together they set out just as a chorus of insects greeted the dawn.

It was midday when they came upon the charred remains of a small group of houses. Grace did not see them at first. She had dropped back a bit, lost in thoughts about the burnt man in Tarafel. Just ahead, Lirith and Aryn spoke in low voices, then the young woman laughed: a cool sound.

Grace jerked her head up as Aryn's laughter fell short. At first she feared some sort of sudden attack, like the bear. Then she reached the top of the slope up which they rode and gazed down into the valley along with the baroness and the witch. Durge was already riding among the ruins. Around him were the blackened stone foundations of several houses.

It would not have been enough to qualify as a village—a small collective of farms was more likely. Otherwise, it looked exactly as Tarafel had. The destruction was complete. None of the houses had survived. Nor, Grace saw as she guided Shandis down the slope, had any of the people.

"There are no signs that the fires spread from house to house," Meridar said. "The ground is not burnt between them. I fear these fires were set by intention."

Durge scratched his stubbled chin. "But why, Sir Meridar?"

Plague, Grace wanted to answer. *Fear. Purification.* But she could not give sound to the words. She could only stare at the twisted forms on the ground, black as coal, shriveled limbs twisted in final poses of agony. So much for Tarafel being an isolated incident.

"We have to leave here," Aryn said, her voice half whisper, half shriek. "We have to leave here now!"

Lirith laid a hand on the baroness's left arm, her dark eyes intent. "Steady yourself, sister."

Aryn swallowed, then nodded, and her trembling eased a bit.

Kalleth spat on the ground. "Her Highness is right. There is nothing for us here."

No, Grace tried to say. *No, we have to look.* There could be evidence in the ashes, something that might let them know the origin of the plague—and the direction it was moving. Had it struck Tarafel first? Or this place? They had to know if they were riding away from it . . . or toward it. However, fear locked her jaw like tetanus. Shandis followed after the other horses. Grace could only hold on as they left the scorched shapes behind.

They did not stop to eat a midday meal, and no one spoke as they rode along a track that led among rolling fields and vine-tangled trees. Grace wished they could have pushed the horses into more than a fast walk, but there were many more leagues before them on this journey, and they didn't dare exhaust the horses now.

After a time, dark clouds pressed from the west, and thunder rolled across the land. Grace hoped for cooling rain, but it did not come. Instead the air grew still and oppressive as the clouds built. Finally, Grace clenched her teeth, certain that if the pressure increased another fraction she would scream. Aryn's enthusiasm had vanished again, replaced by tight-lipped silence. Even Lirith looked wan, and the knights wore grim miens. Sweat poured down their faces, and their mail shirts exuded a sour, metallic reek.

All of them let out breaths of relief when, just as a

few straggling rays of the setting sun slipped through
a gap in the western clouds, Durge rode back from
ahead to say he had caught sight of a village.

"Is it . . . is it all right?" Aryn asked, twisting a
lock of hair with her left hand.

"There is no sign of fire, my lady, except for cookfires. If we have ridden as far as I believe, then this
village is called Falanor."

"It is Falanor," Kalleth said. "I squired under Baron
Darthus along with the current lord, and I have vis-
ited here once before. Eddoc should offer us good
hospitality."

"I could use a little hospitality," Meridar said. He
shifted in his saddle and winced. "Especially the part
I've been—"

Lirith raised an eyebrow, and Meridar clamped his
mouth shut, his sun-reddened face deepening another
shade.

"Sir Knight," the witch said, "if you mean to let
your hindquarters beg hospitality of the local lord, I
hope they won't be expecting a separate room from
yourself. Otherwise, I fear your discomfort could
increase."

Meridar opened his mouth to reply, but his words
were lost as a ruddy fork of lightning split the clouds
overhead, and a clap of thunder broke the air.

"I don't like the looks of this storm," Durge said.
"It is too hot. Let us make haste to Falanor."

33.

It was nearly dark as they passed the tall shadows of
two trees and followed a well-worn track into the
village of Falanor. There were no torches in sight, no
oiled sheepskin windows glowing with the warm
light of candles. Nothing moved. Grace clutched

Shandis's reins, afraid this village had suffered the same fate as Tarafel. Then a jagged line of red arced from horizon to horizon, and in the hot strobe Grace caught the outlines of two dozen structures. All stood unharmed.

She forced the breath from her lungs. Even in Calavere most people went to bed at dark. And here, in a village on the fringes of the Dominion, it was doubtful they had much fat to spare for luxuries like lamps or candles. Everyone was asleep, that was all.

"This way," Kalleth said above the moan of the wind. "The manor is just ahead."

Another flash of lightning honed the hard lines of the knight's face. Slow thunder rolled. The other riders followed after him.

"Do you feel it, sister?"

Grace jumped in her saddle at the whisper, the sound of which was somehow more unnerving than the crash of the electrical storm. She glanced to the side and saw that Lirith had guided her palfrey close to Shandis.

There are eyes upon us.

Lirith's lips did not move, but Grace heard her voice clearly. This might have startled her, but the witch's words were more troubling than their means of conveyance. Grace glanced in either direction, but it was impossible to see in the alternating blackness and glare. She clenched her teeth, then shut her eyes and reached out quickly to touch the Weirding.

It was difficult, and once she did touch the web of life she lost it a second later. However, it had been enough to feel the lives huddled inside each of the houses. And the fear that crackled on the air along with the lightning.

She opened her eyes. "I don't understand. What are they so afraid of?"

Lirith met her gaze. *Us.*

She winced at the word that sounded in her mind.

Had Lirith used the Weirding on purpose, to call attention to Grace's inability to hold even the scantest thread of magic together?

Stop it, Grace. This is your problem, not Lirith's. Just because you can't seem to use the Touch anymore doesn't mean every other witch has to stop.

The horses came to a halt as a stone wall rose before them. They had reached the manor house. To her relief, Grace saw lights glowing behind translucent windows. Someone was home.

The riders dismounted in the manor's courtyard, then Durge and Kalleth approached the door while the others watched. Kalleth raised a fist and knocked three times, but the third blow was lost in a clap of thunder. He raised his hand to knock again. However, just then the door swung open, and gold light spilled onto the steps.

It was difficult to make out the silhouette in the doorway. A man, Grace decided, although whether old or young, serf or noble, she couldn't tell. Regardless, his hunched posture spoke clearly of fear. Would the man refuse to let them in? But that was impossible. Afraid or not, one did not deny a request for hospitality made by knights of the king on behalf of a baroness, a duchess, and a countess of Toloria.

Durge gestured, and the man jerked his head up to cast a wide-eyed look at the ladies. Grace couldn't help but smile. *Care to bet he wasn't expecting nobility for dinner?*

The man made a hurried motion with his hand. Kalleth stepped inside, and Durge returned to the others.

"It seems Lord Eddoc is away," the Embarran said. "However, that man is the reeve of Falanor. He is overseeing the manor in his lord's absence and has opened the house to us." He glanced at Grace. "Sir Kalleth has gone to see to the rooms, to be certain they are adequate for your needs."

"I'm certain they'll be fine," Grace said, grateful they would not have to try to sleep outside in the storm.

"When will Eddoc be back?" Aryn asked.

"Jastar—that's the reeve—did not say," Durge answered.

The baroness shuddered. "It doesn't matter as long as we can go inside. This storm is so queer. It makes me feel like . . . like screaming."

Durge glanced at Aryn, concern on his craggy face. Her shoulders crunched in and she hung her head, obviously embarrassed at the words she had spoken.

It's all right, Grace wanted to say. *It makes us all feel like screaming.* But Lirith moved first. The witch laid a hand on the young woman's arm.

"I always wait until the thunder sounds." Her full lips turned upward. "That way no one can hear me."

Aryn nodded and gave her a grateful smile.

Durge looked to Meridar. "Accompany the ladies inside. I will see to the horses."

Grace was glad when the door swung closed behind them, shutting out some of the din of the storm. They stood in a narrow entry hall. Candles infused the air with oily light, and benches lined the wall, that travelers might sit and lay down their burdens. There was no one besides the four of them.

Really, Grace? Then who closed the door?

She turned and saw a boy of perhaps eleven or twelve standing beside the door. A squire? Grace took in his bare, dirty feet, his ragged knee pants, and his heavily patched shirt. A peasant's son, then, come to work as a servant in the lord's house.

"Where is the reeve?" Meridar said.

The boy turned his face toward the knight. Though smudged with grime, his skin was clear of disease, and his green eyes were bright beneath a crooked fringe of brown hair. He smiled, showing teeth that were already stained with rot.

"Reeve Jastar has gone with your brother, my lord. They look at the rooms in the manor, to choose the best."

Grace coughed. The air was dry and metallic, and it was hard to swallow.

"Can I get you some water, my lady?" the boy asked.

Grace lifted a hand to her throat and nodded.

"Can I, my lady?"

Grace frowned. "Yes," she croaked. "Yes, thank you."

Still smiling, the boy moved to a sideboard and lifted a pitcher. It wasn't until he poured the water that Grace realized the truth. He didn't stop pouring until liquid ran over the rim of the pewter cup and onto his hand. Then he turned and held the cup toward Grace, missing her direction by only a few degrees.

He's good—he's adapted well. But then children usually do. Still, you should have noticed it sooner. No eye contact. And he didn't see your nod in answer to his question. You're losing your touch, Doctor—in more ways than one.

She took the cup from his outstretched hands. "What's your name?"

"Daynen, my lady."

"Are you Eddoc's son?"

He laughed at this. "No, my lady. My father works the farm by the hill north of the village. When I lost my sight, he begged the lord to take me, because I was no use to him on the farm and he could not feed me."

Grace's jaw dropped. A man would cast his son out just because he went blind? But she shouldn't have been surprised. She knew the rules of this world, and they were harsh ones. Love was a luxury, not a necessity.

She started to speak, but Kalleth stepped into the hall, the reeve Jastar on his heel.

"This way," Kalleth said without preamble.

Durge entered at that moment, and together the travelers followed Jastar. Now that Grace could get a clear look at the reeve, she saw he was a plain man: short and sturdy with a pockmarked face, just like most men on this world. He wore a tunic and hose of forest colors, with a brown gorget around his neck, the hood pushed back. By the sour odor he exuded, bathing was not as frequent here in the hinterlands as it was in Calavere. However, his face was cheerful if homely, and his bow and gesture for them to follow were polite, although Grace caught the trembling of his hand.

Poor man. This is probably the first time in his life that a baroness has come to stay at this manor, and here his lord is away.

They followed the reeve up a flight of steps to the second story and found themselves in a hall that ran the length of the manor, doors on either side.

"This is your room, Sir Knights," Jastar said to Durge and Meridar, pausing before a door. He moved on, then gestured to another door. "And I hope this chamber will please the ladies. It is the largest in the house."

As Grace followed down the hall a fly buzzed past her face, and she caught a whiff of a putrid scent. She wrinkled her nose and batted the fly away.

"There is a foul humor on the air," Durge said to Jastar.

The reeve spread his arms in apology. "I fear the cook allowed a joint of meat to spoil in the kitchen, my lord. I am having difficulty purging the bad air from the house."

"I hope he had an easier time purging the bad cook," Lirith murmured.

Aryn moved to a door across the hall. "What of this room, reeve?"

The man winced. "I'm afraid, my lady, that by

some trick of halls and angles the odor is strongest there, in Lord Eddoc's chamber."

Aryn hurried away from the closed door, then bent her head toward Grace. "I hope for the reeve's sake that the air clears before his lord's return."

Grace could only nod as she concentrated on breathing through her mouth.

The knights retreated into their chamber and the women into theirs. The room was large, as promised, and surprisingly clean and odor-free. There was one large bed with a straw-tick mattress, which Lirith said she would share with Aryn, and a smaller cot, which would be Grace's. An oiled parchment window was shut tightly, and every few seconds it glowed with a flash of lightning. The rafters above creaked from the wind, but there was still no sound of rain. The storm was all heat and energy with no release. Grace hoped it would pass soon.

After a short while Durge came to the door to see if they were well settled. Before Grace could answer, Daynen appeared in the door behind the knight.

"Forgive me," he said, gazing with blind eyes, "but the reeve asked me to tell you that supper has been set on the board."

By the time the women and Durge reached the manor's main hall, Kalleth and Meridar were already there, along with Jastar. They sat on benches at a well-worn table, and the reeve offered them a meal of bread, cold venison, cheese, and dried fruit with cream. It was simple enough, but Grace had had far worse meals. Apparently the cook had mended her ways.

Jastar was pleasant, if dull, company. He inquired after their journey, but he did not ask for details; Grace knew that, in the Dominions, a common man did not question the motives of nobles. Throughout the meal the reeve sweated profusely, until his tunic was stained with moisture. It was clear that speaking with knights and ladies was not something the man was accustomed to. But he performed well enough, and Grace hoped they'd be able to relay a message to Eddoc saying this. She felt bad for imposing on the poor reeve.

As they finished, Daynen entered the room to begin clearing plates. Grace watched him work, amazed at how few mistakes the boy made despite his disability. Then another, smaller figure caught Grace's attention.

She slipped into the room as quietly as a shadow: a girl of no more than seven years. A sleeveless gray shift was her only garment, and her feet and thin, freckled arms were bare. A cascade of flame-red hair hid much of her face and tumbled over her shoulders. She started to help Daynen gather plates, and Grace stared, although she was unsure why. Something about the girl demanded her attention.

"What's your name?" she said, as the girl took the cup in front of her.

The girl only shook her head, her face cast downward, and clutched the cup. Grace glanced at Daynen, then realized he could not see her questioning look. However, he must have sensed the pause and answered anyway.

"Her name is Tira. She can't talk."

Grace absorbed this information, then leaned forward in her chair. "Hello," she said. "My name is Grace."

Still the girl did not look up. Grace reached out, cupped her hand under the girl's chin, and gently lifted her face. The child's fiery hair fell to one side. Grace nodded; she had expected something like this.

The left side of the girl's face was remarkably pretty: pale, smooth, delicately formed. The right, however, was covered with tight rivulets of scar tissue. These dragged down the corner of her mouth, and her eye drooped within shiny pink folds. The right ear was gone altogether. Grace made her diagnosis: third-degree burns to the face and head, now healed. Her hand slipped down to the girl's right arm and turned it over. Slick tissue covered the underside. Grace guessed there would be more burns beneath the thin fabric of the shift, on the right side of her torso. It was remarkable the girl had not died of infection. On Earth, skin grafts and cosmetic surgery would have helped rebuild her face. Here she would be scarred for life.

"You're a beautiful girl, Tira," Grace said in a soft voice, and she meant it.

The girl pulled her hand back, bowed her head, and carried an armful of dishes from the room. Daynen followed her. Grace watched the two go.

"Does Eddoc have any children of his own?" she asked.

Kalleth answered. "His wife died while heavy with their first child some years back, and I do not believe he's taken another wife since." He glanced at the reeve, who nodded in agreement.

Lirith rested her chin on a hand. "Lord Eddoc must be a very kind man to take in the children of others."

"Too kind, sometimes," Jastar murmured.

Grace glanced up. What had that meant? Did the reeve fear that the children were too great a burden for his lord? However, before she could ask more, Kalleth stood.

"We will leave early in the morning."

"Then I will be up to see you off, my lord," the reeve said.

However, Grace knew the knight's statement had been as much a suggestion that the ladies retire to their chamber as it had been an announcement for the host.

Following Lirith's lead, Grace and Aryn rose, bid the men good night, and headed upstairs. When they stepped into their chamber, they found Daynen and

Tira within. The children had replaced the linens on the beds with fresh ones. When he heard them enter, Daynen hastily gathered up the old sheets and moved to the door. Tira followed after him, then halted when she drew close to Grace.

"Come on, Tira," Daynen said.

"No," Grace said. "It's all right."

She knelt and laid her hands on the girl's shoulders. They were far too sharp and bony. She brushed the girl's fiery hair from her face.

"You don't need to hide," she said. "Not with your pretty face."

Tira went stiff, but Grace didn't let go. The girl relaxed and looked up, grinning to show perfect white teeth. Grace grinned back.

"You have a good manner with children, sister," Lirith said.

Now it was Grace's turn to go rigid. In the ED she had avoided pediatric patients with grim determination. Children could be too disarming. Too honest. Yet somehow she felt at ease with Tira. What was different?

Isn't it obvious, Grace? Mute kids have a hard time asking difficult questions.

"When did Tira stop talking?" she asked Daynen.

"She was like this when Lord Eddoc found her."

Aryn took a step closer. "The lord found her?"

Daynen nodded. "It was when he journeyed to Perridon this spring, to visit his cousin. On his return he found her wandering by herself, in the wilds of southern Perridon. There was no way to know what had happened to her—she couldn't say. So in his kindness Lord Eddoc brought her home."

"How is it you know her name?" Lirith said.

"We don't, not really. Tira is what my lord calls her. I think it was the name of his wife."

With deft fingers Grace probed the girl's throat, but she detected no abnormalities. Mostly likely Tira was physically capable of speech. However, the wounds she had suffered were more than enough to induce behavioral changes. It was not uncommon for a child to respond to trauma by refusing to speak. But how had she gotten burned?

Don't you know, Grace? How else have people been burned in this Dominion?

Again she saw the charred remains of the village, and the man on the cot writhing as he underwent his impossible metamorphosis. But it couldn't be the same, could it? Tira's wound had healed—it was just a mundane burn.

"Tira and I should go, my lady," Daynen said.

Grace nodded. "You heard him," she said to Tira. "Go on—we'll see you tomorrow."

Daynen stepped into the hall, and Tira turned and trotted toward him. However, when she reached the door she stopped and turned. She looked at Grace, pointed through the open doorway, then formed her hand into a stiff shape and brought it up and down in a jerking motion.

Daynen frowned. "What's Tira doing?"

Grace glanced at Lirith and Aryn, then back at the girl. Tira continued to make the peculiar motion, her face an impassive mask.

"I'm not sure," Grace said. "I think . . . I think she's trying to tell me something."

Daynen shrugged. "Tira's funny sometimes." He groped forward, found her shoulder, and gently pulled her to him. "Come on, Tira. The ladies need to sleep, and so do we."

The boy and the girl left the room, shutting the door behind them. Grace looked at the other women, but any words she might have spoken were lost as another clap of thunder shook the stones of the house.

34.

Grace woke to ashen light.

She sat up in her bed, pushed snarled hair from her eyes, and blinked. Something was strange—her ears seemed to throb, and the stuffy air of the chamber pressed in on her. Then she realized what it was.

Silence.

She wasn't certain when she had finally fallen asleep. The storm had raged on long into the night. Even through her closed eyelids she could see the metallic flashes of lightning, and despite a feather pillow mashed over her head the thunder drummed through her skull. At some point she must have fallen into a fitful sleep. And now . . .

Grace cocked her head, listening, but she heard nothing except the steady breathing of Aryn and Lirith in the bed across the room. The storm had finally passed.

She rose and dressed, careful to make as little noise as possible. There was no point in waking Aryn and Lirith yet. By the light, dawn was still some time off, and given the restless night all were certain to have had, she guessed their departure from Falanor would be later than usual.

Unless Sir Kalleth marches in here with his spurs on and kicks us all into motion.

Grace wouldn't put it past the stern knight.

She slipped through the door and pressed it shut. As she started down the hall, her nose wrinkled. Yesterday's putrid scent still hung on the air, stronger than ever. What had the cook done with that joint of meat? Shoved it up in the rafters? She hurried down the hall to the head of the stairs.

When she stepped into the main hall, she found

she was not the only one who had arisen early, for Meridar and Durge sat at the long table. A fire burned on the hearth. No matter how hot the day, Grace had observed, people in the Dominions always lit a fire. As far as she could tell, it was some sort of obsessive-compulsive need in medieval people.

The boy, Daynen, was in the act of setting a tray of bread, cheese, and dried fruit on the table. Tira followed behind him, carrying with studious care a clay pitcher of some grainy-looking fluid. She set it on the table without spilling a drop.

"Hello," Grace said from the doorway.

The knights rose to their feet, and Daynen smiled.

"Good morrow, my lady," he said. "Did you sleep well?"

Grace raised a hand to the back of her aching head, glad the boy couldn't see the pained expression on her face. "Just fine," she said.

"Reeve Jastar left early to see to affairs in the village, but he bade me to be sure you had anything you needed."

"How is Lady Aryn?" Meridar asked before Grace could thank Daynen. "And Lady Lirith," the knight added belatedly, his pitted cheeks brightening.

A twinge of regret pulled at Grace's heart. She wished Meridar didn't feel the way he did about the baroness. Then again, he was hardly a stupid man. No doubt he wished the same.

"They're still sleeping," Grace said.

She felt a tug on her skirt and looked down. Tira pointed to the table: *Eat.* Grace crouched down, bringing her eyes on a level with the girl's.

"Thank you," she said.

Tira gave a hesitant nod, then ducked her head, letting her red hair cover the shiny, melted scars on her face. She hurried to a corner of the hall. Grace sighed. Something told her that the smile she had glimpsed last night was a rare gift.

She sat down and surveyed the breakfast fare. The soupy brown liquid in the pitcher turned out to be beer, although if someone had whirled together stale bread and water in a blender she wouldn't have known the difference. Grace would have preferred a blistering-hot cup of *maddok* laced with a single curl of cream. Her growing suspicion was that the entire Dark Ages on Earth would have lasted about three weeks instead of ten centuries if there just had been an ample supply of coffee to get everyone's brains jump-started.

She sipped her beer, then looked at Durge. "Where is Kalleth?"

Durge's expression was as somber as his gray attire. "I do not know. During the night I went to see to the horses, to be certain fear of the storm had not driven them to harm. When I returned sometime later he was gone."

Meridar broke open a loaf of coarse bread. "Kalleth rose very early this morning, just as the storm was waning. He told me there was something he wished to see, but he did not say what it was, and he has not returned since."

Grace frowned. That was peculiar news. Kalleth hardly seemed like the type just to wander off in the night. He must have had a task of specific import to see to. "What should we do?" she said.

"We will wait," Durge said. "For a time."

The piece of bread Grace had started to swallow stuck in her throat.

They continued eating in silence, and when they finished the knights headed outside to ready the horses for the day's journey. Daynen cleared some of the dishes, leaving out the food for those who had not yet risen, and Grace found herself alone with Tira. She tried to speak to the girl, but Tira sat on a bench, staring into the fire, and did not move. Whatever

Grace had done to reach the child last night, it es-caped her now as surely as the Touch. She was glad when Daynen returned to the hall.

"May I ask you a question, Daynen?" she said in a careful voice.

He nodded and sat on a bench. "Of course, my lady."

"I'm a healer," she said. "I was wondering about your eyes. Can I ask how you lost your sight?"

He turned his face up, his tousled hair falling back. "I looked into the sun. I looked and never turned away."

Grace's jaw dropped. She had expected fever, or perhaps a blow to the head, but not this. Staring at the sun would sear the retinas and fry the optic nerve to a crisp. There was nothing Grace could do to repair that kind of damage.

"Why?" she said, the question startled out of her.

"They come in fire. That's what my father said. So one day I woke up and knew I had to look into the sun, because that's the biggest fire there is. I knew that if I looked long enough, I would see what we're supposed to do to stop them."

Grace shook her head, fighting for understanding. "Who are you talking about? Who comes in fire?"

"The Burnt Ones."

Grace clutched the edge of the table. "You've seen the Burnt Ones?" Her voice was an urgent whisper. "Tell me, Daynen. Have you seen them?"

He shook his head. "No, but my father spoke of them. He heard about them from a man who came from the east. The man said that people get a fever, and that some of them die, but that some don't, that they turn black as night and become the Burnt Ones and come back to burn everyone up. He used some other word, too. *Kren . . . krem . . .*"

"*Krondrim,*" Grace murmured.

He nodded. "Yes, that was it. He said the *krondrim*

would come for us here just like they had in his village."

Grace laid her hands on the boy's shoulders and spoke in precise words. She had to know, she had to be certain. "This is important, Daynen. Did anyone touch the man—the one who came from the east? Did anyone have contact with him?"

Daynen frowned. "I don't think my father touched him. He said there was something wrong with the man, that he smelled bad. The man went to talk to Jastar, I think, but then I didn't see him again. He must have kept traveling west."

Dread trickled into Grace's stomach. She wished she hadn't drunk the sour beer.

"And I did see something, my lady. In the sun. Just before everything went dark, I saw it so clearly."

She moved to him. "What was it, Daynen? What did you see?"

A smile touched his lips. It was a strange expression—distant yet joyful. Beatific, that was the word. The expression on the face of a painted saint whose pale body was pierced with arrows.

"It was me, my lady. I was carrying a girl in my arms while I walked on the bright fields of the sun. It was beautiful."

Grace could find no words. She couldn't tell him that it had been only a hallucination, one last-ditch effort by the vision center of his brain to make sense of the searing stream of photons before the whole system overloaded. He had looked to the sun for answers but had found only darkness.

He sighed and stood. "I'm going to go upstairs, my lady. I aired out Lord Eddoc's chamber yesterday, but I think it still needs another try."

Grace gave a stiff nod as he left the room, even though she knew he couldn't see it. Then another figure stepped through the door. Grace gazed up into mysterious brown eyes.

"That child has the Sight," Lirith said.

"Do you think so? Or is he just a stupid kid who stared at the sun too long?"

Lirith shrugged. "Who can say? But the simplest explanation is not always the truest, sister. Remember that."

Grace thought about this, but things seemed no clearer. She stood. "I don't like this, Lirith. There's been no sign of the Burning Plague here, but there's something wrong about this place all the same. Let's wake Aryn and get the others. We need to find Sir Kalleth and go."

The two women headed upstairs. When they reached the door to their chamber, Grace saw that the door on the opposite side of the corridor was ajar. Lord Eddoc's chamber. Daynen must have gone in to open the window.

It hit Grace a second later: the choking atmosphere of decay. It poured almost tangibly through the open door. Flies buzzed on the air. Before she thought about it, she approached the door to Eddoc's chamber. Daynen stood beside the open window, nose wrinkled, fanning his face with a hand. Grace's eyes slid past him to the bed.

The decomposition was advanced. Death had occurred three days ago, maybe four. It was hard to say, because even from the door Grace could see that Lord Eddoc had been in the intermediate stages of the Burning Plague. The blisters were apparent, as were the first black patches showing through the skin. The cause of death was easy to determine: The cut in his throat was so deep it had nearly decapitated him. So not all of his flesh had been toughened yet.

The bloated remains of Lord Eddoc held Grace's eyes for only a moment. Her gaze continued on, to the form lying facedown on the floor in a pool of blood. She didn't need to see his face. His stocky shoulders and gray-shot hair were enough. The knife still protruded from his back. By its position, Grace guessed it had slipped through two ribs to pierce his heart. Sir Kalleth had died before he even knew he had been struck.

There was a gasp behind her. Lirith.

Daynen looked up at the sound. "Lady Grace? Is that you? Or is that Lady Lirith?"

Grace shook her head. Daynen had been in this room yesterday. But he couldn't see. He didn't know what lay on the bed.

The boy frowned. "What is it, my lady?"

Grace did not answer him. Motion caught the corner of her eye. She turned and glanced down. Tira stood just outside the door. The red-haired girl stared forward, her scarred face blank. As she had done last night, she moved her arm up and down in a stiff chopping motion.

Grace looked up into Lirith's startled eyes.

"Get Durge," she said.

35.

The five travelers stood outside the open door to Eddoc's chamber, shocked into silence. Only the drone of flies sounded on the air. Aryn had stepped from her room at the same moment Durge and Meridar ran, boots clomping, up the stairs. Her scream had frozen everyone's blood.

As if through great force of will, Aryn turned away from the grisly scene in the lord's chamber and pressed her face against Sir Meridar's chest. For once, Grace noted distantly, the baroness's action appeared genuine rather than manipulative. The anger on the homely knight's face was replaced by astonishment. He stiffened, then reached up and enfolded the slender young woman in strong arms.

Lirith was the first to find her voice. "So that was what Tira was trying to tell you last night, Grace."

Durge looked at Grace. The Embarran's face was as hard as wind-battered stone. "What does Lady Lirith mean?"

"Tira." Grace folded her arms over the bodice of her gown. "I think . . . I think she must have seen what Jastar did. When he killed Eddoc."

Daynen stood in the hallway now, staring with wide, blind eyes. He gripped Tira tightly. The girl gazed forward, her half-melted expression as placid as ever, twirling a lock of her fire-red hair with a finger.

"Kalleth must have suspected some sort of foul play," Durge said. He glanced at Meridar. "That was what he went to see last night, when he left our room."

With careful but deliberate motions, Meridar pushed Aryn away. Lirith took the young woman and circled an arm around her shoulders.

Meridar clenched his hand into a fist. "Jastar must have been waiting in Eddoc's chamber, knife in hand, afraid one of us would see his handiwork. Then Kalleth did. Blast that cursed reeve. I will have his blood!"

Grace shuddered. The kindly knight she knew was gone. Now a queer light shone in his eyes.

"Wait." Grace took a step forward. "I don't . . . I don't think you understand everything."

Meridar stared at her. "What is there to understand, my lady? The reeve has slain his lord and our companion. His life is forfeit."

She licked her lips. "Eddoc had the plague. The Burning Plague. Look, you can see it—the change . . . it had already started. I think that was why Jastar killed him. To keep it from spreading in the village."

Meridar's eyes narrowed. "And Sir Kalleth? Did he have the plague then, my lady?"

Grace stepped back, her face stinging as if struck with the flat of a blade.

Meridar looked to Durge. "Are you with me?"

Durge gazed into space, as motionless as if carved of stone, then he let out a breath and met the other knight's eyes. "Get your sword, Sir Meridar."

Grace placed a hand on the Embarran's arm. "Durge—please . . ."

He shook his head, his words both regretful and hard. "We must do this, my lady."

With care, but without hesitation, he pulled his arm free; then he and Meridar moved past her.

Grace watched them go, gripping the doorframe. No, she wouldn't let rage seize her. That was how lives were lost. Meridar was out for revenge, and she knew Durge would not be able to control him. There was no telling what the Calavaner might do to anyone who got in his way. They were just peasants out there. It would be a bloodbath.

She pulled the door to Eddoc's chamber shut, then turned and caught Lirith's gaze. This time there was no need for magic to transmit the message.

Lirith pushed away the sobbing baroness. "Sister, do you need to stay in our chamber?"

Aryn roughly wiped her wet cheeks and forced her shoulders back. "No, I can't stay here. Not with . . ." Her eyes flickered to the closed door.

"Come on," Grace said. "We'll go together."

She started down the stairs, and the others followed.

"What do you intend to do, sister?" Lirith said behind her.

Grace spoke the truth. "I don't know."

The three women left the manor house and stepped into the mists of dawn. Dim shapes hovered like specters around them: houses and trees. Navigating half by what she could make out in the gloom and half by memory of the evening before, Grace led the way through the village.

It was only when they reached the edge of Falanor's common green that Grace noticed two smaller forms following behind Lirith and Aryn.

You idiot, Grace. You should have told Daynen and Tira to stay at the manor. If something happens, they could get hurt.

But it was too late by then. There wasn't time to take them back. "Stay behind us," she said to the children.

Daynen nodded, tightening his hold on Tira's shoulders. The mute girl gazed into the mist as if she could see something in its folds. Grace shivered.

"Sister," Lirith whispered, placing a hand on Grace's arm. "The Touch."

Grace halted. She peered into the fog but could make out only fleeting shapes. Shutting her eyes, she forced herself to reach for the Weirding. There—she caught the shimmering threads of life that criss-crossed the commons just before the web slipped from her hands. Her eyes flew open. They were not alone.

"Blast you, reeve! Where are you?"

Grace jumped at the voice that sounded no more than twenty paces away. She recognized the gruff tone, even though she could not see him. Meridar.

"It is better if you show yourself, Jastar." This voice was lower, more somber. Durge. "You cannot hide for long. The sun comes, and it will burn away the mist."

Silence, then a harsh bark of laughter. "The mist is not all that will burn!"

Chain mail jingled. Grace could imagine the knights turning around, searching for the speaker. But the fog had a queer effect on sounds, muffling some, amplifying others.

"I can't see what's happening," she hissed.

"But it's so clear, Grace. Use your mind, not your eyes."

She stiffened. Then she felt a slender hand on hers. She turned and found herself gazing into frightened but now strangely steady blue eyes. Aryn.

"It's all right, Grace," the young woman said. "We'll help you."

Grace swallowed hard, then gave a nod. Lirith took her other hand, and Grace stood between the two witches. She shut her eyes and could feel the warmth pouring from them, filling her. A sigh escaped her lungs, and she felt her dread melt. Before, when she had attempted the Touch, the web of the Weirding had slipped from her grasp. Fear was the reason—fear she would see it again, the hideous blot attached to the thread of her own life. But now there were other, brighter threads to surround her. She let the power of the two witches fill her, then reached out and touched the tapestry of life woven across the commons.

A gasp escaped her. Durge and Meridar shone like cold blue steel in the center of the commons. The villagers were dimmer but still clear, milling about the edges of the square. And there, on the farside of the green, stood one who—like a coal—was black and fiery at once. Her eyes flew open.

"Jastar," she breathed. "He has it."

Both Lirith and Aryn cast questioning looks at her. She opened her mouth, but she didn't have time to explain.

"Get out of here." The reeve's harsh words cut through the fog. "Get out while you still can."

"Not without justice," came Meridar's reply. "Lord Eddoc and Sir Kalleth are dead by your hand, Reeve Jastar. You must be made to pay."

Grace pressed her eyes shut again. Meridar and Durge stood together, swords drawn, facing in the direction of Jastar's voice, crouched and ready. But the

knights couldn't see the villagers who even now shuffled from the left and right, feet silent on damp grass.
Fear and hate choked the air as thickly as fog.

"Durge!" she cried out. "Durge, they're coming
from the sides!"

She heard the clank of chain mail as the knights
spun around, as well as a hissed curse from across the
square. But it wasn't enough. She shut her eyes again.
The lines of villagers hesitated, then kept pressing
inward, toward the center of the commons. There
were too many of them.

"We have to do something," she whispered.

Aryn trembled. "What, Grace?"

Desperation flooded her. She didn't know. What
could she do against an entire mob? If only this fog
would lift . . .

That's it, Grace.

There was no more time to think about it. "Help
me," she said.

A calm presence touched her mind. Lirith. *What
are you doing, sister?*

I'm not entirely sure. If it works, you'll see.

That she had replied to Lirith without spoken
words registered only dimly. She gripped the hands to
either side—so tightly she heard soft moans of pain.
Warm power flooded her body. The Weirding flared in
her mind, its brilliant threads running in every
direction.

Then she saw it: shadowed and sickly, pulsing just
on the edge of her vision. Grace recoiled, knowing
that if she followed her own thread it would lead
straight toward the darkness. She steadied herself;
she had other threads to follow. With substanceless
fingers she clutched the silvery strands rooted to either side of her and followed them out into the
greater web of the Weirding.

For a moment she was perilously intoxicated. The

Weirding was so vast, endless and shimmering, coursing between all living things. It would be so easy to lose herself to fascination.

Weave, Grace. You've got to weave.

At first she used imaginary hands, pulling the threads together, running one over the other. However, that was too slow. She imagined more hands, and more, gathering the strands and binding them together. Then it was done. It drifted in the air, covering the entire commons, like a mesh fashioned of starlight. Grace felt astonishment radiate from both sides, but there was no time to explain. The villagers were ten paces from the knights. Five paces. Three.

Pull! Grace shouted without words.

There was confusion, then understanding. She reached out with her mind and gripped the shimmering net at the same time she felt Aryn and Lirith do so. Together, the three witches cast the net aside.

Grace felt as much as heard the rushing noise. She opened her eyes in time to see the fog before her swirl and break apart. Like a sudden dawn, sunlight poured through the rift, illuminating the commons as the last shreds of mist retreated to the edge of the square. There, a gray wall undulated, rising twenty feet into the air.

Aryn gasped, and Lirith gazed at Grace with an expression not of amazement, but of deep interest. Grace shook her head. She would explain it to Lirith later—if she even could. Right now there was no time. She felt hollow but oddly exultant, as she did after a twenty-hour shift in the ED in which she had not lost a single patient.

Cries of fear and dismay sounded as the mist broke. The villagers skidded to a halt on the wet grass, clubs and wooden hoes in their hands, their boldness dissipating with the mist. It was one thing to sneak up on a man who could not see you. It was another to face two angry knights, their blades sharp, drawn, and ready. Durge flicked his gigantic great-sword. The villagers stumbled back a step.

"No!" a shrill voice cried. "There are more of us than them. We must kill them before they kill us!"

The villagers hesitated, staring with dirty, scarred, and battered faces. What had Jastar told these people?

Grace gazed across the commons. Now that she knew to look for the signs they were obvious enough; she should have seen them before. But then, from what little she knew, onset was sudden. His tunic was sodden, not just with the fog but with sweat, and his hair was plastered to his soot-smeared forehead. There were a few small blisters on his neck and on the backs of his hands. His eyes were already starting to darken.

"Get back," Meridar barked at the villagers. "Get back and you won't get hurt. It's him that we want."

"Jastar," Durge said, "do not let your people be harmed for your own folly. Call them aside and stand forth to meet your judgment with dignity."

"It is you who shall be judged, Sir Knight." Jastar's lips pulled back from his teeth. "You and your kind, who would bring death upon this village. It was your Sir Kalleth who killed Lord Eddoc. I saw it with my own eyes, and I killed the murderer before he could strike again."

Hisses ran among the crowd. A few of the villagers stepped forward again, gripping their hoes and pitchforks. Dread filled Grace's chest. She had to stop this. But how? Fog she could clear from the air—but this anger, this deceit, this hate? She opened her mouth, but no sound emerged.

"Your words are easily proven false, reeve," Meridar spat. "Eddoc's body is putrid. We arrived only last evening, yet he has been dead for days."

Again uncertainty flickered in the eyes of the villagers. They looked to Jastar, then to the knights.

Grace understood. These were people who had followed an authority figure all their lives. Right now all they wanted to know was who they should listen to, who would tell them what to do.

Fear pulled the air taut as a drum. Everything was still, then a slight figure moved forward to stand beside Grace. A small hand snaked up to grip her own. Tira.

Jastar's face twisted into a mask of horrid glee. "Look! Look at the burnt child. They consort with her!"

A woman clad in a shabby dress the color of soil pointed at Tira. "She will bring the plague upon us. Jastar says she will."

Durge's mustaches drooped in a frown. "What is this madness you speak, goodwife?"

The woman wrung gnarled hands together. She was toothless, wrinkled, and hunched with osteoporosis. Grace supposed she was just over thirty.

"It's the Burning Plague." Fear filled her puffy, red-rimmed eyes. "Those stricken will burn up, but they won't die. They'll turn black as night and come back to burn us all. She'll do the same. She'll put fire to us all, she will!"

Now Daynen stood beside Tira. "You're wrong!" he shouted, his face flushed. "Tira wouldn't hurt anyone."

Grace clutched his shoulders, pulled him back. A smooth voice spoke beside her. Lirith.

"Was not the girl burned before Lord Eddoc brought her here, goodwoman, before this scourge began?"

Even as the witch spoke these words, Grace knew they were wasted, that reason was pointless.

Jastar raised a fist. "Maybe she started it all then. She should have died. Don't you see? She's the one who brought it on all of us. Take her with the knights!"

An energy coursed through the throng of villagers at these words, like a wild wind through a stand of trees. The knights positioned themselves before the three women and the children, swords ready, faces hard. It was going to be a massacre.

Then, just like the mist clearing, she understood.

"You're wrong, Jastar," spoke a voice that was so cool, so clear, so filled with authority that all were forced to cease motion and listen. Grace was only dimly amazed to realize the voice was her own.

Still holding Tira's hand, she stepped forward, away from Daynen and the witches, past the stunned knights. The villagers pulled away from her. A few even started to bow, then caught themselves, faces puzzled at their own actions. Grace felt a power, and it had nothing to do with the Touch. It draped her like a gold mantle, and she did not resist. These people wished for someone to obey, and it would be her.

Jastar shook his fist at her, sputtering for words. "You have the plague! You and that monster of a girl."

Grace took another step forward. "No, it is you who has the plague, Jastar. You have all the symptoms. Can't you feel it? The heat rises in you even now."

The villagers turned to stare at Jastar. He opened his mouth, but only a strangled sound emerged. Grace advanced again, and he moved back.

Her voice was soft and relentless. There was no need to raise it. "Even now you're becoming one of them, Jastar. You know it. You slew Sir Kalleth because he discovered the truth. And that's why you want them to kill Tira. Because she's the only one who saw you touch Eddoc when you killed him. But then, you didn't know at the time that was how it was transmitted, did you, Jastar? That even as you killed Eddoc to stop the plague, you brought it on yourself."

Tremors coursed through his body. She could see the first telltale wisps of smoke rise from the shoulders of his tunic. So stress seemed to exacerbate the symptoms, she noted with clinical detachment.

"No, you're wrong!" His voice was a wet shriek of fury. "Kill them!"

Durge and Meridar hastened forward to protect Grace, but they were too slow. Jastar pulled a knife from his belt and with weird speed lurched forward, until his face was inches from her. Heat shimmered from him in sick waves, and the stink of burnt meat filled her nostrils. Even as she gazed into his eyes, the last vestiges of white and brown faded, leaving only blackness.

"Die," he hissed.

The knife slashed down—

—and passed inches from Grace's throat. The expression on Jastar's face was one of confusion. Grace had seen the look many times before. People seldom expected to die.

She stepped back with Tira and watched Jastar's body fall facedown to the turf. A pitchfork protruded from his back. Even as Grace watched, the wooden tines blackened with heat. She looked up into a broad, coarse face and caught a peasant man's eyes. He gave a shallow nod. The villagers stared at the dead reeve, then one by one they turned and walked from the commons. The man who had struck the fatal blow started to follow them.

Grace held out a hand. "Where are you going?"

The man's leathery face was without expression. "I will wait in my house," he said in thick words.

She shook her head. "Wait for what?"

"For them to come, my lady. And for all the world to burn."

The man turned his back to her, walked to the edge of the commons, and disappeared into the wall of fog. He was the last; the villagers were gone. Grace was aware of Lirith and Aryn to one side of her, Daynen between them. To the other, Durge and Meridar still gripped their swords, faces grim. But Grace did not look at them.

Instead she followed Tira's calm gaze upward, to the red star that shone low in the morning sky, turning the mist to fire.

PART THREE

THE SHATTERED MAN

36.

The rain poured down from a gray sky, washing away everything he was and ever had been.

"Blood and bones!" a man's voice said, muffled by the din of the storm. "What was that?"

"What was what?" This voice was deeper and coarser, the final word merging with a crash of thunder.

Travis blinked water from his eyes. It was hard to see where he was. Dark walls pressed against him from every direction. He was cold—terribly cold. How had he come to be here?

Ashes to ashes, dust to dust. . . .

The raspy words drifted through his mind. He shut his eyes, and images came to him: the old graveyard on the hill, the scarecrow preacher clad all in black, the rectangular gash in the earth. Again he read the fresh, sharp words incised on the slab of stone. *In death do we begin.* . . .

He opened his eyes and gazed at the walls of wet soil. Mud oozed between his bare toes where he crouched. Yes—he understood now. That was why he was so cold. He was dead. What other reason to lie naked in a grave?

The thunder rolled away.

"—so get back to digging. It'll be full dark soon. Or sooner, with this queer storm." A scraping sound punctuated the coarser of the two voices as it spoke.

"I can't dig. Not when we're being watched. I tell you, I saw something."

"Like what?"

"I'm not . . . I'm not sure."

The scraping sound ended in a *clank*. "Well maybe you'd see better if you quit looking out your arse, Darl."

"Sulath slit me! I know what I saw, Kadeck. Something is over there. Like a light, it was. And it wasn't lightning, mind you. It was all silvery and low to the ground."

There was a groan, then, "All right, all bloody right. If that's what it takes to make you dig, then let's—"

A clap of thunder drowned out all other sounds, and a flash illuminated the rough planes of the grave. By its light, Travis saw a wadded-up bundle of cloth lying at his feet. On instinct he reached for it, and only then did he realize he already gripped something in his right hand.

He unclenched his fingers and peered at the object. It was a small half circle of silver metal, gleaming dully on his palm. That was right; the preacher had given it to him just before he climbed into the grave. He seemed to recall a story, something about dead men needing a coin to pay the one who would ferry them across a wide, silent river. But wasn't the coin supposed to go under the dead man's tongue? Yes, he was sure of it. He opened his mouth, then slipped the cool piece of metal into his mouth. It tasted like blood.

A crunching sound, as of boots on gravel, drew

near, and he huddled against the muddy wall of the grave. Craning his neck, he saw two shadows appear in the murk above. He froze. Something told him he did not want to be discovered—not here, not now, and not by these men.

The shadows hesitated—had they seen him? Then they passed on, and he let his sigh merge with the rain. After a time, he heard again the faint scraping sounds. It seemed to be growing darker; the light was failing. This disturbed him somehow, but he wasn't certain why. What was light to the dead?

By Durnach's Hammer, you're not dead, Travis. Now get out of this hole!

This time it was not the rasping voice of the preacher that spoke inside his head. Instead the voice was angry and familiar. Travis answered with a faint thought.

Jack?

However, the voice was already gone. Still, he had to think that maybe the voice was right. His legs ached from crouching, and his jaw was chattering so hard it was difficult to muffle the sound of it. If this was death, then it was remarkably similar to sitting in a cold, wet hole in the ground with no clothes on.

But if he wasn't dead, then what was he supposed to do? It was so hard to think. Whatever he did, he had a feeling this was not a good place to stay. The two voices above did not strike him as particularly kindly. He had to get out of here, to find someplace warmer and drier where he could concentrate.

He rose up in the grave, wincing as he straightened stiff legs. The hole was shallow, and his head reached the edge well before he reached his full height. He cocked an ear, listening, but there was no break in the rain or in the rhythmic *chunk-scrape* of shovels. Travis picked up the cloth bundle, set it outside the hole, then gripped the edge to pull himself up.

Saturated dirt liquefied under his hands. His purchase melted. He slid back into the grave, landing with a grunt. The sounds of the shovels ceased.

"There! Did you hear that, Kadeck?"

A pause, then, "Aye, that I did."

"See, I told you."

"*Hssst!* Be still, you lump."

Panic flooded Travis's chest. He rose, turned his head, and through the gray veil of rain saw a spark of crimson light. His head snapped back, and he clawed again at the edge of the grave. Gobs of mud peeled off under his hands, covering him. But he kept moving, fueled by fear, using his feet as well as his fingers, half digging and half climbing his way out of the grave.

With one last heave he lurched over the edge, then fell facedown to the rain-soaked turf. He nearly choked on the half-coin, clenched his teeth to keep from swallowing it, then stumbled to his feet, grabbing the bundle of cloth on the way up.

A white-hot knife sliced apart the slate-colored sky, and light burst forth. In that disarticulated moment Travis witnessed a strange tableau. Headstones leaned at all angles, casting crazed shadows, and wind-worn statues gazed with dark, moss-filled eyes from atop pedestals. No more than ten paces away, two men hunched beside a grave. A skinny one with a beaklike nose and chinless jaw clutched a shovel. The other—short, squat, and pig-faced—was in the act of reaching for a pick with a thickly muscled arm. The grave between the men had been crudely torn open. A well-rotted corpse spilled out, lipless mouth gaping open as if thirsty to catch the rain, withered arms flung out as if eager to be free. Lightning glinted off gold bracelets, jeweled rings, pearled necklaces.

Gloom cast its cloak back over the scene. The graverobbers were lost from sight.

"There! I told you I saw something."

"Well, bend me over and Sulath bugger me."

The voices were hoarse whispers, but by some trick of the damp air Travis could hear them perfectly. Or was it something else—some other trick that had to do with understanding the speech of others? If only he could remember.

"We've got to get out of here. He's one of the dark ones, risen again and coming back to murder us!"

"Blast your dented skull, no he's not. It's mud, Darl. That's all. He's a man, and he just saw what we were doing, and if he tells the earl we'll be the ones who get burned. And I promise you *we* won't be back after that."

Rain spilled into Travis's eyes; it was impossible to see what was happening. He stumbled back, slipped on a stone, then regained his balance and looked up. There was the red spark again. It was bobbing now, drawing nearer. Then he understood. It was a lantern.

"Ho, there!"

This time the voice was a shout, meant to be heard.

"Ho, there, come on out, friend! It's not a night to be staying in a place such as this. We'll be making a fire. Why not come with us and get yourself warm?"

The voice was bold and cheerful. He could almost believe the words were sincere. Then Travis saw a curve of metal gleaming bloodred in the lantern light.

"Don't fear, friend! Tell you what—if you come out now, we'll share our booty with you. The old countess here doesn't need her jewels anymore. And she's got more than enough to make us all rich men. Come out and we'll give you more gold than you ever dreamed."

Along with a pick in the back of my head, Travis added to himself. If he wasn't dead yet, he was certain that would do the trick. He backed away another step.

Whispers again, yet somehow almost as audible as

the shout. "Let's just be gone from here, Kadeck. I don't like this place."

"Shut up, worm. Now follow after me. And when you see him, brain him with your shovel."

The red eye of the lantern drifted nearer. Then it blinked out of existence. Travis turned and ran. Energy coursed across the sky, and for a heartbeat light stilled motion.

"There he is!"

"Get him!"

Night constricted around Travis. He careened on, bare feet slipping on soaked grass. Then pain flashed through him, bright as lightning, as he struck the sharp corner of a grave marker. A grunt escaped his lungs. He stumbled, nearly dropped the bundle, then clutched it tighter and ran on.

"I heard him. This way!"

The shout was horribly close, but he didn't dare look over his shoulder. Rain pelted down, lashing his naked skin, and his breath came in sick gasps. Just a little longer and he would fall, unable to go on. Just a little longer until sharp metal drove through his skull.

You were wrong, Jack. I am dead.

Another flash of lightning illuminated the night. A black pit appeared in front of Travis: an open grave waiting for its fresh, new denizen. There was no time to veer to either side. Travis cried out and flung his body forward. The ground yawned beneath him—

—then he struck the other side, fell to his stomach, slid through sheets of mud, and came to a rough halt against a tumbled chunk of marble. He looked up as the sky shattered into shards of silver fire and saw his pursuers bearing down on him, murder on their faces. Too late they saw the open pit in front of them. They flung their arms out, but their boots skidded on the oily mud. As one the graverobbers tumbled over the edge and into the grave. Curses of anger became groans of pain.

Travis did not wait to see if they would climb out again. He used the oddly shaped stone he had struck to push himself to his feet, and only then did he see what it was: a fallen statue, broken in half, its gray visage battered by the elements and by the angry hammers of vandals.

Travis stared down at the stone man in the long robe, gazing into the pits of eyes that, although shattered, remained somehow serene. Then he turned, stumbled past the statue, and ran from the graveyard.

37.

Sharp stones cut into the soles of Travis's bare feet as he ran, and nettles scratched at his naked shins. The gloom was impenetrable, save for disjointed moments of brilliance when lightning clawed across the sky. Each time Travis would jerk his head up and try to lock his eyes on a crooked tree or a crumbled stone wall—any landmark he might possibly navigate by. When the darkness snapped back he would stumble on, hoping he was moving away from his pursuers rather than toward them. He could hear no shouts, no sounds of booted feet behind him, but then he could hardly hear thunder and the howl of the wind over the rasping of his own breath.

Just when he felt both heart and legs failing he saw it, outlined by a livid streak of greenish lightning. In a blink the sight was gone, but the outline remained, seared onto his retinas: the blocky shape of a building.

Travis knew he should keep running, that the thieves could not be far behind. However, he had to rest, if only for a minute. His lungs were molten, but he was shivering, and his limbs felt as if they were molded from cold clay. He lurched in the direction of the building.

A flash revealed the wall too late to stop him from running into it. Pain fizzed through his head, and he stumbled back. Before the lightning faded, he made out the squat stone structure before him. Part of one wall had fallen outward in a heap of rubble. Where was he? He tried to think of what structures stood near the Castle Heights Cemetery. Except that was pointless, wasn't it? He spat into his hand and gazed at the silver half-coin. This was not Castle City.

Eldh needs you, son. They're calling for you even now. Can't you hear?

No, he was someplace very far away from Colorado. A thrill coursed through his chest, but it quickly became a shudder. He had to try to get warm. Scrabbling over the pile of stones, he clambered into the building.

The hovel was barely more than ten feet square, the floor covered with clumps of dirt and some kind of thorny weed. The roof had mostly fallen in, but there was a corner that was still covered and relatively dry. He huddled in the corner, pressing his back against the stones, and tried to catch his breath. It felt as if he were breathing hot water. However, after a time the laboring of his lungs eased.

Only then did he remember the bundle still pressed beneath his arm. Curious, he held it before him, but he could not make out what it was.

You need to see, Travis. Give yourself light.

The voice speaking in his head should have alarmed him. But it sounded so much like his friend Jack that instead it made him feel warmer and less lonely. Before he even knew what he was doing, he murmured the word.

"Lir."

A pearl-white glow sprang from nowhere to hang upon the air of the hovel.

Travis blinked, able now to see walls, wreckage, and the object in his hand. Dull shock gripped him. What was this light? He had to think about it, to understand what he had just done, but someone had wrapped his brain in cotton. He focused on the bundle instead.

It was caked with mud, but as he wiped away the dirt he found the ends of a knotted cord. He undid it with fumbling fingers, then set the bundle down and peeled the covering back.

The outer layer of cloth must have been waxed, for it was stiff and crackling, and it had kept the mud and water away from what things lay within. With his fingers, Travis brushed soft fabric. Then he lifted the folded garment and shook it out. It was a robe of mist-gray.

The robe seemed familiar to him somehow, but he couldn't say why. Not that it mattered. It was dry and looked warm. He shrugged the garment over his head—the rain had done a good job of washing the mud from his skin—then smoothed the gray fabric down. He sighed. The robe felt . . . *right*.

The bundle was not yet empty. He bent down and this time came away with a cloak in his hands. The cloak was frayed along the edges, but it was thick, and as gray as the robe. Except, as he moved it in the pale light, a rainbow sheen danced across the fabric of the cloak, like a skim of oil on a puddle. He cast the cloak over his shoulders.

A quick examination revealed more objects inside the bundle. The first was a small pouch of soft leather attached to a cord. It was empty, but Travis thought he could guess its purpose. With careful motions he placed the silver half-coin in the pouch. He hesitated, then took the bone talisman—the rune of hope—from around his neck, coiled it up, and placed it in the pouch as well. Then he cinched the pouch tight and slipped the cord over his head.

Next in the bundle was a thick leather belt, and he used that to cinch the robe around his waist. Then there were his familiar buckskin boots. He pulled them on. The last object in the bundle was a slim stiletto with a single bloodred gem in its hilt. He touched the tip of the knife, winced at the keenness, then tucked it into his belt, shifting it toward the back where it was covered by the cloak.

It was time to go; he couldn't stay in this hovel. The graverobbers knew he would be seeking shelter. And they were men used to dealing with corpses. One more would mean nothing to them. He moved to the gap in the wall. Even as he thought it would be good to banish the light somehow, it ceased without a whisper. Night stole back into the ruin. Travis moved in the opposite direction.

The rain had dwindled to a light mist, and thunder rolled away in the distance. The storm was ending, but the night seemed darker than ever. Crimson specks danced on the air before him. They vanished each time he blinked, then one by one swam back into his field of vision.

He made his way by feel more than sight, and after only a few steps he stumbled through a break in the weeds. A pale swath stretched away from him in the gloom. A road. Hope flooded his chest. He still didn't know where he was—not exactly, anyway—but a road meant people. People who could help him.

Travis started along the road. It was more of a path, really, winding around trees and small boulders, but it was easy to follow even in the murk. The cloak kept the drizzle off of him, but sweat poured into his eyes and trickled down his sides beneath the robe. The spark-motes kept hovering before his eyes, and he started to wonder if perhaps he wasn't ill, if that wasn't why it was so hard to think and remember.

Yes, that was right. Hadn't there been something about a fever or a sickness? There had been a man. No, not a man—a friend. He had been burning with the fever. Except then Travis saw flames. It didn't make sense. Had the man, his friend—Travis couldn't seem to remember his name—had the man touched him? He wasn't sure why, but that seemed important for some reason.

Brighter sparks appeared in the dark before him, gold rather than red. Travis tried to blink them away, but this time they did not waver. As he drew closer the lights grew into bright squares. Windows.

He raised his eyes and saw more lights in the distance. A town? Maybe. But if it was a town, it was too far way. His legs ached, and his throat felt as if he had swallowed a handful of ground glass. He stumbled toward the nearer structure. Where there were lights, there had to be people.

Travis halted before the building. Had it not been for the lights glowing behind the translucent windows, he might have thought it abandoned. Thistles sprang up all along the stone foundation, and the thatch roof sagged precariously. A board hung above the peeling door, but if it had once borne words then the gloom made a mystery of them. Over the wind he caught the sound of rough voices and raucous laughter.

Hunching his shoulders inside the gray robe, he moved to the door. There was no knob, so he pushed against the weathered wood. There was a groan as the door swung inward.

The laughter ceased in a ragged edge of sound, as if cut off with a dull knife.

Smoke-blackened beams hung low over a long room, and dirty straw covered the floor. A fire sputtered on an open hearth, while a scattering of candles produced the wan light along with a rancid odor. A trio of plank tables took up most of the cramped

space. Sitting at these on benches were a half-dozen
men. They wore coarse, brown tunics, mud-stained
hose, and close-fitting leather caps. To a one they
were short, crooked of limb, and powerfully muscled.
They stared at Travis with small, dark eyes.

*Villeins. Freemen, yes, but barely more than peas-
ants in manner. Do be careful, Travis.*

Travis stepped into the room. A gust of wind
slammed the door shut behind him.

Ducking his head to avoid the glares, he sat at the
end of the least-populated table. Whoever these people were, they did not appear glad to see him. Perhaps
they feared strangers. But Travis wouldn't bother
them. He just needed a place to sit for a moment, to
rest and decide what to do next. He knew he wasn't
on Earth anymore, but he had to find out exactly
where he was. That way he would know where to go.
He had friends here, he was sure of it, even if he
couldn't remember their names just now. He had to
find them.

Mutterings broke the silence, and this time the
half-coin did not help Travis comprehend. He
hunched over the table. Even the dim illumination
cast by the candles distressed him. The light seemed
to throb, expanding and contracting on the air.

A shadow appeared before him, and he lifted his
head, although this action sent a wave of dizziness
through him. A woman stood above him. It was impossible to tell if she was young or old because her
face was a mass of thick scabs. Food, sweat, and blood
stained her brown dress, and a shapeless cloth cap
covered her head. The only features Travis could
really make out were her eyes, and they were clear
and filled with fear. Hand trembling, she set a small
clay pot on the table, then hurried away, vanishing
behind a curtain.

Travis stared at the chipped clay pot. He reached

for it, but it was hard to make his hand move precisely the way he wanted, and he nearly knocked it over. Using both hands, he managed to grip the pot and bring it to his lips. A metallic scent flooded his skull, and his gorge rose in his throat so quickly he barely had time to swallow it back. He set the pot down with a clatter, fumbled, and managed to keep it from tipping over. However, some of the liquid within spilled onto the table: thick, brown, and gritty as vomit.

Finally he understood: the proximity to the town, the tables, the freemen, the woman who brought him beer. This place was an inn of some sort. A tavern.

No, a saloon. . . .

Sharp knives of remembrance laid open his brain. He stiffened. How had he possibly forgotten? Travis didn't know, but now it came back to him in flashes hotter and brighter than lightning: the Mine Shaft, Max, the fire.

Oh, Max. . . .

The pain in his chest was fresh, as if it had only just happened, as if he had only just seen his friend taken by flames. He shut his eyes, probing his mind, and found he remembered everything now. Deirdre, the Seekers, Duratek. Child Samanda and Sister Mirrim with her blind eyes. But none of this explained what had happened. Why had Brother Cy sent him here?

One last memory oozed from the wound in his mind.

The key . . . Yes, it is you to whom I must give the key.

This time it was another Travis saw in the flames, black robe billowing, curling like burnt paper.

Beware—it will consume you. . . .

Travis shuddered. This memory was important, maybe more important than all the others. He searched for a reason, but it was impossible to concentrate. The shaking was worse now, his hands flopping against the table like dying fish, leaving damp trails. His tongue was a lump of lead in his mouth, and it felt as if someone had jammed hot, hard stones into his armpits.

His thoughts were drowned out by a scraping sound, followed by the thuds of heavy, booted feet. Travis opened his eyes and forced his head up. He gazed into a pair of small, suspicious eyes.

"Get you away from here," the man said.

His accent was so thick and slurred that even the magic of the silver coin rendered it barely comprehensible. Travis tried to speak, but no sound came out. He ran a sandpapery tongue over dry lips and tried again.

"I just . . . I just need to sit for a little while."

The man's thick-fingered hand moved to the eating knife at his belt. A reek poured off of him, and hate and anger played across his lumpy, bearded face. Shadows hovered on the edges of Travis's blurred vision. His gaze flickered to the curtain in the wall, and he saw frightened green eyes peering out at him. Then the curtain was jerked closed, and the eyes were gone.

"Your kind aren't wanted here," the villein said.

Travis looked back at the man. He knew he should be afraid, but it was hard to feel anything other than the heat rising within him. How long would it be before the fire took him like the man in black? Like it took Max?

Travis forced the words out. "What . . . kind?"

"Gray man," the villein spat.

Travis started to shake his head. Then he looked down at the soft gray robe he wore, and he remembered the cast-down statue in the cemetery. Maybe he understood after all.

Speak a rune, Travis.

Shadows became men as two more of the villeins stepped into his field of vision. Their eyes were flat with loathing.

"Get out of here, gray man," one of them snarled.

The air was melting, turning colors to smoke. Travis clutched the edge of the table to keep from falling.

Now, Travis! Speak a rune. These men mean to kill you.

It was so terribly hard, like moving through molten rock. But Travis forced himself to obey. He started to open his mouth, started to reach a hand toward the men, started to form his lips into a single word.

Krond.

Then, before he could give the word voice, he pulled his hand back. Something was wrong, awfully wrong. There was a reason he didn't want to do this.

Travis!

It was too late. Travis slumped back. He could not have obeyed the voice now if he wished to. Hard hands grabbed his shoulders, pawed at his robe, pulled him back away from the bench, and shoved him up against a wall. There was a crunching sound, and pain sparked through his body, although he hardly noticed it through the heat and fire. Any moment now, and it would come. He opened his eyes and saw a clenched fist poised before his face.

Crack!

At first Travis thought it was the sound of the fist striking his face. Then, through his wavering sight, he saw the tavern's door fly apart in a discharge of splinters.

"Hold!" a voice commanded.

The men froze, the hate on their faces transmuting to dread. They cowered, no longer fierce attack dogs but mangy curs.

"Unhand him this instant!"

The voice was noble and clear as a horn, and the sound of it made Travis's heart leap. He tried to make out the speaker, but a veil had descended before his eyes, and all he could see was a tall figure standing amid a corona of fey light. The figure approached, and the farmers fell back. A cool hand touched Travis's arm.

"Do not fear," the shining man said in a musical voice. "I am here now."

Travis smiled and tried to tell the shining man it was all right, that the fire would take him now. However, before he could speak, the last remaining strength drained from his legs, and the dirty floor rushed up to meet him.

I'm coming, Max.

Then the world was lost, not in fire, but in darkness.

38.

It was very late. Or very early.

From her makeshift bed on the ground, Grace stared up at the dome of the sky and watched the moon sink toward the black line of the horizon. She supposed Earth's own satellite would seem odd to her now—so small, so cold, so terribly distant. In her time here she had grown used to the gigantic, honey-gold moon of Eldh.

Grace counted carefully in her mind—she had almost lost track of the days—but the moon confirmed her conclusion. The orb was waxing, and nearly a perfect quarter.

Today will be the seventh since we left Calavere, Grace. That means just eight more days until the moon is full. Eight more until—

Grace gasped. To the south, a silvery wisp of cloud

dissolved, revealing a pulsing red spark in the sky. Crimson light tinged the moon like blood.

A faint jingling drifted on the air. Grace caught a flash out of the corner of her eye, then came the low, comforting sound of a familiar voice.

"My lady, are you well?"

She spoke the word like a prayer. "Durge."

The knight squatted beside her where she sat. In the dimness his face looked as craggy as that of the moon, but she caught the concern shining in his deep-set eyes. As often, Grace was struck by his solidness. Durge was not a large man, but even in the dark she could make out the thickness of his stooped shoulders, the depth of his chest, the hardness of his arms and legs. At forty-five years of age the knight might have considered himself old, but to Grace he was like a wind-worn stone which seemed only stronger for having stood so long against the fury of the elements.

He cocked his head. "My lady?"

"I was just looking at the moon."

Durge nodded. She did not need to explain further.

"You should return to sleep, my lady. Dawn is yet two hours off."

"Yes," she said, but she did not move, and nor did he.

"Will we reach Ar-tolor today?" she said after a time.

"That was my hope, my lady. However, we were . . . delayed at Falanor. My wish now is, at the least, to make the bridge over the Dimduorn before nightfall, and to cross into Toloria. From thence it is but five more leagues to the queen's castle."

Grace took these words in, then she looked past Durge. In the dim glow of the fire's remains she could just make out five sleeping forms. Two curled close to one another: Daynen and Tira. Lirith and Aryn slept nearby. However, the last figure huddled some distance apart. Grace's eyes flicked up to meet Durge's in the darkness.

"How is Meridar?"

"He . . . rests now, my lady. The wine you gave him appears to have calmed him."

Grace almost grinned in the darkness, but her face was so brittle she feared it would crack. It was not mere wine she had given Meridar after dinner, and Durge knew it. Grace did not feel good about slipping the herbs into the knight's cup. Drugging a man seemed more the methods of a witch like Kyrene rather than a Lirith or an Ivalaine.

However, all day yesterday as they rode from Falanor, Meridar had seemed increasingly troubled. He had not talked to the others, but instead hunched in his saddle, riding apart, and often muttering and shaking his head. At first Grace thought it to be remorse for Kalleth's death. Perhaps Meridar blamed himself for not saving his companion. However, as their shadows stretched out toward evening, she became less certain of that diagnosis. She dared to bring Shandis near to Meridar's charger, and to ask the knight if he was well. To her shock, he laughed.

"Fury makes a fine armor of fear, my lady," he had said in a hard voice. "And hate does forge a sharp sword of cowardice."

Grace had had no answer for that, and had let Meridar spur his warhorse ahead.

After a mirthless supper, during which Meridar had not eaten, Durge had drawn Grace aside and had whispered to her. *Sleep would be a good balm for his spirit, my lady, if it could be made to come.*

These words had stunned her. In the past, Durge had studiously avoided all things related to witches. But she had nodded, and had gone to her pack to retrieve the herbs.

Now Grace shivered, drawing her arms around her

shoulders. Strange how the days could be so muggy while the nights turned so chill.

"Will you return to sleep now, my lady?"

She nodded, not wanting to tell Durge that sleep was an impossibility. "What about you?"

"I will keep watch. That is rest enough for me."

Grace gazed at Durge and once again marveled at the man. She wished she could find a way to make him see what a wonder he was. But even an X-ray machine, had she had one there, could not have captured on film the depth, strength, and kindness of his soul. Instead, without really thinking, she leaned forward and pressed her lips against his rough cheek. His eyes went wide.

Grace yawned as a heaviness stole over her, and suddenly she wondered if perhaps she could sleep after all. She lay back down on her bedroll. "Will you be near, Durge?"

She heard the creak of leather as he stood. "I am ever here, my lady."

Grace drew in a deep breath. Maybe she would never love another. Maybe that kind of closeness was beyond her. But maybe, in a way, this was better. How could love ever offer a safeness like this?

Above her, a shooting star streaked across the sky, but Grace did not make a wish. Instead she closed her eyes and slept.

When she woke the eastern horizon was ablaze, and everyone else was already up. Grace rose, joined the others in a breakfast of hard bread, currants, and water—no one seemed to have the desire to stir the coals into a fire—then helped break camp. They set off just as the red ball of the sun heaved itself into the sky.

Sir Meridar seemed better for his sleep. At breakfast he spoke with control, and once on the road he followed Durge's lead without question. Perhaps he was over the worst of it. Then Grace happened to catch his gaze for a moment, and in his once-kindly brown eyes was a look so haunted that she quickly turned away. Whatever was wrong with Meridar, it would not be cured with a few dried leaves or a few hours of sleep.

As they rode, both Durge and Meridar spurred their horses ahead often, or dropped far back only to come pounding up from behind to meet the others. Grace did not need to ask them to know what they were doing, to know what they were keeping watch for.

I will wait in my house.

Wait for what?

For them to come, my lady. And for all the world to burn.

Grace clutched Shandis's reins. She was not ready to give up and hide. Not yet, not while Travis still needed her help. And not while there was still hope of a cure.

Sometime the day before the road had veered southward, away from the Dimduorn. Grace knew it was cutting the corner made by the river and now angled southeast toward the bridge that would let them cross into Toloria. The road wound through low valleys and over long ridges.

Aryn rode nearby Grace, gazing forward with sapphire eyes. What was the young woman thinking about? However, Grace couldn't guess. The baroness had been subdued since Falanor, but not distraught, not as she had been after Garf's death. Yet somehow her calmness troubled Grace more than tears.

Just behind the baroness came Lirith, and riding before her on the withers of her horse was Daynen. He swung skinny legs inside tattered knee pants as they rode, face turned up to the sun, chatting blithely, often asking Lirith about the land they rode through. When he did, the witch would bend her head toward his, as if her answers were for him only, and each time a smile would cross his face.

In many ways Lirith was still a mystery to Grace. What she thought of any of this—their journey, the Burning Plague, Sir Kalleth's death—she had not said. All the same, Grace was glad for her presence. No matter what happened, Lirith seemed to have the power to remember what was really important. It was she who had first spoken the obvious truth: They could not leave Daynen and Tira in Falanor.

Grace glanced down at the slight form perched in the saddle in front of her. So light and so quiet, sometimes Grace almost forgot Tira was there. Her bones were as thin as a bird's beneath the fabric of her smock. Only her hair seemed to have real substance: thick, curling, and bright as fire.

As if sensing Grace's gaze, the girl glanced up. As always Grace was struck by the contrasts of Tira's face: one side soft, dimpled, and exquisite, the other a shiny mask of scar tissue. A fleeting smile touched the corner of Tira's mouth, then she hung her head again, letting her hair tumble forward to conceal her face. However, her little body scooted back in the saddle, pressing against Grace's stomach. Grace stiffened, then forced herself to relax and accept this closeness. After all, what did she have to fear from a broken child?

Grace's examinations last night had confirmed her earlier suspicions; large areas of the right side of Tira's body were covered with scar tissue. How she had survived the burns was as much a mystery as how she had gotten them. Before they left Falanor, Grace had tried once again to encourage Tira to speak. The girl had not seemed particularly bothered by Grace's questions, but nor had she made a sound in response. Instead she hunched over, playing with a small object Grace could not see, cradled in her lap.

Finally, frustrated at not connecting, Grace had tried a different tactic, asking if she might see what Tira was playing with. Tira held out the object: a small, crude doll, fashioned from a piece of wood wrapped in a frayed rag. Accepting the doll, Grace turned it over in her hand, then sucked in a sharp breath. The side of the doll's head was charred black, as if it had been deliberately stuck into a fire. Tira stretched out small fingers, taking the doll back, gently stroking tangled string hair.

After that Grace had run out of questions. But she had known Lirith was right, that neither Tira nor Daynen must be left in Falanor. The villagers had shut themselves in their hovels in fear. There was no one to care for the children.

She had thought Meridar might protest, but the knight hardly seemed to notice Daynen and Tira.

"Where shall we take them?" Durge had asked.

"To Ar-tolor," Lirith had said. "Ivalaine will see that they are cared for."

At this Daynen had smiled. "I have heard the queen is very beautiful."

Grace had grimaced, glancing at the boy's sightless eyes.

Now, as they rode in the morning sun, Grace felt Tira's slight, warm body against her own, and while the sensation was strange, it was curiously compelling as well. She lifted a hand to touch the girl's tumbling red hair—then halted. Tira was playing with the wooden doll again, making it dance on the back of Shandis's neck, stroking its fire-blackened face.

Grace swallowed and let her hand fall.

It was afternoon when they reached the edge of a wood. The road passed beneath an arched canopy of branches and wound its way among tall, gray-skinned trees.

Grace was tempted to reach out with the Touch, to try to sense the life all around her, but she did not. The magic she had woven on the green of Falanor had astonished no one more than her. Aryn had expressed admiration at the way Grace had been able to draw on hers and Lirith's threads, and the Tolorian woman had questioned Grace long and pointedly on the manner in which Grace had accomplished this feat.

"I have seen the Weirding woven in such a way before," Lirith had said, her dark eyes intent, "but never have I seen a weaving so great, nor one that could move such a wind. How were you able to manage this, Lady Grace?"

Grace had thought about this question, then had shaken her head. "I *didn't* manage it. I wove the Weirding, but that was all. I couldn't . . . I couldn't touch my own thread. All the power came from you, Lirith. And from Aryn."

Both women had gazed at the baroness, but Aryn turned her head, staring into the far-off distance, as if she saw something there.

Lirith had returned her dark eyes to Grace. "We will speak more of this in Ar-tolor."

Grace had only given a stiff nod. *I'm sure we will.*

The road dwindled to a narrow track between the trees, and they were forced to ride single file. Durge led the way on Blackalock, with Grace, Tira, and Shandis just behind. The others followed, and Meridar brought up the rear.

Grace sighed. It was dimmer and cooler in the wood. Yet before long her sense of relief faded. The forest was too quiet. Shouldn't she have heard the movements of small animals, or the trill of birds? Instead, aside from the clopping of the horses' hooves and the jingle of the knights' mail shirts, there was only the faint creaking of trees which, the more Grace listened to it, the more it sounded like the whispering of dry, distant voices.

Just when Grace thought the silence might drive her to scream, the track widened, and a clearing opened before the riders. Grace brought her horse to a halt beside Durge's, and an acrid scent filled her nostrils. A breeze stirred up grit, flinging it into her eyes.

The clearing was not natural. In a perfect circle a hundred paces across, everything—trees, vines, shrubs—had been burned to a fine, gray ash. The ground was blackened and cracked, like a clay pot left too long in the kiln. Aryn gasped, lifting a hand to her mouth, and Durge muttered a low oath.

"What is it?" Daynen said. He tilted his face up, moving it from side to side. "It smells like fire."

Grace could only nod.

"There's something over there," Lirith said, pointing across the burnt area. "Near the edge of the circle. I cannot . . . see what it is."

Grace glanced at the witch. Something told her it was not with her eyes that Lirith had been looking. She turned her gaze forward again. Yes, she could see it now—something dark and shapeless lying on the scorched ground.

"I will see what it is," Meridar said.

Durge glanced at him. "Be careful, Sir Meridar."

However, the knight had already spurred his mount ahead. The charger pounded across the circle, clouds of ash flying up from its hooves. They watched the knight bring the horse to a halt, dismount, and kneel to examine something. Then he stood and signaled to them with a hand.

By the time they reached the far edge of the circle, Meridar had mounted again. Shandis whickered, her ears back, and Grace glanced down at the shriveled form on the ground. Relief coursed through her, and only then did she realize what she had dreaded she would see. However, the body was not human.

"I think it was a wolf," Meridar said.

Durge lifted a gloved hand to his chin. "Indeed. But I have never known a wolf to wait for a forest fire to overtake it. Why did it not run?"

"But don't you see?" a soft voice said. "It wasn't a forest fire."

The others turned surprised glances on Aryn. Had

she sensed something Lirith had not? But maybe none of them needed magic to know who—no, *what*—had started this fire. Grace gazed back down at the burnt husk of the wolf, and she thought of the bear—the animal that had burst from the woods to attack Durge and kill Garf. She remembered the way it had snarled madly. And the burnt, blistered patch in its pelt.

A jolt of understanding stabbed her. She drew in a gritty breath and opened her mouth to tell the others what she had remembered and what it meant.

Her words were lost in the bright, high call of a trumpet. The sound drifted among the trees and reverberated across the clearing. Before any of the riders could speak, a man stepped from the shadow between two trees. He was tall, but beyond that Grace could see nothing, for a long brown cloak draped his body, and a green hood hung low over his face.

An oath sounded beside her—Durge—and Grace snapped her head up in time to see a dozen more figures step from the forest to stand on the edge of the circle. All wore cloaks and hoods of forest colors. Here and there Grace saw the hilt of a sword protruding from beneath one of the cloaks.

A small hand clutched at Grace's. She looked down into Tira's frightened eyes, then circled an arm around the girl and held her close. Lirith and Aryn cast startled looks at Grace, and Daynen stared forward, silent, his face taut. He did not need eyes or magic to sense the danger.

"We wish no trouble with you," Durge said. "Let us pass, and none shall be harmed."

The Embarran sat straight in his saddle, face grim. Meridar's hand crept toward the hilt of his sword; but Grace knew it was no use. No matter how skilled Durge and Meridar were, they were two against a dozen. And the armed men had them surrounded.

Durge's eyes flickered to Grace. She caught the

message in them: *When it begins, ride.* Durge nodded to Meridar, then reached for the gigantic sword strapped to his back.

Another sound broke the silence of the barren circle. It was laughter.

"Stay your hand, Sir Durge. It's been a bad enough day already. I really don't want to finish it by dancing on the end of your greatsword."

Durge froze as the figure closest to them stepped forward, raised his hands, and pushed back the green hood. Grace stared, breath suspended, then in a warm rush fear melted into joy. With one swift motion she disentangled herself from Tira, slid from Shandis's back, and ran forward to throw herself into the arms of a tall, rawboned man with thinning blond hair and a smile like dawn after dark night.

"It's good to see you again, too, Lady Grace," Beltan said with a chuckle, and tightened strong arms around her.

39.

"It is not much farther, Your Radiance," the tall, red-haired man leading Grace's horse said.

Grace gazed down at him where he walked and sighed. She had thought she had left that title behind leagues ago, but apparently she had been mistaken. The man—no, the *knight,* she corrected herself, for despite their simple garb he and his companions were all knights of the Order of Malachor—had bowed low when Beltan had spoken her name.

Yet, as she rode, she was less and less certain it was the title and the obeisance that had bothered her, and increasingly sure it was something else. But what?

It feels right to you, Grace. That men bow to you seems only as it should be.

No, the thought was absurd. She was nothing and no one. The day she believed she was truly royalty was the day she drank enough tea of barrow root to turn her brain to jelly and send it running out her ears. She clutched Shandis's golden mane with one hand, held Tira tight with the other, and let the knight lead her through the silent forest.

Grace hoped they would reach the knights' camp soon. She ached to tell Beltan about the real purpose for her journey, but he and the majority of the men had gone on ahead to make things ready for the travelers.

"There's a lot for us to talk about, Grace," Beltan had said in the clearing, his bright expression falling dim. "But it's better not to speak of it in this place. We can talk more where it's safe, and after you've rested and eaten."

He and the others had disappeared back into the trees then, vanishing as quickly as they had appeared.

"Come, Your Radiance," the red-haired knight had said, taking Shandis's reins in hand. "We must lead the horses by a longer trail than those who walk on foot."

Two more knights had stepped forward to lead Aryn's and Lirith's palfreys. All three of the knights seemed frightfully young—none of them could be more than twenty-five—but she remembered hearing that it was mostly the younger, landless men who were joining the Order of Malachor. For a moment she had been reminded of Garf, but she had forced the thoughts from her mind. This forest was already too damn somber.

"Sir Tarus," Durge spoke now from atop Black-alock. The Embarran rode alongside Meridar at the rear of the party. "What can you tell us of the burnt circle?"

The red-haired knight who led Grace's horse glanced back. "You had best ask Sir Beltan of that when we reach our camp, my lord. It was he who discovered the place."

"What is there to know?" Aryn said in a quiet voice. "It's dead. Utterly dead."

The baroness hugged herself with her left arm, and Grace chewed her lip. Had Aryn tried to touch the Weirding in the burnt circle?

Durge gazed at the young woman, then blew a heavy breath through his mustaches. "It was ill fortune to come upon that place so unexpectedly."

"And yet," Lirith said in a musing voice, "it was good fortune to come upon Lord Beltan, was it not?"

Durge opened his mouth, but the solemn Embarran seemed to have no reply to that. Lirith's lips curled in a smoke-red smile, and Grace found herself smiling as well. Only Lirith could manage a jest in a place such as this. Once again Grace was grateful the witch had stolen away with Aryn to come on this journey.

It was a good thing the Malachorian knights were leading the way, for even had Grace walked right past the camp, she would have missed it completely. Tarus brought Shandis to a halt before a thick wall of silver-barked trees that looked to Grace exactly like every other part of this forest. He lifted a pair of fingers to his mouth and let out a soft whistle.

Two shadows separated themselves from the murk beneath a tree and stepped into a shaft of golden light. Grace lifted a hand to her chest, startled. The men were no more than five paces away, but she had not seen them. Their garb blended perfectly with the surrounding woods—although here and there she caught the glint of steel beneath the green-and-brown cloaks. The knights saluted Tarus with a fist against the chest, and the red-haired man returned the gesture.

"They're waiting for you," one of the knights said.

Tarus glanced up at Grace. "Come, Your Radiance. Our journey ends just ahead."

They moved through an arch of trees, and only then did Grace see that there was in fact a fairly broad track leading through the wood. They followed it for no more than a minute before Grace caught the sound of water over stone. The trees parted, and the bright note of a horn pierced the air. Grace stared, and Tarus grinned, displaying crooked but white teeth.

"Welcome to our humble fortress, my lady."

Grace handed Tira down to the knight, then gazed around as she and the others dismounted. It was not exactly a glen, but the trees were more open there, where a small brook widened and flowed in a frothy cascade over a series of flat rocks. On the ground were a handful of canvas tents, but it was toward the forest canopy that Grace's eyes were drawn. Tira disentangled herself from Tarus's big, gentle hands and walked forward, gazing upward with solemn eyes.

Twenty feet above the ground, rope-and-plank walkways stretched between a dozen gigantic trees. Ladders were nailed to the trunks, leading to and from wooden structures tucked among stout branches. Grace opened her mouth, but before she could find words, a tall form parted from a nearby group of knights and strode toward them on long legs.

"Grace, there you are."

Beltan grinned as he approached, and as always Grace was struck by the way the simple act of smiling could transform the blond knight's face. Unlike his uncle, King Boreas, Beltan was not a handsome man. He was tall and straight but rangy, with long, white-blond hair far on its way to thinning at the crown. His green eyes were bright but small, and his face—adorned by a sparse yellow mustache that framed either side of his mouth—was broad and plain. However, when he smiled it was like a light shone upon him, concealing in shadow what was jovial but homely, and highlighting what had been hidden, and which was noble and beautiful.

Grace returned the knight's grin. It was good to see him smile. There had been a time at Calavere when the expression had been all too rare.

"I was beginning to wonder if Sir Tarus had lost you." Beltan winked at the red-haired knight.

Tarus spread his arms in mock apology. "I was just taking them by the scenic route."

Beltan lifted a hand to give Grace a half-whispered aside. "Sir Tarus isn't the brightest fellow, and he hasn't quite discovered the fact that one tree looks much like another. But he's pretty to look at, so I keep him around."

The red-haired knight only smiled, as if he had not heard a word. Grace stifled a laugh.

Lirith drifted forward, holding the hem of her riding gown just above the leaf litter. "Are you certain you and your men are working here?" She raised her eyes to the trees. "To me, this all appears suspiciously similar to fun."

Tarus scratched the red goatee on his chin, giving the witch a sheepish look. "The tree forts were Sir Beltan's idea."

The big knight shrugged. "And which king decreed that work can't ever be fun?"

Lirith laughed, but then Beltan's smile faded.

"And there are other reasons for not staying on the ground at night."

They followed Beltan through the camp to a circle of stumps gathered around a fire pit. Along the way, Grace counted about fifteen men in the camp, and she supposed, from the number of tree structures, that an equal number were out on patrol or standing watch on the camp's perimeters.

Daynen chattered as Lirith guided him by the elbow, asking what the knights looked like, how many tree forts there were, and other questions the witch was more hard-pressed to answer. Luckily, Tarus came to her side and helped by explaining how the knights had built the encampment. As they reached the circle and sat, Daynen moved on to ply another one of the men with more questions, his face shining. Lirith cast a grateful look at Tarus. The red-haired knight bowed.

"You should think twice before you show me such respect, warrior of Calavan," Lirith said.

"And why is that, my lady?" Tarus said, straightening.

Lirith tapped a dusky cheek, as if searching for just the right words. "Queen Ivalaine is my . . . *mistress.*"

Tarus raised an eyebrow. The expression seemed genuinely startled, but only for a moment, then his grin returned. "I see. And does this mean you're going to wave your fingers and turn me into a shrub, my lady?"

"Are you not afraid, warrior?"

"Oh, trembling."

Lirith laughed, but the sound became a sigh, and when she spoke again the playfulness was gone from her voice. "I hope the time does not come when that is the case, warrior of Vathris. Indeed, there are those among your brethren who would believe that time has already come upon us."

"And among your sisters, my lady."

Lirith nodded.

Grace watched this exchange with interest. She knew the followers of Vathris tended to mistrust the Witches. But what had Lirith meant? What time did some believe had already come?

Before she could ask, Beltan was there, gesturing for her to sit on one of the stumps and pressing a pewter cup into her hand. Only then did she realize how thirsty she was, and she lifted the cup and drank: cool, spiced wine.

The other travelers joined her in the circle. Soundlessly, Tira clambered into Grace's lap. Grace's shock lasted only a moment, then she gathered the girl in close.

She needs you, Grace.

Or was it the other way around?

"What's your name?" Beltan said in a gentle voice, kneeling before Grace and the child.

Shyly, Tira looked up, then just as quickly bent back over her doll, letting her crimson hair hide her face. Beltan glanced at Grace.

"What happened to her?"

Grace licked her lips. "Fire."

Beltan stood and made a sharp gesture to Tarus. The young knight nodded and left them. Grace knew they would not be disturbed while they talked.

"That's why you're here, isn't it, Beltan? Because of the fires."

All looked at Aryn. Grace expected to see fear on her face, but instead the baroness's visage was as smooth and serene as water at twilight.

Beltan paced inside the circle. "I was at our fortress in Galt when we first heard of them. It was two months ago, and I was just getting ready to lead a group of knights on patrol for an exercise. Then we heard that several villages had been burned, two in the northeastern region of Calavan, a few more in the marches of Toloria, beyond Ar-tolor. We thought maybe some of the wildmen who dwell in the Fal Erenn had organized themselves into raiding parties and had managed to ford the Dimduorn. I took thirty knights, and we rode here to set up an encampment and keep watch."

For the first time since entering the camp, Meridar spoke, his voice hoarse. "But it was not wildmen you found, was it?"

Beltan clenched his jaw, then nodded.

"Have you seen them?" Grace said, surprised at the trembling in her voice. "The *krondrim.*"

Beltan rubbed his chin. "*Krondrim.* Yes, I heard an

old man use that word to describe them once. But usually they're just called the Burnt Ones." He shook his head. "No, I haven't seen them. Just some of the work they do."

"How long?" Durge said.

Beltan shrugged. "How long have they been coming down from the Fal Erenn? It's hard to say. Two months, three. Maybe even longer. But we didn't learn of their existence until a few weeks ago. When they . . ."

"When they burned a part of the forest just a league from here," Durge finished.

Beltan turned toward the Embarran, his face hard. "That wasn't forest, Durge. That was the village of Carnoc."

It took them all a moment to find their voices again. They had come upon burnt villages before, but in each of them at least some ruins had remained. However, the destruction in the circle had been complete. Only the charred carcass of the animal—which Grace supposed now had been a dog—had remained. She had to tell the others what it meant.

"There was a burnt bear," she said before she lost the courage.

Beside her Aryn stiffened, and Lirith reached out to grip the young woman's left hand. Beltan cocked his head, listening.

"It came upon us just a league from Calavere. It . . ." This was still so hard to speak about. "It killed a friend of ours. The bear had a horrible burn in its pelt. The pain had driven it mad. I thought it must have been caught in a brush fire, but . . ."

Beltan shook his head. "That's dark news. From what I've seen, they—the Burnt Ones—usually stick to the Dawning Fells. What you've said makes it possible that at least a few of them have made it across the highlands of Galt and have crossed into the Fal

Sinfath." He ran a hand through his thinning hair. "But I suppose in a way that makes sense."

A frown creased Lirith's brow. "How does it make sense, Sir Beltan?"

The big knight squatted, picked up a stick, and scratched a vertical line in the dirt. "Here are the Fal Erenn," he said, then he drew a pair of rough shapes below the line. "And here are the marches of Calavan and Toloria. For the last few months, stories and incidents involving the Burnt Ones have been sparse, and all of them have been confined to these regions"—he pointed to the areas just beneath the mountains—"here, and here."

"And now?" Durge said.

"Now we're hearing new stories almost every other day, and they're coming from"—Beltan hesitated, then circled his entire map—"they're coming from all over this area."

"Of course," Grace murmured, her brain working quickly, piecing together all of the evidence. "It's the progression in every pandemic. The first incidents are isolated—the infection cycle is so rapid that it kills faster than it can spread. But now the contagion has had time to adapt. It's not killing its hosts as quickly, and that means the affected area can begin to grow. Only the lack of traveling in this world has kept it from spreading faster."

She looked up and saw the others staring at her.

Durge shook his head. "What does it mean, my lady?"

"It means," Beltan said, setting down the stick and standing, "that the Burnt Ones—the *krondrim*—are on the move."

"But why?" Lirith said. "What do they want?"

No one had an answer to that. The silence of the forest settled over them. Grace drew in a deep breath. It was time to finish this.

"Beltan," she said in a low voice, "there's more."

She wasn't sure how he knew. Maybe it was something about the tone of her voice or the expression on her face. Or maybe it was something else, some thought she projected. Regardless of what it was, the blond knight met her eyes.

"It's Travis Wilder," he said. "Isn't it?"

She could do no more than give a stiff nod. Beltan knelt before her, reaching around Tira to lay big hands on Grace's shoulders, his eyes hard as flint.

"What's happened to him, my lady? You must tell me."

At last air rushed into her lungs, and she was able to speak. In dry, emotionless words she explained the dream, the vision, and the purpose of her journey. She was dimly aware that she had told none of this to Meridar. However, if the knight was angry he did not show it. He still stared at the map Beltan had drawn in the dirt.

When she was finished, Beltan stood.

"It is not far from here to the bridge over the Dimduorn," the knight said. "We can cross into Toloria tonight, then be to Ar-tolor before this time tomorrow."

Grace shook her head. "I don't understand."

"I'm coming with you," the blond knight said.

40.

Travis was on fire.

The world should have been brilliant with the flames, but instead it was dark and suffocating. Hot, black fabric swaddled him, tangling around his limbs. The place seemed a tomb—confined and lightless, walled in stone. How had he gotten there?

The hands. Yes, that was it. The hands had reached out of the darkness, batting at him, tearing off his clothes so that he was naked once again. They had dragged him through swirling murk, jostling his body cruelly, piercing his flesh with fiery needles and sinking them deep into the joints between his bones. Then the motion had ceased, and he had been here, the walls compacting the gloom against him. The hands had wrapped him in a shroud of shadow, and the flames had risen up to lick at him.

Did they think he was dead? They had set him on a funeral pyre. He had to shout, to let them know they had made a terrible mistake, but the heat fused his jaw shut, melted bone and snapped tendons. They were burning him alive.

Master Wilder?

The roaring voice of the flames phased into words.

Master Wilder, can you hear me? Try to move your head if you can understand what I am saying.

The voice was kind yet stern. Travis wanted to obey, but molten bands encircled his body, paralyzing him.

Do you know what ailment afflicts him?

This voice was different from the first. Smoother and more sibilant, but sharper somehow.

I am not certain. But it is a fierce fever that has seized his body. Master Eriaun has spoken many runes of cooling over him, but I fear they have had little if any effect.

Is it the fire sickness, then?

By Olrig! Do not speak such a thing. How could it be such when he comes from so great a distance?

Forgive me, All-master. It is only that I have heard it said it begins this way. Yet you are right, of course. It is impossible the sickness could have reached so far as the place from which he came.

The soft voice was contrite, yet somehow this made it all the more damning. The kinder one—the one called All-master—answered with only a grunt.

Travis knew he had to speak, to tell them they

were wrong, that the sickness they spoke of had indeed reached his world. He tried to open his eyes, only he wasn't certain if he had done it. Then, like red dawn, a brightness stabbed into his skull. He recoiled, sinking back into darkness. However, just before the light vanished, he thought he saw a shadow against it. No, not a shadow, but a man with keen blue eyes and a white beard. Jack? Was it Jack come to put out the flames?

The voices were receding now.

Master Wilder!

It is no use, All-master. He cannot hear you.

No, you are wrong, Master Larad. Did you not see? He opened his eyes—for only a moment, yes, but he did.

If you say it, then it is—

The voices dissipated, smoke before a wind, and the roar rose again around him.

It was sometime later that he was aware of waking. He lay still, listening, but there was no sound, and the silence was like a balm for his shriveled soul. Perhaps the flames had done their work. However, if this was death, it was certainly better than dying. The tomb was cooler now, filled with silvery light.

He heard a rustling sound. Travis turned his head to one side. That he could see impinged upon him only after a moment, for he did not remember opening his eyes.

He could not see much. Even this soft illumination drove shards of glass into the backs of his eyes. The tomb was mostly a gray blur, although Travis could make out what might be stone walls, and he sensed that he was lying down on some sort of bed or bier. He blinked, and one more object came into focus.

At first Travis wondered if the man was one of the two speakers he had heard earlier, then something told him this was not so. The man seemed young. His face was broad, homely, and beardless, and even sitting he seemed short, although his arms and shoulders looked powerful. The man wore a robe of drab brown, and for some reason that struck Travis as wrong. Shouldn't the robe have been gray?

The man smiled—a grotesque expression, yet not frightening. He must have seen Travis's movement, and he stood and moved out of view. This sent a jolt of panic through Travis, but a moment later the man reappeared, a cup in his hand. A cool scent reached Travis's nose. Water.

How long had it been since he had drunk? He tried to work his tongue, but his mouth might as well have been filled with cement. The man knelt beside the bed, slipped a thick arm beneath Travis's neck, and lifted his head. Travis tried to drink, but most of the water spilled down his chin and onto his chest. However, a small amount passed between his lips, and he tasted metal. The man lowered him back to the bed.

The gray light was collapsing against the weight of darkness. Travis knew he didn't have much time.

Where am I?

But he had spoken the words only in his mind. That wasn't good enough. He forced his brittle lips to form sounds.

"Where . . . ?"

This time Travis was certain he had managed to speak the word. However, the man only shook his head, smiling again, and touched a finger to his lips. He set down the cup, then patted Travis's hand. Travis tried to speak again, but now exhaustion stole over him, dragging him down. The last thing he remembered was something damp being pressed against his forehead. The light contracted to a pinhole and vanished.

After that the world oscillated in and out of darkness, like a screen catching stark frames from a black-and-white movie. At times, in the periods of light, images racked into focus before Travis: the man in the brown robe again, now an empty chair, then blank stone, now men in paler robes, standing in a knot, murmuring. Once, two figures who shone like fairies hovered over him: one onyx and silver, the other azure and gold. It seemed a cool hand soothed his brow.

Do not let go of life, dear one, the gold fairy said. *We must go, but we will return soon.*

Then the lens of his vision fogged, and the image was gone. For a long time there was no light at all, and he feared the end had come and gone, and that this was all there would ever be. Then the flames rose again around him, and he knew this was not over yet.

This time the fire was urgent, as if desperate to burn him, to reduce his being to ash. As the flames reached their crest, hallucinations came again: shadows, then hands reaching out for him, the leering oval of a man's face floating above, and a whispered word. *Krond.*

"Get you away from here!" a voice screamed.

He knew the voice was his own, yet he had no power over it.

Olrig help us, he's burning up. Can you not do something, Master Eriaun?

It is beyond my power, All-master.

No, it is beyond all our power. As so many things are in this age. Even Olrig cannot help us now.

The end was close now. One final time the hot fabric of darkness covered Travis, draping him like the folds of a black, smoldering robe. At last he understood. He was the burning man now. This was to be his own transformation.

Fire forged his body into a rod. His spine arched, and his head went back as once more words that were not his own ripped themselves from his scorched lungs.

"It will consume you!"

Then the fire closed in and burned everything to cinders.

Darkness.

Silence.

And after a time . . . light.

A thin, gray line appeared against the blackness. The line expanded as Travis opened his eyes.

He blinked, and the light throbbed in time to the dull thudding in his skull. However, it was bearable. His body ached as if it had been bludgeoned, but at least he was aware of it beneath the rough blanket, and he could move his fingers and his toes. They had not burned after all.

Before he thought about what he was doing, he sat up. The motion sent dizziness surging through him, but he clenched his jaw and was able to ride it out. When he was able to open his eyes again, he let them move about the small, dimly lit space.

It was not a tomb, that much was clear. Nor was it exactly like a bedchamber. More like a cell. The room was barely long enough to contain the narrow cot on which he rested, and the stone walls were bare. A slit of a window had been cut near the ceiling, and it was through this that the light filtered. The only other objects in the room were a chair and a table, both austere and fashioned of wood.

There was a rattling sound, and he moved his eyes in time to see the low wooden door open. A short, stout man in a brown robe stepped through, holding a cup and a pitcher. He stopped short when he saw Travis, his brown eyes wide in his lumpy face. Then he grinned, a lopsided expression, and turned to step back through the door.

Wait, Travis tried to say, but the word was only a harsh croak. The door shut, and the man was gone.

Should he get out of bed and go after the man? Travis wasn't certain he could, and before he decided whether to try the door opened again. This time two men in gray robes stepped into the cramped cell, the man in the brown robe limping behind them. One of the men was about Travis's age, with black hair, black eyes, and a face crisscrossed by scars. The other man was old, his hair and beard white, and his eyes like blue stones. He leaned on a staff of ornately carved wood, but despite his age there was an air of solidness about him.

"Well," the dark-haired man said, his tone sour, "he doesn't exactly look like a runelord."

The older man frowned. "Think before you speak, Master Larad. He hears you."

The scarred man gave a penitent nod, but his eyes gleamed as he studied Travis.

The older man drew close to the bed. "Do you know what has happened?"

Travis thought, but it was like trying to cut fog into meaningful shapes with a dull knife. "I've been sick," he said, the words hurting his throat.

The old man nodded. "And do you know who I am?"

Travis studied the man's lined face. It was quiescent now, wise and peaceful—but this face could hold anger as well, could it not? "I saw you in the tavern. You're the shining man."

The dark-haired one laughed at this. "Shall that be your new title, Oragien? And a fine one it is. So much more dramatic than 'All-master.'"

The older man shot the other a hard look before turning back to Travis. "Yes, it was I who came to your aid at the tavern near the town. But that is not important now."

Travis's eyes moved to the mist-colored robes the two men wore, surprised to find that he understood. "This is the Gray Tower, isn't it?"

The old man—Oragien—gave a solemn nod. "It is."

"And you're runespeakers."

"We are."

Travis attempted to wet his lips, but his tongue was like a block of wood. "How . . . how did I get here?"

Oragien gripped his staff. "We summoned you."

Travis rolled this over in his mind. He remembered words from the old cemetery on the hill. *They're calling for you even now. Can't you hear?*

So that's what Brother Cy had meant. But it still didn't explain why he was here, on Eldh. Travis opened his mouth, but he had moisture and energy for only one word.

"Why?"

Oragien started to speak, but the dark-haired man answered first, his words digging in like splinters.

"It's simple, Master Wilder. According to the Allmaster, you're going to save the Runespeakers."

41.

The door shut, leaving Travis alone in the little cell.

He sank back against the hard cot, trembling and sweating. The fever had broken, and the sickness that had gripped him—whatever it had been—had passed. However, Travis felt dry and hollow: the husk left behind by a molting insect. He had talked with Allmaster Oragien and the other runespeaker, the sharp-tongued one—Larad—for only a few minutes. All the same, the act had left him as drained as if he had run a marathon after a week without sleep.

"It will be some time before you are truly recovered," Oragien had told him. "What the source of your fever was, I cannot say. At first I thought it simply an ague caught from the rain, but the sickness seemed to be more than that. Regardless, you were caught in its throes for three days. You should not try to stir from this bed until you are strong enough."

Larad had directed his sharp gaze at the elder rune-speaker. "And what of this evening's chorus? The others grow weary of waiting, All-master. They want to see this hero you've summoned for them."

Oragien had drawn shaggy white eyebrows down in a scowl. "Hush, Master Larad. The man has been ill, and—"

"No, it's all right. I'll go to your . . . your chorus."

Travis supposed his own expression had been as surprised as that of the two runespeakers. However, it was clear there was some disagreement between the two concerning him. That made it seem even more important to understand why they had called him from Earth.

And better yet, Travis, how *they did it. The Runespeakers aren't supposed to have that kind of power. Not anymore, at any rate.*

Attending this chorus of theirs seemed like the best way to start understanding what was really going on. And while he still felt weak, Travis supposed he had enough energy to sit and listen to a few men in gray robes sing some songs.

At least, that was what he had thought when he told Oragien and Larad he would attend. Now, as he lay on the cot, he wasn't so certain. Sweat rolled off his forehead in rivulets, and the blanket that covered his body was soaked. Maybe he would have to tell them he couldn't go after all.

It was only when the door creaked open that he realized he had dozed off. His eyelids fluttered up, and he saw a short, brown-robed figure enter the cell.

"Hello," Travis said.

The young man jumped, then his rubbery lips parted, pushing his lumpy features into a cheerful grin. Despite his weariness, Travis couldn't help but grin back. The man hurried forward, then set a tray down on the small table beside the cot. On the tray was a clay crock, and from it rose a savory scent.

"What is it?" Travis said, pushing himself up a notch. His stomach growled. That was a good sign at least.

The man formed his hand into a scoop and brought it to his mouth. The message was clear: *Soup—eat.* He moved to the door.

"Wait," Travis said, although he was uncertain why. Maybe it was just that, in the delirium of his fever, he had felt so alone. He searched for something to say. "Would you like to stay for a while, to talk?"

The man shook his head. Travis frowned. Why didn't the other ever speak?

A thought struck him. Maybe the man couldn't understand his words. Travis groped beneath the blanket, then his hand found the small pouch that contained the silver half-coin; they had left it around his neck. Of course—he had been able to speak to Oragien and Larad. Why not this man?

The other pointed to his mouth and shook his head again, and Travis understood.

It makes sense, Travis. Who could possibly be a better servant for the Runespeakers than someone who's mute? There would certainly be no danger of him speaking any runes he happened to overhear.

"I'm sorry," Travis said.

The man shrugged, then smiled. Obviously it was no great concern to him.

"I'm Travis Wilder. What's your name?"

As soon as Travis asked the question, he regretted it. How could the other answer? However, the man pointed to himself, then to the narrow opening high in the wall.

Travis frowned. "Window? Ledge?" He snapped his fingers. "Sky."

The man beamed, pointed to himself, and nodded.

Travis grinned, then opened his mouth to say something more. However, instead of words, a great yawn escaped him. The young man—Sky—folded his hands and pressed them next to his cheek. Travis needed neither words nor half-coin to translate that message.

"Yes, sleep sounds good. After soup."

Sky nodded, limped through the door, and shut it behind him, leaving Travis alone again.

The complaints uttered by his stomach grew more insistent, and Travis leaned over the table. The soup was thin, but salty and delicious. At first he tried using the wooden spoon Sky had left, but his hand shook, and he got more soup on the blanket than in himself. It was easier to pick up the crock and drink.

Even the simple act of eating was wearying. Travis set down the crock, arms trembling, then lay back. He wanted to think more about everything that had happened to him, but before he could, cool sleep stole over him.

When he woke again the light seeping through the window had dimmed to pewter. The soft trilling of doves drifted in. Evening.

He blinked, realizing he felt shockingly better for the soup and the rest, and sat up in bed.

"So, our runelord finally wakes."

It took Travis a long moment to find his voice. "Master Larad. I did . . . I didn't know you were there."

"How could you?" the dark-haired runespeaker said. "You were asleep when I entered."

Travis winced at the edge in the other's voice, then wondered how long Larad had stood there, watching him.

The runespeaker gestured to the window. "The sun has passed below the horizon. The chorus will meet now."

"Where's Oragien?" Travis said.

"And is a simple master not fine enough escort for you?"

Travis cringed. *That's not what I meant,* he started to say, then swallowed the words, knowing there was no point. Larad's black eyes were like stones, and the scars that marked his face glowed in the pale light, rendering his face into a shattered mosaic.

"Your clothes are there." Larad nodded toward a stack of folded garments on the chair.

Travis started to slip from beneath the blanket, then realized he was naked. However, Larad showed no signs of leaving or even turning his back. Being clothed around others who were not gave one a sense of power—a concept Larad appeared well aware of. Travis clenched his jaw, swung his legs over the edge of the cot, and set his bare feet on the cold stone floor.

Modesty was superseded by a desire just to stay conscious as vertigo rippled through him. However, the dizziness passed, and with help from the table and none from Master Larad, Travis was able to stand. Although, when he did, he was hunched over, shoulders crunched inward. He knew this light, dry brittleness was exactly what it felt like to be old.

Travis moved to the chair and saw all his belongings neatly stacked. He picked up the gray robe and, with stiff motions, shrugged it over his head. It was clean and fresh-smelling, all traces of soil and blood gone. The same was true of his buckskin boots. He pulled them on, then—drained of energy by these simple acts—left the stiletto on the chair, folded inside his mistcloak. Belatedly, he wondered what had become of his spectacles, then gave a wry grin as he realized they were on his face. No doubt the runespeakers had not known what to make of them—few on this world did—and so left them in place.

"Darkness falls, Master Wilder," Larad said. "The chorus awaits."

Evidently the Runespeakers took their singing seriously. Travis nodded, drew a breath into his withered lungs for strength, and moved to the door. Larad reached for the handle to open the way.

"You're not glad I'm here, are you, Larad?" Travis said to the runespeaker.

Larad froze, then raised an eyebrow that was made a black lightning bolt by its intersection with a thin scar. "All-master Oragien believes you have the power to aid the Runespeakers in their time of need."

Travis tried not to laugh at the absurdity of that thought. He could hardly even stand up. "But that's not what you think, is it?"

Larad shrugged, his gaze impenetrable as smoked glass. "What I think is not important."

But it should be, Travis added the unspoken implication. Short hairs on the back of his neck stood up. Every instinct told him this man was intelligent. And dangerous.

Travis licked his lips. "This isn't . . . my world, Larad."

The master studied him, then nodded. "We are aware of all the facts concerning you, Master Wilder."

"Then tell me—how was I summoned here? To Eldh."

Larad's nose wrinkled, etching white scars deeper into his flesh. "Oragien sought help in the matter."

"From who?"

For the first time the angular pieces of Larad's face rearranged themselves into a readable emotion: anger. "From a source I do not care for. And were he not All-master, some might even dare to speak the word heresy."

As you just did, Travis wanted to say. However, Larad's visage was already calm again, a funeral mask of alabaster in an ancient tomb: shattered and serene. He opened the door of the little room.

"Come, Master Wilder, it is time to go."

42

The Gray Tower of the Runespeakers was seven centuries old—that much Travis knew from the stories Falken Blackhand had told him. If he shut his eyes, he could still hear the bard telling tales of the three towers that were raised after the fall of Malachor: bastions of learning founded to preserve the knowledge of the Runelords.

However, as he followed after Master Larad, Travis did not need Falken's tales to remind him that this tower was ancient. The stones themselves bespoke an archaic and alien viewpoint. All around he saw triangular arches, twisted columns, and unsettling curves molded by a lost craft to please eyes long since dimmed with dust. The gray stone itself was smooth and without seam, ledge, or crack. Nothing he had seen on Eldh—certainly not the crude keeps and castles—looked like this place.

Except that wasn't true, was it? It had been a ruin when Travis had set foot within it, but he had seen these same polished walls, these same queer lines and angles inside the White Tower of the Runebinders. Only the color of the walls had been different there—bone instead of fog. However, the White Tower had fallen centuries ago, its foundation corrupted by the folly of its builders, and the Black Tower had fallen as well. This tower was the last of the three.

Despite Travis's recent illness, Master Larad set a swift pace. Travis followed down a wide flight of steps that spiraled through the heart of the tower. There was no railing on the inside edge, and in the center of the staircase was a hollow shaft about a dozen feet across. When Travis looked up, he saw twilight filtering through slits in the dome a hundred feet above, adding a tincture of violet to the gray walls.

Every few steps the two men passed a wooden door set into the outside wall. Travis guessed each led to a small, trapezoidal cell like the one he had awakened in, all of them arranged around the staircase like vertically offset wedges from a wheel of gray cheese.

As he descended, Travis's foot caught the hem of his gray robe, and he stumbled toward the edge of the inner shaft. A hard hand clamped around his arm, pulling him back.

"I would not recommend falling, runelord. Not unless you know how to speak the rune of flying. It is a long way down."

Travis swallowed hard, eyes round behind his spectacles, and gave the runespeaker a nod. Larad grinned. However, it was not an expression of humor. He turned to continue the descent; Travis frowned as he followed. That was at least the third time now that Larad had called him *runelord.* But why?

Travis wasn't certain who the Runelords were or where they had come from. He did know they were the greatest wizards Eldh had ever known, and that they had guarded the Imsari after the three Great Stones were won in the war with the Pale King over a thousand years ago. Then, a few hundred years later, just after the fall of the ancient kingdom of Malachor, the Runelords had vanished along with the three Imsari.

So why did Larad keep referring to him as *runelord?* Travis was neither a wizard nor seven hundred years old. Unless the runespeaker meant it as mockery. And the more Travis thought of the harsh look on Larad's scarred face, the more he thought that was the likely explanation.

The staircase ended in a small, egg-shaped chamber, although the shaft continued down through the floor into some open space below. Travis did not have time to peer in and see as Larad took his arm.

"This way, Master Wilder."

Three corridors led from the heart of the tower. He followed Larad down the nearest; then they came to one of the odd triangular arches. On the other side of this was another, smaller spiral staircase. The stone felt thick and heavy here, and although his sense of direction had been muddled by his fever and the twisting descent, Travis had the sensation this staircase lay within the tower's outer wall. After fifty steps, the staircase ended. Pale light welled through a second archway, along with the hiss of whispers off stone.

Now Larad moved behind Travis and propelled him along in front. As Travis stepped through the archway, a gasp rushed from his lungs. So this was the space he had glimpsed through the shaft of the stairwell.

The chorus chamber of the Runespeakers filled the entire base of the Gray Tower. However, *filled* was certainly the wrong word, for the chamber seemed not forged of rock but rather conjured of air and pearl-gray light. Its design was simple, but this made it all the more wonderful, leaving one to marvel how so vast a space could be defined with so few lines.

The chorus chamber was neither a circle nor a triangle, but something in between. Stone benches lined the walls, rising in seven tiers, surrounding a dais in the center. Rows of vertical slits pierced the walls, and while each of these was too thin to see anything meaningful through, if Travis moved his head he could see—like blurred images through a spinning zoetrope—the shapes of mountains fading to black against a charcoal sky.

While there were benches enough for several hundred runespeakers, Travis saw no more than a hundred men in gray robes sitting on only the lowest tiers. But that wasn't really a surprise. Hadn't Falken said the Runespeakers were not as popular as they once had been?

A constant susurration wove a soft tapestry of sound upon the air, almost like the voice of an ocean caught within a shell. Then words rose above the background murmur.

"Good eventide, Master Wilder."

The greeting was not uttered in anything above a normal speaking voice, but Travis heard it clearly, and in that moment he understood the true purpose of this chamber's design: Everything about this place had been fashioned to carry and amplify the faintest sound.

But that makes sense, Travis. To speak a rune without invoking it, you have to say it quietly, without any force or feeling. So in this place a master could whisper a rune, and the apprentices would still be able to hear it.

The words of the greeting faded, but they did not vanish, instead merging with the gently modulating backdrop of sound. If Travis concentrated, he could still pick them out from among the sea of whispers.

Another whisper—this one sharp and directed—spoke in Travis's ear. "You are above answering the All-master's greeting then, runelord?"

Travis winced, then blinked and saw that Oragien indeed stood before the central dais, blue eyes gazing in his direction. Travis nodded at the All-master.

"Hello," he said, then winced again at the way the loudly spoken word ricocheted around the chamber. Larad glared at him, and even Oragien pressed his lips into a white line. Travis bit his tongue.

Larad directed Travis toward one of the front rows of benches. As Travis walked, he was aware of a hundred pairs of eyes on him. He concentrated on not tripping on his robe, then let out a breath of relief as he sank onto the bench.

"Well, you're looking considerably better," a reedy voice said beside him. "If you don't mind my saying, the last time I saw you, Master Wilder, you looked like a joint of meat that Sky had forgotten to turn on the spit."

Focused on just getting to his seat without winning more glares from Larad, Travis had not noticed the runespeaker he had sat down next to. Now he turned and found himself looking at a short, plump, middle-aged man whose otherwise neat gray robe was spotted here and there with bits of food and wine. Despite the lines around his mouth and eyes, and his thinning hair, his face had a boyish quality. For some reason, the runespeaker seemed vaguely familiar. Had Travis seen him somewhere before?

"This is Master Eriaun," Larad said, speaking in a voice that seemed low by exaggeration, no doubt for Travis's benefit. "He helped attend to you while you were ill."

Of course. That was why the other looked familiar; Travis must have seen him during his delirium. "Thank you for helping me," Travis said.

Master Eriaun smiled, dimples forming in his cheeks. "Why, you're welcome. I'm simply glad to see you well. Your fever was quite dire. For a time I feared it to be the burning sickness."

These words sent a chill through Travis. Once again he saw the sharp words of the newspaper headline: *One Doctor Calls It "a New Black Death."* He opened his mouth to ask Eriaun more.

"This chorus has begun," a voice intoned before Travis could speak. "Let our words join together as one word, and our thoughts as one thought."

He looked up and saw that Oragien had ascended the dais. The All-master leaned on his staff, but somehow he looked anything but frail. His eyes were as piercing as a hawk's, and his white hair and beard shone in the colorless light that drifted from above.

Except there were no torches or candles in sight. How was the chamber being lit?

On instinct Travis cocked his head, listening. Then he caught it: a single word amid the ceaseless tide of murmurs that ebbed and flowed, faint yet still distinct. *Lir.*

He sighed, amazed anew. How long would the rune linger on the air, filling the chorus chamber with gentle light? Travis wasn't certain. Most likely it would last until someone spoke the rune *Bri*, dropping a curtain of darkness over the chamber again.

Travis leaned toward Master Eriaun. "So, is this when you all start singing?"

"Singing?" A frown crossed the runespeaker's plump face. "Why, there's to be no singing, Master Wilder."

Now it was Travis's turn to frown. "But I thought this was supposed to be a chorus."

"And so it is—a time when all may speak, and when all voices become one."

Before Travis could question further, Oragien spoke again, each of his words reverberating before it joined the thrumming background. "As all of you can see, Master Wilder has awakened from the illness that gripped him since he came to us. Now it is time for us to tell him why we summoned him from his homeland far away."

Nods and murmurs of assent traveled around the chamber at Oragien's words. The All-master turned on the dais, directing his gaze and his words directly at Travis.

"Master Wilder, I know you studied for a time with Master Jemis at Calavere, but I do not know what he taught you. I was never able to speak with Master Jemis before . . . before he passed from this world."

Travis clenched his jaw. *You mean before Jemis was strangled by his student, Rin, who had been made into an ironheart and a servant of the Pale King.* But he did not interrupt.

"The Runespeakers have a history that goes back many centuries," Oragien said. "It is a proud tale. However, it is also one that most have forgotten. I do not know if Jemis imparted this knowledge to you, but the Runespeakers are not as . . . favored as they once were."

A harsh laugh sounded beside Travis. Master Larad. "We are not many things we once were."

Oragien cast a disapproving glance at Larad. The black-haired runespeaker did not retract his words, but he did clamp his mouth shut.

"Of late," Oragien went on, "that dislike has grown into hatred on the part of some. As I fear you encountered in the town below."

Travis shook his head. "But why? Why do people dislike the Runespeakers so much?"

Oragien shrugged. "It is a question we have asked ourselves many times. Once nearly all noble lords sent a younger son to study at the tower. So many came that only those with the greatest talent were accepted. Now few come willingly up the road to our tower, and we take in whoever fate sends our way. As you see, there are not many young men among us."

Travis gazed around the chamber. There was one small knot of a half-dozen boys, and a few men here and there who looked to be in their twenties, but nearly all the others in the chamber were older than Travis.

"Now the common folk have new reason to mislike us," Oragien said, "although their fear is misplaced."

"The burning sickness," Travis said before he even really thought about it.

Oragien gave a solemn nod. "They came in the spring of the year, along with the terrible heat that has withered the land. The Burnt Ones. No one knows their origin or their purpose. But we do know their touch induces a plague that causes the afflicted to burn from within and die."

"Or to become like them," a runespeaker across the chamber—one of the few younger men—said.

Oragien glanced at him. "We do not know that, Temris. Not for certain. There are only stories, and ones spoken by peasants at that."

No, Travis wanted to say. *No, he's right. I've seen the pictures. It's not a sickness. It's a transformation.*

But he couldn't find his voice. It was all impossible. Yet in a way it made sense. Why else had Brother Cy shown up? The burnt man, the twisted forms in the pictures Hadrian Farr had shown him, even the heat. All of it was tied with what was happening on Eldh.

"It was we who gave a name to the Burnt Ones," Oragien said. "*Krondrim*, we called them. The Beings of Fire. However, doing so was a mistake. Because we named them, some began to believe that it was we who made them."

It was ludicrous but believable. People always had a way of blaming the message on the messenger. And it explained the welcome Travis and his gray robe had received in the tavern; the townsfolk had thought him a bringer of plague. But that still didn't explain why he was here, on Eldh, in the Gray Tower. He drew in a deep breath. It seemed an awfully self-centered question, but he had to ask it.

"So what does any of this have to do with me?"

Travis kept his eyes on Oragien, but he was aware of the others shifting on their benches, and of new whispers being added to the ceaseless drone on the air.

Oragien tightened his hands around his staff. "The Runespeakers have been unfairly blamed for a great evil. There is only one way we can bring respect to our name and our order again. We must find a means to drive the *krondrim* away. And we summoned you to help us do it."

Motion was impossible as Travis fought to comprehend these words. He was not as certain as the Allmaster that driving away the Burnt Ones would redeem the Runespeakers in the eyes of the common folk. Demonstrating power over them might only make it seem all the more plausible that the Runespeakers had created the *krondrim* in the first place. And by the mutterings around him, Travis guessed he was not the only one who held this same concern. However, there was a greater flaw to the Allmaster's logic. His voice was like a dying man's croak.

"But how can I help you against the *krondrim*?"

"Who else can help us, if not you, Master Wilder?" Oragien said. "Are you not the heir to the runelord Jakabar?"

The whisperings in the tower rose to a rushing noise that filled Travis's skull. "Jack? Do you mean Jack Graystone?"

"Yes, Master Wilder. Jakabar of the Gray Stone was a runelord." Oragien lifted his staff and pointed it directly at Travis's chest. "And so are you."

43.

"What did you want to tell me, Grace?" Beltan said, a solemn note entering his usually bright tenor.

Grace glanced over her shoulder. She and Durge had drawn Beltan aside, leaving the others in the circle of stumps around the fire pit. Daynen asked questions Grace could not hear and which Lirith was evidently trying to answer, while Tira squatted on the ground, playing in the dirt with her burnt doll as Aryn watched. Meridar stood apart from them, hand on the hilt of his sword, his homely face hard—all except for his eyes, which were soft as they gazed upon the young baroness. Grace sighed and turned back to the two men.

"Beltan, there's nothing I want more than for you to come with us. I think—no, I know we can use your help. And I've missed you. We've missed you. But"—she gestured to the tree forts all around—"are you sure you can leave?"

The knight's yellow mustache curved down around his mouth. "What do you mean?"

Durge cleared his throat. "I believe, Sir Beltan, that Lady Grace is concerned your orders will not permit you to part from your troop."

Beltan stared at them, then grinned. "Well, then there's nothing to worry about. I get to make my own orders. That was part of my bargain with Sir Vedarr when I joined the Order of Malachor."

"Sounds convenient," Grace said.

"It is." Beltan met her eyes, and his grin faded. "But I haven't forgotten my duty, Grace. I was charged with the task of finding the source of the fires. And now we know that means the Burnt Ones. So it's only right that I go with you."

A frown chiseled furrows even deeper into Durge's brow. "How is that so?"

Grace looked at Beltan—like Durge, she failed to see the logic of his conclusion.

The blond man scratched his chin. "So you mean you don't think there's a connection between Travis's coming and theirs? The *krondrim*, I mean."

Grace's mouth dropped open, but she could find no words to speak. How could she have not seen it before? Everything had been right there in her dreams about Travis: the firedrake, the red star, the flames. And, once, the perfect black eyes with which he had gazed at her. But the dreams had ceased after her vision of Travis at the Gray Tower, and in her urgency to get to him she had forgotten them. Now all the images rushed back to her, and she found herself shaking.

Two sets of strong, callused hands reached out to steady her.

Grace managed a weak laugh. "Well, a girl knows she's in a bad spot when she needs two knights in shining armor just to prop her up."

Durge raised an eyebrow. "My lady?"

She shook her head, then waved a hand, indicating she could stand on her own. And indeed, when the knights released her shoulders, she did not fall face first to the ground.

Beltan's eyes were still concerned. "Are you all right, Grace?"

Odd for someone to be asking the doctor that question. However, she gulped in air and gave a nod. "You just caught me by surprise, Beltan, that's all. I hadn't thought about the . . . the connection between Travis and the Burnt Ones. I don't think Durge had either."

The Embarran shook his head.

Beltan shrugged broad, rangy shoulders. "Sorry. I thought if I could see it then it had to be pretty obvious. I usually expect you and Durge to have everything all figured out ahead of time."

Grace's lips turned up in a sharp smile. "I wouldn't expect too much, if I were you."

They returned to the others then, and informed them that Beltan would indeed be joining them on their journey to the Gray Tower. At this news, Aryn's face lit up.

"Oh, Beltan!" she cried, and in that moment she seemed more like a girl just on the edge of adulthood than a young woman experimenting with newfound power. She rushed to the big knight and threw herself into his arms.

Beltan's smile twisted into a grimace, and a grunt

of pain escaped his lips. A troubled look replaced the joy on Aryn's face as she stepped back. The knight pressed a hand to his side, his visage pale.

Lirith moved forward and laid a brown hand on the sleeve of Beltan's green tunic. "Are you well, Sir Knight?"

Grace answered before he could. "It's the wound. The one you received on Midwinter's Eve. It's been bothering you, hasn't it?"

He straightened, and the expression of pain left his face, but Grace could see the tightness along his jaw, and she knew the effort had cost him.

"A little," he said. "And only every once in a while. But it's well closed now. So what's there to worry about?"

Plenty, Grace wanted to say. The wound in his side he had suffered at the claws of the *feydrim* should have killed him. And it would have, had it not been for the intervention of the fairies. She pressed her lips together and said nothing.

Beltan gave a cheerful laugh. "Besides, what's a knight without a few battle scars, eh?"

Grace had a feeling these words were for the benefit of Daynen and Tira, whose respective ears and eyes were locked on the big knight. The boy grinned, and even Tira smiled, although the expression was fleeting, and she bent back over her doll.

"I've got to talk to Sir Tarus," Beltan said to Grace and Durge. "Get your things together, then come find me."

Fifteen minutes later they found Beltan on the other side of the camp, beneath the largest of the tree forts, speaking with the red-haired Sir Tarus. The two knights stood close, shoulders touching, heads bent together. They looked up as the others approached.

Tarus grinned at Lirith. "And was it something I said that is causing your swift departure, my lady?"

"No, good sir." She rested her chin on a hand. "But

tell me, does the need for wearing armor necessarily preclude the ability to bathe frequently?"

The handsome young knight did not back off from the charge. "No, my lady. We simply prefer it like this. It's all very manly."

Lirith's small nose wrinkled. "Indeed."

Tarus laughed, and Lirith flashed one of her mysterious smiles.

"Sir Tarus," Beltan said, and at once the red-haired knight snapped around.

"Yes, my lord?"

Beltan held out a piece of rolled vellum sealed with wax. "Here's the missive I penned for Sir Vedarr. It explains I'm accompanying the duchess of Beckett to Ar-tolor and beyond, and the reason why. See to it that it gets to him."

"Without fail, my lord." Tarus's words were crisp, but there was a softness in his eyes, almost like sorrow. His gaze lingered on Beltan as he took the missive.

Beltan turned with a muffled jingle—he wore a mail shirt beneath his forest-colored cloak now. "Sir Meridar," he addressed the knight, "weren't you going to join the Order of Malachor after seeing Lady Grace to Perridon?"

Meridar gave a jerk, as if startled, then nodded. "That was my intention."

Beltan nodded. "It's hard to say how long it will be before we can fulfill the king's orders and take Lady Grace to Castle Spardis. If you'd like, you can join the order now and remain here with Sir Tarus. I will write a missive to Boreas, releasing you from your duty to him."

Grace started to agree—it seemed a logical suggestion—but Meridar spoke in a stony voice.

"I will not forsake my duty, Sir Knight."

Beltan took a step back, and Grace stared at Meridar. His plain face was flat and without emotion, but she thought she caught a momentary twitching of his cheek. Before she could be certain, Meridar turned his back and strode to his charger.

Beltan cast a look at Grace. "Is he all right?"

To Grace's surprise, Aryn answered first, her voice soft. "I'll go talk to him."

The baroness followed after the knight. Grace watched her go. Maybe she had underestimated her friend these last days. Or maybe it was just that Aryn was like any young woman of nineteen: a child trying to turn herself into an adult, and trying not to lose herself in the process.

Durge glanced up at fragments of sky through the canopy of the trees. "The day is wearing on."

"We'd better go then," Beltan said. He gazed at the red-haired knight. "Good luck, Tarus. I know you'll be a fine leader for these men. Better than me, I'm sure."

Crimson flushed the young knight's cheeks. He saluted with a fist. "Vathris speed you on your journey."

Beltan nodded.

"And Beltan"—Tarus drew in a deep breath—"I will . . . that is, we will miss you, my lord."

Grace studied Sir Tarus, then nodded, making her diagnosis. The signs all had been there: the closeness with which they had stood, the long glances, the way their hands had touched when the missive was exchanged. Whether they had shared a bed or not, she didn't know, but it was clear the young knight worshiped Beltan. And she supposed Beltan had not been opposed to accepting Tarus's interest. Tarus was bright and kind, and certainly more than handsome enough.

However, while the smile Beltan cast at Tarus was fond, it was also transitory, and as he turned away his eyes were distant, as if already focused on the gray spire at the end of their journey. He did not see the way Tarus's shoulders crunched inward, but Grace did. It was always so much easier for the loved than the lover, wasn't it? She vowed not to forget that, as if she needed another reason to avoid such intimacy.

As they approached the horses, Grace heard the sound of low voices. Aryn spoke to Meridar, her blue eyes intent, and he stood stiffly, half-turned toward her, half-away. However, what they were saying Grace did not hear, and the two broke away from each other as the rest of the traveling party approached.

Meridar mounted his charger. "I will bring up the rear," he said, and he wheeled the horse around—although not before throwing one last look at Aryn.

They all climbed onto their horses and followed Beltan's bony roan charger down the trail. At once trees closed in behind them, and the camp of the knights was lost to view.

All afternoon they rode through the woods. As before, Tira sat on Shandis in front of Grace, and Daynen shared Lirith's horse. The women traveled together, while Durge and Beltan kept a short distance ahead. Meridar was usually out of sight behind them, although from time to time Grace heard the clopping of his warhorse's hooves.

The hush of the forest should have put Grace at ease—usually she enjoyed the quiet. However, for some reason she couldn't explain, the silence chafed against her nerves, and she gripped Shandis's reins in tight-fingered hands. After riding for an hour, Grace thought about bringing Shandis close to Aryn's horse. She wanted to ask the baroness about what Meridar had said. However, the idea of breaking the silence was too discomforting. Even Daynen, who usually chattered like a squirrel, spoke little, and when he did his piping voice echoed harshly on the air, so that Lirith took to hushing him.

Just as the light was fading from green to gray beneath the trees, the forest ended in an abrupt wall.

Grace let out a sigh as they found themselves on the edge of a narrow, sloping plain that ran parallel to the forest. Not two furlongs away was a broad swath of silver reflecting the waning daylight. Grace searched with her eyes, then saw it nearly directly ahead: a series of five symmetrical arches spanning the swift-moving river.

"The air has changed," Daynen said. "I smell water."

"You have a good nose," Lirith said. "It's the Dimduorn that you smell. We've left the forest, and now the River Darkwine is just ahead."

Durge eyed the failing light. "Should we cross the river on the morrow?"

Beltan shook his head. "No, we'll want to cross the bridge now. The ground is higher on the other side. It'll be better for making camp." His grin flashed in the gloom. "Unless some of you happen to like sleeping in a marsh."

Marsh lost by consensus, and the travelers rode toward the bridge.

It was hard to say exactly why, but for some reason Grace was relieved when Shandis's hooves echoed off timeworn stone. For the entire journey east, the Dimduorn had seemed like a barrier between them and Travis. It would be good to finally leave the river behind them. Gathered in a close knot, the riders started across the old Tarrasian bridge.

They were halfway to the other side when Daynen tilted his head back and sniffed the air. "Now I smell smoke."

Aryn frowned in the twilight. "So do I."

Grace drew in a lungful of air, then she caught it, faint but acrid. Beltan lifted a hand, and hooves scraped against stone as the party came to a halt on the bridge. Grace stiffened in the saddle. *Why are we stopping?* she started to say, but the words turned to ash on her tongue.

On the other side of the river, forms moved across the undulating landscape, approaching the bridge. They were shadows in the gloaming, shaped like spindly people, but as dark as the coming night. A parched wind sprang out of nowhere and blew across the bridge, like the air from an oven. Grace heard a stifled scream beside her, followed by a low oath from one of the knights.

A small hand reached up to touch Grace's cheek. She looked down into Tira's frightened eyes.

"The Burnt Ones are coming," Grace whispered.

Tira nodded, looked back down, and cradled her doll.

44.

Silver twilight stretched across the land on either side of the Dimduorn: a thinner and thinner membrane separating day from night.

"How many of them do you see?" Durge said. The Embarran's grim face shone like a ghost in the gloom.

Beltan nudged his charger forward, peered past the end of the bridge, then shook his head. "It's hard to say. There might be three, maybe four."

Grace tried to count the *krondrim*, but it was impossible to hold them with her eyes. They melted in and out of the gloaming, vanishing only to reappear in a different—and closer—place. Then she caught the red flickers low to the ground, like crimson blossoms unfurling in the dusk. The grass of the plain was igniting under their feet, burning brightly for a moment, then dimming to ash. By the telltale light she was able to guess the number of the dark beings.

"Five," she said, her voice turned into a croak by the hot wind. "There are five of them."

Already the Burnt Ones were less than a furlong

from the river, lurching forward in a rough semicircle so that there was no clear route past them. Grace guessed they had two minutes, maybe three until the *krondrim* reached the bridge.

Hooves rang out on stone as Meridar pressed his charger forward. "Sir Beltan, were you and your men not tracking the movements of these creatures? Did you not know they would be in this place?"

Beltan threw his cloak back over his shoulders, and his chain mail gleamed in the pale light. "We had heard reports they were traveling along the river. But I had no idea they had come this far south, or this close to Ar-tolor."

"What must we do?" Lirith said, her calm voice like a salve to Grace's sizzling nerves.

Beltan glanced at the witch. "From all the stories I've heard, they don't move fast. And they only burn what's in their path. If we go back the way we came, we should be able to outride them easily enough."

A cold needle injected panic into Grace's chest. "But that means not crossing the bridge. Is there another way over the river?"

He met her eyes, then shook his head. "I'm sorry, Grace."

She nodded. There was no other choice; if there were, Beltan would have offered it. How they would cross the Darkwine now and get to Travis before the full moon, Grace didn't know. But they would do Travis no good if they were burned to cinders here. They had to turn back.

Durge nudged Blackalock's flanks and brought the charger alongside Shandis. The knight reached out, hesitated, then laid a gloved hand on Grace's arm. "Come, my lady."

She pressed her hand over his, then let go. Together, the travelers turned their horses around and started back over the bridge. Tira squeezed her thin body back, and Grace did not resist the closeness. She held the girl against her.

Just as they reached the west end of the stone span, Lirith spoke in a quiet voice. "Lord Beltan, do the men of your company ever patrol this near to the river?"

He frowned, glancing at her. "Sometimes. Why?"

"I see torches among the trees."

Grace sucked in a breath. Even as Lirith spoke, she saw them: red sparks winking in and out of existence against the dark line of trees four hundred yards away. Then the lights moved from the trees, onto the open land between river and wood.

"Those aren't torches," she said, her voice rising.

Beltan swore a low oath.

"There must be ten of them," Meridar said. "Twenty."

Durge let out a rumbling breath. "More."

Spindly, onyx forms lumbered from all directions, approaching the west side of the bridge, leaving snaking trails of fire in their wake.

A strangled sound escaped Aryn's throat. "I don't understand. What do they want from us?"

"Maybe nothing," Beltan said. "We don't know what their purpose is. I suppose we were just lucky enough to get in their way."

"We must head back over the bridge," Durge said. "There are fewer of them on the east side of the river."

Beltan nodded. "And if we can get past those, then we can outride the ones coming from the west."

And how are we going to get past even five of them? Grace tried to say. But the parched air had fused her throat shut.

They wheeled their mounts around and pounded over to the Tolorian side of the bridge. The horses snorted and rolled their eyes; the beasts smelled fire.

"I'm afraid," Daynen said, his voice warbling.

Lirith circled her arms around the boy and held him close.

The five *krondrim* on the east side had continued their approach. They were thirty yards from the bridge now and closing, setting the grass ablaze wherever they stepped.

Beltan swung his legs over his charger's back and hit the ground with a dissonant ringing of chain mail. "Everyone, get off your horses. It's going to be hard to control them when those things get close."

Durge reached up and drew his greatsword from the sheath on his back. Colorless light reflected by the river shone off the flat of the blade, and its edge was stained with crimson. "My lady," he said to Grace. "You and the others must stay behind us. Be sure to keep the children with you."

Grace gave a wordless nod.

They left the horses in a knot to the right side of the bridge. Grace, Aryn, and Lirith stood in the place where stone met turf, Daynen and Tira in their midst, while the three knights fanned out in front, swords raised. Grace watched the lines of fire draw closer and wished Melia were here. On Midwinter's Eve, the amber-eyed lady had managed to hold dozens of snarling *feydrim* at bay in the great hall of Calavere. If only Grace had such power.

But don't you have power, Grace? Maybe it's not like Melia's. But you were able to conjure a wind in Falanor, enough to move fog, at any rate.

However, she didn't know what good that did her. It was going to take more than a breeze to hold the *krondrim* back. The Burnt Ones were ten paces away now. Five. Still, Grace could make out no distinguishing features: only the sharp outlines of their bodies, so dark she saw them as holes in the gloom.

"Get ready," Beltan said to the other knights. "And whatever you do, don't let them touch you."

Durge and Meridar tightened their grips on their

swords. The *krondrim* covered the last remaining distance and reached out sooty hands. Heat rolled off of them in choking waves.

Durge's sword was the longest, and he struck first, a powerful blow aimed at the center of the nearest creature's body. There was a harsh clanging, as of metal on stone. Both Durge and the *krondrim* stumbled back. The Embarran recovered, then raised his sword again. The tip of the blade glowed a dull red, as if it had just been pulled from the coals of a forge, then dimmed as it cooled again. The Burnt One staggered, then started forward once more.

Two other *krondrim* closed in, and—like Durge—Beltan and Meridar were able to beat them back with their swords. However, the blades did not seem to harm the creatures. Their skin was like rock hardened from lava. The Burnt Ones moved forward again, joined now by the rest of their kindred.

In ones and twos the *krondrim* lurched toward the foot of the bridge, only to fall back under the onslaught of the knights. Sweat poured down the faces of the men, and they shifted their grips constantly against the hilts of their hot swords. How long could the knights stand the furnace? And how long would the *krondrim* attack only one or two at a time?

A puff of hot, gritty air struck Grace's face, and tears ran from her stinging eyes. She blinked the tears back—

—and saw Tira walking away from her.

"Tira!" she hissed, snatching out her hands to clutch the girl. She was too slow. Tira started forward, in the direction of the battle, and Grace let out a strangled scream. Then the girl turned, dodged the stamping legs of the terrified horses, and squatted beside the bank of the river, just to the right of the bridge. Small waves lapped at her bare toes. She pulled her charred doll from her smock, dipped it into the water, and looked back in Grace's direction.

Grace stared, paralyzed. What was the girl doing? Then Tira submerged the doll again, and Grace understood.

"The water!" she shouted to the knights. "We have to get them into the water. It's the only way to harm them."

None of the men looked her way, but a grunt from Durge let her know he had heard. He started to back away, toward the strip of shore just left of the bridge, opposite Tira and the horses. Beltan and Meridar followed, as did the *krondrim*. Tira dashed back to Grace's arms. Grace gripped the girl tightly, then pushed her behind Lirith and Aryn, up onto the bridge. How the girl had known what to do was a mystery that would have to wait for later.

"Stay here," she said to Tira. "You too, Daynen." She nudged both boy and girl a dozen paces up the bridge. Daynen's face was a mask of fear as he found Tira with blind hands and held her close. Grace turned and moved back down to the other women, at the foot of the bridge.

"Come!" Meridar hissed. Flames reflected off his eyes. "See if you can melt this blade before it cuts you in two!"

He shook his sword at the Burnt Ones. Blisters dotted his face. The knights' armor gleamed in the light of small grassfires, and Grace knew they were baking inside the metal.

"Keep moving them toward the water!" Beltan called.

Durge grunted in assent. The knights kept falling back and left, and the *krondrim* staggered after them. Five feet from the river, now three, now one. The heels of Beltan's boots touched the waves washing up on the bank.

The Burnt Ones stopped.

The knights moved back another pace, letting the water rise up to their knees. The *krondrim* milled back and forth on the shore, reaching onyx hands toward the men. But they did not step into the water.

Grace saw it—the flaw in their plan. Water had the power to harm them. And that meant the Burnt Ones would never follow the knights into the river. Hot tears blurred her vision.

"Grace."

Lirith's voice was soft, but somehow it cut through the smoke and despair that dulled her mind.

"Grace, look."

There was a muffled gasp beside her. Aryn. With her fingers, Grace wiped her eyes clear. Unwilling to tread into the river, the *krondrim* had turned away from the shore. Now they walked in a new direction—one, thanks to Grace's plan, no longer blocked by the knights or their swords.

"Grace!" Aryn's voice was a hoarse whisper. "What do we do?"

Grace hesitated, then reached out and took the hands of the others into her own. Lirith gave a solemn nod, and Aryn squeezed back tightly. Together the three women watched as the Burnt Ones shambled toward them.

45.

With a great frothing, the knights pounded out of the river and onto the shore. However, the water held them back, slowing their action. The *krondrim* were well away from them—and only a matter of feet from the foot of the bridge.

Grace glanced over her shoulder at the children who stood on the bridge twenty feet behind her. "Daynen, stay put. And hold on to Tira. Do you understand me?"

He nodded, his blind eyes wide, and tightened his

grip on Tira's shoulders. Grace turned back, and a searing wave of heat struck her in the face. She willed her legs into columns. If she could delay the Burnt Ones, even for a few seconds, the knights might have time to save the children.

And how will you accomplish that, Grace?

But she already knew the answer to that question. For all its frailty, flesh was not so easily consumed. Even the white-hot fires of the crematorium at the hospital took time to reduce a body to ashes.

A shout rose above the crackling of burning grass. "Adagar! Lunge!"

At the call, one of the horses reared onto its hind legs: Meridar's charger. The charger let out a trumpeting call, its muzzle wet with foam and the whites of its eyes showing. However, such was its training that the warhorse heeded the command of its master. It burst from the knot of horses and charged directly into the line of approaching *krondrim*. Hooves crashed down, striking sparks against hard flesh. Several of the Burnt Ones tumbled to the ground—then clambered to their feet again. Black hands reached out to stroke glossy flanks.

The charger screamed: a squealing, impossibly high-pitched sound that shredded Grace's nerves. The horse crashed to the ground, legs flailing, as the flames engulfed it far more swiftly than she had thought possible. She heard oaths from the knights, but they were lost in another animal shriek. Then the sound ended as the horse's legs went stiff. The *krondrim* moved past the smoking carcass, continuing on their path toward the bridge.

Now, at last, the beings were close enough for Grace to make out details of their features. In a way they still seemed human. Here and there lumps suggested noses, chins, breasts. Their skin was smooth and textureless, like volcanic glass, but lined with a

webwork of cracks through which a dim, red luminescence welled like blood.

Durge and Beltan labored after the creatures,
swords before them. Meridar followed just on their
heels. However, Grace knew the men would not
make it in time. She gazed into eyes like black stones:
hard, reflective, and utterly dead.

Next to her, Aryn whispered a prayer to the goddess Yrsaia. Lirith chanted something as well: Grace
caught the word *Sia* once, then again. She opened her
own mouth, but what words could she speak? What
god could she pray to? If she believed in one, she
would have asked it to part the river, to raise the
water into the sky, then have it come crashing down
on those who would pursue and slay. But she did not
believe.

*Then you do it, Grace. Play God. Isn't that what
doctors do every day?*

There was no more time to think. Obsidian hands
stretched toward her. Aryn screamed. There was an
odd sizzling sound, and dimly Grace knew it to be the
sound of her own hair shrinking and curling from
the heat. She shut her eyes, then reached out with the
Touch.

This time she was not afraid of the shadow lurking
on the edge of her vision. She did not need to follow
the thread—her own thread—that led to it. Without
hesitating, she grasped the silvery lines she knew belonged to Lirith and Aryn. Now what?

*You did it with fog, Grace. Water is the same stuff,
just a little denser. You need a better net, that's all.*

There was no time to weave the threads of the
Weirding. Instead she imagined the net in its entirety,
and it was there, shimmering in her hands. She cast it
toward the flowing stream of silver she knew to be
the river, then gasped at the flood of power that
washed through her. There was a life in the river that
mist could never hold. She nearly lost herself in the

myriad of swimming, floating, darting sparks of energy in the water. Then she forced herself back from the edge, clutched the net, and pulled.

It was heavy, terribly heavy. She couldn't do it; the force of the river was far too great, dragging her down. Then two pairs of cool, shining hands reached out alongside hers.

We're here, Grace.

Together they pulled, but still the net she had woven would not budge. Then Grace understood. They were struggling against the vast, endless flow of the Weirding in the river, and against so great a force they could never win. But what if she was to draw on that force rather than fight it?

With a single thought Grace reshaped the net into a glowing cup, and she let all the threads of the river pour into it.

Now!

Three sets of bodiless hands touched the cup and—in a simple motion—tipped it over. Silver poured out, streaming in a new direction.

There was a great rushing noise, followed by a crash and a terrible hissing. Grace's eyes flew open in time to see the *krondrim* stumble back as a wave spilled over the banks of the river and onto the land. She scrambled up onto the bridge with Aryn and Lirith, avoiding its flow.

The wave was not large. It came no higher than the knees of the Burnt Ones. All the same, the creatures flung their arms up as it washed around them, the black pits of their mouths open but unable to scream.

The cold water screamed for them, shrieking and bubbling around their legs, sending plumes of steam into the air. The *krondrim* fell into the water, stiffening as they did, like molten steel hardened in an instant in a quenching bucket. More steam billowed upward. Then the water receded, draining back into the river, leaving the stiff, twisted forms of the Burnt Ones to cool upon the shore.

Grace staggered to the foot of the bridge, still clutching Aryn and Lirith. Beltan reached them first, followed by Durge. However, Meridar lingered, gazing at the now-extinguished husk that had been his warhorse, his eyes as flat and unreadable as those of the Burnt Ones.

Beltan gripped Grace's shoulders with strong hands. His green eyes were wide with many questions, but the one he asked was, "Are you well, Grace?"

She gave a shallow nod—all the answer she could manage.

Durge stepped forward. "Lady Aryn? Lady Lirith? You are safe as well?"

The two women embraced one another. Lirith opened her mouth to reply.

She was interrupted by a sizzling sound. The steam had hidden it, but now it stepped from one of the roiling clouds, its feet hissing against the damp ground with each step. Grace stared, unable to move. So she had miscounted after all. But it must have followed the rocky line of the shore, where no fires would betray its presence.

Before any of them could react, the Burnt One lurched forward. Grace and Beltan were the nearest. She went rigid, wondering how quickly the flames would take her. The *krondrim* gazed at her with eyes as flat as death—

—then shambled past her and up onto the bridge.

A thin, piteous scream knifed the air. Grace jerked her head around. On the center of the bridge, twenty feet away, Tira scrabbled at Daynen's tunic, staring as the Burnt One approached. The left side of her face was twisted by terror, while the scarred flesh of the right remained smooth as ever.

"Daynen!" Lirith called. "Don't move!"

"What is it?" the boy cried, tears streaming from his sightless eyes. He clutched Tira's trembling body.

Durge sprang forward onto the bridge, then let out a curse and leaped back. He stamped his feet, and only then did Grace see that his boots were smoking.

She looked back at the bridge and gasped. Pits marked the stone where the Burnt One's feet had sunk into it. A dull red glow spread outward from them, and in moments the entire surface of the bridge between the shore and the *krondrim* glowed in the thickening dark. Just beyond the Burnt One, the children huddled together on as yet cool stone.

"It's hot," Durge said through clenched teeth, still stamping his feet.

The *krondrim* neared the two children. Tira screamed again. Grace clutched at Beltan, thinking this the end, but instead the Burnt One halted. It seemed to gaze at the children—no, at Tira. Then, in a slow, stiff motion, the *krondrim* bent forward. What was it doing? Ice replaced fire as Grace understood.

It's bowing to her—showing obeisance.

Tira's scream ended, and the fear drained from her face, so that both halves were tranquil. She gazed at the Burnt One with calm eyes, then reached a small hand toward its body.

"It's going to burn them!" Aryn cried. "Somebody do something!"

Jump, Grace started to shout, but she was startled into silence by a dull blur that moved past her and dashed onto the bridge. Another scream shattered the air—the deep, horrible scream of a man in agony. Meridar.

The knight stiffened as smoke rose from his boots, and moisture poured down his face. Clenching his jaw, he ran across the half-molten stone of the bridge, his chain mail glowing in the bloody light. The *krondrim* turned around, but its reaction was too slow. Meridar reached out, then coiled his arms around the Burnt One, hugging it close to his body.

The sizzle of flesh cooking was audible on the air. Another scream ripped itself from his lungs, and only after a second did Grace realize it was a word.

"Aryn!"

Then the momentum of Meridar's dash carried him forward, along with the Burnt One. In a ball of flame they toppled over the side of the bridge and plunged into the swift waters of the river below. There was a hiss, quickly extinguished, then silence. After several heartbeats a pair of dark, intertwined forms bobbed to the surface of the water. Then they sank again and were gone.

Aryn took a staggering step forward. "Sir Meridar . . ."

Lirith reached out and caught the young woman, holding her back from the foot of the bridge.

"Vathris keep him," Beltan said in a hoarse voice.

Grace disentangled herself from the blond knight's arms and gazed at the fiery trails snaking on the other side of the river. They had almost reached the west side of the bridge. She licked parched lips, then spoke the words softly, so Daynen and Tira could not hear.

"The others are coming."

Beltan followed her gaze. "We've got to get the children off the bridge."

Durge approached the foot of the bridge, then was driven back by the fierce heat. Half the bridge, between the eastern shore and the children, still glowed dull red. "We must wait for the bridge to cool," the knight said.

Beltan shook his head. "We can't wait. In two minutes the other *krondrim* will reach the west side of the bridge. If Meridar made it across, then so can I."

With a powerful hand, Durge gripped Beltan's arm and halted the big knight. "I have never heard it spoken that Sir Beltan of Calavan was a man who would discard his life without purpose. Sir Meridar made it across the stones, yes, but by the time he reached the children he was already dead. Would you join him, then, along with the children?"

The two men locked eyes, then Beltan grunted. Durge released him.

"So what do we do?" Beltan said.

The crimson light played across Aryn's pale features. "The river. They can jump in the river."

"No," Durge said. "The Dimduorn is too deep here, and its undercurrents too swift. Surely they will drown."

Beltan started to shrug off his mail shirt. "You're right, Durge. But it's still their only chance. Once they jump, you and I will have to—"

"*Daynen! No!*"

Grace had never heard Lirith scream before, not even when Garf was attacked by the bear. She looked up, and her heart became ash in the pit of her chest. Daynen had lifted Tira onto his shoulders. Even as Grace watched, the blind boy took another step along the bridge, placing his bare feet on hot, glowing rock.

Sickness strangled Grace's throat. There was nothing any of them could do but watch. Pain contorted Daynen's face as he moved down the bridge. He stumbled as his feet became lifeless blocks, but he did not halt. Tira sat still on his shoulders, her small hands pressed against his cheeks.

It seemed an eternity Grace was forced to watch, but it was only seconds until Beltan was able to reach out with long arms and snatch both Daynen and Tira off of the bridge. Tira coiled her arms around the big knight's neck and gazed down as Lirith fell to her knees beside the boy. Grace knelt beside her, but she already knew what the diagnosis would be.

They made him comfortable on the grass. His face was pale, smeared with sweat and soot, but it was peaceful now. That was the one blessing of burns like this—there were no more nerve endings in his charred legs to transmit pain.

Daynen gazed up, searching with his unseeing eyes. "Lady Lirith?"

"I am here." Tears shone in her eyes, but her voice was low and soothing.

"Is Tira all right?"

"She is well. Do not fear."

"I'm not . . . afraid."

His words were getting fainter now, and the trembling in his body was easing. Shock was setting in quickly. It wouldn't be long now.

"It was just . . . just like I saw it, Lady Lirith. Only now I know who it was . . . who I was carrying."

The witch smoothed damp hair from his brow. "What do you mean, Daynen?"

"It was Tira. That's who I saw. I carried her over . . . the bright fields . . . of the sun." Daynen's lips curved into a smile. "It was . . . it was so . . ."

Grace watched the life flow out of him, and his thin body grew still. A small form slipped from Beltan's arms and padded across the ground. Tira. She squatted down and touched Daynen's face, running her fingers over his lips, his nose, his staring eyes. Then she turned and clambered into Grace's arms. Grace watched the approaching fires.

"We must go," Durge said. The knight had gathered the frightened horses back together.

Beltan knelt and, as if lifting a small bundle of rags, rose with Daynen in his arms. Lirith remained kneeling, Aryn's hands on her shoulders, as Beltan walked to the edge of the river, bent again, and let the small body go into the dark, swirling waters. He returned to Lirith and helped her to her feet.

"Can you ride?" he said.

"I can."

They mounted their horses. The animals stamped and snorted, anxious to run from the reek of smoke and fire.

From the back of her palfrey, Aryn glanced at the bridge, then spoke in a quiet voice. "In the forest, before we left the camp, Meridar told me that he was ashamed of what he had done in Falanor. He said he had acted without honor, that for revenge he would have harmed the innocent and weak. He said he wanted to redeem himself, and to prove himself good in . . ." She swallowed hard. ". . . in my eyes."

Grace stared at her, then spoke the only words she could find. "Did he?"

Aryn shook her head, the wetness on her cheeks shining in the cast-off light of flames. "What was there to prove?"

The baroness turned her horse around and started down the road. The others followed. As they galloped, Grace looked down at the red-haired girl wedged before her on the saddle. In her mind she saw the way the *krondrim* had bowed before Tira. But what had it meant?

Maybe it was like a greeting, Grace. One burnt one to another . . .

Despite her scorched skin, Grace shivered as she urged Shandis after the other horses, into the east and the night, leaving the fires behind.

46.

Maybe Oragien was right. Maybe he really was a runelord. All the same, Travis had the feeling he was far from one of the greatest wizards Eldh had ever known.

Master Larad glared at Travis's wax tablet. "You've transposed *stone* and *sky*. Again, You've crossed *iron* on the wrong side. Again. And you've made *water* look like something a child might scrawl in the dirt with a stick." He tossed the tablet onto a table. "This work would shame an apprentice."

Master Eriaun moved across the small room, gray robe whispering, and picked up the tablet. "Now Master Larad, this is not so . . . well it isn't . . ." He sighed. "I do think he's improving."

Travis slumped in his chair. He had warned Oragien he didn't know many runes. Despite this, the All-master had given him to Larad and Eriaun, so that the two might make an assessment of his abilities.

Larad crossed his arms, his black eyes hard. "How can he help us decipher the runestone if he can't even read and write the simplest runes?"

"He is a runelord, Larad."

"So we've been told. But how can we know for certain?"

"He can speak runes, bind them, and break them. One with all three abilities has not been known in Falengarth since the Runelords vanished." Eriaun spread his pudgy hands. "What more on Eldh do you need, Larad?"

By his grunt he needed something else, but what it was he would not say. Larad turned his cutting gaze on Travis. "Evening chorus begins in an hour. I suggest you rest until then. We will resume our work afterward." The master turned and left the windowless chamber.

Eriaun gave Travis a sympathetic look. "You must forgive Master Larad. He is . . . that is to say he . . ." However, if there was in fact a reason to forgive Larad, then Eriaun could not seem to voice it. He smiled weakly, then moved through the door, leaving Travis alone.

Travis leaned back in his chair and lifted a finger to each of his throbbing temples. For three days now

Larad had railed at him, demanding answers, raking his brain for knowledge.

"Once we have made certain you are ready, you will help us read the runestone," Oragien had said the morning of Travis's second day in the tower. "In it you will no doubt see something we have not, some power that will help us work against the *krondrim*."

Travis had almost laughed—he doubted he would ever be ready for *that*—but the seriousness in Oragien's blue eyes had made him choke his laughter back down.

He pressed his aching eyes shut and thought back to the stories Falken had told him about the runestones. Once there had been nine of the stones, forged by the Runelords, containing the keys to all their knowledge and learning. Most of them were lost in the fall of Malachor seven centuries ago. And Travis knew another lay buried—and most likely shattered—beneath the White Tower of the Runebinders. However, at least one of the runestones still remained, here in the Gray Tower.

"Much knowledge has been lost over the centuries," Oragien had told him. "For all our studies, we can comprehend only a fraction of what is carved upon the runestone. You, Master Wilder, will help us learn more."

Travis sighed and opened his eyes. He wished Falken and Melia were here. He was certain they would understand what was happening far better than he did.

Only they're not here, Travis, and you are.

He looked down at his right hand. He had grown used to the tingling beneath his palm, but it was still there—the symbol Jack had somehow branded into his flesh that terrible night beneath the Magician's Attic.

Jakabar of the Gray Stone was a runelord. And so are you.

Oragien's words still echoed in his mind. Even now they stunned him. But hadn't he heard them once before?

It is you who drew me to this place. You are Jakabar's heir!

Yes, it was the final piece of the puzzle. The burnt man was connected to Eldh—maybe even had come from Eldh. The same was true of Jack Graystone. And it was Jack who, just before Travis's first journey to Eldh, had given Travis the Great Stone Sinfathisar. The Stone of Twilight.

The gray stone, Travis said to himself.

Falken's stories told how the Imsari, the three Great Stones, were scattered after the fall of Malachor seven hundred years ago, taken and hidden by the last three runelords. And Deirdre and Hadrian had said that Jack had been alive for at least several centuries. There was only one answer that fit all the evidence. Jack was one of the three runelords who had fled with the Imsari. Somehow he had found his way to Earth. And somehow, that night beneath the antique shop, when the Pale Ones had attacked, Jack had given his power as a runelord to Travis.

But what did it all really mean? Eriaun was right— Travis had spoken, bound, and broken runes. However, he didn't really know how he had done any of those things. It had always simply come to him, usually in a moment of panic.

So Oragien spoke truth. Travis was a runelord—or at least a runelord's heir. He could accept that; he had no choice, given what he knew. But the All-master was wrong in thinking that Travis could help the Runespeakers. It was all he could do to lock up the power inside him, to keep from harming more people as he had in the past.

Maybe Jack gave this power to you, Travis. But that doesn't mean you have to use it. You've got to tell Oragien you can't help him. Tonight.

Resolved, he stood up. However, before he could step into action, a knock sounded at the door. It opened, and a stout young man in a brown robe entered the room.

Despite his troubles, Travis smiled. "Hello, Sky."

The young man's lumpy face twisted into a grin. He nodded and held out a hand, his meaning clear. *Hello to you, Master Wilder.*

"What is it?" Travis said.

Sky spread his arms in a circle, then made jabbering motions with his hands, opening and closing them.

Travis smiled. "The Runespeakers are meeting downstairs. It's time for chorus."

The young man's grin broadened, and he nodded.

Travis knew there would be no chance to talk to Oragien privately during the chorus. And afterward Master Larad and Master Eriaun would have him in their clutches. He supposed it would have to wait for tomorrow. He let out a sigh, gave Sky a faint smile, then gestured to the door.

"Lead the way, my friend."

Those next days moved more swiftly than Travis would have thought. The greater part of each was spent in the windowless chamber high in the tower. There he was subjected to the tortures of Master Larad—cruel and repetitive activities ameliorated only slightly by Eriaun's gentler interruptions.

"This is madness!" Larad erupted during one session, after Travis had mispronounced *Sirith*, the rune of silence, as *Silith*, the rune of stench. "We could better teach a lump of clay to speak runes."

"Calm yourself, Master Larad." Master Eriaun's tone was soothing, although slightly nasal from the way he held his nose against the putrid reek that filled the room. "Take a deep breath and . . . oh, well, perhaps that's not a good idea. But remember Olrig then, and how he surrendered his right hand to the jaws of the dragon Asgarath that he might steal away with the secret of the runes. Knowledge comes only by great sacrifice."

"And I'd rather have both my hands chewed off than instruct such an imbecile." Larad stamped from the room.

Eriaun cast a wan smile at Travis. "I'm sure he didn't mean that like it sounds."

In contrast, Travis was rather certain Larad had meant it *exactly* as it had sounded. But he nodded all the same, then bent back over his tablet.

Despite the tedium of his work with the two masters, it was hard not to be interested in the Runespeakers. Dwelling in the Gray Tower was like seeing one of Falken's tales come to life. Travis doubted there was another place on Eldh where the name Olrig—as well as the names of Ysani and Durnach and the other Old Gods—was still spoken in reverence.

Before long, he found himself looking forward to each evening's chorus. Usually the Runespeakers discussed mundane matters of the tower, but always they ended the chorus by softly speaking a chant of runes. Although he could understand few of the runes, Travis would let himself drift on the tapestry of voices the Runespeakers wove, layer upon layer, voice upon voice, on the thrumming air of the chorus chamber.

While most of his time was spent with Master Eriaun and Master Larad, or in the chorus chamber, Travis did have some time to himself, and this he used to explore the tower. One afternoon he climbed the entire staircase, counting 251 steps—and many more thudding beats of his heart—along the way. At the top he found a triangular platform no more than five paces across, wedged between the three horned minarets that crowned the tower.

After years of driving narrow Rocky Mountain

passes, Travis was used to heights and the feeling of exposure, but the lightness of vertigo filled him all the same as he gazed at the sheer drop below. It was two hundred feet down arrow-straight walls to the spur of rock from which the tower had been carved, and another thousand feet from the crag itself to the tawny plains that swept southward to the horizon.

Travis moved to the other side of the platform. This view was more to his liking, and he looked across a gap to see range after range of knife-edged peaks marching ever more dimly into the north. Those were the Fal Erenn—the Dawning Fells. Below, a narrow ridge connected the tower crag with the nearest mountain, and upon the causeway was carved a narrow, winding track.

With his eyes he followed the path back toward the spire. Just before the tower's door was the only level space on either ridge or crag, a rough half circle perhaps a hundred feet across. In the center of the plateau was a shape so dark that at first Travis thought it to be a pit. Then he squinted and realized the truth.

It was a standing stone. From this distance there was no way to get a sense of scale, but he knew all the same that, were he to stand beneath it, the stone would tower over him. What was its purpose? It seemed so forlorn, all alone on the plateau.

Several more minutes of peering over the edge yielded no answers—only a pair of eyeballs parched from the hot, dry wind. Travis let it blow him back to the stairs.

He had nearly reached the level of his chamber—at the midpoint of the tower—when he rounded a curve and ran into Master Eriaun. Literally. In fact, had he not reacted quickly and shot out an arm, hooking Eriaun's robe, the master might have made one last, interesting discovery in his life: how long it took to fall to the bottom of the tower.

"Well, then," the runespeaker said as he smoothed

his rumpled robe, "that was a most exciting happening. And from it I would gather no one has yet told you the rule of the stairs."

Travis straightened his spectacles on his nose. "The rule of the stairs?"

"Up on the inside, down on the outside."

"Oh. I'll remember next time."

"I'm certain you will." Eriaun's myopic eyes brightened. "But it's by the hand of Olrig that we have come upon each other. For I was just coming to look for you."

They started down the staircase—on the outside of the spiral.

"What is it you wanted, Master Eriaun?"

"It's a small thing, really. Each of us has our own pet subjects, you see. Matters of interest to us. And for many years I have made a study of the Imsari."

Travis cast a startled look at Eriaun. "The Great Stones?"

"Quite right. Most particularly, I've searched many years for knowledge concerning which runes, spoken in what order, might allow one to handle one of the Stones without harm. Not that there will be much cause for doing so, I am sure. But of course, you understand, one most often studies out of curiosity, not need. And I wanted to speak to you because . . . well, it has been said . . . that is to say, you have had some contact. . . ."

"I've held it, if that's what you mean," Travis said in a quiet voice. "The Stone of Twilight."

Eriaun halted on the steps, his eyes distant, and spoke the word like a sigh. "Sinfathisar."

"But I never spoke any runes before I touched it," Travis said. "I'm sorry."

The master's gaze snapped back to Travis. "No? But then, you are a runelord. What else is to be expected? Olrig help me, but I should have thought of that. You need no runes!" Eriaun touched his arm.

"But if thinking back you happen to recall that you *did* in fact speak runes before touching the Great Stone, you will let me know what they were, won't you?"

Travis fumbled for words. "Sure. Of course."

The master beamed, then headed down the steps, leaving Travis at the door to his chamber.

"Thank you, Master Wilder." Eriaun's reedy voice drifted up the staircase. "I shall see you at chorus."

Travis shrugged at his encounter with the peculiar little master, then opened the door to his chamber.

It was only as he shut the door that an odd thought struck him. Eriaun had said he was just coming to see Travis. But at the point where they ran into each other, Travis had not yet descended to the level of his chamber.

So how had Eriaun known to look for him higher in the tower?

47.

The next day, Travis woke hoping to venture outside the tower, to breathe air not confined by stone. However, his work with the Runespeakers lasted from just after dawn until the evening chorus, leaving him no time for explorations. All the day after that, another of the violent thunderstorms—such as the one the night Oragien had found him—held the world captive. It was a queer storm: boiling, angry, and shattered by streaks of sickly yellow lightning.

The morning after the storm dawned hot and clear, and at breakfast Travis learned from Sky—through a series of uncannily descriptive hand gestures—that both Masters Larad and Eriaun were to be occupied until noontime. This was his chance. As he approached the high, triangular door of the Gray Tower, he expected someone to rush up and stop him. Yet no one did.

And why should they? You're not a prisoner here. Even if it feels like Larad is your personal inquisitor.

Although huge, and covered with carved runes, the wooden door swung easily when he pushed it open. He slipped through, into the world beyond.

The path that led from the Gray Tower was narrow and worn deep into solid rock by the passage of countless feet. Travis followed it across the plateau, then walked out onto the causeway, enjoying the heady pull of the drop to either side. After walking halfway across the ridge, he turned back, not wanting to cause any master who happened to look out his window a conniption at the sight of the Runespeakers' last, best hope walking away.

As he moved back onto the plateau, he let his gaze be drawn by the tall shape that dominated the half circle. The standing stone was indeed large, although not so large as he had thought. It was perhaps half again his own height and thick enough that it would take the arms of two good-sized men to encircle it. The stone was nearly black, carved of some volcanic rock that bore little resemblance to the gray stone of the Fal Erenn.

Travis stepped off the well-worn path. As he drew near the stone, the world receded into the distance, and the beating of his heart seemed to cease. Then he saw the single rune incised into the pitted surface of the stone. It was *Sirith.* The rune of silence.

Curious, he tried an experiment. Softly, and without much force—just in case he was wrong—he opened his mouth and spoke a rune. *Sharn.*

It was like speaking into cotton. He felt the rune of water leave his mouth, then it was swallowed in the folds of enchantment surrounding the standing stone.

Travis attempted another experiment. "Hello," he said.

This time the word carried on the air, although muffled. So it was only runes that were silenced by the stone. He stepped away from the artifact, and both world and sound rushed back.

Travis gazed at the stone. Why would an object bound with the rune of silence stand before the Gray Tower? After all, this was the fortress of the Rune*speakers*. In silence, how could they work their craft?

Travis shrugged. The stone certainly wasn't going to answer his question. Above him, the sun was nearing its zenith; Master Larad would be waiting for him. With a sigh, he turned to trudge back to the tower.

It was not until a week after he had resolved to talk to Oragien that Travis finally gained a moment alone with the All-master.

"I spoke with Master Eriaun this afternoon," Oragien said before Travis could open his mouth. "He believes it is nearly time for you to begin searching the runestone."

The words caught Travis off guard. He had come upon the All-master quite by accident in the refectory. It was a large room with tables and benches enough for three hundred runespeakers to sit and eat at once. However, these days there were never more than a third of that. Travis was hungry, and he had come to the refectory in hopes that Sky might be there, preparing the evening meal with the help of the tower's few other servants, and that the young man might be convinced to part with some cheese or an apple a bit early. Instead he had found Oragien, sitting by himself, taking a simple meal of bread and figs.

At last Travis gained the use of his tongue. "Search the runestone for what?"

"For the key, of course." Oragien's eyes were sharp and blue as a winter sky. "The key to defeating the *krondrim*."

Travis stared at the All-master. The burnt man in the saloon had spoken of a key. But what was it?

Beware—it will consume you.

Was it the key he was supposed to beware of? Maybe that was what the burnt man had meant. What was he supposed to beware of if not *them*? The *krondrim*.

Travis drew in a deep breath, then asked the question that had been on his mind ever since waking in the Gray Tower. "All-master, Master Larad said that the Runespeakers had help in summoning me here to Eldh."

"Master Larad says many things," Oragien answered before Travis could go on. His words were not harsh or angry, merely crisp and factual.

"But you did have help, didn't you?"

Oragien nodded. "And does that alter anything?"

"No, of course not." Travis licked his lips. "It's just that . . . I just wanted to know who they were."

To Travis's shock, Oragien laughed, slapping the table with a gnarled hand. "A very good question, Master Wilder. And, if you are lucky, perhaps one day they will tell you. Even I am not certain I truly know the answer to that question."

Travis frowned. This was not the response he had expected. He decided to try one more tactic. "If the Runespeakers summoned me, then why did I appear in the town below the tower?"

Oragien sighed, and the laughter faded from his wrinkled face. "I do not know, Master Wilder. There is much we no longer understand. The runechant with which we summoned you has not been spoken in many centuries. Indeed, it had been long lost, and only recently was revealed to us again."

"But if you didn't know where I would end up, how did you know to find me in the tavern?"

Now a hint of laughter returned. Oragien's eyes

sparkled. "My son, I am the All-master. We have forgotten much, but I am not without my tricks."

Travis decided that was all the information he was going to get. He took a deep breath, then spoke the words he had been rehearsing for the last seven days. "All-master, I say this with respect, but I don't think I have the power to help you against the *krondrim*."

Oragien waved the words aside. "Humility becomes you, Master Wilder. Indeed, it is good and all too rare to see one whose pride has not grown in accordance with his ability. But do not forget you are a runelord. The power to discover the key *is* yours." Oragien's voice grew soft. "If you would so choose to aid us, that is."

Travis opened his mouth, but speech was lost as he realized what had just happened. Oragien, All-master of the Gray Tower of the Runespeakers, had just begged for his help.

Oragien picked up his staff and stood. "Come, Master Wilder. It is time for chorus."

That night, in the chorus chamber, Travis was asked to recount the tale of his first journey to Eldh. As he ascended the dais in the center of the chamber, his knees shook; he was not used to being the center of attention. The air around him whispered with voices past; here, at the focus of the chamber, they abided the longest. How ancient were some of the sounds he could just barely hear? Days? Weeks? Centuries?

Somehow, the thought of all those others standing where he stood now was comforting. Travis spoke, the descriptions of all that had happened to him tumbling out of his mouth. His words echoed around the chamber, each one fading but never quite to silence, weaving a tapestry of sound, until it was almost as if he could see them all there, the ones he spoke of: Melia and Falken, Grace and Beltan, Aryn and Durge.

When he reached the part of his tale that concerned the White Tower of the Runebinders, master, journeyman, and apprentice alike leaned forward, eager to hear of their ancient brethren. Then he spoke of the folly of the Runebinders, and of the blood that had spilled forth with the second breaking of the Foundation Stone. Now cries of dismay mingled with the whispers on the air.

"Master Wilder, you cannot expect us to believe what you say," a harsh voice rang out.

Travis looked up and saw Master Larad striding toward the dais. Heads nodded as he passed; the dark-eyed runespeaker was not the only one who doubted Travis's story.

"How could the Runebinders have spilled the blood of a Necromancer at the founding of their tower? All the Dark Ones were destroyed in the War of the Stones. And even had one survived, how might the Runebinders—who were mortal just as we—have captured such a being?"

Travis opened his mouth, although he was unsure what exactly he would say, but another voice spoke first.

"I believe," a quiet voice said.

All eyes turned toward Oragien, who stood beside his seat, staff in hand.

"Ever were the Runebinders the proudest of the orders," the All-master went on. "They traced their line directly to the runelords who bound the Rune Gate in Shadowsdeep. Mikelos, last All-master of the Runebinders, once said that his order might bind the sun in the sky, if they so wished, so that it would ever be day. A year later, the White Tower fell, and the Runebinders were no more." He turned his gaze on Travis. "Now, at last, we know why."

Heads nodded around the chamber, and some wiped their eyes at the tragedy that had befallen the Runebinders over three hundred years ago. Larad frowned, although he sat and said nothing more. However, all throughout the rest of his tale, Travis felt black eyes on him.

The next evening, just as the sun was sinking into fire, Travis looked up, startled to see Oragien standing in the doorway of his chamber.

"All-master!" Travis rose from his bed—where he had been sitting cross-legged, working with a tablet of runes—and smoothed the wrinkles from his gray robe.

"It is time," the white-haired man said.

"For chorus. Yes, of course. Just let me—"

"No, Master Wilder. There will be no chorus tonight."

Travis froze. There was quiet power in Oragien's voice.

With his runestaff, the All-master pointed through the door. "This way."

Travis managed a nod, then walked after the elder runespeaker. As they started down the staircase, two figures fell in just behind, one short and plump, the other taller, sharper, and darker, and both clad in mist-gray. Larad and Eriaun. They did not speak to Travis, and he did not dare to break the silence himself.

When they reached the lowest level of the tower, Travis thought the procession would stop. Instead, Oragien led the way through an opening Travis had never noticed before: In fact, such were the queer angles of the arch's design and the way it was set into the wall that it was impossible to see the opening until one was already stepping into it.

Beyond the arch was another staircase: smaller, narrower, and lit by a colorless light that sprang from no visible source. Travis lost count of the turns as they continued down. A great weight pressed on the air, and he knew they were descending into the crag from which the spire had been hewn.

Just when Travis was certain that the invisible
force was going to crush his body into so much jelly,
the staircase ended, and he followed Oragien into a
cavernous space. The makers of the tower had left the
walls of this chamber rough, but everywhere inclu-
sions of pale crystal marked them, and these caught
the sourceless light, fracturing it and scattering the
cool shards in all directions.

"What is this place?" he murmured. Unlike the
chorus chamber, the air in this place muted his
words, although it did not smother them as had the
standing stone outside the tower.

Oragien gestured with his staff, pointing to the
center of the chamber. Travis took a halting step
forward.

The stone was half the height of a man, three-
sided, and fashioned of onyx. At first Travis thought
it rested on a stand that was the exact same color as
the walls. As he drew nearer he saw the truth: The
stone floated four feet above the floor of the chamber,
suspended without aid of pedestal or wire.

Gray shapes moved on the edges of Travis's vision—there were others in the chamber, perhaps
twenty masters in all. However, he did not glance in
their direction, for his gaze was caught and held by
the stone.

*No, not stone. Runestone. There's nothing else it
could be.*

Incised over every inch of black stone were small,
angular shapes. Runes. Here and there Travis recognized one of the symbols. Most were alien to him.

He stopped before the runestone and breathed in a
sharp, metallic odor, like the scent of lightning. His
right palm itched, and he reached toward the polished
surface.

"Stay your hand!" a harsh voice spoke, although
the echo was cut short by the stillness of the
chamber.

"No, Master Larad, let him try," another, softer voice said. Eriaun.

Oragien's deep tones cut through the preternatural hush. "Surely the runestone will know its own kind."

Travis held his breath, then laid a finger gently atop one of the runes.

Fhar.

The voice that spoke in his mind sounded like Jack's. But somehow Travis knew it wasn't really Jack who had spoken. It was a part of Jack, that was all. A part of the runelord he had once been, and that he had given to Travis.

Travis shut his eyes, and he could see the rune glowing against the blackness. *Fhar. River.* Yes, of course, it was so clear.

A gasp sounded behind him. Travis opened his eyes, then saw it was not only in his mind that the rune shone. The grooves that formed the rune *Fhar* seemed filled with molten silver, except it remained cool. Travis touched another rune.

Meleq, the voice whispered in his mind. *Wood.*

Like the other, this rune glowed when Travis touched it, and a jolt of energy coursed through him, delicious but fleeting. With light motions, Travis touched three more runes. Each of them burst into silvery life as he listened to the words.

Tisra. Kael. Pehr.

"That is enough, Master Wilder," a voice said, but it was dull and distant. The light of the runes filled him, singing through his veins. He spread his fingers out and with both hands touched the runestone.

Indar. Sefel. Ris.

Brilliant light streamed from the stone as the runes sounded in Travis's mind, each one louder than the last.

Uthen, Halas, Lor.

He stepped back, but still the runes echoed in his mind, no longer spoken in Jack's voice alone, but rather in a chorus of voices that rose in a deafening cacophony. In front of him, the stone began to rotate in midair, spinning like a top, faster and faster, sending wild splinters of silver light careening about the chamber. Travis clutched his hands to his ears, but the voices only grew more clamorous, threatening to split apart his skull.

LavethKrindorAreshJevuWista—

"Dal!"

This rune was spoken, not in his mind, but by a roaring voice that thundered across the chamber. As if a door was shut, the jabbering symphony in Travis's mind ceased. The radiance dimmed to black, and the runestone jerked to a halt, motionless again. Travis stumbled back, his body as brittle as cracked glass. He turned and found himself gazing into bright, angry eyes.

"Why did you not heed me when I told you to stop, Master Wilder?" Oragien said, his voice low now, but no less hard.

Travis fought for words. "I'm sorry. It was . . . it was just so . . ." But he never could have explained how it had felt to be filled with the buoyant light. It was like every possibility come true.

"Never disobey me again, Master Wilder."

The only answer Travis could manage was a shallow nod.

"Do you see now, All-master?" Larad said. His scar-crossed face was flat and emotionless, but a smug light glinted in his black eyes. "This is the danger I warned of. This is what comes of meddling in what we do not understand."

Oragien whirled around and advanced on Larad, his staff gripped in white-knuckled hands. "And what precisely do we understand, Master Larad? Anything?"

The All-master did not wait for a reply. He turned on a heel and strode from the chamber.

Master Eriaun cast a worried glance after him, then sighed, pressing his hands together. "Olrig will guide us."

"Will he?" Larad said. Then he, too, left the chamber.

A sickness swam in Travis's stomach. He gripped his right wrist and gazed down at his hand. On the skin of his palm, the rune of runes shone faintly.

Why, Jack? Why did you have to do this to me?

But this time the voice in his mind was silent.

48.

There was no chorus again the next evening. Master Eriaun told Travis it was because there were many questions to be considered and researched before they could be properly discussed. However, Travis knew the real reason Oragien had canceled the meeting. After the incident with the runestone, there were likely to be many in the tower who agreed with Master Larad—that in letting Travis touch the stone they had dabbled in something perilous and unknown. Were a chorus to convene, those voices would likely speak the loudest and prevail. By avoiding the chorus, Oragien avoided that dissent—and perhaps outright rebellion.

It was nearing sunset when Sky brought a tray with a light supper to Travis's cell.

"Thank you," Travis said. There was bread, soft cheese, and a crock of herb-and-vegetable soup.

Sky smiled and gave a half bow. *You're welcome.*

The homely young man turned, but before he could leave the room, Travis spoke.

"If you can do something, Sky, does that mean you should?"

Travis winced, uncertain what had made him speak the words, and to Sky in particular. Maybe it was simply that there was a peace about the mute young man that Travis envied.

"I mean, even if you have a . . . a power to do something, is it all right not to do it?"

Sky didn't move, and Travis feared he had offended him. Or maybe the young man hadn't understood his words. Then Sky stepped forward. He brought a hand to his throat and the other to his lips, and his eyes went wide, as if he was surprised at a sudden discovery. Opening his mouth, he moved his hands outward, like birds flying from him. Then he lowered his arms and regarded Travis with solemn eyes. The message was clear: *Had I a voice, then I would sing.*

Shame warmed Travis's cheeks. But it wasn't that simple, he wanted to tell Sky. Singing couldn't hurt other people. However, when he looked back up Sky was gone.

By the time Travis finished his supper, twilight drifted through the window, along with a light as silvery as that which had welled forth from the runestone. He lifted his eyes to the window. Outside, the moon was nearly full.

A restlessness stole over Travis. There was no chorus, but that didn't mean he had to stay cooped up in this cell. He moved through the door, onto the great spiral staircase. Before he could decide which direction to go, his feet started taking him upward.

At first he passed doors behind which runespeakers dwelled. Some were ajar, and here and there he caught glimpses of light or snatches of murmured conversation. Once, as he passed a door, loud words spilled forth.

". . . that it is impossible. We have forgotten too

much over the centuries. Far too much. We should not . . ."

Travis hurried up the staircase, leaving the angry voice beneath him.

The tower grew silent. He had ascended above the cells still used by the runespeakers. Now the doors he passed had drifts of dust in front of them. How long had it been since some of these doors had been opened? Years? Decades? More, perhaps.

Travis halted before one of the doors. There was nothing to distinguish it from the others; it was fashioned of the same gray wood, unmarked by rune or symbol. He gripped the tarnished bronze knob and turned. It was not locked. Curiosity filled him, and guilt. He glanced down the staircase, but it was empty.

Curiosity won out.

Travis pushed the door open and stepped inside. At once he choked as dust filled his nose and lungs. He blinked, clearing the grit from his eyes, but still could not see. Even if this room had a window—and he could not tell if it did—night had fallen outside. He considered leaving. Instead he hesitated, then spoke a single, quiet word.

"Lir."

A soft radiance flickered into being, centered in the air just above his head, driving the shadows back to the corners of the wedge-shaped room. Part of him winced at this display of power. But of all the runes he had ever spoken, the rune of light was the gentlest, and it gave him the most comfort. And there was no one else here—no one who might get hurt.

Now that he could see, he peered around the cell. However, it was empty save for a moth-eaten cot and a chair that listed on three legs. With a sigh he stepped back through the door.

Travis knew he should return to his cell. However, as it usually did, boredom got the best of sense. He walked up several steps of the staircase, then opened another door. But the room on the other side was completely empty—without even a scrap of furniture—as were the next three after that.

He shut the last door and leaned against it. A peculiar disappointment filled him. But what had he hoped to find behind the doors? With a shrug, he started back down the staircase, toward his cell.

After three steps he stopped. Had it not been for the pale light hovering above his head—which he had forgotten to banish—he never would have seen it. As it was, there was only a thin shadow, like a crack in the wall.

But the walls of this place don't have cracks, Travis.

He ran his hand along smooth stone. His fingers reached the shadow—then touched nothing. It was an opening in the wall, like the arch that led to the runestone beneath the tower. He only meant to explore it, to see the optical illusion by which the builders of the tower had managed to conceal it, but before he realized what he was doing he had stepped through the arch to the room on the other side.

There was no need of his light there. With a thought, he let it dissipate. A misty glow permeated a space as large as three of the smaller cells put together. Like the other rooms, a veil of dust and cobweb draped the walls and floors. Unlike the others, this room was not empty.

Kneeling, Travis examined one of the pieces of shattered stone that scattered the floor. It was smooth on one edge, sharp on the other. At first he thought the stones must have fallen from above, but a quick look up revealed the ceiling to be as flawless as the rest of the tower. So where had the rubble come from?

He picked up another piece, then stared. It was a hand, broken off at the wrist, larger than his own but perfectly proportioned. He turned the stone hand over, and a thrill coursed through him. Carved into the palm was a symbol. No, not a symbol. A rune, one made of three intersecting lines:

Travis knew the rune well. It was a mirror to the one that, at times, shimmered on his own right palm. The rune of runes. The mark of a runelord.

A quick search of the room confirmed his suspicion. The stones were the remains of a statue. It was a man—or had been at any rate—clad in a flowing robe. From what Travis could make out, his features had been sharp and stern, but the corner of a mouth Travis found seemed to curve upward in a knowing smile, softening the harshness of the countenance. Beyond that, Travis could tell little, save that the entire statue seemed to still be here. He had found two eyes, two ears, and two feet. But, now that he thought of it, only the one hand. Perhaps some of the pieces were missing after all.

Nonsense, Travis. Of course it's all here. And you know perfectly well who it is.

Travis winced at the voice—Jack's voice—as it sounded inside his skull.

Who was it that gave up his hand to the dragon's maw that he might steal away with the secret of the runes?

It never ceased to amaze Travis that Jack could still chastise him even when he wasn't around anymore. But he was right—Travis did know who the statue depicted. In some ways, Travis supposed, he had been the first runelord. Olrig, the Old God called Lore Thief, who stole the secret of rune magic from the dragons and granted it to men.

But not to women. At least Travis had never seen

any women runespeakers. Only witches. Why was that? Perhaps it was simply that women had more sense than men did.

He sighed and gazed at the hand. "Maybe it would have been better if it had all stayed a secret."

"Tell me, Master Wilder, do you often speak to broken statues?"

Travis spun around, still clutching the stone hand. A steel ball of dread wedged itself in his throat. "Master Larad, I didn't see you there. I'm sorry. I know I probably shouldn't have been in here, but . . ."

Larad stepped into the room, the pale light illuminating the fine net of scars that covered his face. "So, can you put it back together?"

Travis gaped. What was Larad talking about?

The dark-haired runespeaker gestured to the stone hand, then to the other pieces. "The broken shards of our lord Olrig. Can you not make them whole again?"

There was a bitterness in Larad's voice that Travis suspected was not reserved for him. All the same, instinct told him this man was dangerous. Travis chose his words one by one.

"I suppose I could try. If I had the right tools."

Larad laughed: a short, mocking sound. "Well, that's more than they would say, I will grant you that, Master Wilder. In all these years, they have never even spoken of trying." Larad walked among the shards of the statue, then he looked up, his gaze piercing. "Tell me, Master Wilder, did you know that it is possible to feel greed for knowledge?"

"What do you mean?" Travis spoke before thinking, but the runespeaker's words were both puzzling and intriguing.

"It is true." Larad bent down, brushed a stone arm, then stood, dusting his hands. "Many of the All-masters of the past were selfish of what they knew. They held their secrets precious, and they perished without passing all their knowledge to their students, clutching it instead to their breasts as they died."

He gestured to the fragments. "There is an enchantment in this statue, one worth recovering. Five centuries ago a journeyman runespeaker working alone could have put it back together. Now all of the masters in the tower together could not do so. Not that any of them have tried." He met Travis's eyes. "Do you understand what I am saying, Master Wilder?"

It was strange, but Travis thought he did understand. "The Runespeakers have given up trying. They think everything's impossible."

"Yes! They're like men dying of thirst, trying to keep the last droplets of water they have from running through the fingers of their cupped hands, when beneath them lies a great well of water, if only they would dig for it."

"That's why they called me here, isn't it?" Travis drew in a breath. "Because they think I can do what they're afraid to try themselves."

Larad's silence was answer enough. Travis gazed down at the hand of Olrig. What Larad had said was important, only he wasn't sure exactly how. With a thumb, he started to trace the rune of runes carved into the hand, then stopped and looked up.

"Why did you come to the Gray Tower, Master Larad?"

The runespeaker's face tightened. At first Travis thought it was anger, then he knew it was something else, something more.

"I was eleven winters old when a runespeaker came to my village." Larad gave a humorless smile. "In those days, our kind could still walk abroad without being stoned. But nor were they greeted with joy. Still, a few boys went to be tested by the runespeaker. My mother sent me, for she still followed many of the old ways, although she did not tell my father."

"And the runespeaker discovered your talent," Travis said quietly.

Larad nodded. "I was the only one in the village with promise. My mother was pleased when I showed her the mark the runespeaker had drawn in ink on my hand. But when my father saw it he flew into a rage. He took up a knife and swore he would cut out my tongue to keep me from speaking runes. But I was of a mind to keep my tongue. I struggled, and so I got these instead." He traced a finger along the white lines marking his face. "That night, after my mother bandaged my wounds, I stole from our house. I could barely see for the blood in my eyes, but all the same I found the campfire of the runespeaker outside the village. He spoke runes of healing over me and brought me back to the tower. And here I have been since."

As Larad spoke, Travis's fingers had curled tighter and tighter around the stone hand. Now he forced them to unclench, then bent to set the hand back on the floor with the other fragments.

"What if you had kept it a secret?" Travis said as he straightened again. "What if you had never told anyone about your power, and had never used it?"

Larad raised a dark eyebrow. "And would that not have slain me more surely than my father's knife?"

The runespeaker did not wait for an answer. He moved to the archway, which was clearly visible on this side.

Travis took a step forward. "Wait," he said, surprised at his own action. "How did you know I was here?"

Larad paused, his eyes unreadable. "I didn't, Master Wilder."

Then the runespeaker was gone, and Travis was alone with the broken remains of a mostly forgotten god.

For several minutes, Travis stood as still as a statue

himself, then the shards came together in his mind, and he knew what he had to do, although the knowledge terrified him. Oragien had summoned him so he could help the Runespeakers. And there was only one way Travis could do that. Before he could consider it further, he hurried from the hidden room and down the staircase.

He half hoped he would run into a runespeaker as he went—someone who might grip his arm, ask what he was doing, and order him to stop—but the stairway was empty. The masters were all in their cells. Travis reached the bottom of the staircase, then moved to another hidden archway. It took him only a moment to find it this time. Then it was down another staircase.

The stairs ended. Travis stepped into the rough-hewn chamber far beneath the Gray Tower. The sourceless glow fell from above, illuminating the stone that hovered in the center.

With deliberate steps, Travis approached the runestone. His mouth had gone dry, and he was trembling beneath his robe, but he did not stop. A thrumming sounded on the air, like the beating of a heart. Travis halted before the stone and ran his eyes over the countless runes incised into its surface. What knowledge, what power, what secrets might they grant him if only he touched them and let them speak in his mind?

No, Travis. It's not you that needs the knowledge. It's the Runespeakers. They have to learn to try for themselves. It's the only way.

He lifted both hands, hesitated, then reached out and touched the runestone. It was so much easier than he ever would have thought. He opened his body and, like a conduit, let the power flow through him as he whispered a single word.

"Reth."

The preternatural hush that hung on the air swallowed the sound of his voice. The faint hum ceased, leaving only silence. Travis took a breath and felt . . . nothing. So he had no power to help after all. He started to move away from the stone.

Crack!

The sound was like a thunderbolt passing through his skull. Travis clutched his hands to his ears, but his flesh might as well have been tissue paper. Before him, the runestone shone blue-silver, then like dark serpents they snaked across the stone's surface: deep, lightless gashes.

"Master Wilder! No!"

The voice was lost in the roar of sound. Travis stumbled back even as the runestone flared, then went dark. Like so much rubble, the shards of the stone fell in a heap to the floor. The noise of thunder receded and was gone. Travis was aware of dim, gray shapes rushing forward. One with a white beard appeared in front of him, blue eyes blazing.

"What have you done? By Olrig, what have you *done*?"

I've just saved you, Travis tried to say. But he could not speak as rough hands grabbed him and dragged him away from the broken remains of the runestone.

49.

Grace stood on the flat knoll beneath which they had made camp the night before and watched as dawn set fire to the sweeping plains of northern Toloria. A wind sprang out of the east, tangling hot fingers through her ash-blond hair. She didn't need to look over her shoulder to know the pale circle of the nearly full moon was just setting in the west. One day. They had one more day.

Boots sounded against the dry grass behind her, and she turned around.

"Grace, what are you doing up here? I finally convinced Durge to lie down and get some rest last night. If he wakes now and sees you're gone, the man will never sleep again."

She smiled at the tall, fair-haired knight, then turned back to face the north. "I know, Beltan. I should go back. But I was just wondering if I could see it from here. The Gray Tower."

Grace heard him move in behind her.

"And can you?"

A sigh escaped her lips. "No, not yet."

His strong hand cupped her shoulder. "We'll save him, Grace."

"How do you know?"

"Because we have to."

She did not look at him, but she nodded, staring at the sharp, gray shapes that hovered on the north horizon like storm clouds.

When they reached the bottom of the knoll, they found that Lirith and Aryn had risen, along with Tira. The women spoke in soft voices as Lirith gathered things for a simple breakfast and Aryn helped Tira dress the girl's stick doll. A lumpy shape still snored beneath a blanket nearby. Grace held a finger to her lips, and the others smiled at her. Then she tiptoed and knelt beside the huddled form.

"Sir Knight," she said in a gentle voice, "it's time to wake up."

Grace was nearly knocked flat on her back as Durge sat bolt upright, brown eyes wide. He had slept in his armor, and his hand groped for the sheathed greatsword that lay next to him.

"What is it, my lady? Brigands? Wild boar? Dragons?"

"Breakfast," she said with a grin.

Durge blinked, then blew a breath through his mustaches. "Oh."

"Come, Sir Knight. This way."

She gripped his hand, leaned back, and pulled him to his feet—although not without effort. The Embarran was *dense*.

"And you can leave the greatsword. I think it's a bit more than you need for spreading butter on a trencher. Let's let Lirith handle things."

"And I am an old knight indeed if I need a noble lady to butter my morning bread."

Now it was Grace's turn to blink. Durge's grumblings had sounded dangerously close to humor. However, the expression on his craggy face was more wounded than wry. It was all too much. Grace clapped a hand to her mouth, but she couldn't keep the laughter from escaping. The others joined in, and even Tira's lips drifted upward in a fleeting smile. Durge only let out a pained breath.

They made their breakfast in a circle on the ground, and they even risked a fire to brew a pot of *maddok*. Grace sipped the hot, energizing liquid and thought perhaps she could face the day—and the end of her journey—after all.

They had not stopped in Ar-tolor. The morning after crossing the bridge over the Dimduorn, they had seen seven high towers crowned by bright banners: yellow on green. Durge and Beltan had started toward the castle, but Grace had stayed them with a word.

When she was pressed to tell the others why she did not want to go to Ar-tolor, it was difficult to put the reasons into words. Part of it was urgency. The days were passing quickly, and the moon was waxing to full. But that was only part of it.

"I'd just rather Queen Ivalaine didn't know where we're traveling," she said finally. "Or why."

She had not needed to glance at Lirith to know the

woman's dark eyes were on her. After all, it was Lirith who had confirmed what Grace had suspected—that the Witches feared Travis was the one they called Runebreaker.

Grace licked her lips. "I'm sure if anyone wished to stay in Ar-tolor, the queen would be happy to receive them."

"I am certain she would," Lirith said in a crisp voice, then mounted her palfrey.

Grace breathed a sigh of relief. She was glad the witch was staying with them. She tried not to wonder if she should be worried as well.

A league from the castle they came upon one of Ivalaine's household knights, and Grace gave him a message to take to the queen, begging permission to ride through her Dominion. After that, Grace expected to be waylaid at any moment by a company of knights who would drag them to Ar-tolor. However, the only people they saw on the road were peasants, and then no one as the castle vanished in the distance behind them.

They had made good time across Toloria, although not as good as Grace might have wished. Horses were not cars, and they couldn't be driven all day without food or rest. In addition, Durge and Beltan chose their routes carefully, making certain they never found themselves in places where they might be surrounded with no avenue of escape, as they had been at the Tarrasian bridge, and these maneuverings caused some delay.

It had been hard these last days to speak about what had happened at the bridge. Or maybe it was simply that there was no need to speak of it. They had all witnessed Meridar's horrible death in the molten embrace of the *krondrim*. And they had all watched, helpless, as Daynen gave himself for Tira, smiling even as he walked over fire to save her.

Often as they rode, Grace would clutch the girl's

small, thin body to her. *You saved one, Grace. You know you'll take that over nothing. In the ED you'd call it a stalemate and move on.*

But this wasn't the hospital. At night she would lie on her back, staring at the red star pulsing low in the sky, and would try to weep for Daynen. But her eyes were a desert, and she had already forgotten what he looked like.

Although they remained always watchful, they saw no more *krondrim* as they rode. They were cutting deep across Toloria by then, and all Beltan's reports had indicated that the Burnt Ones were staying close to the river and the mountains.

"Or close to borders," Beltan said one night as they camped beside a stream.

Durge grunted. "What do you mean?"

"I'm not sure. Not completely, anyway. It's like they're looking for something. Or someone. Only it's not in one place. It's on the move."

"Of course," Aryn said, looking up from the rent in her riding gown she was mending with thread and needle. "It's simple tactics. If you want to find something that could be anywhere, and that's most likely moving, then you should keep watch at the borders that lead from one Dominion to the next."

Grace regarded the baroness, jaw open. "How did you know that, Aryn?"

The young woman shrugged. "I'm the ward of a king, Grace. I pay attention now and then."

"This explains their movement," Lirith said, gazing into the flames of the campfire. "Yet it still doesn't tell us what it is they hope to find."

Her words met only silence. None of them had a theory to explain that.

As they journeyed, Grace kept a close watch on Aryn. The months since Midwinter's Eve had been a dark time for the young woman. First she had used the Weirding to kill Leothan in self-defense. Then

Garf, who had clearly loved her, had died in front of her eyes. Finally Meridar, who had loved her as well, had shouted her name even as he walked into the arms of death. Grace had seen catatonic patients in the ED who had been through less.

However, much as Grace searched for signs of distress, the baroness seemed better than she had in many months. At times Aryn was sad and thoughtful, at others quietly happy. There was an air about her that was calm, even assured, but in no way prideful or smug. The coy and secretive girl who had begun this journey had not crossed the Dimduorn with them. It was a strong and noble young woman who had made it to the other side.

Finally, one evening, Grace dared to approach Aryn and ask her how she felt about Meridar.

Aryn bent her head, then looked up, her sapphire eyes refracting the last light of day. "He died for me, Grace. I didn't ask him to do it, and I didn't want him to. But he did, and I can't change that. So I have to be strong. For him. If I'm not, then what would it all mean?"

Grace had tried to speak, but there were no words she could say that would be more true than what the young woman had spoken. Aryn was growing up—really growing up. However, there was yet a long road ahead of her, and many burdens to carry upon it, of that Grace was certain. With a gasp that might have been joy or sorrow, she reached out and embraced her friend. Yes, her friend, the best she had on any world. Aryn hugged her back, and the gesture was no less fierce for the fact that it was made with only one arm.

"I love you, Grace. I love you so much."

I love you, too, Aryn, Grace wanted more than anything to say. But she was weak, and words failed her, so instead she had held the young woman more tightly yet.

It wasn't until the next day—their fourth since the

crossing of the Dimduorn—that Lirith spoke of what Grace had done at the bridge.

The Tolorian woman's words came without preamble. "The Weirding has never been woven like that before, sister."

Startled, Grace dropped the knife with which she had been cutting a hard loaf of bread for their supper and looked up. Lirith sat on the ground, watching her. Grace cast a startled look at Aryn, who picked flowers with Tira nearby, then forced her gaze back to the witch.

"What do you mean?" Grace's voice was quiet. Durge and Beltan had walked off to gather wood for a fire, but the knights were not so far away the wind couldn't bring them into earshot.

Lirith's visage was smooth as ebony, but there was an intensity about it all the same. "The best of us—and that is only a few—can pluck some threads of the Weirding and weave them into a new strand. It is a great talent, but the magics we can make with it are small and private. We might cause the eye to see a shadow that is not there, or the mind to perceive a voice the ears alone cannot hear. These are useful things, yes, even powerful in their own way, but they are illusion."

Aryn had stopped all pretense of picking flowers and stared at Lirith outright. Grace could not move, as if cast of stone. Tira undulated in a silent dance amid tall grass.

"I don't understand," Grace managed to say.

A fleeting smile touched Lirith's deep red lips, then was gone. "Nor do I. What you did at the river was not illusion, Grace. It was real. You did not weave the Weirding. You hardly seemed to Touch its threads. Instead, it was as if you made yourself a vessel and simply let all the force of the river pour through you to drive the *krondrim* back."

Grace clutched the handle of the knife. Maybe it

seemed strange to Lirith to have worked magic in the way she did, but Grace had had no other choice. She could not weave the threads of the Weirding because the strand that connected her to it led to the shadow. To reach the Weirding, she would have to pass through the shadow first.

In her mind she saw the pulsing blot of darkness, and it gathered itself inward and upward, taking on shape: fire-darkened walls, jagged cupolas, and windows staring like empty eyes toward barren peaks. No—that was the place her thread would take her, and she could not go there. She had escaped with her life and her sanity once; she could not possibly hope to do so again.

"You helped me." Grace didn't realize she had spoken the words until she saw Lirith's shocked expression. She clung to them. "You helped me, Lirith. And Aryn did, too. What I did . . . I couldn't have done it if you hadn't been there."

Lirith's eyelids closed halfway, and her look of astonishment was replaced by one of mystery. "Yes, it was not only from the river that the flood came. There was another source."

Her gaze flickered toward Aryn who stood nearby, forgotten flowers crushed in her left hand. The young woman swallowed hard, then nodded toward Grace.

"You're bleeding, Grace. You've cut yourself."

Grace lifted her hand. The knife had nicked her finger, and now blood oozed forth in a thin, red stream.

"I'll get a rag," Lirith said, and that was the last they spoke of the incident at the river.

Now, three days later—the sixth since their crossing of the River Darkwine, they finished their scant breakfast in the shelter of the knoll. As the sun rose above the horizon, they readied themselves for the day's journey.

When she was finished packing their foodstuffs

into Shandis's saddlebags, Grace took a pair of water flasks and walked the short distance to the brook that ran beneath the knoll. She stepped past a stand of willows to the edge of a clear pool.

By the time she saw that she was not alone, the other was already moving. In one action he rose from a crouch, grabbed his sword from the stone where it lay, and spun around with the blade raised before him.

"Grace!"

Beltan lowered the sword as recognition flashed in his eyes. Water streamed from his white-blond hair, running down the bare skin of his chest.

Grace raised a hand to her throat. If she had been a robber, she knew she would be dead right now. It was a valuable reminder for her. Beltan was kind and good-natured, and because of these things she had forgotten what he was: a disciple of Vathris and a man of war. The scars that crisscrossed his pale, lean chest bespoke a violence she had never witnessed firsthand. Prominent among them was a thick band of knotted scar tissue that snaked down his side—the wound he had received on Midwinter's Eve. It had healed, but by the looks of it just barely.

Grace realized she was staring. She forced herself to take a breath. "I'm sorry, Beltan. I didn't mean to startle you."

"It's all right. I just didn't see you there in the shadow." He slicked his wet hair back from his brow, then bent to sheathe his sword again.

Grace frowned. Her startlement had faded, but there was something else that had unsettled her— something about what had just happened.

Beltan gazed at her, concern written across his plain face. "What's wrong?"

She stared at him, then she had it. Her name. It was the way he had said her name.

Grace!

In her vision, when she saw Travis bound to a stone before the Gray Tower, he had turned, his eyes had gone wide, and he had spoken her name in surprise just as Beltan had. She had thought he couldn't have seen her, that he must have been calling her name in despair. But what if that wasn't so? What if he *had* seen her?

I just didn't see you there in the shadow. . . .

A certainty flooded her. Yes, it had to be—Travis had said her name because he really had seen her. Except he couldn't have glimpsed her vision-self. There was nothing, no body, for visible light to bounce off of. Which left only one possibility.

"You were there, Grace," she murmured. "I mean, you *will* be there. That's how he saw you."

Beltan cocked his head. "Grace, are you all right?"

She grinned at the knight. "We're going to make it, Beltan. I know it now. I was there, at the stone. I mean, I'm *going* to be there. That's what I saw in the vision. I'll be there to help Travis."

The blond man grinned back. "I have absolutely no idea what you're talking about, Grace. But if you say we're going to be there, then we're going to be there."

For the first time since the bridge, Grace felt hope—real hope—rise inside her. With a laugh, she threw her arms about his wet, bare shoulders, stunning him anew.

50.

This time the chorus of the Runespeakers met at dawn. Red light oozed through the window slits high in the domed chamber. Travis knew it was just the morning sun. But the light looked like blood, and for all the quiet murmurs of the masters in their gray robes, he knew he was in danger—perhaps greater than any he had ever faced before on Eldh.

Although he dreaded what it might bring, Travis was glad to see morning come. The night had been a dim and silent eternity, spent alone in the confines of his cell. He had not needed to try the door to know it was shut with *Banu,* the rune of closing. Instead, he had spent the hours sitting on his bed, listening for Jack's voice, begging it to tell him what to do. But the only voice he heard was Oragien's, echoing in his mind.

By Olrig, what have you done?

Despite Oragien's words, breaking the runestone had had nothing to do with Olrig. Travis had done it for the Runespeakers, and he had done it for himself. That was his only consolation through the lonely hours of darkness—that if given the opportunity to change what he had done, he would not. But something told him he was going to have a tough time selling the Runespeakers on the idea that destroying their one link to the knowledge of the ancients was a good thing.

They came for him in the gray light before dawn.

There was no knock, but he heard and felt the whisper of magic as *Urath,* the rune of opening, was spoken on the other side of the door. When the portal swung inward, he hoped he would see Sky there. Instead, two grim-faced runespeakers stepped into the cell. Travis had seen them both at chorus, but he did not know their names.

The elder of the two masters glanced at the younger. "Speak the rune of silence upon him."

You don't need to do that, Travis wanted to say. *I won't try to speak a rune to get out of this.*

However, even as he opened his mouth, the runespeakers chanted a single word in harmony.

"*Sirith.*"

Silence enshrouded Travis, smothering his words.

A spark of anger rose in him, along with an urge to speak the rune *Reth*, to break their rune, and to turn it back on them. It would have been easy, despite the fact that they were two and he was one. The magic of the rune they had spoken was weak, barely held together by their combined will—he could feel it.

Instead, Travis clenched his jaw, letting the silence close around him. He could hear sounds perfectly, but as long as the power of the rune lasted he could make no noise himself.

"Come with us," the younger master said.

They passed no one on their descent through the tower. Then, as they entered the chorus chamber, Travis understood why. A low murmur surged on the air of the domed chamber: waves on a deep, sullen ocean. All the runespeakers were there, filling the lowest third of the stone tiers.

On the dais in the chamber's center stood Oragien. Travis knew the All-master had reached his eightieth winter, and for the first time since Travis had met him he looked his years. His skin was nearly as gray as his robe, stretched thinly over the sharp bones of his face, and he stooped over the runestaff as if it were the only thing propping him upright.

And perhaps it was. He had brought Travis there to help study the runestone, to discover its secrets. Instead, Travis had shattered the stone. And just maybe, from the way he stared at the floor with blank eyes, Oragien with it.

Guilt seeped into Travis's lungs like cold fluid. He forced the feeling aside. *Remember, Travis, you didn't ask for this. You didn't sing a little song about rainbows, and you didn't wish to be whisked from Colorado and dumped here. If they thought they could just wave their hands and summon you and have you do their every bidding, then they were wrong.*

Now indignation bubbled into his chest, as it had

when he spoke to the Duratek agent in Castle City, and then to Deirdre Falling Hawk and Hadrian Farr. It seemed like everyone wanted to use him for something: Duratek, the Seekers, the Runespeakers. Even Jack Graystone had used Travis without asking. It wasn't fair. However, he knew none of this had anything to do with fairness. A sigh escaped his lips, although it made no sound.

"This way," the younger of the two runespeakers said with a jerk on his arm. They led him to the bench closest to the dais. It was empty. "Sit."

Travis hesitated. However, even if he were to escape this place, where would he go? He would find no more love outside the walls of the tower than he could find right now within.

Travis sat on the empty bench, and the two runespeakers withdrew. He could feel angry eyes on the back of his head, but he did not turn around. Instead he hung his head and gripped his right wrist. He found himself thinking of Grace Beckett, and wishing she were there. He could have used a little of her cool logic just then, to help make some sense of all this. But Grace was leagues and leagues from the place, safe behind the stone walls of her castle.

"This chorus has begun!"

Oragien's voice echoed and reechoed around the chamber. The words were not loud—they did not need to be in this place—but they were hard and solid. The All-master stood straight now, his blue eyes bright as lightning. So there was strength left in Oragien yet.

The murmuring of the runespeakers ceased, leaving only the sigh of ancient voices on the air. Oragien did not look at Travis as he spoke, but rather over him.

"I have summoned this chorus as our laws demand, although there is little enough to speak about now. We know well the crime and the one who committed it." Here the All-master's gaze did flicker for a moment in Travis's direction. "And what our order will do now that our one trove of knowledge is no more is a matter that will take not one chorus to decide, but a hundred. So the question before us today is simple." Oragien pointed his staff directly at Travis's heart. "We have only to decide the fate of this heretic."

Travis clenched his jaw. At least he wasn't going to have to go through all the fuss of a trial.

Oragien lowered his staff. "Is there any who would speak in defense of this runebreaker?"

A laugh escaped Travis—who would be mad enough to defend *him*?—but fortunately the rune of silence swallowed the sound. Then movement caught Travis's eye.

His was not the only jaw agape in the chamber as a short, rotund form waddled down the steps to stand before the dais. Oragien's bristling eyebrows knit together in a scowl.

"Master Eriaun, you would speak for this man?"

"Yes, All-master." The runespeaker's myopic eyes bulged as a hiss ran around the chamber. "I mean, *no*."

Oragien's frown deepened. "Which is it, Master Eriaun?"

Eriaun clutched his hands together before him. "I mean, I simply want to speak, All-master. May I?"

Oragien hesitated. "Very well, Master Eriaun. But be brief."

Eriaun cleared his throat, his voice rising tremulously to the dome. "I just wonder if we understand what we're doing, that's all. It seems like there's so much we don't understand these days. We don't understand the runestone." He bit his lip. "Or we didn't, at any rate. I don't understand how we managed to summon Master Wilder here, even with the help we had. And I certainly don't understand this power of his. Why, here he is a runelord and breaking rune-stones and all, and he can hardly read an apprentice's first list of runes." Eriaun's eyes went wide. "Oh, no offense intended, Master Wilder!"

Despite himself, Travis grinned. *None taken.*

Eriaun opened his mouth, then frowned, then spread his arms. "Evidently that's all I have to say. But we've been a bit rash with things that are a bit beyond us, and I think we should be careful not to do the same now."

Eriaun waddled back to his seat. It had been a brave effort on the part of the stout runespeaker. However, even before the next voice spoke, Travis knew it had only made things worse.

"Master Eriaun is right," a hard voice splintered the whispering air. "There *is* much we don't understand. And it's time we did."

Master Larad descended the steps toward the center of the chamber. He did not look at Oragien or Travis, but rather turned to address the other runespeakers.

"It's time we understood why he was brought to us. It's time we understood how some believed he was to help us. And it's time we understood who truly has the ability to lead our order now that the runestone has been broken." Larad shrugged, then let his dark gaze flicker toward Oragien. "But perhaps it is not quite time for those things . . . yet."

Oragien's eyes blazed, but he clutched his staff and said nothing. Larad went on, stalking before the dais like a gray cat, the angular shards of his scarred face tinged red by the dawn light.

"While Master Eriaun speaks truth, there are some things we do understand. For five centuries there have been no runebreakers in Falengarth. Those of the black robes and the Black Tower were forbidden long ago. Their kind and their craft have not been known since." Larad gestured toward Travis. "Yet when one came into the world again, what did we do but invite him into our own tower? Runelord we called him. And perhaps, somehow, he is that. Even so, it does not change what he is: a breaker of runes."

Another hiss circled the chamber, louder this time. Travis clutched the sharp edge of the bench.

Now Larad's voice rose to the high dome. "Have you all forgotten? Was it not the Runebreakers who brought the fear and hatred of men upon all of the runic orders? The black robes were forbidden for good reason—one we now have seen for ourselves all too well. So I call for an end to this talk, and for a chanting of the chorus. There is only one punishment for a heretic and a runebreaker."

Without glancing at Oragien, Larad strode back to his place. On the dais, fury drained from the All-master's visage, leaving it gaunt and pale. He nodded.

"Master Larad has called for a chanting. Let it be so."

Travis didn't understand what was happening. Each of the masters closed his eyes and sat still upon his seat. A hush fell over the chamber. Then it began. A single tone rose on the air. More notes rose to join it, and still more, until the walls resonated with the sound. The Runespeakers were chanting, each man voicing a single, droning note that blended with the others.

At first there was a dissonance to the tone, but in moments this was overpowered by a bright harmonic that shimmered off polished stone. Still the tone grew in force and volume. Travis's hands scrabbled for his ears. The rune of silence did nothing to muffle the sound, and the chanting filled his brain. Another second and he knew it would shatter his skull, just as he had shattered the runestone.

"Stop!"

The ragged shout sliced through the air, marring

the perfect, shimmering harmonic. The chanting ceased, but the corrupted sound of it still ricocheted off the walls, cascading into a deafening roar, until shards of sound flew through the chamber like pieces of broken glass. All clutched hands to their ears to keep their minds from being cut to shreds.

The riot of sound faded to a hiss. By force of will, Travis pulled his hands from his ears. It was only when he saw all eyes turned toward him that he realized the shout had been his own, that he had broken the rune of silence cast upon him.

"I did it to help you," he said. His voice was a hoarse whisper all could hear, merging with the fragments of the chant. "You have to understand that, Master Oragien. I did it so you could learn for yourselves. Without me, without anyone."

His words faded away. Then Oragien spoke in a quiet voice.

"The chant was in harmony, Master Wilder. All voices were in accord. The chorus has decided."

Travis looked up into Oragien's blue eyes. There was a new light shining in them now: sorrow. Travis opened his mouth, but a gesture from the All-master silenced him more certainly than could any rune.

"At sunset tomorrow, when the moon is at her full, Master Wilder will be bound to the null stone outside our tower, where no rune may be spoken."

Oragien hesitated, but Travis already knew the words that would come next.

"And there he shall die."

51.

They rode steadily all that day—Grace and Tira, Aryn and Lirith, Durge and Beltan—pushing the horses as hard as they dared as the leagues slipped past and the tumbled slopes of the Fal Erenn edged ever higher into a sky that phased from dull jade to jasper.

The air grew dryer as they neared the mountains, and the verdant floodplains gave way to broken grasslands interrupted by steep gulches and ridges of weathered stone. If she had paused to think about it, the landscape would have reminded Grace of her childhood in Colorado, of the mountains near Castle City, and of the Beckett-Strange Home for Children. However, only one thought consumed her as she rode.

You were there, Grace. You will be there. It was in your vision.

Had she let herself, Grace might also have wondered at this fierce need to save Travis Wilder. He was her friend, of course—that was reason enough. And even more, he had helped rescue this world on Midwinter's Eve. Didn't he deserve at the very least not to be burned alive?

Yes, but these were not the real reasons she pressed her legs against Shandis's sides, urging the palfrey on. It was the same need that had propelled her without rest, without thought, from patient to patient in the ED at Denver Memorial Hospital: the ceaseless drive to heal others, to take their shattered bodies and make them whole. Garf's life had slipped through her fingers. Meridar and Daynen had been beyond her reach. Losing Travis was not an acceptable outcome.

"My lady!"

Belatedly, Grace jerked on the reins, bringing Shandis to a skidding halt on a patch of shale. The others had stopped their mounts several yards behind Grace—she had almost kept on riding without them. She turned her horse to move back to them, and that was when she saw it.

Before and above her, a rough crag protruded from the looming wall of the mountains, connected to them by a knife-edged ridge. Upon the crag, tall and impossibly slender, rose a single spire of mist-gray stone.

She lowered her gaze and saw the beginning of a narrow trail carved into the steep slope, marked by a pair of wind-worn stones. In her haste she had ridden right by it. Even as she watched, the westering sun tinged the tower's walls crimson, as if setting them on fire. A dizziness swept through her, and she clutched Shandis's mane. She was below it now, not soaring above, but the tower looked just as it had in her vision.

No, Grace, it's not like the vision because the moon won't be full tonight. Not quite. You've got one more day. You made it—you really made it.

A small hand brushed her cheek, and she looked down into Tira's placid eyes. The girl smiled, the left side of her face lifting upward in a pretty expression, while the right remained a mask, as hard and emotionless as pink plastic. Grace held the child tight against her, as if she could transfer love with the gesture, rather than simply pressure and heat. Then she looked up at the others.

"Well, we're here."

Beltan eyed the three horned minarets that crowned the tower. "I can't say this is the most inviting place I've ever seen."

"And what exactly might that be, warrior of Vathris?" Lirith said in a musing tone. "A tavern where strapping young men were handing out free pots of ale to fair-haired knights?"

Light sparkled in Beltan's green eyes. "Something like that."

Durge swung down from Blackalock's back, his boots grinding against the ground. "There's no room for the horses on the path. And it looks to be a treacherous climb. I shouldn't wonder if one of us turns an ankle on a loose stone and falls off the edge before we get to the top."

"Well, Durge," Aryn said as she let Beltan help her down from her palfrey, "you've just assured we'll all make it to the top in good form."

Durge frowned at her. "Your Highness?"

Aryn sent a radiant smile in the knight's direction. "Really, Durge—surely you know that if you speak aloud some ill is going to happen, then it never does."

Beltan scratched the gold stubble on his chin. "You know, I think she's right. The days you wake up and think, 'I'll most likely get a sword in my gut before lunchtime,' it never happens. It's when you're just out for a jaunt through the countryside, whistling a cheery tune and thinking about strapping young men giving away pots of ale, when someone jumps out of the bushes and sticks a knife in you."

Lirith laughed, a brilliant sound that echoed off lifeless stone. "So you mean, on this entire journey, every time Durge has voiced his worries about a particular disaster or danger, he has actually ensured that these things would never come to pass?"

"Precisely," Aryn said.

Plucking up the hem of her riding gown, Lirith curtsied low before the Embarran. "Why, thank you for this protection, Sir Knight."

Durge's eyes bulged, and he opened his mouth to reply, but evidently he had no idea what to say, because instead he shut his mouth, emitted a wordless grunt, and turned to rummage through Blackalock's saddlebags.

A warmth flooded Grace's chest, and she smiled despite her weariness, despite her urgency. She would never know how she had managed to deserve any friends at all, let alone such improbable and marvelous friends as these. However, over the last months, she had learned to accept the fact that sometimes— bizarre as it seemed—good things happened for no reason at all.

The shadows cast by the mountains lengthened. Grace's smile softened as a sigh escaped her lungs.

"I suppose we should get going. I've noticed, on this world at least, that people seem to prefer getting unexpected visitors when it's still light out."

Both Durge and Beltan nodded.

Aryn glanced at Lirith. "Will we be . . . welcome at this place, sister?"

Lirith smoothed her russet gown. "It has never been with the Runespeakers that the Witches were concerned. Nor do I believe they are concerned by us."

Beltan cast a puzzled look at the witch, but Grace understood her words well enough.

She still thinks Travis is this Runebreaker, Grace, that maybe he shouldn't be saved at all. Are you sure Lirith should really come with us to the tower?

This suspicion sickened Grace, and she forced it aside. She had to believe in her friends. After all, the gods of this place knew she couldn't believe in herself.

"I think that's a stable there," Beltan said, pointing to a low, stone structure Grace hadn't noticed before. It blended with the outcrop it was built against.

The blond knight went to investigate, then motioned the others over. They brought the horses.

"It's a stable, all right," Beltan said. "Although I don't think it's been used in years."

Aryn stroked her palfrey's neck. "But will the horses be all right here? Someone might try to steal them."

A flinty light stole into Durge's eyes. "Then someone will find one of Blackalock's hooves planted neatly on the back of his skull."

The Embarran's sooty charger let out a snort with such perfect timing that Grace could only take it for what it seemed: an equine affirmation of the knight's words.

The men tethered the horses inside the stable, then the six travelers made their way to the stones that marked the beginning of the path. A silver-blue flash caught the corner of Grace's eye. She looked up and saw a light gleaming at the horned tip of the tower. Then the light was gone.

"They know we're coming," Durge said.

Grace gave a stiff nod, then, holding Tira's small hand inside her own, she started up the trail.

The going was as steep as Durge had feared, but not so treacherous. The trail was cut deep into the rock and had been cleared of loose stone by the passage of numberless feet. The only parts that proved difficult were three stairs cut into the rock face in places where the cliff was all but vertical. The stairs were worn and slippery, without rail or handhold, and gave Grace the unnerving sensation that the ground below was pulling at her. Only Tira seemed unconcerned by the stairs, and she scrambled up ahead of the others with a speed that wedged Grace's heart into new and completely incorrect anatomical locations.

By the time they reached the small plateau before the tower, the sun had vanished behind the high peaks, and twilight crept from deep valleys to cloak the mountains. As they approached the gate of the tower, they moved past a tall, hulking shape. A shudder passed through Grace as she recognized the standing stone from her vision. So this was where they had bound Travis. Where they *would* bind him.

But you'll be there, Grace. I don't know how yet, but you'll find a way to save him.

The standing stone fell behind them, and the tower's triangular gate loomed before. Even as they drew near, the gate swung inward. Standing in the opening—bathed in a light as pale as the moon, but which came from within the tower rather than without—was an old, bearded man in a gray robe. His eyes were like an eagle's amid the sharp planes of his face, and he gripped an ornate staff in his hands. Behind the old man were others in gray robes, including one whose face was lined with thin, white scars. They came to a halt as the old man spoke.

"One knight of Calavan, one knight of Embarr, three Daughters of Sia, and a burnt child." The old man shook his head. "This is a curious party that has come to my door."

Grace opened her mouth. A single, surprised word escaped her. "Runes . . . ?"

A faint smile played about the old man's withered lips—or perhaps it was simply a shadow. "No, Your Radiance. It is no magic that tells me who you are. We have all heard the tale of Travis Wilder and his companions. It is easy enough to recognize you all. Save for the child. And you, my lady." He nodded toward Lirith. "A countess of southern Toloria, are you not?"

Lirith nodded in reply.

A thrill coursed through Grace. "Travis. He's here, isn't he?"

The old man nodded again, any trace of a smile gone now.

Beltan moved beside Grace, his face grim. "We have to see Travis. Now."

"You will see him," the old man said. "But not just yet."

He made the barest gesture toward the scar-faced man. Too late Grace understood his meaning. Next to her Beltan reached for his sword, but he was far too slow.

"Sinfath!"

A dozen voices spoke the word in resonating harmony, and shadows leaped forth, casting a suffocating veil of twilight over Grace. She heard the muffled cries of the others and knew they, too, were lost. Then the twilight deepened, filling her mind like mist, and everything went gray.

52.

Through the window slit of his cell, Travis watched the first flecks of copper gild the azure sky. It was almost time.

He looked down at his hands and saw they were trembling. Maybe it was fear. Or maybe it was just hunger. They had not given him food that day—just a pot of metallic-tasting water brought by a grim-faced journeyman shortly after dawn. After that no one had come, and he had sat on the bed, watching the narrow line of sunlight creep across the wall.

He had tried the door, of course. Not because he thought it might be unlocked, but just because it seemed required. However, the door wouldn't budge, although he sensed no rune of closing upon it; they must have chosen more solid and mundane barriers to keep him in this time. For a while he stared at the door, willing it to open, and for Sky to be on the other side, grinning, there to set Travis free. After a while he gave that up.

You're alone, Travis. They're keeping Sky away from you. And Beltan's not going to come save you this time, not like at the Rune Gate. This is it.

He sighed as he thought of the good-natured knight. Travis wished he would have a chance to see Beltan again. It would have been nice to see his friend, to see how he was doing. But that wasn't going to happen, was it?

Although he tried not to, Travis couldn't help wondering how long it would take to die. Once, in the Dominion of Eredane, he had seen a runespeaker lashed to a pole by the Raven Cult. They had let him hang there like a scarecrow. A heretic, the sign on the post had branded him.

Heretic. That was what Oragien had called him as well. But then, wasn't that what they were always called—people who spoke a truth no one wanted to hear? Weren't those who were different always crucified like this . . . on crosses, on fences, on stones?

Outside the window, the flecks of copper ignited into flame and spread across the sky. The first echoes of boots against stone sounded outside the door.

"No good deed goes unpunished," Travis murmured.

But maybe this wasn't really such a bad way for things to end. Maybe the Runespeakers would never understand, but he *had* helped them. They would learn now—because they had to. He supposed a lot of people died having done less. He folded his hands in his lap and waited for them to come.

By the fire of Durnach's forge! Are you just going to let them do this to you, Travis?

He winced as the voice spoke in his mind. "Jack."

Travis wasn't certain whether he was glad or not to hear the voice finally speak to him. Yes, it had helped him in moments of danger. But sometimes it seemed more like an affliction than a blessing—a reminder of what had been done to him, of how he had been changed.

This is absurd, Travis. These fools are the barest shadows of the Runespeakers of old. And you're a runelord. They should be obeying your commands, not questioning your actions.

"I broke their runestone, Jack." He spoke aloud because somehow this seemed a little less insane.

And what a show that was, Travis. By Olrig, you're bolder than I ever guessed. I'm not certain many of us could have done that. But then, you're the only one left now. You're everything we ever were.

For a moment it seemed there were other voices in

his head besides Jack's—a vast chorus speaking in harmony. Then it was just his old friend once more.

There is no need for this, Travis. Once they open the door, you can drop them all with a single rune and be away from this place. You have the power.

Travis clenched his right hand into a fist. "No, Jack. I won't hurt them. I won't hurt anyone. That was my vow, and I'm going to keep it. I didn't ask for this power."

What utter nonsense! No one asks for power—except for idiots and madmen. But you have it, Travis, and it's your duty to use it.

Travis shook his head. "Not if it means hurting people. If I could get away from the null stone after they leave me there, I'd do it. But you can't speak a rune there—I know, I tried. So there's nothing that can help me."

There was a silence so long Travis thought that even the voice had fled him now in this final hour. Then it came again, a whisper deep in his mind.

You're wrong, Travis. The null stone is ancient, but there are powers more ancient still. The hand of Olrig will aid you.

This was a cruel joke. Travis pounded his fist against his thigh. "But Olrig isn't here anymore. Don't you remember? The Old Gods are gone."

Are they?

Travis opened his mouth, then closed it. There was no use in replying. As if a door had shut in his mind, the voice was gone. At the same moment another door—the one to his cell—swung open. Three journeymen entered. Travis stood.

"You don't need that," he said, as one of them lifted a strip of leather. However, the man ignored him and tied the strip over his mouth, gagging him. Apparently they weren't going to risk his breaking their rune of silence again. The others took his arms and shoved him through the door.

A half-dozen times he nearly saved them the work of taking him to the null stone by stumbling and just about breaking his neck on the steps as they pushed him down the staircase. However, with rough jerks they kept him upright, and he made it to the bottom. They forced him through the gate.

The light of the dying day spilled like blood across the plateau in front of the tower. The runespeakers were all there, gathered in a semicircle facing west. He could not see past them to the null stone, but he knew it was there, for it weighed like a blot on his mind. Hard hands propelled him toward it.

Sweat trickled in rivulets inside Travis's robe, and he was unable to walk without knocking his knees together. It was difficult not to entertain thoughts of escape. If somehow he could get the gag off, just for a moment, he could freeze his captors with *Gelth*, or burn them with *Krond*. Then he could run far from here. Where he would go, he didn't know. Maybe back to Calavere, to see Grace and Beltan, and . . .

The runespeakers parted, making way for him to pass, and all of Travis's thoughts ceased. His eyes locked on the black outline of the null stone—then moved down to the heap of sticks piled at the base. Fear transmuted into panic. He strained against the grips that held him, but more hands reached out, pulling him toward the stone. Travis tried to scream but only choked against the gag instead. He had been wrong. Horribly, stupidly wrong. They weren't going to just tie him to the stone and leave him.

They were going to burn him alive.

53.

This wasn't how it was supposed to happen.

"There has to be a way out of here. There has to be."

One more time Grace pawed at the rough wood of the cell's door, digging her nails into every crack, groping for any sign of weakness.

"Grace." Aryn's voice was soft but urgent. "Grace, it's no use. You have to stop."

She hesitated, then lifted her hands to gaze at them: Blood oozed from the raw fingertips. With a stiff nod she stepped away from the door. Aryn let out a sigh, then cast a worried look at Lirith. The witch's lips were pressed into a line, but she said nothing, her hands resting on Tira's thin shoulders.

Grace paced around the boundaries of the wedge-shaped cell. They had found themselves in the cell upon waking—sometime after sunset the previous night—once the effects of the rune had worn off. Somehow Tira had already been awake, for Grace had opened her eyes to see the girl's placid face bent over her. Now it was nearly sunset again. Grace knew that, when it rose over the western mountains, the moon would be full.

She considered shouting again, but her throat was as ragged as her fingers. Not that there was a point to it anyway. They would not come again. At least not until after nightfall. Oragien had made that much clear.

The old man who had met them at the tower's gate had come to their cell just after dawn, and had spoken to them through a crack in the door, identifying himself as the All-master of the Gray Tower.

"Why are you keeping us?" Aryn demanded before

either Grace or Lirith could speak. The baroness's blue eyes blazed with ire. If Grace had forgotten Aryn was nobility of the highest degree, she had remembered it then.

"It is for the best that you remain here," Oragien said, his voice weary but resolute.

"And for what crime are we being imprisoned?"

"For no crime, good sister. After sunset tonight we will release you, and you will be free to leave the tower."

Grace clenched her jaw. After sunset . . . and after they had murdered Travis. Wasn't that what the old man meant?

Aryn's tone was frosty steel. "I am a baroness of Calavan, here with a duchess as well as a countess of Toloria. And all of us are companions to Queen Ivalaine. Do you truly believe you won't have to answer for this deed?"

Oragien passed a withered hand before his eyes. "In the end, we each must answer for our deeds, good sister."

At that, the color had drained from Aryn's face, and words had seemed to flee her. Lirith gripped her shoulders, pulling her back from the door. Oragien stepped away from the crack.

Wait! Grace had tried to shout. *You still haven't said why you're doing this to Travis!*

But the door had already shut, and since then no other had come to the cell.

Now Grace sat on one of the two cots that occupied the cramped room. She shut her eyes and lifted a hand to her forehead. They had all awakened with headaches that still lingered. An aftereffect of the rune magic, perhaps.

"Here. Drink this."

Grace opened her eyes and saw Lirith holding a wooden cup. At least they had been left a pitcher of water, along with some bread and raisins. Grace accepted the cup and drank, and the throbbing in her skull receded a bit.

"Maybe we should try again," she said as she handed back the cup, meeting Lirith's dark eyes. "To use the Touch."

Lirith laid a slender hand on Grace's arm. "The walls are stone, sister. The door wood and iron. Not mist, not water. You tried this morning when you were fresh and rested, and you could not move them. How can you now when you are weary?"

Grace stiffened. *And maybe you just don't want me to open the door. Sister. After all, you think he's the Runebreaker. Maybe you don't want me to save him.*

But these thoughts were madness, brought on by exhaustion and fear. Lirith was her friend.

Grace drew in a breath. "You're right. And even if we weren't all too tired, the Weirding is weak here. I don't think there's enough life in this tower to fill a thimble."

Aryn ran a hand over one of the impossibly smooth walls. "No, that's not true. I know it seems odd, but there *is* life in this stone. It's like the Weirding, but it's different as well. Colder. More distant. I can't . . ." She shook her head. "I just can't seem to grasp it."

Grace shot Aryn a grateful look. At least she had tried.

"My lady . . ." came a deep, faint voice.

At once Grace stood, moved to the farside of the cell, and knelt beside an opening at the base of the wall—so small even Tira would not have been able to slip her hand through it. The opening would allow water from this cell and the next to pour into a common drain. More importantly, it let Grace see into the adjacent space. She peered through and saw a stone floor and two sets of boots.

"Durge. Beltan."

"We are still here, my lady," came the Embarran's somber voice.

"We're sure as steel not going anywhere with these things on," Beltan's tenor followed.

Chains rattled. They sounded heavy.

"So you haven't been able to get free?" Grace said without even attempting to sound hopeful.

"I'm sorry, Grace," Beltan said, his voice hollow through the opening. "I don't think a troll could break these chains."

"My lady," Durge said, "I called because I wondered what time of day it was. There is no window in here."

Grace glanced at the glowing slit in the wall behind her. "It's almost sunset."

There was silence from the other side, then the chains rattled again, louder this time, and a shout of effort, rage, and pain echoed off stone.

"They can't do this to him! By Vathris's bloody blade, they can't do this! Oh, gods . . ."

Grace squeezed her eyes shut as Beltan's words ended in a strangled sound of anguish.

"Forgive us, my lady," came Durge's quieter but no less heartrending tones. "We have failed you. And we have failed Goodman Travis."

No, Grace wanted to say. *No, I'm the one who failed—failed to be where I was supposed to be.* But she couldn't give voice to the words.

She still couldn't understand how this had happened. Her vision was going to come true, but she was not going to be there by the standing stone as she had believed. But that didn't make sense. In the vision, Travis had seen her standing there, she was sure of it. But how was he going to see her now that she was locked in this cell?

Grace opened her mouth to say something, anything, that might comfort the knights—

—and stopped as a knock came at the cell door.

She jerked her head up. Both Lirith and Aryn stared at the portal. Tira only played with her burnt doll. The knock came again, louder this time. Then the cell door opened—not a crack, but all the way.

Grace was so astonished she could not move, could not bolt for freedom as she should have given the opportunity. Instead, she watched as a man—robed not in gray, but in brown—stepped into the cell. He was young, no more than twenty, his rubbery face misshapen but kindly.

"Who are you?" Grace said.

The young man drew something from inside his robe and held it toward her. Grace drew closer. It was a hand made of gray stone. She cast a puzzled look that was returned by Aryn and Lirith, then met the young man's eyes.

"What is it?" she whispered, certain that something important was about to happen.

The young man opened his mouth. As he did, she saw the stump of flesh where his tongue had once been. He worked his jaw, his face contorting even further. Then sound issued from his lips.

"Oh . . . hrig."

Grace stared. Her instincts told her this was the first time this man had spoken in many years, perhaps since he was a child, when his tongue was taken from him. Shaking, he held the stone hand out farther and spoke again.

"Oh-*hrig.*"

Grace gazed at the hand. It was broken at the wrist, as if once part of a larger sculpture. Ohrig. Was that a word for hand?

No, Grace. That's not it. Think—he doesn't have a tongue. That means he can't form lingual sounds.

She took the hand and looked up into his eyes. "Olrig. This is the hand of the Old God Olrig."

He nodded and grinned, his eyes bright.

Aryn stepped forward. "Grace, what's going on?"

She shook her head. "I don't . . ."

The young man handed her another object. Grace's fingers closed around soft fabric. She shook the garment out and gasped. It was a robe the color of mist.

The young man gestured, his movements as eloquent as gently spoken words: *Put it on, my lady*.

She cast a shocked look at Aryn and Lirith.

Lirith's eyes were intense as coals. "You must go, Grace. I looked out the window just a moment ago. Already the runespeakers are gathering."

Grace clutched the robe. "But . . ."

"But there's only one robe." Aryn stepped forward and touched her shoulder. "We'll do our best to free Beltan and Durge. Now go, Grace. You're Travis's only chance."

Grace gazed at the two women. Then Tira moved between them. She patted Grace's hand, then looked up and cast a beautiful half smile at the young man. He grinned back at her. Grace held up the robe.

"Well, here goes nothing," she said.

54.

Travis strained against the hands that held him, but it was no use. His boots scraped against hard slate as they dragged him toward the heap of wood waiting beneath the standing stone.

Next time you're sentenced to death, Travis, remember to ask what method they're going to use. That way you can avoid these nasty little execution-day surprises.

Amidst the crowd of gray robes, Travis glimpsed a pair of myopic brown eyes. Eriaun. The stout master wrung plump hands as Travis stumbled past. Then he was lost to sight as the runespeakers closed the half circle behind Travis.

His captors thrust him toward the null stone, and all sounds receded, becoming muffled and indistinct, as if heard in a dream. His right hand itched, and he knew that if he tried to speak a rune, his tongue would cleave to the roof of his mouth.

He slipped on the sticks as his captors grabbed his shoulders and pressed him hard against the stone. Air rushed from his lungs in a sickening *whoosh*. Before he could move, they had bound him to the stone with thick lengths of braided cord. One of them jerked the gag away from his mouth. There was no danger of his speaking a rune now.

The runespeakers retreated, their gray robes melding with the others, and a queer peace stole over Travis. At least he didn't need to decide what to do anymore.

Just a little while longer, Max. Then I'm going to burn, just like you did.

"It is sunset. Let us be done with this."

The voice was strong and carried even past the dullness surrounding the null stone, but the sound of it was weary all the same. Travis raised his head and saw two runespeakers standing in front of the others. One was Oragien, his white hair and beard fluttering on the listless breeze. The other was Master Larad. The shattered fragments of his face were arranged in an expression as lifeless as that of a statue.

Travis looked past Larad, searching for one kind, homely face—but there was no sign of Sky. However, he did see one who stood slightly apart from the others, as if reluctant to be close to them as they did this thing. Travis couldn't see who it was—the hood of his gray robe was drawn up over his face—but maybe not all the runespeakers thought like Master Larad did.

Oragien leaned on his staff. "Do you understand

the crime for which you are to be punished, Master Wilder?"

Before Travis could speak another, harsher voice answered.

"He has defiled the runestone," Larad said with a sneer. "The runestone, which is the heart of our tower and the source of all we are. His punishment has been decided."

Oragien kept his gaze fixed on Travis. "Have you any words to speak before the end?"

Again Larad answered first. "He's spoken enough lies already."

This time the master's words won a sharp glance from the All-master. The scar-faced man fell silent, but his eyes did not move from Travis. Somehow, Travis drew a scant breath of air into his lungs. He forced his voice to carry past the stillness that weighed over the stone.

"I've only told you the truth, Oragien."

He could see the All-master's frail hands grow white as they tightened around his staff. Oragien pressed his eyes shut but said nothing. Larad made a sharp motion with his hand. Two runespeakers moved forward, each holding a burning torch. They plunged the brands into the pile of sticks beneath Travis.

Instinct forced Travis's body against the ropes that bound him, but they were far too strong to break. His mind screamed the rune *Sharn*. Water. But when his lips tried to form the word, the presence of the null stone pressed down on him like an iron weight. A curl of smoke wafted against his face, stinging his nose and throat. He turned his head away—

—and saw Grace Beckett standing beside the null stone.

Wonder replaced fear. How could Grace be there? She looked just as he remembered her, clad in a violet gown, her green-gold eyes as brilliant as summer gems. Except her hair was longer now, framing the fine, regal features of her face. But she seemed so pale, as if ill, and her expression was stricken. Why didn't she speak to him?

"Grace!" he said, barely able to utter the word.

Still she did not speak. His first thought was that he was already dying, that this was one final hallucination brought on by smoke and pain. But the fire was still crackling its way upward through the wood, and when he blinked she was still there, standing just a few feet away.

No, not standing. He saw now that her form drifted above the ground, and while all things cast long shadows in the setting sun, she did not. Only then did he realize that he could see the faint outlines of rocks through her translucent body.

The heat was rising now, growing uncomfortable against his legs. More smoke drifted past his face, choking him. A few more seconds, then he would die. Was Grace dead as well? Was this her ghost coming to welcome him?

Not her ghost, Travis. Her spirit.

In that second he understood everything. It was just like the circle of standing stones outside Calavere, when Grace had cast a spell on the conspirator's knife, and had flown from her body to see the two would-be murderers speaking there. How he could see her vision-self he didn't know. But once, in the petty kingdom of Kelcior, it had seemed as if his gunslinger's spectacles had helped him see auras of light around Melia, Falken, and Beltan. Wasn't a spirit like an aura?

There wasn't time to think about it. All that mattered was that Grace had seen him here. And if it was anything like the last time, then she had glimpsed all of this days ago. Maybe even weeks. This was her future. Which meant . . .

*You could be here, Grace. If you saw this happen,
if you cared enough, you could be here.*

It was beyond desperate: a dying man's fantasy. But
if there was even one shard of possibility left for his
existence, however small, he had to reach for it.
Wasn't that what Brother Cy had showed him?

*But what do you do, Travis? Even if she saw you,
even if she's here, how do you help her help you?*

His mind was blank. The heat rose to the threshold
of pain—and moved beyond it. Smoke filled his eyes
with tears, obscuring the ghostly vision of Grace.
Then, like a whisper, words echoed in his brain.

The hand of Olrig will aid you. . . .

So that was what Jack had meant. He had to tell
Grace—both then and now. A roaring filled Travis's
skull. There was no more time.

The fire leaped up, and he threw his head back to
scream.

55.

Grace stumbled after the young man in the brown
robe, following him down a twisting staircase, nearly
biting her tongue with each jarring step. She was tall,
but the gray robe was still too large, and it caught
around her ankles, threatening to trip her and send
her tumbling down the steps.

There were so many questions she wanted to ask
the other. What was his name? Why had he come to
the cell? And what did he want? But even a single
word had been nearly beyond him. Nor was there
time to stop and chat. The young man was helping
her try to save Travis—that was all she really needed
to know.

The staircase ended, and they stood before a triangular opening as tall as three men. Hot crimson light

poured through, infusing the air like plasma. Grace stepped forward, then realized she was by herself. She looked back over her shoulder. The young man stood on the other side of the line between light and shadow.

"Aren't you coming?"

He pointed to the ceiling, then brought his wrists together and snapped them apart. *I must help the others free the knights, my lady.*

Grace froze. Alone. How could she do this alone? Those men out there meant to murder Travis.

Get a grip on yourself, Doctor. Just change the gray robes to white coats and you've got a bunch of attending physicians who made a bad diagnosis. All you have to do is tell them the procedure they're about to attempt is wrong. It's not as if it's something you haven't done a hundred times.

Grace sucked in a breath like a woman just taken off a respirator: alive, for the moment. She nodded to the young man, and he smiled. He moved his hands from his collar to the top of his head. *Pull your hood up, my lady.*

Grace did this, then looked up to see he was already gone. She turned and stepped into the light.

It took several blinks for her eyes to adjust to the full glare of sunset. The sharp summits of the Fal Erenn stabbed at the sky like black knives, and red light rained down. When she regained full vision, she saw that the last few runespeakers were falling into place in a semicircle thirty yards away. Grace picked up the hem of the robe and hastened after them. She fell in behind the last man just as he was stepping into place. There seemed no more room for her in the formation, so she stood a pace to one side and a pace back. Her heart thudded against her ribs, and she knew at any moment one of the runespeakers would turn toward her, point a finger, and shout the word *impostor.*

Instead, all faced forward as a weary voice spoke. "It is sunset. Let us be done with this."

Grace pushed her hood back an inch—just enough to get a clear view. Two runespeakers stood near the stone. One was Oragien. The other was the man she had seen at the gate last night, the one whose face had been rendered a broken mosaic by countless white scars.

Oragien's voice drifted thinly over the plateau. "Do you understand the crime for which you are to be punished, Master Wilder?"

It was the scarred one who answered, his words like the lashes of a whip. "He has defiled the runestone. The runestone, which is the heart of our tower and the source of all we are. His punishment has been decided."

Grace licked her lips. She had to do something. But what? Inside the sleeve of her robe she clutched the stone hand of Olrig. It had to be important—why else would the young man have given it to her? However, Grace had no idea what she was supposed to do with it, and time was running out. On the farside of the standing stone, two men stood ready with torches.

You've got to say something, Grace. Anything. It doesn't matter—just so it makes them stop what they're doing.

Grace opened her mouth, but Oragien beat her. "Have you any words to speak before the end?"

Again the scarred man answered for Travis. "He's spoken enough lies already."

This time a glare from Oragien silenced the scarred one.

"I've only told you the truth, Oragien," a quiet voice said.

Travis gazed at the All-master. His face was ashen, his sandy hair dark and damp with sweat, but his gray eyes were calm behind his wire-rimmed spectacles. The hot wind snatched a whisper from Grace's lips.

"Oh, Travis . . ."

Oragien hung his head, and the scarred man made a sharp gesture. The men with torches approached the standing stone. As they did, the scarred one moved back, his gray robe melding with those of the other runespeakers, and Grace lost sight of him. She looked back at Travis. Torches contacted dry wood. In seconds thick smoke rose upward.

Now, Grace. Just scream. Scream for them to stop.

But this wasn't a trauma room in the ED. Nor was this Castle Calavere. She was neither doctor nor duchess. Her commands would not be obeyed here.

Travis had turned his head away from the smoke, and now he seemed frozen. What was he doing? Then she saw his lips form a word, and she knew what it was.

Grace!

Shock coursed through her. So he *had* seen her— not her true self, but her vision-self.

Which means you weren't supposed to be there, Grace.

This thought filled her with sudden hope. She had not failed her destiny after all. Instead, she could still shape it. But she had only seconds now. Travis's body went rigid with pain. He threw his head back, and just as had happened in the vision, a scream ripped itself from him.

"Olrig's hand will save me!"

Grace started to step forward, to throw herself on the heap and beat the flames back with her body if she had to. Hard fingers gripped her arm, halting her.

"The hand!" a dagger-sharp voice hissed in her ear.

She turned and stared into a pair of dark eyes set deep in a shattered face.

"What are you waiting for?" the scarred man spat. "The hand of Olrig—throw it to him! The rune of runes bound into it will counter the power of the null stone."

For a frozen moment Grace stared in mute confusion. Then, like a needle, understanding pierced the dull membrane that shrouded her mind. *Olrig's hand will save me.* It was not a plea to a god for help. It was a set of instructions. She stepped forward, drew the stone hand from her sleeve, and threw it toward the flames at Travis's feet.

Grace had never been the athletic type; this time her aim was perfect. The runespeakers stared as sparks flew up where the hand landed on the burning wood. Travis looked down, a fierce grin added to the pain upon his face, then he spoke a word just as the sun dipped beneath the western mountains.

"Reth."

The fire was snuffed out, and a crash like thunder rolled across the plateau. Then the arc of the rising full moon cleared an escarpment, and by its cool light Grace saw a scene that made her gasp as one with the runespeakers.

Travis stepped away from the pile of half-burnt sticks, trailing the ropes that had bound him, his face smudged with soot. Behind him, the standing stone lurched at an odd angle. A deep crack ran through its center; the stone was broken.

"Yes!" a voice whispered behind Grace. "By Olrig, yes!"

Grace cast a stunned glance back at the scarred man. The shattered fragments of his face had rearranged themselves into an expression of triumph. Grace didn't try to understand. Instead she ran toward Travis. He stared at her, his gray eyes confused. Then she laughed and threw back her hood. Now his eyes went wide behind his spectacles, and he staggered toward her.

"Grace?"

"I'm here, Travis. I'm really here."

Tears made tracks down his fire-darkened cheeks.

"Grace," he said, and threw his arms around her. "You came."

She stiffened, knowing she should push him away, should examine his legs to determine how severely they were burned so she could prescribe the proper treatment. But she let herself melt against him instead. This was a kind of healing as well.

A murmur rose from the gathering of runespeakers, and both Grace and Travis looked up.

Oragien stared at the broken stone. "This is impossible. . . ."

"No, All-master, it is not."

Another runespeaker approached, thin scars gleaming in the light of the moon.

"Master Larad," Travis said.

Larad cast a feral grin at him, then looked back at Oragien. "Too often we have called something impossible when what we really meant was we were afraid to try."

Another runespeaker approached: a plump little man with small, blurry eyes. He clasped and unclasped his hands. "But what does this mean for Master Wilder's punishment?"

Master Larad let out a chuckle. "Do not fear, Master Eriaun." Now he raised his voice so all could hear. "The null stone has cracked. The old laws speak clearly on this: The judgment is void, and Master Wilder is free. Go back to the tower and think on what has happened until we meet again for chorus!"

The runespeakers muttered among themselves, then several of them turned and walked slowly back to the tower. More followed, and more, disappearing through the tower gate, until the plateau was nearly empty.

"You understood my message, Grace." Travis lifted an object he had been holding: the stone hand. "You realized this would help me break the null stone."

"Actually, I didn't." She glanced at Master Larad. Travis frowned. "But I don't understand."

Oragien leaned on his staff. "Nor do I."

"I knew the statue of Olrig was as ancient as the null stone," Larad said, "that both were forged by the Runelords of Malachor. And I suspected that the rune of runes bound into the hand would counter the rune of silence bound into the null stone. For the All-rune is supreme above all other runes. That is why I had Sky give the hand to your friend."

"But why?" Travis said. Gently, he disentangled himself from Grace. "I thought you wanted me dead. Why did you help me?"

"For the same reason I did my best to convince you to break the runestone—to wake my brethren, to show them that nothing is impossible if we haven't tried it, to make them give up the shadows of the past so that we can learn anew for ourselves. That is how the Runespeakers will regain their place in Falengarth—not by one runelord's hand, but by the hands of all of us."

Oragien's face was grim as wind-worn stone. "You might have spoken to me, Master Larad."

The harshness crept back into Larad's voice. "Yes? And what would you have said, All-master?"

Oragien clenched the staff. "You mentioned the old laws, Master Larad. They speak clearly on this matter as well. I do not know if what you have wrought is for good or for ill. I will hazard that likely it will be for both. But either way you will be punished for these acts."

Now the sharpness fled Larad's face. "I know," he said.

Grace stepped toward Larad, but before she could ask him more—why he had given her the stone hand, and why Larad had not used it himself—several figures appeared in the tower's gate, then ran across the plateau.

"Travis!" a bright voice called.

Travis looked up, then laughed. "Beltan!"

The blond knight was the first to reach them, followed closely by Durge, Aryn, and Lirith leading Tira. Behind them came a crooked figure in a brown robe.

"I knew you'd return to us," Beltan said. He threw his arms around Travis. "I knew it."

The two men embraced as the others laid their hands on Travis's shoulders. Finally, Travis stepped back and cast a smile toward the mute young man.

"Sky—I should have known you had a part in all this."

The young man bowed low. *You're welcome, Master Travis.*

Durge eyed the smoldering pile of sticks and the broken standing stone. "What has happened here?"

"That is a question I would very much like to hear the answer to," a shimmering voice spoke.

All looked up to see two figures step out of a shadow and into the moon-drenched twilight. Grace's heart fluttered in her chest, but it was wonder and not fear that filled her.

Oragien made a stiff bow in the direction of the regal, amber-eyed lady in blue and the man with silver-shot hair and one black glove. "Lady Melia, Master Falken. It is good you have returned."

Grace searched but found she had no words that could possibly express her feelings. By the looks—and silence—of the others, they were in a similar predicament.

Melia glided forward, her blue kirtle whispering. "Well, I see you're causing trouble as usual, Travis."

Grace could see Travis's wince. Falken's low, musical laugh rose on the evening air.

"By the gods," the bard said, "it's good to see all of you again."

Now Melia smiled, her amber eyes glowing. "Oh, Travis."

She pressed her cheek against his chest. He blinked, then sighed and folded his arms around her. Finally, she pulled away and moved to Grace.

"My dear one, you're more beautiful than ever."

Grace didn't know what she could possibly say, so she hugged Melia tightly instead.

"All right, dear. You mustn't break me."

"Sorry," Grace murmured, releasing the small woman. Grace seemed to have only two modes for expressing affection: off and maximum power.

"Of course, dear." Melia smoothed her kirtle, then she paused and moved toward Lirith and Tira. She knelt before the girl. "And who is this?"

"Her name is Tira," Grace said, but before she could say anything more, the girl flung her arms around Melia's neck and pressed her lips against the coppery skin of the lady's cheek.

"Yes, dear, I love you, too," Melia murmured.

Apparently satisfied by these words, Tira let go and pressed her small body against Lirith's skirts once more.

Grace marveled at the girl's unusual display, but she could wonder about it later. "Melia, Falken," she said. "What are you doing here?"

Melia gestured to them all. "Why, we've been waiting for you, of course."

"That's right," Falken said. "And it's about time you're all here. We have to go find Krondisar."

PART FOUR

FOOTSTEPS

56.

At dawn, two days after the full of the moon, the companions gathered beneath the Gray Tower of the Runespeakers to continue their journey east. Travis was amazed at how quickly they fell into their old traveling routines.

"I'll get the horses ready," Beltan said.

"Of course you will, dear," Melia said, her coppery skin glowing in the warm morning light.

Falken glanced at Melia with faded blue eyes. "So, are you sure you know how to find this place?"

"Don't you trust me?"

"Not entirely. Why?"

The amber-eyed lady folded her arms across the bodice of her blue kirtle. "I'm sure I'll manage."

Travis pushed his spectacles higher on his nose. "So, where is it that you want to go?"

Both the bard and the lady turned looks of displeasure on him. "Please don't interrupt us while we're having a discussion, Travis."

He sighed as the two bent their heads together to speak in low voices. "Here we go again."

However, his sigh phased into a laugh as he caught Grace's brilliant green-gold eyes. She laughed as well, and at their combined mirth Falken and Melia halted their conversation and looked up.

"What's so funny?" Falken said with a frown.

"Oh, you wouldn't understand," Travis said, then he linked arms with Grace, and the two strode after Beltan to the stable.

"Someone's getting just a trifle pert, isn't he?" Melia said behind them.

Falken's only answer was a snort. Travis leaned his head against Grace's, and she clutched his elbow as she shook with glee.

"I've missed you, Grace."

"I know."

Besides his laughter, there were other differences between this journey and the trek Travis had made once with Falken, Melia, and Beltan from the Winter Wood to Calavere. For one, Durge moved to help Beltan with the horses, the Embarran knight's chain mail absorbing the sunlight while the Calavaner's reflected it. For another, Aryn stood near Melia and Falken, and while the baroness seemed both paler and quieter than Travis remembered, her sapphire eyes were even brighter.

With Grace and Aryn had come two Travis didn't know. In some ways Lirith reminded him of Melia. Both had black hair and mysterious smiles. However, Lirith's tresses fell in tight coils about her shoulders, unlike Melia's smooth, midnight wave, and Melia's skin was copper, while Lirith's reminded Travis of dark, polished wood. And while Melia's mysteries were as distant as stars in the night sky, Lirith's were shadowed and inviting, like a cool, deep cave beckoning in a blazing desert.

Then there was the other Travis did not know. He searched with his eyes, then found her perched on a rock apart from the others, cradling a small object in her arms. Yesterday, Travis had listened as Grace told the harrowing story of their journey to the Gray Tower, including the events in Falanor. Several times Travis tried to introduce himself to Tira, but on each occasion the girl turned from him, circled her arms around Grace's or Lirith's neck, and hid her half-scarred face behind a cascade of fiery red hair.

Now Tira looked up, and Travis caught her eyes— one perfectly formed, the other drooping in the melted ruin that was the right side of her face. He froze. For a second, as had happened once before in the ruins of Kelcior, it seemed an aura of light shone around each of his companions.

The aura about Grace was as green-gold as her eyes, although muted, and dimmer than he would have thought. In turn, Aryn's aura was sapphire blue and so bright he could hardly look in her direction, while Lirith's was as warm as honey in sunlight. Durge had appeared from the stable, leading a trio of horses, and while Travis would have guessed the knight's aura to be as gray and somber as mist, instead it was blue steel. Then his eyes moved again to Tira. For a moment he saw it flickering around her thin body: a corona of hot fire.

"Travis?"

He adjusted his spectacles, and the auras were gone. He looked at Grace and managed a grin that was nearly all genuine. "Let's help with the horses."

Grace nodded and followed after.

Travis recognized the three horses Durge had led from the stable. One was Melia's pale, slender-legged mare, and another Falken's proud jet stallion. Travis laughed as he saw the third: It was the same shaggy, sand-colored gelding he had ridden all the way from Kelcior to Calavere.

"I haven't seen you in a while, old friend," he said, as the horse nuzzled his hand. Upon finding no carrots the beast let out a disgruntled snort, and Travis laughed. "I suppose I'm going to have to name you now." He reached up and stroked the white spot on the horse's flat face. "How about Patch?"

The gelding rolled its eyes, but since it didn't suggest anything better, Travis made a command decision.

"Patch it is."

Durge and Beltan had already lashed Travis's things to the gelding—a bedroll, a pack of food, and a saddlebag containing his gray robe. Travis had traded the garment for the green tunic and brown hose he wore now—clothes Falken had produced, and which looked so similar to those the bard had once obtained for him that Travis wondered if Falken had stolen these from some peasant farm as well. They were certainly ragged enough, but they were clean and would serve well for riding.

He checked the saddlebag, making sure his mist-cloak and Malachorian dagger were safe inside. Then his fingers brushed one more object tied to the saddle. It was long and slender, wrapped in felt. Once again he heard the words Oragien had spoken to him last night.

This runestaff was forged by the Runelords long ago. As their heir, it is only right that it should be yours.

It was not the ending Travis had expected to his stay in the Gray Tower of the Runespeakers. Yesterday, the runespeakers had gathered for chorus at dawn, and they had not left the domed chamber until sunset. What they spoke of Travis didn't know. However, Falken and Melia took part in the chorus, and from time to time, standing outside the chamber, Travis heard the ceaseless whispering rise into more heated debate.

As evening approached, Melia and Falken left the chamber to let the runespeakers deliberate. Travis swallowed hard when he saw them. The lady's cheeks were flushed, and Falken's black-gloved hand was clenched in a fist.

"I told you we shouldn't have left while he was still recovering from the fever," Falken said.

Melia's eyes flashed. "Well, how was I supposed to know how much trouble he could cause in such a short time?"

"You'd think we'd have learned by now, wouldn't you?"

Understanding hit Travis like a rock on the head. "It was you! You were the two that helped summon me to the Gray Tower."

Melia sighed. "And what other completely obvious things did you wish to tell me, dear?"

"But I don't understand. How did you call me here?"

Melia shrugged. "I have connections."

"And quite a lot of luck," Falken said.

Melia treated the bard to a withering look.

Travis did his best to absorb this information. He knew there was something . . . *special* about Melia. But he wouldn't have thought this was a feat she could manage, summoning him across worlds. Then he thought of Brother Cy, and he wondered if Melia had indeed been lucky—if perhaps her call had been heard by another.

"I saw you, Melia," he said quietly. "When I was sick. I saw you bending over me, and you were shining. But I thought it was just the fever showing me what I most wanted to see."

Melia's gaze softened. "I'm sorry we had to leave you, Travis. But we received an important message, and we had to pay a visit to an old friend of mine."

Before he could ask more about this old friend, the bard and the lady were summoned back into the chorus chamber.

A short while later he watched as a stream of rune-speakers passed by. Some cast glances at him, but what their looks portended he didn't know. Finally, two last figures stepped through the triangular opening: Melia and Falken.

"He wants to speak with you, dear," Melia said, touching his arm.

Travis frowned. "Who?" But even as he asked, he knew.

"Go on," Falken said. "He's waiting for you."

Travis hesitated, then stepped into the chorus chamber. The sound of argument had faded; only the murmur of ancient voices drifted on the air. A single, stooped figure stood below the dais at the center.

Oragien spoke as he approached. "I hope you can forgive us, Master Wilder."

Travis nearly choked. Why should the Rune-speakers forgive *him*? He had broken their runestone, destroying their one link with the past. Had he really saved them? Or had he simply hastened their inevitable fading? He halted before Oragien. To Travis's surprise, the old man was smiling.

"You know, you are fortunate to have friends such as Falken Blackhand and Lady Melia. There were those among the masters who felt you should stay, to help us learn as we begin to rebuild the runestone. But those two argued strongly that you were needed elsewhere."

"You mean I'm free to go?"

"Yes, Master Wilder, you may go. The null stone has broken, and all judgments against you are void." The All-master ran knobby fingers over the timeworn wood of his runestaff. "But are any of us truly free?"

Travis didn't know how to answer and so said nothing.

After that, despite his protests, Oragien had pressed the runestaff into his hands, and Travis had felt quiet power coursing up and down its length.

Use it well, and only when you must, runelord,

Oragien had said. *And when you can, come back to us.*

Then the old man had turned and limped from the chamber, leaving Travis alone.

For a time Travis had stood alone in the chorus chamber, listening to the echoes of voices past. However, if they had any message for him, he could not make out the words. He had left the chamber and spent the next hour searching the tower for one other person whom he wanted to bid farewell. Again that morning he had searched. However, Sky was nowhere to be found.

"Perhaps he was needed somewhere else," Melia had said last night when Travis asked if she had seen the young man, not looking up from Beltan's cloak, which she was mending.

Travis had thought this an odd answer, but maybe she was right. Melia usually was. He had finally given up his search, but he hoped one day he would find Sky again, and have a chance to thank him for his kindness.

Strangely, Sky was not the only person in the tower to go missing. To everyone's puzzlement, Master Eriaun was gone as well. The last time anyone remembered seeing the plump little master had been just after Travis broke the null stone. Travis hoped the nearsighted runespeaker hadn't wandered off the edge of a precipice in the twilight. However, no one had seen any trace of him—although the runespeakers had not given up their search. Travis hoped Eriaun was all right.

"It's going to be a hot day."

Travis blinked as Durge's words jerked him back to the moment. He let his hands fall from the felt-covered staff.

"You'd better get used to the heat," Falken said. "It's only going to get hotter where we're riding."

Travis wanted to ask the bard about their destination and their quest, but he knew better. Falken would tell them when he was ready. All he had said so far was that this had something to do with one of the Imsari, the three Great Stones—the one called Krondisar.

Travis glanced up at the sun. He knew enough about runes now to translate that word. The Stone of Fire.

"Travis, will you assist me?"

Melia stood beside her white mare. Travis hurried over and with his fingers wove a step for her tiny boot. Once in the saddle, she arranged her kirtle into an elegant cascade. Travis reached to buckle one of her saddlebags—

—and it hissed at him.

He snatched his hand back, but not in time to keep needle-sharp claws from tracing a red line across his skin. He lifted his stinging hand to his mouth, then saw the fluffy black ball peeking out of the saddlebag with moon-gold eyes.

"You!"

The kitten let out a purr, cleaning a tiny paw with delicate laps of its pink tongue.

But it can't be the same kitten she had in Calavere, Travis. That cat would be full-grown by now.

All the same, Travis eyed the kitten warily. Something told him he was going to have to be careful on this journey if he wanted to finish it with skin still on his ankles.

The others had begun mounting their horses, and Travis turned to do the same. He halted as a man in a gray robe stepped between the two standing stones that marked the trail to the tower. He noticed the pack strapped to the other's back. So he wasn't the only one about to embark on a long journey.

"Master Larad," he said.

The scar-faced man nodded. "Master Wilder."

"Where are you going?"

Larad's lips twisted in a mocking smile. "Anywhere I wish, as long as it's not here."

"So they banished you," Falken said from aback his horse.

"It would seem that way, Falken Blackhand."

Travis studied Larad's face. For a time yesterday, while the chorus recessed, Travis and Grace had spoken with Larad in an alcove near the chorus chamber.

So you set everything up, Travis had said. *Getting me to break the runestone, then showing that escape from the null stone wasn't impossible.*

Yes, Larad had said. *The Runespeakers had to learn how to forget that word.*

What word?

Impossible.

Grace had spoken then. *But there are still some things I don't understand, Master Larad. Why didn't you just use Olrig's hand yourself? Why give it to Sky to give to me?*

Because I was to stand near the null stone as one of Master Wilder's accusers. If I were holding the hand, its power might have been revealed by the null stone too early to help him.

Then it had been Travis's turn to express his confusion. *But if you wanted me to go free, why go to such great lengths to punish me in the first place?*

I wished for you to break the runestone, Master Wilder. To reforge it the Runespeakers must truly come to understand it. But this required punishing you for the deed. While we must think of the future, the ancient laws must still be obeyed. Without them we have no foundation upon which to build.

Travis had thought about these words all last night. Now he approached the runespeaker. "I think I understand, Master Larad. Why you did things the way you did, I mean."

Larad nodded. "It was important for you not to like me."

"Well, you did a good job of that." Travis's smile faded. "But why didn't you just tell me what you wanted me to do? Wouldn't that have been easier?"

"And if I had told you the truth, and what your punishment would be, would you have done it?"

Travis thought about this, then answered with the truth. "I'm not sure."

"Nor was I."

Travis hesitated, then held out a hand. "It's all right, Master Larad. I'm not mad at you."

"I did not ask for your forgiveness, Master Wilder."

Ignoring Travis's hand, Larad started away. Then he paused to cast a glance back over his shoulder, his dark eyes gleaming in the shattered mosaic of his face. "I wish you well on your journey. Runelord."

"You too," Travis whispered, but Larad had already disappeared around an outcrop of stone.

Travis let out a soft breath, then turned toward the others. They all sat on their horses. It was time to go. He moved to Patch, grabbed a handful of mane, and climbed into the saddle. He looked up to see amber eyes upon him.

"Are you all right, dear?" Melia said.

Travis gripped the reins. "Let's get away from this place."

57.

They kept close to the Fal Erenn as they journeyed, and with every league that passed, Grace's spirits rose higher. Maybe it was Travis they had helped to save at the Gray Tower, but Grace felt like she was the one who was suddenly free. The road to the tower had been shadowed, and marked by fire and death. But all of that was behind her now. Despite Falken's admonition to the contrary, the air grew cooler and moister as they traveled east and—if Grace recalled her maps rightly—nearer the ocean.

She spoke little that first day of riding, instead content to keep Shandis back and watch her companions. One by one, her gaze alighted on each of the others. Travis laughed at one of Beltan's bawdy jokes. Melia bowed her head toward Falken as the two spoke in low voices. Aryn gazed at the world with brilliant blue eyes, her visage pale but exquisite, while Lirith rode nearby, her expression as calm and deep as still water. Then there was Durge—good, kind, true Durge—spurring his charger ahead and searching so very hard for any signs of bandits, monsters, or unlikely natural disasters.

A small hand reached up to brush Grace's cheek. She looked down into Tira's half-melted face. The girl nodded, as if she had merely wished to remind Grace of her presence, then turned her placid gaze forward again. Fingers tightened around Grace's heart, but it was a good pain.

You're never alone, Grace. Even when sometimes it feels like you are. You have to remember that.

Just after midmorning, Melia and Falken guided their mounts close to Travis's to ask him what seemed a never-ending series of questions. At the Gray Tower, the same evening they had freed him, Travis had told his story. All of them had listened in rapt attention, shuddering as they learned the fire evil walked not one world, but two. Grace couldn't hear much of their conversation now, but the bard and the lady seemed to be probing Travis for finer details of his story, especially about the man in the black robe who had come to Travis's saloon. Grace shivered as she remembered Travis's description of the other.

Beware—it will consume you.

Had the man in black been speaking of the Burning

Plague? It was the only answer that made sense. She almost wished she could go back to Denver, so she could study one of the plague victims at the hospital—to run blood tests and biopsies, to take X-rays and MRIs, to probe with modern tools and see if she could comprehend the nature of this disease.

Then she thought of the man in the farmhouse, the one she had ended with an iron poker, and she knew no tools or tests, however advanced, would be able to truly explain this affliction. Besides, if a door to Denver were to open before her at that moment, Grace was not so certain she would step through. How would it feel to put on a stark white lab coat again after wearing bright gowns of violet and gold?

Her eyes moved again to Lirith. The Tolorian woman sat straight atop her palfrey, not as stiffly as Melia, and perhaps not as regal, yet commanding all the same. No, *commanding* wasn't the right word. Compelling—that was it. Lirith didn't order you to do things, not like Melia did. Instead she made you *want* to do them.

It had been interesting observing the two women these last days. At the Gray Tower, Melia and Lirith had stared at each other like two women who had worn the same expensive dress to a party. Now, as they rode, Lirith cast surreptitious but frequent glances at the amber-eyed lady, and while Melia didn't look up, there was something about the set of her shoulders that made Grace think Lirith's looks had not gone unnoticed.

At last curiosity won out, and Grace guided Shandis toward the Tolorian woman's palfrey. "What is it, Lirith?" she whispered without preamble.

"What do you mean, sister?" Even as Lirith spoke these soft words her eyes moved past Grace to the lady on the white horse.

"That," Grace said. "You can't take your eyes off her. Lady Melia."

"It's nothing," Lirith said far too quickly.

Grace's lips twisted into a wry smile. "Of course. I always stare at other people for absolutely no reason."

Lirith raised a slender eyebrow. "I see you learned much indeed from the Lady Kyrene."

"Oh, no you don't," Grace said with a fierce grin. "You're not going to get out of this by throwing it back to me. You know something about Melia— something you're not telling."

Again Lirith's eyes moved past Grace, and she spoke in a quiet tone. "If I know anything, it is only what she chooses to reveal to all of us."

Before Grace could ask anything more, Lirith lightly touched the neck of her palfrey, and the horse leaped into a canter, leaving Grace behind.

They made camp as the long shadows of the mountains reached into the east. Beltan had brought down a small mule deer with a snare, and while Grace's heart had fallen to see the young animal get captured, her stomach was more than happy to give purpose to the creature's death.

That night there was an almost festive air around the campfire. Beltan told colorful anecdotes about drunken warriors, Falken sang songs, and Lirith astonished them all by performing tricks of magic with a coin. These feats relied on sleight of hand rather than the Weirding, but Grace gasped all the same as Lirith made the coin vanish in her hand, then pulled it from the ear of a wide-eyed Durge. Tira clapped her hands and laughed, and Grace hugged her.

This is dangerous, Grace. You know it is. You're letting yourself get used to Tira being here. You're letting yourself get too close.

But suddenly it was hard to remember exactly what her reasons were for keeping others at a distance. She tightened her arms around the girl, and Tira did not resist.

Melia fashioned the fresh venison, along with herbs collected by Aryn and Lirith, into a fragrant stew, and once bowls were passed out Lirith lowered her gaze and spoke in a reverent voice.

"Joy from pain, life from death. In endings are beginnings born. May Yrsaia bless the gains of this hunt."

When she looked up, Lirith's gaze fell on Melia.

"What a lovely prayer, dear," the regal lady said with a smile, then ate her stew.

After supper, Beltan began to tell another joke, this one involving a hapless knight who couldn't manage to remove his armor in time when the fair maiden he had rescued wished to express her gratitude. Then Falken spoke, and while his voice was not loud, it silenced the mirth all the same.

"It's the Stone of Fire that's creating them somehow."

"The Burnt Ones," Grace said without thinking.

Firelight glinted off Travis's spectacles. "Of course, it makes sense. *Krondrim*. Krondisar. I should have guessed it sooner."

"What is it you have learned, Falken?" Durge said. "It is not so apparent to some of us as it is to others."

"It was Melia's friend who told us," the bard said.

Melia smoothed the folds of her kirtle. "The Great Stone Krondisar has been found. And it is in the possession of one who would use it for evil. Who does so even now."

"But who is it?" Grace said.

Falken met her gaze. "That's what we have to find out."

"All right," Beltan said, speaking the question on everyone's mind, "so where are we going?"

Firelight played across Melia's visage. "To the place from which Krondisar was stolen."

All of them stared at the amber-eyed lady—all except for Tira, who stretched small hands toward the fire and laughed.

They woke before dawn the next day to continue their journey. Now that they knew something of their destination, the holiday air of yesterday's ride had given way to a more somber mood. However, the rugged landscape about them was beautiful, and while a shadow had touched Grace's thoughts, they were far from dark.

It was only when Beltan mentioned that they were nearly to the southern border of Perridon that Grace remembered the mission King Boreas had given her. She had been so focused on reaching the Gray Tower and saving Travis that she had forgotten entirely about her orders. But one did not dismiss the commands of a king on this world. Not and live long to regret it.

Grace moved Shandis closer to Falken's jet stallion. "We're riding into Perridon, aren't we, Falken?"

The bard frowned. "Is something wrong, Grace?"

There will be if Boreas finds out I've gone AWOL on him.

"I was just wondering if we're going to Castle Spardis. King Boreas gave me a task to do there, and I'd like to finish it."

Falken turned his faded blue eyes north. "I've been hearing some dark news out of Spardis lately, ever since old King Persard died. Queen Inara is only sixteen, and her son, Perseth—Persard's heir—is still at her breast. It's not a good position to be in. At least not in a Dominion where every five-year-old peasant has a dagger and a plan." He glanced at her. "I take it you agreed to survey the situation for Boreas?"

Grace nodded, lifting an unconscious hand to her neck.

"Don't worry." The bard grinned now. "You'll get to keep your head attached to your shoulders, Your

Radiance. After we make this one stop, we'll be heading straight for Spardis. We're supposed to meet Melia's friend again there. I think we'll each be very curious to hear what the other has learned."

That evening they camped inside a broken circle of stones that tilted like a crown atop a hill. As they ate leftover stew, Falken explained that these were the remains of a watchtower built by explorers from Toringarth over a thousand years earlier.

Durge stroked his mustaches. "I did not know men of Toringarth ever sailed this far south."

"And farther," the bard said. "They were the greatest mariners ever to navigate the four seas. Many towers they raised near the sea, all up and down the coasts of Falengarth."

Grace thought back to her lessons in politics. She remembered seeing Toringarth on Aryn's map—a jagged finger of land north of Falengarth, across the Winter Sea—but she recalled no other reference to the kingdom, save in Falken's stories when he told how long ago King Ulther of Toringarth helped defeat the Pale King with the help of Elsara, Empress of Tarras.

She glanced at Falken. "Why didn't anyone from Toringarth attend the Council of Kings at Calavere?"

"No word has come across the Winter Sea from the kingdom of Toringarth in many centuries, and no ship made in Falengarth can navigate the churning ice that fills the Winter Sea, not as the ships of the Toringarders could of old, bound with runes of strength and swiftness."

Grace chewed her lip. The bard's answer was wholly unsatisfying. An entire kingdom couldn't simply vanish. What had happened to Toringarth after Ulther slew the Pale King and helped found Malachor?

Maybe you'll just have to go there yourself someday and find out, Grace.

Night fell, and one by one the travelers lay down

inside the ruined tower, but sleep eluded Grace. Instead she watched meteors streak across the star-strewn disk circumscribed by the ruined walls of the tower.

She must have drifted off at some point, because she blinked, and the stars jerked across the circle. Now a crimson spark had joined them: the red star. Something pressed uncomfortably against Grace's bladder. She sat up. Black fur blended with night, but amber eyes shone in the gloom.

"What do you think you're doing?" Grace whispered.

The kitten only purred as it continued to knead with small paws at her stomach.

Grace removed the kitten, considered what to do with it, then placed it in the crook of Tira's elbow. The kitten turned three times, then lay down, resting its head against the girl's arm. Tira sighed in her sleep.

Lying back down, Grace shut her eyes, but she opened them again a moment later. The kitten's cruel paws had done their work, and there would be no chance of sleep if she didn't pay a visit to a conveniently located bush.

As quietly as she could, she rose and picked her way among the sleepers, then passed through a gap in the wall. She circled around the ruined tower until she finally found her bush. Once finished, she kept circling in the same direction, since she was already more than halfway around the tower.

"I should never have left you."

Grace froze at the sound of the soft, tenor voice.

"I've been fine," another, cooler voice whispered. "Besides, we talked about this, and we both agreed it was for the best."

Grace edged around a jumble of mossy rocks. In the starlight a half-dozen paces away two figures sat on stones. One was small and slender, her dark hair merging with the night. The other was tall and rangy, his mail shirt and fair hair glowing in the shine of the just-rising moon.

"Well, regardless, I'm here now," Beltan said. "And I'm still your knight protector."

Melia touched his hand. "I hardly wish to turn you away, dear. I don't know what I would have done without you these last years. When I met you, Falken was lost in a dark pit into which I could not reach. Without you, I might never have done so. You will always be my protector." She drew her hand back. "But, in time, you might find that you wish to be other things as well."

"My duty is to you, Melindora Nightsilver."

"Your duty is to your heart, Beltan of Calavan. And you must never forget that."

Beltan grinned, but it was a sad expression. "In this case, I don't think it's my heart that's requested of me."

"And how do you know that? Have you asked?"

Beltan said nothing, but Grace knew she had already heard much more than she should have. She moved back a step.

Beltan's hand started toward the hilt of his sword. "I heard something."

Melia stayed his hand with a light touch. "It is nothing, Beltan. A startled animal, that's all."

"You're sure?"

Amber eyes flickered in Grace's direction. "Yes, I'm quite certain of it."

Snatching up her skirts, Grace turned and stumbled back the way she had come. Once in the tower, she found her place and lay down. She started to close her eyes, then stopped. Two golden sparks watched her; the kitten still rested against Tira's arm, eyes open and gazing in her direction.

"She saw me, didn't she?" Grace whispered. "Just like you do now."

The kitten licked a paw. With a shiver, Grace turned on her blanket and curled up. And all that night she dreamed of amber moons watching her from an onyx sky.

58.

On their third day of traveling from the Gray Tower, the tumbled line of the Dawning Fells made a sharp bend to the north, and the riders turned to follow it.

Travis sighed as he gazed from his vantage atop Patch's swaying back. The land they traveled through was beautiful and utterly empty. Before, Travis had seen the occasional daub-and-wattle hovel, or the ruins of an old wall. But now there were no such signs of civilization, abandoned or not.

"It has been many more than a thousand years since people dwelled in this place," Falken said over the *clop* of hooves when Travis nudged Patch close to the bard's mount and asked about the history of this land. "We have passed beyond the marches of Toloria, and we are near the Dawn Sea and the southern reaches of what is now called the Wild Coast. But the folk who once walked this place called it DunDordurun, which in their tongue was the In-Between-Land. To them, it was a place of magic."

Travis looked at the mist-shrouded mountains and at the rugged plains below. A single hawk wheeled against the endless blue sky as a wind sprang up, carrying on it, faint but sharp, the scent of salt and the ocean.

"Who were they, Falken? The ones who lived here?"

The bard gazed at the low, distant line of a ridge

that was too straight and too long to be entirely natural. Lirith and Beltan had guided their horses closer to listen to the bard's story.

The wind blew Falken's silver-shot hair from his brow. "Those who remember them call them Maugrim, which means *the Wild Ones*. But in their tongue they were the Gul-Hin-Gul, which as far as I know meant *the True People*. I'm afraid little is known of the Maugrim."

Beltan laughed. "But I'd be willing to bet my sword that every bit that *is* known is locked up inside your skull, Falken."

"You'd likely win that bet," Melia said, drifting closer on her pale mare. Aryn rode just behind, as did Grace and Tira. Only Durge, who scouted the land ahead, was not in earshot of the bard.

"What happened to them?" Travis said. "The Maugrim."

Falken grinned at their expectant faces. "I'm sorry to disappoint you all, but I'm afraid I don't know. By the time the folk of Tarras ventured into the north of Falengarth, the Maugrim were already just a fading memory. Some believe they vanished into the Twilight Realm along with the Little People. But I fear it's more likely they simply dwindled and died out, as many peoples have throughout history."

Travis frowned. "That's it?"

"Not every tale makes a good telling." The bard gazed again at the straight line of the ridge. "Of course, there were always stories whispered in ancient days, about shadows glimpsed in forests or on high hills at twilight. Goblins, the Tarrasians called them. But I've met some who thought these shadows and spirits were a remnant of the Maugrim, lingering still in the deepest woods, and atop forlorn hills that were said to be vast and hollow inside, with secret entrances only the Wild Ones could find and open."

Above, the hawk let out a lonely cry, and the treeless hill slipped away behind them.

It was just after midday when Travis saw the giant. His stomach was growling, and he was beginning to think that complaining to Melia and Falken was almost worth the stark glares he knew such action would win him, when the riders crested a rise, and found themselves gazing into a shallow valley. The land angled down to the thin line of a stream, then rose again on the far side. It was on the green, facing them, that the giant rested. Travis's jaw dropped open, and he heard gasps to either side.

The giant stretched the entire height of the opposite ridge, his outlines traced in white stone that shone brightly against the jade background. The lines that formed the figure were crude, but powerful and wildly expressive, and the whole made Travis think of drawings he had seen of Paleolithic cave paintings.

Although the giant was manlike in form, his crooked legs and clawed feet reminded Travis of a bird's. His face was featureless save for the sharp line of a mouth and a single huge eye. Lower down the slope, his barbed phallus jutted above a pair of boldly drawn circles. Despite the enormous organ, there was something about the drawing that kept Travis from thinking it was some ancient symbol of fertility. Maybe it was the two triangles that stuck out from the smiling line of the giant's mouth like teeth. Or maybe it was the shapes protruding from one of the giant's clenched hands. Shapes which, if Travis squinted, looked almost like the small, broken forms of people.

Travis glanced to his left at a hissing sound. Melia sat stiffly aback her horse. She clutched the black kitten, fur standing up on the back of its neck, to her chest. Which of them had made the sound, Travis couldn't say.

"What is it, Melia?" he said.

"I had not thought I would ever see your likeness again," the lady said, not to Travis. "We destroyed all such images. Or so I thought."

Falken moved his horse beside Melia's and laid a hand on her arm. "Calm yourself, Melia. It's just a drawing. Lines in the dirt, that's all."

Her eyes flashed. "And do not lines have power, Falken? Is that not what you always tell me when you speak of your precious runes?"

The bard pressed his lips shut but said nothing.

"Who is it, Falken?" Travis said without really meaning to.

Falken spoke in a hard voice. "It's Mohg, the Lord of Nightfall. One of the Old Gods."

"Like Olrig, you mean?"

The bard shot him a look so sharp that Travis bit his tongue.

"No. Not like Olrig. Even in the beginning Mohg was different from the other Eldhari, and in the end he was their foe."

"Not just theirs," Melia said, her amber eyes narrowing to slits. "All of ours."

Grace nudged her palfrey forward. "I've heard you talk about the Old Gods, Falken. And the Runespeakers did as well. But no one else I've met has spoken of them. Did people ever worship them?"

"The Eldhari had little to do with people. Not like the Nindari, the New Gods who ventured into Falengarth from Al-amún and Tarras to the south, and whose fates were ever caught up with those who followed them. The Old Gods were creatures of stone, and forest, and sky. They had little understanding of the ways of people. Although some few did seek them out, and were befriended by them, and gained great gifts. Gifts like the runes. And for a numberless age the Maugrim knew of the Old Gods, and of their children, the Eldhrim—the Little People."

As the bard spoke, Travis's gaze was drawn again to

the figure outlined in white stones. There was something about it that seemed almost . . . familiar. Something about the single eye that stared from the center of its face. Then he saw something he had not noticed before: a shape perched on the old god's left shoulder, a shape with folded wings and a curved beak. Almost like . . .

Like a raven, Travis.

But that couldn't be. The ravens were all gone—they had been burned away. Wasn't that what Sister Mirrim had seen with her blind, bloody eyes?

"Who made this drawing, Falken?" Durge said in his rumbling voice. "Was it the Maugrim?"

The bard shook his head. "No, the Maugrim made no drawings. Nor did they make music or adornments for their bodies, save such pigments as they could gain from soil or plants. My guess is that this was forged later by some of the first people who journeyed into Falengarth from the south, and who encountered the Old Gods here."

Beltan snorted, gesturing toward the struggling stick figures caught in the giant's hand. "Call it a hunch, but something tells me it was an encounter they didn't much care for."

Lirith studied the drawing with dark, intent eyes. "It's fascinating."

"No, it's hideous," Melia said with quiet vehemence. She turned her amber gaze on Falken. "And you profess to wonder why people forgot the Old Gods."

The bard only grunted.

"But what *did* happen to them?" Aryn said. "Where did they go?"

Falken sighed. "Their time passed. When the New Gods came with men out of the south and marched across Falengarth, the Old Gods and the Little People knew their age had ended, and so they faded away into the Twilight Realm."

"It was hardly that simple," Melia said.

The bard studied the drawing on the hillside. "No. No, I suppose it wasn't at that."

Grace brushed strands of ash-blond hair from her eyes. "There's something I don't understand. Last winter, the Little People of Gloaming Wood were roaming the halls of Calavere. You were the first one to say they had come back, Falken. So if the Little People can come back from this Twilight Realm, does that mean the Old Gods can as well?"

Before Falken could reply Melia made a sharp gesture with her hand. "Let us leave this place. There is nothing for us here." She urged her white mare down the slope.

Travis frowned at Falken. "What was that about?"

However, the bard did not meet his gaze. "Come on," Falken said, and together the riders followed after Melia.

59.

The next day they rode between a pair of stone watchtowers set atop twin mottes—mounds of soil raised by the builders—and passed into the Dominion of Perridon. Evidently the fabled mists of the place had been lurking just across the border, for as soon as the travelers reached the towers a thick fog rose from low hollows in the ground, swirling around the legs of the horses and up to the knees of the riders.

Durge looked up at the silent watchtowers as they slipped past. The narrow windows high in each tower were dim. "Should not these forts be manned, Falken?"

"Given that this is Perridon, you'd think so." The bard's wolfish mien was grim.

Beltan snorted. "I didn't think a mouse could slip

into Perridon without someone demanding its name and a tax of three whiskers. The Perridoners have garrisons at pretty much every road, river, and footpath that leads into the Dominion. Every time I've come here, I've had to stop and tell them who I am, why I'm here, and what I had for breakfast two Melinsdays ago."

Travis guided Patch past Lirith and Aryn, toward Grace's horse. "Cheerful place, isn't it?" he said to her under his breath.

Grace smiled. "Actually, I've always sort of enjoyed foggy days."

"You're not kidding, are you?"

She shrugged. "I like the way fog hides everything. It's sort of nice to be able to move through the world and have it seem like you're the only one on the planet. It feels . . . safe."

Travis shuddered. Grace's words didn't sound nice at all, but instead horribly lonely—dwelling in a world of gray, unable to see or touch the people all around you. He opened his mouth to reply, but at that moment Tira looked up and gazed at him with her one perfect, one drooping eye. She held her half-burnt doll out toward him.

"She wants you to hold it," Grace said. "It's an honor, really—she doesn't offer it to just anyone."

Travis stared at the girl, certain that he did not want to hold the charred doll, to feel the dry, scorched wood under his fingers. But she lowered neither doll nor disarming gaze, and he started to reach for it.

"Go back!"

The riders brought their horses to a halt at the sound of the rasping voice. Even as Travis watched, a figure stepped from a bank of mist. The man's hair was plastered to his skull, and his cheeks were shadowed by dark stubble. His cloak was as gray as Travis's own.

"Go back!" the man shouted again, his voice a dry

croak. "You are fools to enter here. Go back from where you came."

Falken guided his horse forward. "We mean no harm to you." He reached his ungloved hand down toward the man.

"No! Don't touch him!"

A figure surged past Travis. It was Grace, spurring her palfrey toward Falken. The bard jerked his hand back and stared at her, as did the man in the gray cloak.

It was then that Travis saw the man's eyes: They were black, without whites, without irises. A sickness flooded his gut. Next to him, Aryn clasped a hand to her mouth, and Lirith let out a soft sigh.

"Yes," the man said, gazing up at Grace with his impossible eyes. "I see you understand."

"How far?" Grace said. Travis had never heard her voice so cold before. "How far has it spread in Perridon? The Burning Plague."

The man passed a hand before his face and staggered to one side. Travis wondered if he would collapse. Then he spoke, his voice quieter now.

"I don't know. Some villages here, some there. There is no reason, no pattern to it. They come, they strike, then they are gone again."

There was no need for Grace to ask whom he spoke of. They all knew: the Burnt Ones.

Beltan nudged his roan charger forward—but not too close. "How long ago were they here?"

The man crossed his arms over his sunken chest. "I cannot say. When I came to this place they were already ashes." He made a vague gesture toward the two towers.

"Do you know what they want?" the blond knight said.

The man laughed now, a crazed sound that chilled Travis's blood. "To burn us all, I suppose. But there was one. I saw him in the duchy of Varsarth. One who still could speak, near as he was to the end. The key, he said. He wanted the key to fire. Yet what does that mean?" He held shaking, skeletal hands before him. "But then, perhaps I will know before long."

"It's not too late," Grace said, her voice without emotion. "To end it."

He smiled now, his lips pulling back in a rictus from rotten teeth. "I know, my lady. I came here to watch, and to warn others as long as I could. But that time is nearly over. I will make one more trip up the steps of the western guard tower. And when I descend again, it will not be by the stairs, but rather by the very swiftest of routes." His black gaze flickered toward Falken. "Now, will you turn away from this place, for fear of plague?"

"It is for fear of plague that we must ride here."

The man considered the bard's words, then nodded. "So it was that I guessed. I've heard it said that trouble precedes you, Falken Blackhand. It seems the stories of the Grim Bard are true. But may the other tales be right as well." He pressed blistered lips together. "Find an end to this, Blackhand. Find an end for all of us."

Falken opened his mouth, but the man had already slipped back into a swirl of mist and was gone.

"Do you want me to find him?" Beltan said, gripping the reins of his charger.

Falken held up his gloved hand. "You won't find him. Didn't you see what he wore?"

"A mistcloak," Durge said. "He is a Spider, then?"

The bard nodded. "One of the king of Perridon's personal spies. It's said that a Spider can walk through a city at midday and not be seen by a single pair of eyes."

Travis scratched his chin—the gold-and-copper stubble had grown into a thick, full-fledged beard—and glanced at the bard. "But if that man was one of the king's spies, what was he doing here?"

"King Persard is dead," Grace said in a low voice.

Lirith's eyes glittered. "And a new king has new spies."

"But we have heard nothing of a new king in Perridon," Aryn said.

Beltan fingered the hilt of his sword. "Maybe we just have."

"What now, Falken?" Melia said, folding her arms.

"We ride," the bard said. "This changes nothing. Except perhaps to make our errand more urgent yet. Come on." He nudged the flanks of his stallion.

Travis hesitated, then cast a glance back at the two towers. The mist was rising, and the towers floated like islands in a colorless sea. He squinted through his spectacles. Was that a small shadow he saw moving atop the westernmost spire? Before he could be certain, a gray wall heaved upward, obscuring his view. He turned and followed the others, riding into the thickening fog.

60.

It was midmorning four days later when Falken, who rode at the head of the traveling party, raised his black-gloved hand and brought the group to a halt.

At least Grace assumed it was midmorning, but this was a vague supposition at best, with little visual evidence to support it, and only the growling of her stomach. The mist-heavy air was so dim that Grace nearly continued on past the others after they had stopped. If Shandis had not snorted—recognizing the location of her companions by smell—Grace supposed she would have kept riding until she and Shandis and Tira all fell over a cliff or into a pit. There had certainly been enough such perils as they made their way north through Perridon, across the rock-strewn moors at the broken feet of the Fal Erenn.

With one hand Grace held on to Tira while she used the other to tug on the reins, bringing Shandis hard around. Squinting, she made out a number of darker patches of gray against the fog ahead. Either she had found her friends or a group of stumps shaped remarkably like people on horses. As she drew near, the fog parted a bit, and she glimpsed rocks and thorny shrubs along with her companions—all of them slicked with moisture.

Despite the words spoken by the Spider at the guard towers, their ride through Perridon had been mostly uneventful. They did come upon a few isolated farms and villages after crossing the border, but all had appeared to be fine. Or at least as fine as any medieval village with open gutters for sewers and a population rife with rickets, scrofula, and other diseases of malnutrition. At any rate, there had been no signs of another, far more virulent disease—the Burning Plague.

Along the way they had been able to pick up a few supplies to replenish the foodstuffs packed at the Gray Tower—but only a few. These were the hinterlands of Perridon, far from any major castle or keep of power, and the folk who lived there were both shockingly poor and fearful of strangers. In one village they had managed to purchase a small amount of dried fruit, unleavened bread, and sour wine.

"We'll have better luck in the next village," Beltan had said, a slightly desperate crack to the big knight's voice. "Don't you think we'll have better luck, Grace?"

But there had been no next village. After that they had ridden across only barren plain and moor, intermittently choked with fog and crisscrossed everywhere by jagged ravines and broken stretches of loose, rain-slick slate that placed both horse and rider at peril.

Despite the fog and moisture, the coolness of the wild lands between Toloria and Perridon had vanished at the border along with the sun. Instead, the misty air was hot and dank, like that of a steam room that had been allowed to mold. The damp permeated everything—armor, tunics, gowns—and the heat conjured sweat which had no chance of evaporating, but only soaked their garments further.

As they traveled, Falken had spoken little more of their destination—only that it was the place where he believed the Stone of Fire had dwelled for a time. While she had heard Falken tell stories about the Imsari—the three Great Stones—Grace still didn't really understand what they were or where they had come from. All she knew was that the Pale King had been willing to go to any lengths to gain Sinfathisar, the Stone of Twilight, but instead Travis had given it to the Little People to guard. Understanding that, Grace knew it was possible Krondisar could be used in the manufacture of many evils.

Including plagues of fire. It looks like you've finally got your disease vector, Grace.

But whether or not she could find a vaccine or a cure was another question altogether. However, wasn't that what they had journeyed there to find out?

Falken swore, waving a hand at the swirling mist. "Can't you do something about this, Melia?"

Somehow Melia could gracefully perch sidesaddle upon a slender-legged white mare and exude menace all at the same time. "And what exactly would you propose I do, Falken?"

"I don't know." The bard made indeterminate weaving motions with his hand. "Can't you just . . . you know . . . use your . . . and sort of . . . ?"

The mist did not soften Melia's glare, and Falken's words faded into the gloom.

Beltan smeared damp, pale hair back from his high forehead. "And here people say *I'm* not too bright. At least I know better than to ask questions like that."

Lirith's lips curved in a musing smile. "Silence is the oft-forgotten seasoning in the stew of wisdom."

Beltan groaned and clutched his stomach. "Don't talk about stew. I'm starving."

Melia turned her gaze on the big knight. "I thought you said you were fasting in order to gain the blessing of Vathris."

"Actually, I just said that so I wouldn't have to feel so bad about not having anything to eat."

"Are you entirely certain that makes sense?" Aryn said, casting a puzzled glance at the knight.

Beltan shrugged. "It does to me."

Melia gave the blond man a withering glare. "You should know better than to make a jest with the name of a god, Beltan."

Falken grinned, clearly glad to have Melia's displeasure directed elsewhere. "And we should know better than to take large knights on long journeys without carting along a packhorse loaded with food."

"And ale," Beltan said with an emphatic nod.

Durge guided Blackalock closer to the others. The Embarran knight's sooty charger blended with the mist, so that it seemed Durge was floating in midair. "Why have we stopped here, Falken?"

Falken turned in the saddle and pointed. "That's why."

Even as the bard spoke, a gust of warm, sodden wind sprang out of nowhere, tearing a rift in the fog and sending the tatters scudding across the moor. Grace craned her neck, following the bard's gaze. A sheer wall of black stone loomed before the travelers, jutting into the slate-colored sky.

"Well," Melia said. "We're here."

Travis peered over the rims of his spectacles, the lenses clouded with moisture. "What is this place, Falken?"

"A place of death."

Grace shuddered despite the muggy air.

They dismounted, picketed the horses, then approached the wall. Except it wasn't truly a wall, Grace saw as the mist continued to unravel, but rather a sheer cliff—part of the eastern escarpment of the Fal Erenn. The entire face of the cliff had been hewn flat and polished smooth as glass. Grace lifted a hand, and her fingers danced across the wall's surface. The stone felt slightly oily to the touch, but her fingers came away without residue. She looked up, but as far as she could see the wall was without mark or feature.

"I've found something," came Aryn's voice from off to the left.

Grace was the first to reach the baroness. On instinct she reached out and gripped the young woman's left hand as both of them stared.

"It's a door," Grace murmured, and Aryn nodded.

The arch was a foot or two taller than Grace and protruded slightly from the surface of the wall. Etched into the stone were intricate geometric designs. The designs were difficult to trace with the eye, and they were like nothing she had ever seen before. Shadows lurked inside the arch, suggesting an opening beyond, but when Grace reached forward her hand met hard, smooth stone after only a few inches, confirming her suspicion. It was a door, but it was shut.

The others arrived, crowding around Grace and Aryn to look at the door. Beltan pushed on the stone inside the arch, but despite his straining muscles, the door did not budge.

Melia looked at Falken. "In case you hadn't noticed, it's locked."

"And you were expecting a friendly greeting instead?"

Melia tightened her arms around a purring ball of black fur. "No, I suppose I didn't. Not here."

"What is this place, Melia?" Grace said. However, if the lady heard the words she did not choose to respond.

Lirith ran slender fingers over the markings on the arch. A frown touched the dusky skin of her brow. "These designs are clearly Tarrasian, but they are not quite like any others I have seen. I would guess them to be very ancient."

"And you would guess right," Falken said. "This door was forged well over a thousand years ago. Long before the Dominions were founded. Before even Malachor was built." He drew in a deep breath. "And we have to go through."

"All right," Beltan said, hands on his lean hips. "So how do we open it?"

Falken opened his mouth, but Durge, who had been peering inside the archway, now pulled his head back. "There are markings on the stone within. I am not certain, but I think they might be runes."

"Light," Falken said. "We need light."

Beltan turned and started toward one of the horses—to get a torch, Grace supposed—but before he could move two steps Travis reached out and spoke a soft word.

"Lir."

A pale radiance sprang into being, driving back the shadows inside the arch and glinting off fine, silvery lines. Falken gave Travis a sharp glance, but Travis did not meet his gaze. The bard turned back, then peered at the glowing lines traced upon the recessed stone inside the arch.

"You're almost right, Durge. The markings do remind me of runes in a way. But they're not quite runes—they're just a row of lines and dots."

Lirith lifted the back of a hand to her chin. "I don't understand. If the door is Tarrasian in design, why are there runelike symbols inscribed on it? Runic magic has never been practiced in Tarras."

"This place was built by one who came from the south," Falken said. "But it's another—one who came after—that we're concerned with."

"Can you read what the symbols say?" Aryn asked, her words breathless.

Falken shook his head. "I'm afraid not. If they are runes, then they're too worn and fragmentary to read. But I think maybe they're some sort of code. After all, he would not have left the way open for anyone."

Melia glanced at him. "What are you talking about, Falken?"

"My guess is that it's a message meant only for a runelord. Only another runelord would be able to decipher it."

"But do we not have a runelord with us?" Lirith said.

Travis held up his hands and took a step back. "Don't look at me. I have no idea what it means."

All gazes returned to the bard.

He let out a sigh. "Let me work on it."

A small form slipped between Grace's and Aryn's skirts. Tira. She reached out and brushed the bard's black-gloved hand. For a moment his grim expression lightened, and he smiled down at her. The girl nodded, then turned and ran back to Grace.

"Olrig help me," the bard muttered, and turned again toward the ancient door.

61.

They made camp around midday, after it became clear Falken was not going to open the doorway anytime soon. Travis kept a prudent distance away as the bard worked, but by the periodic curses that rose on the damp air, Falken wasn't having a great deal of luck. Sometimes the bard leaned deep into the arch, and at others he paced in front of the doorway, head down, black-gloved hand to his head.

"Just try to ignore him," Melia said after a particularly loud and colorful burst of swearing.

"Does it help him concentrate?" Aryn asked.

Melia smiled. "Not that I know of, dear. But it certainly makes things easier for me."

They made a scant and cheerless meal as the fog closed back in, but even Beltan seemed to have no appetite. The iron-gray sky pressed down on them, and any good-natured words they attempted to speak fell like lead weights to the ground. Beltan and Lirith tried to start a fire to dry out their clothes, but what little wood they managed to scrounge was soaked through, and after much trying they finally threw down flint and tinder in disgust.

Travis knew he could have started the fire. After all, *Lir* had come easily enough to his lips. Too easily, in fact, for he had spoken the rune before even thinking to do so.

That's how you'll hurt people, Travis. By getting lazy, and by forgetting how dangerous it is.

And, as he knew well, *Krond* was far more perilous to speak than *Lir*. He was grateful that no one asked him to use magic to get the fire going.

After a while they all gave up trying to talk. Grace lay down beneath a blanket with Tira, and Lirith and

Aryn followed suit. Both Durge and Beltan attempted to wipe off the moisture that kept condensing on their armor—already the two reeked of rust. By contrast, Melia seemed to have no trouble keeping dry, even though she had covered herself with only a sheer veil of gauze.

Travis huddled inside his mistcloak—the cloak that, except for its frayed edges, was just like the one worn by the dying man they had come upon at the border. A Spider, Falken had called the other. Was it from one of King Persard's spies that Falken had gotten this garment? He resolved to ask the bard about it. But later, he amended at another outburst of curses.

Durge let out a rumbling sigh. "I suppose this means Falken will never open the door." His voice was as dull and heavy as the mist. "We'll most likely all die waiting here."

Grace sat up. "He'll open the door, Durge. You'll see."

The Embarran's shoulders slumped even farther than usual. "Then I suppose we'll go through and get choked by foul air on the other side. Or we'll be bitten by poisonous snakes, or get lost in the dark and never find the light again."

The knight bowed his head, and Grace cast a startled look at Travis. He nodded. Such sentiments were disturbingly gloomy—even for Durge. Travis opened his mouth but was interrupted by an angry voice.

"You'd like that, wouldn't you, Durge?"

All of them looked up at Beltan. The blond knight had leaped to his feet, his face ruddy and eyes hard. "I think you'd like it if something terrible happened, if all of us were killed. You say it so often I have to believe you want it to be true."

The Embarran did not look up.

Beltan's hand slipped to the hilt of his sword. "Tell

you what—I'll give you something to worry about. . . ."

"Beltan!"

Melia's voice was not loud, but it sliced through the mist all the same. Beltan jerked his hand away from his sword and sat down again, but he did not take his eyes from Durge.

"Is that all you knights can think of when you're faced with a problem?" Lirith's voice was a hiss of contempt. The dark-eyed woman was sitting. She braided her hair with rapid movements, then as quickly unbraided it again. "Is the sword your answer to everything?" She twined her hair once more; it was getting snarled.

Beltan snorted, his lip curling. "And what would you do, witch? Cast a spell and have us all do your bidding?"

Dread rose in Travis's throat. Was he really hearing this? He felt as if he was going to scream, although he had no idea why, and he glanced again at Grace. However, she held Tira tightly, her head bowed over the girl.

Another curse sounded from Falken's direction. The bard turned from the ancient door and marched toward them.

"Any luck?" Melia said as he approached.

"What do you think?" he shot back in a caustic voice.

Melia's amber eyes widened, then narrowed to thin, glowing slits. "Maybe if you had thought ahead this problem would not have happened."

"And maybe if your friend had warned us about what to expect we wouldn't be stuck here."

"Are you saying you think Tome did not tell us all he knew?"

"And do your kind ever tell everything they know, Melindora Nightsilver? Do they really?"

Falken's words were as harsh as poison. Melia's

face blanched, and Travis stared along with the others. Before the bard could say anything further, Aryn—who had been lying still on her blanket—suddenly rose.

"Shut up!" The young woman's voice quivered on the edge of a shriek. "All of you shut up! You sound like crows, did you know that? All cackling and cawing and saying nothing. I swear, it's driving me mad!"

The baroness stiffened, then slumped back to her knees, shaking. Grace reached a hand toward her, then snatched it back and looked up. "What's going on?" she said. "Something's wrong—wrong with us. We don't argue like this."

Melia blinked, then glanced at Falken, and he nodded.

"It's like a sickness," Lirith said, her voice a hoarse whisper. "I can feel it on the air of this place. Everything is sick and twisted here."

The witch shuddered, and Tira moved over to sit in her lap and snuggle against her. Of them all, only the girl appeared the same as she ever did.

Aryn's eyes fluttered shut, then all at once they flew open, and her scream drove a spike through Travis's heart. Grace rushed to the young woman's side.

"What is it?" She touched Aryn's brow, cheeks, chest.

The baroness lifted a shaking finger and pointed, her face white with horror. "I saw it. Over there. Like . . . like a rip in the Weirding, filled with . . . with nothing." She bent forward, pressed her face into her hands, and sobbed.

Falken looked up, his face hard. "Beltan, Travis, come with me. The rest of you stay here."

Travis jumped to his feet, and he and the knight followed after the bard, walking in the direction Aryn had pointed, toward a tall clump of dead bushes tangled with vines.

"I should have known," Falken muttered. "I should have known there would be one in this place."

Travis started to ask what the bard was talking about, but then they reached the clump of dead foliage. With a gloved hand, Falken jerked a branch aside.

"Help me."

Travis and Beltan moved forward and tore at the vines and bushes. Thorns bit into their flesh, but Travis ignored them and kept pulling. He could feel it, too—not as vividly as Aryn, but it was still there: a dark, ponderous mass that pulled at him, casting a dusky veil over his eyes even as it drew him on. With a grunt, the three men ripped a knotted mass of branches and vines free and heaved it aside. Travis stared at what they had uncovered.

It was a standing stone hewn of black rock, with four planed sides that tapered toward the top. The stone's surface was worn and pitted, but he could still make out a few of the symbols carved upon it. They were not runes.

Waves of sick, suffocating power radiated from the stone, shimmering on the air, distorting it like the heat waves above a desert plain. Beltan reached a hand toward the standing stone. Travis began to do the same.

A voice cut through the torpor like a cool copper knife.

"You must not touch the stone."

Melia. But she seemed so distant, so small.

"Move away from it, dears. Now."

Travis stiffened, caught between the strength of the lady's words and the inexorable pull of the stone. Then he gasped and lurched backward. The dim veil lifted from his eyes, and only as air rushed into his lungs did he realize he had stopped breathing. Beltan stumbled after him.

Falken glanced at Melia. "Are they all right?"

Melia touched Beltan's brow, then Travis's. Her fingertips were soft and cool as rainwater. "They are unharmed. But we must get away from the pylon at once. Its evil has tainted all of us."

A half hour later they huddled inside a ring of tumbled boulders that was just circular enough to make Travis wonder if it had been, if not built, at least shaped by human hands. He sipped the fragrant liquid in the clay cup he held and sighed. Melia had brewed a tea of *alasai*, and as they drank it their eyes had grown clear and color had crept back into their faces. All except for Tira, who turned her nose up at the tea and ignored them as she scrambled atop one of the boulders to play with her doll.

"What was it, Falken?" Grace set down her cup and regarded the bard with brilliant green-gold eyes. "What was that stone back there?"

It was Travis who answered. But then, it was not the first time he had seen such a thing. "It's a pylon. An artifact of the Pale King."

"No, that's not entirely right," Melia said.

The bard nodded. "It was the Necromancers, the Pale King's wizards, who created the pylons. It was during the War of the Stones. No one is really certain what the pylons were for, but I think they helped the Necromancers communicate somehow—with each other, and with other servants of the Pale King."

Lirith cupped her hands around her tea. "Falken, were not all of the Necromancers slain in the War of the Stones?"

"So it is told."

"And yet you seem to know so much of them."

The bard reached up and fingered the silver brooch that clasped his cloak. "You could say I've had some . . . experience in the subject."

Travis frowned. How could Falken have experience with something that had passed from the world an eon ago?

Durge spoke then. "There is yet one question you have to answer, Falken. Why is there a pylon here?"

"Because it was a Necromancer who built this place, before the War of the Stones began."

All stared at the bard, but no one found words to reply.

Falken stood. "I should get back to the door. I still have to find a way to open it."

"Not alone," Melia said. "It is too close to the pylon."

Travis scrambled to his feet. "I'll go with him."

"And I," Lirith said, rising.

Melia caught and held their gazes. "You must each watch the others for signs of the shadow cast by the pylon."

They both nodded in answer. Falken turned to go. Travis followed several paces behind the bard, Lirith beside him.

"There is more they have not told us," the witch whispered as they walked.

Travis couldn't suppress a soft laugh. "I have a feeling there always is."

They reached the door set into the cliff wall. Travis could feel the power of the pylon, like a shadow just on the edge of his vision, but now that he knew it was there it was easier to close his mind to its call.

Falken let out a breath. "All right, let's start over. Maybe three heads will be able to figure out what all these lines and dots mean. Who wants to take a look at the inscription first?"

"Why don't we all look at the same time?" Lirith said.

Travis shook his head. "The alcove's not big enough for us all to step in and see the inscription."

"Well, then let's bring the inscription out to us," Lirith said.

Falken frowned at the witch. "How do you mean?"

Instead of answering, Lirith moved to a nearby

bush. If pressed for a name, Travis supposed he would have had to call it *not-holly*. Lirith snapped off a handful of bare twigs, gathered several bunches of red berries, then returned to the others. She held out the sticks and berries.

"Lines and dots," she said.

Travis and Falken stared at the witch, then both laughed in understanding.

They took turns stepping into the alcove, studying a few of the symbols, then returning to a large, flat stone on which they re-created the symbols using Lirith's sticks and berries. Soon they had duplicated the entire inscription.

The three gathered around the stone, studying the symbols they had copied. In a way, the markings were familiar to Travis, and not just because they looked vaguely like runes. This was what written words always looked like to him—a chaotic jumble of lines and dots—before he concentrated and sorted them out. But no matter how hard he stared, these markings refused to organize themselves in any meaningful fashion.

Falken groaned and stepped back from the stone. "It's no use. We'll never understand the message." He looked up. "And that's not just the pylon talking."

Lirith held a hand to her brow. "We have to keep trying. Perhaps we made a mistake in copying the inscription. I'll go check again."

Falken heaved his shoulders in a sigh. "I'll help."

The bard and the witch turned back toward the alcove. Travis gazed again at the stone. The sticks and berries seemed to dance, and he gave up trying to make them stop. If there was meaning in the symbols, it was beyond him. He let the dots and lines swim freely before his eyes.

Two of the sticks and one of the berries collided, forming a new shape. Travis sucked in a breath. It was *Urath*, the rune of opening.

He blinked, and the twigs and berries ceased their wandering. The rune *Urath* vanished.

No, that wasn't true. It was still there, wasn't it? He picked up the stick farthest to the right, then placed it on top of the stick and berry farthest to the left. Together, they formed the rune of opening.

Shaking, Travis moved the two sticks that were now the farthest to the right and moved them onto the two sticks next to *Urath*. A jolt passed through him. *Pel.* Door.

He worked swiftly now, moving sticks and berries from right to left, until he had formed seven recognizable runes on the flat stone. Before he even thought about what he was doing, Travis sounded out the runes.

"Urath pel sar bri, fale krond val."

"What are you doing, Travis?"

Travis jerked his head up. Falken approached, frowning at the sticks. Travis opened his mouth to answer, but Lirith, still beside the alcove, spoke first.

"Look at the door," she whispered.

Both Travis and Falken turned to follow her gaze. Deep in the alcove, the symbols glowed with a pale light of their own. A faint *snick* sounded on the air, like a lock turning, and a dark line appeared in the midst of the fragmented runes, running from the top of the archway to the bottom.

"What's happening?" Travis said.

However, his question was answered for him as—with a whisper of dry, ancient air—the doorway swung open.

62.

"By Olrig, they *were* runes." Falken peered through the archway into the opening and ran a hand through his black-and-silver hair. "I just couldn't see it."

"We all have our off days, dear," Melia said, her voice a trifle too smug to be genuinely sympathetic.

The bard shot a sour look in her direction.

Grace gazed past Falken, into the lightless space beyond the arch. It was a passageway. Dusty, faintly metallic air spilled from its mouth—air that Grace was certain had not been breathed in long centuries.

She looked at Travis. "How did you know you were supposed to rearrange the symbols into runes?"

He gave her a sheepish shrug. "I didn't."

Grace studied him. *Of course. It was his dyslexia. He didn't mean to rearrange the symbols—it just happened in his mind when he got tired and couldn't concentrate.*

Beltan shot Travis a wry smile. "Maybe it's not so bad being a mirror reader after all."

"Indeed," Lirith said.

Aryn gestured to the symbols fashioned of sticks and berries. "So what do the runes say?"

Falken opened his mouth, but it was Travis who murmured the translation. "Open this door of dark stone, and seek the king of the valley of fire."

All of them cast startled looks at Falken. It was Lirith who first managed to find words.

"Now that your magic door is open, Falken, who shall step through?"

"All of us."

"Are you certain that's wise, dear?" Melia said.

Falken shrugged. "Is there anyone who cares to stay behind?"

There was not.

"We'll have to leave the horses," Beltan said. "We're not going to get them into that tunnel."

"Will they be all right here?" Aryn asked the blond knight.

Durge stepped forward. "I am certain they will be fine, my lady."

As one, seven pairs of eyes turned on the Embarran. Those had been awfully optimistic words coming from Durge.

The knight smoothed his mustaches. "That is . . . I mean to say . . . I am certain Blackalock and Sir Beltan's charger will guard the other horses against the wolves, mountain lions, and other perils that are certain to come along in our absence."

Grace let out an audible sigh. She turned her attention back to the doorway along with the others.

Melia traced her fingers over the symbols carved into the arch. "Why here, Falken? I believe Tome, of course—he has never been wrong to my knowledge. But why did the Stone come to this of all places?"

Falken rested his black-gloved hand on her shoulder. "That's what we're here to find out."

She reached up and touched his hand. Falken looked at the others.

"There's no need to bring anything besides a little food and water. If all goes well, we won't be long."

The bard's conditional was not lost on Grace. *If . . .* All the same, she brought only a small waterskin and some dried fruit for herself and Tira to share. She wished she had some shoes for the girl—it had never mattered while they were riding—but it was too late now.

I'll carry her if the passage gets too rough. She can't weigh more than twenty-five kilos.

However, as they stepped through the tunnel into the gloom beyond, Grace saw that the floor was as smooth as the cliff wall, hewn of black stone and polished like glass. The passage slanted upward slightly, and within a minute the door was a bright, tiny window floating in the darkness behind them. Then the passage curved to the left, and the doorway was lost to sight. Ancient shadows closed in.

"Travis," the bard said, his quiet words hissing off stone in all directions, "can you give us light?"

Grace sensed Travis hesitate, then he whispered a single word. *Lir*. As before, a silvery radiance sprang into being. However, now the light flickered and contracted under the weight of the darkness. Lines of strain crossed Travis's face, and sweat beaded on his brow—then the light stabilized in a small sphere around him.

Lirith touched his arm. "What is wrong, Travis?"

"I don't know. It feels almost like . . . like the shadows are trying to squeeze out the light."

Falken nodded. "A different magic holds sway here, one of the south, not the north. It is a newer magic, but still strong." He glanced at Melia. "You know, you could—"

The amber-eyed lady raised a hand. "No. I will use no power in this place, not unless there is terrible need. All I might do would be tainted here."

Without further explanation, Melia continued on. Grace started forward, holding Tira's hand, then winced as something pricked through her boots into the flesh of her ankles.

Don't tell me you've already found one of Durge's improbably poisonous snakes.

Grace looked down at her feet. Two small, moon-gold eyes gazed up at her.

Grace sighed. "So it's you. I should have known—Travis warned me about you." She bent down and picked up the black ball of fluff. "Why aren't you with Lady Melia?"

The kitten licked a paw with a pink tongue, obviously above answering to mere humans.

A tug on Grace's sleeve. She looked down to her left. Tira pointed—the others were heading down the tunnel.

"All right," Grace said to girl and kitten. "We'd better get going if we don't want to be left behind."

She bent down, then settled the kitten into Tira's outstretched arms. The creature purred and snuggled against the girl's shoulder. Together, Grace and Tira hurried after the rest of the party.

It was difficult to determine the passage of time as they walked. The tunnel plunged ever deeper into darkness, sometimes making a slight bend to the right or left, but always, Grace felt, heading to the west. In some places the passage became nearly level, while in others it grew so steep it was difficult to gain footing on the glassy floor. Grace began to think that Tira's bare feet weren't a liability at all, but rather an asset, for the girl pranced lightly up slopes on which Grace felt more like Wile E. Coyote trying to get up to speed—spinning her legs without going anywhere.

Travis's light did not so much banish the dark as merely push it back a few feet, like a diving bell fashioned of too-thin glass, dropped into an ocean at night. Only Travis, Falken, and Melia were able to walk in the illuminated bubble. The others came behind, two by two in the narrow tunnel: Lirith and Aryn, Grace and Tira, Durge and Beltan bringing up the rear.

After a time, Grace felt herself drifting into a kind of trance. It seemed she was no longer walking, but floating through dark water, chasing but never able to reach the shining sphere ahead of her.

It was only when she bumped into Aryn that Grace realized the group had come to a halt. Her physician's instincts pricked up—something wasn't right, she was sure of it. Then she made a quick count and understood. One of them was missing.

It took her a moment to realize it was Melia. However, even as she opened her mouth to ask Aryn why they had stopped, and where Lady Melia had gone, two amber sparks appeared in the gloom ahead, beyond the reach of Travis's light.

The sparks hovered low to the ground, moving slightly up and down as they drew nearer. For a moment Grace wondered if it might be the black kitten—the sparks were the same color as the little creature's eyes—but a quick glance to her right revealed the kitten still sleeping in Tira's folded arms.

She glanced back up. The two amber sparks were closer, just beyond the boundary of Travis's light. It seemed she could almost make out a low, sleek black shape behind the two bright points. Then the sparks winked out, and the dark must have been playing tricks on Grace's vision, for it was Melia who stepped into the circle of radiance a moment later.

"There is a stairway ahead," the lady said.

"Good," Falken said. "That means we're getting close."

After a few more minutes of walking they came to the foot of the stairs. Like everything, the steps were hewn of the same onyx stone, their edges sharp as knives.

"We must be careful not to make a misstep," Durge said, and this time his words received nods.

The stairway was even narrower than the passage, and they were forced to ascend single file. In places the ceiling dropped so low Beltan and Travis quickly learned to duck their heads, and if the ceiling were to come down another two inches Grace would have had to join the two tall men.

Grace had never thought of herself as claustrophobic, but, with each step she climbed, the walls seemed to press in a little closer. At three hundred she lost count of the steps, and still the stairway stretched on and up into the dark.

"What if there's no door at the top?" she heard a faint whisper just ahead. Aryn. "What if there's no door?"

These words jabbed at Grace's heart like needles. This was a possibility she had not considered. However, at that moment, the stairway made a sharp bend to the right, and light spilled down the steps—not the magical light conjured by Travis's spoken rune, but real, warm, outdoors light.

Grace squinted, protecting her dark-adjusted eyes, even though she knew it was only the faintest illumination filtering from up ahead. However, with each step the light grew brighter. Then the stairway made another turn, and she could not help gasping as the golden brilliance of the sun struck her full on the face. A few more breathless steps and Grace stumbled through another archway along with Tira. She drew in deep, shuddering breaths of fresh, unconfined air.

"Well," Falken said. "This is it."

Grace stared, knowing her expression contained the same wide-eyed wonder as those of her companions. Sheer cliffs of black, jagged rock ringed the valley on all sides, piercing the thin blue membrane of the sky. The fog of the lowlands was gone, and the sun blazed bright as it hovered just above the far rim.

Lowering her gaze, Grace scanned the floor of the valley. It was utterly barren, without even shrubs or grass, and littered with sharp, broken pieces of shale. Wind hissed over naked stone.

Beltan's boots ground against the loose shale. "What are we looking for, Falken?" The knight's voice seemed far too loud for the silence of this place.

"A temple," the bard said. "A dark temple."

Grace shivered. Unlike the lands below, the air in this place was chill and thin as a knife.

"There is something else here," Melia said, searching the rocks all around.

Falken's eyebrows drew down in a glower. "What is it?"

"Something that watches," Lirith said, opening her eyes. She glanced at Melia, who gave a shallow nod.

Falken sighed. "Well, we won't be here long. We just have to get to the temple, then get out."

Beltan's hand moved to the hilt of his sword. "Are you sure this is the right place? In case you hadn't noticed, there aren't exactly any spooky old temples in plain view. Just a whole bunch of rocks."

"It has to be here," Melia said. "Tome told us it was."

Beltan cringed as he spoke. "I really hate to say this, but could your friend have been wrong, Melia?"

"No," a low voice said. "This is the place. Krondisar was here."

Travis had moved a short distance off, and he pointed to something in the ground. Pits of some kind.

No, not pits, Grace. She drew closer to Travis along with the others.

Time had worn and roughened their edges, but there was no mistaking the nature of the holes gouged into the hard stone, set in two parallel lines. Travis edged a boot forward and slipped it into one of the pits. It fit perfectly.

"They're footprints," Aryn said, her voice merging with the wind. "Footprints in the stone."

Falken opened his mouth, but before he could reply Tira squirmed free of Grace's grip, dashed forward, and—like Travis—placed her small foot in one of the footprints. She looked up, a smile on her half-melted face.

"Mindroth," she said.

The girl laughed—a high, clear sound. Grace and the others could only stare as the sun slipped behind the high rim of stone, plunging the valley into shadow.

63

It was not difficult to follow the footsteps.

Travis clutched his mistcloak around himself as they walked across the hard slate floor of the valley. However, the scouring wind snatched at the edges of the garment, tearing it away, and letting icy fingers of air slip beneath his tunic to stroke his flesh. His gaze fell to the ragged pits in the stone. This was not the first time he had seen footsteps like these.

It had been the day after the burnt man staggered into the Mine Shaft. Deirdre had seen them first, melted into the asphalt of Elk Street. But what did it mean?

His gaze moved to the girl, Tira. Beltan carried her now, wrapped in a cloak on his back; the shards of stone that littered the valley were far too sharp for small, bare feet. According to Grace, the girl could not speak. Certainly Travis had never heard her utter a sound. Yet, minutes ago, she had spoken a single word in a clear, unmistakable voice. *Mindroth.*

A shiver coursed through Travis. Maybe he knew what it all meant after all.

Durge had paused to kneel up ahead, examining a place where the footprints disappeared beneath a loose layer of scree that had tumbled down ages ago. Now the grim-faced knight stood, dusting his hands together.

"They head in that direction," he said, pointing across the valley, "past that spur of rock."

Travis followed the Embarran's gesture. It took him a moment to pick out the ridge that jutted from the valley rim. It was the same dark color as the surrounding stone.

"Let's go," Falken said. "We've got about three

more hours of daylight. I don't know about the rest of you, but I'd rather not be here when night falls."

While it was still afternoon, the sun had sunk behind the high rim of the valley, and the circle of the sky had turned the color of blue ashes. It was an effect Travis had seen many times before in the mountains of Colorado, in deep canyons cast into premature twilight hours before the coming of true night. It seemed the valley was no longer part of the larger world, but instead floated alone in an empty place that was neither day nor night, neither light nor dark.

The clattering of stone ceased as the others came to a halt. Travis skidded to a stop next to Grace, then looked up.

So the valley wasn't a perfect circle after all. Instead it was shaped like a figure eight, with the ridge partially dividing the two halves. Now they had circled around the end of the ridge, and Travis knew this was their destination.

"What is this place?" Aryn whispered, her face pale as she gripped Lirith's hand.

"A place where death rules," Melia said. She bent her cheek to the kitten tucked into the fold of her arms.

Although he resisted, Travis could not help gazing at the temple that hulked before them. He tried to trace the onyx columns, lintels, and cornices with his eyes, but doing so caused his vision to swim and brought dull pain to his skull. The lines of the structure were maddening and alien, its impossible angles giving Travis the feeling that it was he and the world, not the temple, that were grotesquely skewed. Friezes seemed to writhe above the shadowed colonnades, their tortured figures looking not as if they had been carved from the stone, but rather as if they were melting back into it, mouths open in soundless screams.

At last Travis managed to wrest his gaze away from the temple. He looked up and met Grace's eyes. They were haunted in the white oval of her face.

"By the Bloody Bull of Vathris," Beltan said in a hoarse voice, "who built this thing, Falken?"

The bard turned away from the temple. "You speak of Vathris, and that is more appropriate than perhaps you know, for it was one of the kindred of Vathris who built this place."

"No!"

All turned shocked gazes toward Melia. The small woman's face was flushed, and she dropped the kitten to the ground as she clenched both hands into fists.

"Dakarreth was not the kindred of the Nindari." Melia's words edged on a cry. "None of his kind were!"

"You're wrong, Melia," Falken said in a soft voice. "Whatever they became later, the Necromancers were once New Gods, just like the other Nindari. Albeit they were minor ones, far more limited than Vathris, Yrsaia, or any of the other gods of the mystery cults. Then again, once they took bodies to walk Eldh, they gained . . . different abilities."

The color drained from Melia's face, but she said nothing.

Travis took a step toward the bard. "So it was a Necromancer who built this place?"

Falken nodded. "Over a thousand years ago, the Pale King seduced thirteen of the Nindari, the New Gods. He convinced them to take bodies of unliving flesh, and in so doing bound them to him as slaves. They became his Necromancers—his wizards of death. Before the War of the Stones, he sent them out into Falengarth, to raise places of power, like this one, in preparation for the struggle to come."

"So that's why we saw the pylon below," Grace said, her arms folded tightly over the bodice of her violet gown. "You said the Pale King and the Necromancers used them to communicate with their slaves in the war."

"Yes. And it was here, in the pits of this place—and in other places like it—that many of those slaves were forged. Here the Eldhrim, the Little People, were brought in chains of iron. And here, by the magics of the Necromancers, their bodies were corrupted into new and terrible forms."

Fresh sickness rose in Travis's throat. He thought of the *feydrim* he and Grace had once encountered in Calavere, of its monstrous fangs and talons—and of the look of pain and release in its yellow eyes when they managed to kill it.

"You tell a dark tale, Falken," Durge said in his rumbling voice, "but it has not yet told me why we have come to this place seeking one of the Imsari. Were not all of the Necromancers destroyed in the War of the Stones?"

Falken flexed his black-gloved hand. "So the stories say."

"Then how did the Stone of Fire come to be here?"

Before the bard could answer, Travis pointed to the pits burned into the black steps of the temple. "It was brought here."

Falken's voice merged with the mournful chant of the wind. "After the War of the Stones, the Runelords safeguarded the three Imsari in Malachor. But Malachor fell little more than two centuries later, and the Runelords were destroyed—all save three, who each fled with one of the Great Stones, and were lost to knowledge. Their names were Jakabar, Kelephon, and—"

"And Mindroth," Travis said. He saw again the freshly carved words on the tombstone Brother Cy had shown him in the Castle Heights Cemetery. "It was him, wasn't it? The burning man who came into my saloon. It was Mindroth."

Falken nodded. "So I believe."

Travis almost laughed. Yet it made sense in a way. After all, there had been footsteps leading into this valley but none leading out. Mindroth must have left by another sort of door.

"I must be swift," Melia said, her voice as hard as the stones beneath their feet. "We are not alone in this place, of that I am certain. Although what the nature of the other might be, I cannot say."

She glanced at Lirith, but the witch shook her head.

"My senses are not so keen as yours, Lady Melia. I do not know what it might be. But I feel it too—like a shadow always just beyond the edge of sight."

"Keep watch," Melia said. "All of you. I will do my best not to be long."

Beltan stepped forward. "I'm coming with you."

Her amber eyes flashed so brightly that the knight took a half step back. "On this there will be no argument, Beltan. It is certain death for any other than myself to enter this place. If you doubt, ask Falken."

The bard nodded. By the shadow in his eyes, he had had this same argument with Melia—and had lost just like Beltan.

The blond knight touched the lady's shoulder, his green eyes wounded but resigned. "By all the gods, be careful, Melia."

She brushed his hand, her voice softer now. "It is with all the gods that I will enter."

Without further words, the lady turned from them, ascended the steps to the temple, and vanished in the shadow between two misshapen columns.

Aryn clutched her left arm around herself, her blue eyes as dusky as the sky above. "What now?"

Falken sat on a boulder. "Now we wait."

They did not speak. The wind grew stronger and colder, howling as it passed over the rocks, as if their razored edges cut at it. Beltan and Durge paced back and forth, scanning the distance, while Lirith sat, head bowed and eyes shut—keeping watch in a different way. Grace huddled beneath her riding cloak with Tira, and when Travis saw that Aryn could not stop shivering, he opened his mistcloak and wrapped it around himself and the slender form of the baroness.

The minutes eroded as slowly as stone. However, Melia had not lied. No more than a quarter hour later she appeared at the top of the steps before the temple. She staggered and clutched a column for support. Beltan started to spring up the steps, but a sharp gesture from Melia halted him. With careful movements she descended until the knight was able to grip her arm.

"Are you all right?" he said, his eyes intent on her.

"Do not fear. I was able to guard myself from the powers within."

However, Travis noticed that she did not tell the knight to let go. Beltan led her back to the others and helped her sit on a flat rock. The kitten jumped into her lap, kneaded the fabric of her kirtle, then curled up nose to tail.

Falken knelt before her. "What did you find, Melia?"

"It is as we suspected," she said, her voice thin and weary. "Krondisar is no longer here. In a way, Mindroth found a good hiding place. I see why he chose to come here when he fled Malachor with the Stone. If the Necromancers were all destroyed, what better place to hide than in one of their strongholds?"

"How long?" Falken gripped her hands. "How long has it been gone from here?"

"I am not certain. But not long, I think. From what I saw, I believe Mindroth burned here for many centuries, held in thrall by the power of Krondisar."

"But how could that be?" Grace said. "If it's the Stone of Fire that's causing people to become *krondrim*, wouldn't Mindroth have become one as well?"

Falken shook his head. "For two hundred years the Runelords were the guardians of the Imsari, and they understood the power of the Great Stones far better than any who have ever lived—except perhaps the dark elf Alcendifar, for it was the dwarf who first found the Imsari when they fell from the sky, and who bound into them the essences of ice, fire, and twilight."

Grace looked at Travis. "So that's why only Travis could touch Sinfathisar."

Falken nodded. "Only a runelord can resist the power of a Great Stone for long."

"But not forever," Travis murmured. He clenched his right hand. "In the end, even Mindroth burned."

The bard had no answer for that.

"Falken, there is more I found in the temple." Melia returned the grip of his hands. "There were signs of a battle within. A terrible battle. All the defenses of this place were awakened to wrest the Stone from Mindroth. And there is only one who could have done such a thing." She drew in a deep breath. "The one who created this place."

Falken pulled his hands back and stood. He spat out the word like poison. "Dakarreth."

"Wait a minute, Falken," Beltan said. "You told us all of the Necromancers were destroyed in the War of the Stones."

A bitter smile twisted the bard's lips. "The tales say such. But I never have. Dakarreth is alive. Or as alive as any of his kind can be. And he has the Stone of Fire."

Beltan started to protest, but Melia stood, cradling the kitten. "We must go now. Mindroth is not here." She glanced at Travis. "It would seem he found his end on another world, in search of his brethren. We must make haste to Spardis. I have to speak with

Tome, to tell him what we have learned on our journey, and hear what he has discovered on his own."

Travis stood with the others, and together the nine started across the broken floor of the valley, past the ridge, and back to the mouth of the stairway.

They had walked no more than twenty yards from the temple when a dark section of stone separated itself from the top of the ridge to their left.

Travis blinked. Instead of tumbling down the slope, the jumble of stone soared into the sky, traced a circle high above, then with terrible speed swooped down. Someone screamed—Aryn perhaps—and Travis felt sudden pain as Grace's fingers dug into his arm. However, there was no time to turn, no time to run even had there been cover. The shape spread wings like gray sails and stretched forth clawed feet as it alighted on the stones before them. Travis froze, gazing into eyes like colorless gems set into a gigantic, saurian head.

"Move," the dragon said with a hiss of smoke, "and I shall burn you all."

64.

A foul power oozed from the gigantic, winged creature like toxic waste from a forgotten landfill, poisoning every breath Grace struggled to take. She clutched Tira against her so hard she knew it must hurt, her fingers pressing deeply in the girl's flesh, but Tira did not cry out. Next to Grace, the others stood as rigid as statues, eyes locked on the vast form of the dragon a dozen paces before them.

A dragon . . . and how do you know that's what this thing is, Grace?

But what else could it be? What other shape could conjure such shrill, primal terror from the depths of her unconscious? The thing looked like a hundred storybook dragons she had seen as a child, swooping over watercolor castles, being slain by cartoon knights. Yet it looked like none of them.

It was hard to gaze at the dragon—the air seemed to ripple around the creature, distorting everything seen through it, like a warped lens. At first Grace thought the thing's skin to be as colorless as smoke, but then the dragon shifted its mass, and iridescent color shimmered across its hide.

Getting a grip on the dragon's size was as difficult as discerning its color. Grace was left with only relative terms. Bigger than an elephant? Yes. As big as the *Tyrannosaurus rex* skeleton in the foyer of the Denver Museum of Natural History? No, not quite. Except perhaps for the teeth.

Grace had always thought that dragons—presuming they existed—were supposed to be big lizards. However, in many ways this creature looked more like a gigantic, sooty swan. Its neck was long, sinuous, and constantly weaving, and it stood on two crooked legs, spreading its wings for balance. Yet that wasn't right either. For it had no feathers, and the membranous skin of its wings was clearly stretched over elongated digits, as in a bat. And while its snout hooked downward, it was formed of bone rather than beak. Mammalian, avian, reptilian—none of the categories she knew fit. She could see features of all three in the thing.

"Fog and gloom," the dragon said, replenishing the watery flood of dread in Grace's lungs, "but this is a curious band of travelers I have found."

As it spoke, hot air struck her face. She would have thought its breath to be rank and fetid. Instead it was dry and odorless except for a faint, dusty scent—a scent that, after a moment, she realized she had smelled before, in the basement stacks of the old university library.

"Now, what shall I do with such an interesting collection of specimens?" The dragon did not move its lipless mouth as it spoke. Instead the sibilant, strangely sensuous voice emanated from deep in its throat.

It's like a parrot, Grace. It's not really speaking, not like we do. It must have an exceedingly complicated larynx that it uses to mimic human speech.

Mad laughter bubbled up in her throat.

And if you think this thing is just a big, dumb bird, you might as well put on a sign that says "I'm a cracker."

Grace caught movement out of the corner of her eye. With slow but deliberate steps, Falken covered half the distance between the travelers and the dragon. The bard bowed low, then straightened and spoke in a ringing voice.

"Answer me this, and an answer you shall have. One secret for one secret in trade. What is the name we shall call you, Old One?"

The dragon let out another smoky breath, its colorless eyes reflecting the pale sky. "So, you remember the elder ways. Good. Although do not think it will dispose me toward kindness, for of that I am not capable." The dragon stretched its neck upward in what seemed a proud gesture. "You may call me Sfithrisir. He Who Is Seen And Not Seen. Osthrasa was my dam, who was one of the brood of Agamar the First, Queen of the Sea before Light and Dark, whose waters lap at the beginning and end of the world."

Grace shuddered at its words. They made her feel hollow somehow. Tira squirmed in her grip, but Grace held tight to the girl's thin shoulders.

"I hear your answer," Falken said, "now you may hear mine. The name I am called is—"

At first Grace thought the deep, rumbling sound to be thunder. But a glance up confirmed that the dim bowl of the sky was unmarred by clouds. Then she understood. It was mirth, not thunder. The dragon was laughing.

Heavy smoke oozed from the dragon's mouth. "I already know well the names you are called. Blackhand. The Grim Bard. Cloud-Bringer. Traitor, Fugitive, and Murderer of Kings. Are these not your names, Falken of Malachor?"

The blood drained from the bard's stricken face, and his gloved hand spasmed into a fist.

"I know who all of you are," the dragon said, taking in each of them with its hard, inscrutable gaze. "You see, it is my business to know all things that I can. And so, by your trade, you owe me another secret, Falken Blackhand. And do not presume to think you can best me at my own game."

Falken stared forward, his body rigid. Grace had never before seen the bard miscalculate a situation. But something told her that beating this creature in a battle of wits was not an option. They would be lucky simply to get away with their lives. And at the moment she doubted they would win even that.

"It is . . . strange to see you here, Sfithrisir," Melia said. The lady held a hand to her brow, her skin ashen.

"And what better place is there to learn secrets I do not yet know?" The dragon swung its wedge-shaped head toward Melia. "But you choose curious words, Lady of the Moon. It is not simply strange for you to see me. Rather, it is agony, is it not? Can you not feel your very being scattering? I can see it even now, like a cheap cloth unraveling."

Melia staggered and would have fallen but for Lirith and Aryn behind her, gripping her shoulders. The kitten in the crook of her arm hissed, but at a glare from the dragon the tiny creature's eyes went wide and it burrowed deeper into a fold of the lady's kirtle.

The dragon's head snapped around as if its neck

were a whip. "And do not think your blades can harm me, Sir Knights."

Only then did Grace see that, in the moment of distraction, both Durge and Beltan had stepped forward, reaching for their swords. Now both stood frozen, speared to the ground by the dragon's gaze. "If it is death you want, then I shall be all too glad to grant it to you. A thousand knights have sought me out, thinking to slay me. Your ashes shall join theirs." The dragon drew in a deep breath, its chest expanding.

Run! Grace tried to scream. *You've got to run!*

But the words stuck like burrs in her throat. Cords stood out on Beltan's neck, and the muscles along Durge's jaw bulged, but the knights did not move. The dragon drew its head back and opened its mouth to release the first curls of smoke. Then it thrust its snout toward the knights.

A high, wordless cry of rage shattered the air.

Even as Grace understood what was happening, Tira broke free from her numb grasp and ran barefoot across shards of stone. She interposed her thin body between the dragon and the knights, then looked up and shook small fists at the creature as she screamed again. Grace went rigid, waiting for the dragon to open its mouth and snap up the girl in its massive jaws.

Instead the dragon pulled back, and for the first time there was a readable emotion in the thing's eyes. It was loathing.

"What a hideous little thing you are!" The dragon's voice edged into a shriek. "He should have burned you to nothing. I do not know how he did not. But I shall finish what was begun."

Tira did not move. Instead she gazed up at the dragon, her face placid as ever.

"No!"

The word was not Grace's. She jerked her head to

the side and saw Travis step forward, his eyes queer and distant behind his spectacles. He raised his right hand, fingers splayed, and held it before him.

"You will not harm her."

Impossibly, the dragon scuttled a step back. "You!" Its voice was a whisper now, like that of a dying fire. "You are here! But how? This—this I did not know."

Travis lowered his hand. "Why should you?"

"Why should I know?" Now the dragon's voice was a trumpet call of indignation. "Why, there is no other whose hoard is so great as mine. Not even Eregun, first son of Agamar, in the days before his fall, had knowledge such as I—I who have watched and waited for more eons than you can imagine. There are more secrets in my hoard than stars in the sky."

The wind ruffled Travis's sandy hair. "But what good are they?" he said, his voice so soft it was nearly lost. "What good are secrets if you don't share them with others?"

The dragon's words were sharp and mocking. "But do you not already know? Secrets are power. And there is none in this world who knows more secrets than I."

Travis shrugged. "I'm not from this world."

Lids drew down over the dragon's eyes like hoods, narrowing the orbs to slits. "Yes, I see. So that is how knowledge of you escaped me. But now it is mine, and I know that the end of this wretched creation—this *world*, as you call it—cannot be far off. Not now that you have come, Runebreaker."

A cold razor sliced through Grace's heart. She looked up at Aryn and Lirith. The baroness's blue eyes were wide, but Lirith's gaze was deep and unreadable as that of the dragon. Then there was no more time to wonder, for Tira turned, ran from the dragon, and threw herself against Grace. Kneeling, Grace hugged the girl fiercely, smoothing her wild, fiery hair.

Durge and Beltan stepped back, released from the dragon's spell. Melia moved to Beltan and leaned against the big knight, who circled his arm around her tiny form.

"What now, Sfithrisir?" she said, her voice thin but clear. "What will you do with us?"

Smoke curled from the dragon's snout. Then it seemed to grin. "You have given me something I did not know: a secret I did not have. That has not happened to me in long centuries. And so I feel generous."

Melia's eyes narrowed. "Generous? Are you certain you are indeed one of the Gordrim, Sfithrisir?"

"Oh, I am certain," the dragon hissed. "And for your sharp tongue, you shall be first, Melindora Nightsilver. Here is your secret: That which you crave, you can never have. Any that you love will be doomed to mortal death, and so it shall ever be."

Grace had seen Melia angry, weary, and hurt— even once or twice afraid. But she had never seen this—this look of horror and despair. The lady clasped a hand to her mouth to stifle a silent cry, then she turned her face and pressed it against Beltan's broad chest.

The blond knight glared up at the dragon. "What have you done to her?"

The dragon flexed its wings. "I have done nothing more than speak the truth for her, Sir Knight, as I will speak for you. The one you love is destined to turn from you at the moment your feelings are made clear."

Beltan's jaw dropped, but he said nothing as he held on to Melia.

"You speak lies, not truths," Falken said, his voice bitter.

"That is not so," the dragon said.

Falken clenched his jaw and was silent.

The dragon cocked its head. "Now, who is next?

How about you, Falken? You, who will never forget his hand in the death of a kingdom. Or what of the stout Embarran there?" The dragon swung its head toward Durge. "Strong as stone, you present yourself, Sir Knight, and yet your heart is tender and weak with feelings for another, is that not so? If only you were young and handsome enough to deserve her."

Durge stood stiffly, gazing at the horizon.

"And here are two Daughters of Sia," the dragon crooned, turning its eyes on Lirith and Aryn, "both doomed to betray their sisters and their mistress."

The women clasped hands but did not speak, and the dragon sidled toward Grace, stone cracking beneath its taloned feet. Grace wanted to flee, but her legs were columns of ice.

"And what secrets shall I speak for you?" the dragon said. "Shall I tell you of the girl? Do you not wonder how she spoke the name of a runelord?"

Grace ground the words like glass between her teeth. "Leave . . . her . . . alone."

Again laughter rumbled in the dragon's throat. "No, it is the girl who will leave you before the end—I promise you that, Your Majesty. You should let me take her now. It would be so much easier for you all."

Grace held on to Tira. The girl was still, gazing at the dragon with tranquil eyes.

"Very well," the dragon said, rearing back. "One last secret I will speak. For you, Blademender." Its head flicked from Grace to Travis. "And for you, Runebreaker. Both of you seek the Keep of Fire, where Krondisar is imprisoned. Know that you will find it. And know also that both of you will die there."

Beltan pulled himself away from Melia, his hand dropping to the hilt of his sword, his face solemn. "No they won't—not if I have anything to do with it."

The dragon's eyes glittered. "Oh, you will, Sir Knight. You will."

Beltan's jaw worked, but no words came out. The wind howled over stone, and the sky deepened to slate. The dragon spread its wings: a bank of fog expanding.

"Go now, Runebreaker. Soon this vile world will end—this horrible, finite rock to which we have been chained—and we will return to the beautiful twilight of before. And it is you who shall bring this end about."

Travis bowed his head, then he looked up, and Grace gasped. The expression on his face was one of sorrow, but one of strength as well. He gripped the small piece of bone that hung at his throat: the rune of hope.

"I think you're wrong, Sfithrisir," Travis said quietly. "Secrets aren't power. I think they're like fire. And if you keep them long enough, they'll burn you."

The dragon spoke again, and this time its voice smoldered with hate. "Go before I change my mind and destroy you all." The creature pumped its wings and sprang into the air, soaring into the fading sky. One last cry drifted from above. "Go, Runebreaker! Go destroy the world by saving it!"

For a time they stood as the wind moaned over bare stone. Finally, Grace looked at the others, their faces stricken. She met Travis's eyes, and he nodded. Then, together, they left the valley to the falling night.

PART FIVE

STONE AND SHADOWS

65.

The nine travelers did not speak as they rode into the hot mists of dawn, leaving behind the door, the valley, and the dark temple.

Grace understood their silence. Each of them had something to think about now—a secret the dragon Sfithrisir had revealed to them. As the sheer cliffs of the Fal Erenn vanished in the fog behind them, she cast a glance to her left. Travis bounced in the saddle aback his shaggy gelding. Behind his spectacles, his gray eyes reflected the hazy horizon.

Both of you seek the Keep of Fire . . . both of you will die there. . . .

Despite the already-rising heat, Grace shivered. Her gaze moved down to the too-thin girl in the ragged smock perched before her on Shandis's withers.

It is the girl who will leave you before the end—I promise you that. . . .

As if sensing eyes on her, Tira looked up, her crimson hair tumbling away from her half-scarred face. She grinned, then bent her head to continue playing a game with the burnt doll.

Shall I tell you of the girl? Do you not wonder how she spoke the name of a runelord? . . .

The word still echoed in Grace's mind, spoken in a clear, perfect voice. *Mindroth.* But how *had* Tira known that name—a name that of them all only Travis, Falken, and Melia had ever heard before? And how was it that Tira had never spoken before that moment? Nor had she last night, despite Grace's repeated attempts to coax her into speaking.

Grace lifted a hand, hesitated, then let herself stroke Tira's brilliant, tangled hair. She wanted to tell herself that everything the dragon had said was a lie, even as she knew with that terrible certainty she sometimes experienced that all of it had been truth.

It was late morning when Grace finally dared to break the silence, guiding Shandis close to Falken's black stallion to ask the bard about the dragon.

"I know little enough of the Gordrim to tell you," he said, tightening his gloved hand around the reins. "As Sfithrisir said, the dragons are great acquirers of secrets, but they seldom part with anything contained in their hoards of knowledge."

Grace's brow crinkled. "They. You mean there are more of them?"

"There were, yes. Agamar was the first dragon, and she dwelled in Sinfathmal, the Sea of Twilight which existed before the Worldsmith spoke the First Rune, separating the gray into light and dark, and forging the world Eldh to spin between them. When she saw what the Worldsmith had done, this—" With a sweeping gesture Falken took in the world around them. "—this creation, Agamar was enraged. In her fury, she gave birth to a great brood, which she sent to Eldh to war with the children of the Worldsmith, the Old Gods and the Little People. Most of Agamar's spawn were lesser creatures, small serpents of shadow. But there were a dozen nearly as powerful as herself. Osthrasa, whom Sfithrisir claimed as his dam, was perhaps the most dread and terrible of them all."

Grace thought of the dragon's hissing words. "And do you think he was telling the truth?"

Falken shrugged. "It is said that dragons do not lie, for the truth serves their purposes better. Certainly there are none more wise and ancient than the Gordrim."

"And none more cruel," Melia said. The lady had guided her pale mount close to Grace and Falken. "The dragons speak truth. But they do not speak all of it, and what they do they utter in a way intended to taint, to poison, and to gnaw at the heart. The dragons want nothing more than to bring to ruin all of creation, and to return to the shapeless mists before time. Do not forget that when you think on what Sfithrisir told you."

Falken sighed. "And you as well, Melia."

The lady pressed her lips together, then turned her gaze away and said nothing more.

It was nearing dusk on that first day after leaving the valley when they came upon the first signs of the Burning Plague. While scouting, Beltan espied a village beneath a hill. However, when they reached the track that led to the village, they saw something that brought them all to a halt.

It was a scarecrow fashioned of sticks and rags, lashed to a pole thrust into the dirt. The crude effigy had been set on fire, then deliberately extinguished before the flames could consume it entirely. Even without words, the message of the scarecrow was clear: *The Burning Plague is here.*

They snatched cloaks to their faces against the gritty, ash-filled wind, then steered their horses wide of the silent village below.

The next day dawned hotter than the last. The sun oozed through the mist but did not burn it off, instead transforming it into a ruddy miasma that pulsed on the air as they rode.

The heat made Grace feel dull and weak, and she was always thirsty, no matter how often they stopped to scoop water from a brackish stream or pool. The flies were particularly bad; the insects descended from the hazy sky in black clouds, alighting on every bit of exposed skin. Dozens of times Grace was forced to lean forward and brush the flies from Shandis's oozing eyes. In minutes they were back, thicker than ever.

Twice that day they came upon the half-charred scarecrows that warned of plague, once at a crossing of two tracks, and again in front of the burnt-out husk of a lone farm. At times, when the fog lightened a fraction, they saw columns of smoke rising in the distance, melding with the leaden sky. As dusk gathered, they glimpsed sparks of fire to the north, and they rode long into the night to leave the lights behind.

The next morning they came upon a village that bore no warning sign outside of it because there was no one left alive to raise one.

The others gave the village a wide berth, but despite Falken's protests Grace insisted on riding among the houses. She needed to examine the victims, to see how the pandemic was progressing. She had to know what they were up against.

"I'll go with you, my lady," Durge said, and Grace gave his hand a grateful squeeze.

However, once in the village she wondered if Falken was right, if she should have ridden around it with the others.

Death had come swiftly there, that much was clear. Grace and Durge walked among the rude hovels with wine-soaked rags tied around their mouths and noses. Bodies lay strewn everywhere. It seemed that many of them had dropped in the midst of action—

drawing water from a well, carrying a companion, digging a grave for an infant wrapped in a filthy shroud.

"My lady," Durge said in a choking voice, "we should not be in this place."

Grace swallowed her gorge. "I'll only be a minute or two, Durge. You can wait for me outside the village."

However, the knight planted his feet firmly on the ground as she bent to examine the bodies.

It was the Burning Plague, of that there could be no doubt. All the symptoms were in evidence: the blisters, the darkening of the eyes, the hardening of the flesh. However, in none of the victims was the metamorphosis as complete as she had seen before. All had died before reaching at most the intermediate stages of the transformation.

"We must be getting closer," she murmured.

Durge stepped toward her. "My lady?"

"It's killing them faster," she said, standing and wiping her hands against her gown. "Much faster. But that makes sense. Virulence and mortality are always higher at the center of a pandemic region than at the fringes."

"What does it mean, my lady?"

Grace met his somber brown eyes. "It means we're getting closer to the origin of the contagion."

They returned to the others outside the village, and Grace described what she and Durge had found. As they mounted their horses, Lirith glanced at Grace.

"Do you remember what Daynen said at Falanor?" The witch brushed ashes from her black hair. "About how Eddoc found Tira on his return from a journey to Perridon?"

"What is it?" Beltan said. "Do you think we might be able to find her home here?"

Grace stared at the witch and the knight. What

were they saying? Dread spilled into her chest, and she tightened her arms around the girl on the saddle before her.

Aryn cast a haunted look over her shoulder, at the silent gathering of hovels behind them. "What if *this* village was her home?"

Lirith and Beltan did not reply.

"I believe," Melia said, her amber eyes glowing, "that Tira wishes to stay with Lady Grace."

At these words the girl threw her arms out to either side, tilted her head back, and laughed. Grace cast a startled glance at Melia, but the lady had already nudged her white mare into a trot. The others followed. And after that they spoke no more of finding Tira's home.

It was late afternoon when Melia raised a small hand, bringing the party to a halt.

"Let us stop here for the evening," she said.

Lirith eyed the horizon. "There is yet an hour of daylight left, Lady Melia."

"True," Falken said, nudging his horse forward. "But I think we could all do with a bit of rest in this place."

Curious, Grace gazed past Melia and Falken and saw a ring of tall, narrow trees. The circle of foliage was dense and complete, save for an arch formed of intertwined branches, which provided entrance to a dim space beyond. Grace drew in a breath, and while she could still detect the faint, acrid stench of smoke, a new scent overpowered it, one as sharp, fresh, and invigorating as witch hazel.

"What is this place?" she said to no one in particular.

Travis guided his horse toward hers. "It's a *talathrin*."

Aryn glanced at him. "A *talathrin*. But what is that?"

"It's a Way Circle, dear," Melia said. "The

Tarrasians created many of them of old, to offer a haven to those traveling through inhospitable lands."

"Let's make camp," Falken said.

The travelers dismounted. As Melia started to slide from the back of her mount, Beltan rushed over, knelt, and made a step of one of his broad shoulders. Melia frowned, but it was too late for her to do anything save place her foot on his shoulder and hop lightly to the ground.

She turned and glared at the big man. "You're my Knight Protector, Sir Beltan, not my footstool. I thought I told you not to do that anymore."

Beltan nodded. "You did, Melia."

"And didn't you tell me that you were sorry?"

Again the knight nodded. "I did."

"So what part of this puzzle am I missing?"

A grin illuminated Beltan's broad face. "Just because I'm sorry doesn't mean I won't do it again."

It was one of those exceedingly rare moments when Melia opened her mouth and no words came out. Grace laughed, and the others joined in the mirth.

"I really don't see what's so funny," Melia said, folding her arms across her chest.

A small figure slipped past Grace and ran to Melia. Tira. The girl reached up and touched Melia's arm. The regal lady stared in what could only be shock, then her frown crumbled, replaced by a smile that was sweet and almost shy, and which a quick hand could not quite conceal.

Tira ran back to Grace. Sighing, Grace hugged the girl close. The sound of laughter was as healing as the fragrance of the *talathrin*. Together they approached the arched entrance to the Way Circle.

The thundering of hooves halted them. Grace turned with the others to see Durge charging toward them on Blackalock. Clods of dirt sprayed in all directions as the horse came to a halt. Grace looked up into Durge's craggy face and knew at once that something was wrong.

"What is it?" she said.

"There is smoke to the north," the knight said. "Two leagues, perhaps less. It is moving in this direction."

There was no need to say more. They cast ashen looks at one another, then headed for the horses. In minutes they were mounted again. Grace looked up and saw it: a thick, black pillar rising into the sky.

"They're coming," Travis murmured.

Falken glanced at Melia, then sighed. "Let's go."

The riders followed their shadows into the east, leaving the *talathrin* and the cool scent of water behind.

66.

Once again they rode long into the night, away from the smoke of fires. To the east a pulsing spark of crimson rose above the horizon, as if lighting the way for them.

But we're no traveling magi, Travis. And it's not a birth waiting for you beneath the star. Not if Sfithrisir was right.

He tried to keep the hissing words of the dragon from echoing in his skull, but it was no use. Maybe it would have been better if the dragon had not felt generous, if it had just burned them all. But Jack's voice had spoken in Travis's mind, and it had told him to step forward, to show his hand, and to reveal what he was to the dragon.

Runebreaker.

And what exactly was that? Travis wasn't certain, but the dragon had said he was doomed to bring about the end of the world. It was absurd, of course. How could one person destroy an entire world? Only a monster could do that. But Falken said dragons didn't lie. And maybe Travis wasn't just a person after all.

Quiet voices spoke near him in the gloom.

"Where do you think it has been hidden, Falken?"

"I don't know, Melia. The Barrens, perhaps. But that's little more than a hunch. Let's hope Tome will have found more to tell us when we reach Spardis."

"Yes." A long pause, then, "There is much I hope Tome will be able to tell us."

The voices drifted away, and Travis did not try to follow. He wiped sweaty hands against his breeches, then rode into stifling folds of night.

The next day dawned to fog and swelter as usual. Travis packed his saddlebags, then carried them toward Patch, who was picketed with the other horses. He opened his mouth to say good morning to Lirith and Aryn, but as he approached the two turned and hurried away.

They're just going to get their things, that's all.

However, he knew that wasn't entirely true. Ever since they had left the valley of the temple, he had barely spoken with the young baroness or the Tolorian witch. It was subtle; there was nothing that showed for certain they were avoiding him. However, they always seemed to have something else important to do when he was near them. And more than once he had felt a prickling on the back of his neck, and he had turned to see brilliant blue or smoky brown eyes just looking away.

"Let me help you with those," a bright tenor said as Travis lifted the saddlebags toward Patch's back.

Travis looked up. "It's all right—I can manage."

"I know."

Beltan's calloused hands slipped over Travis's, then took the saddlebags, easily tossing them over the gelding's back. With deft motions the knight lashed them into place.

Travis regarded the blond man. "Thanks, Beltan."
Thanks for not avoiding me even though you know what I am now. However, these last words lodged in his throat.

Beltan grinned. "I'm still your Knight Protector, Travis. I wouldn't want anyone to think I was shirking my duties."

Travis only meant to clap the knight's shoulder, but somehow his arms encircled the other man, and he squeezed Beltan in a hug instead. Maybe it was just that, right then, Travis needed to feel the closeness of another human being, as if that meant he was human as well, and not a monster. The knight smelled of steel, sweat, and leather. It was a real smell, comforting.

At last Travis stepped back, and he saw that Beltan's grin was gone, replaced by a solemn look. Had he offended the knight by being so familiar? He opened his mouth to apologize, but just then Falken's voice rang on the hazy air.

"All right, everyone. Let's get going."

It was midmorning when, after dozing in the saddle for a time, Travis lifted his head to see Lirith just turning her gaze away. She had been looking at him—he was certain of it. Now she leaned to whisper something to Aryn, who rode close by. Grace was on the opposite side of the group. Before he lost his nerve, he nudged Patch's flanks, guiding the gelding toward Grace's slender palfrey. Tira, who sat before Grace, looked up as he approached, then bent back over her doll.

"What is it, Grace?" Travis said in a low voice.

Her green-gold eyes were startled. "What do you mean?"

"You know exactly what I mean. It's those two." His gaze flickered toward the baroness and the witch. "Why are Aryn and Lirith avoiding me?"

She clutched the reins. "I don't know what you're—"

"Yes, you do." He drew in a deep breath. "Grace, after all that we've done together, I think you can tell me."

His words might have been needles for the way they drained the blood from her face. Her gaze moved past him, toward Aryn and Lirith, then moved back, meeting his own.

"I don't really know how to say this, Travis. Maybe that's why I didn't tell you before, even when I should have. But I think the Witches are—"

"Ho, there!" Falken's voice rose above the noise of hooves. "Everyone—we're going to stop here for a minute."

Travis and Grace reined their mounts to a halt. Falken dismounted, as did Melia. The two of them approached something that was all but lost in a tangle of weeds.

Grace glanced at Travis. "Should we go see what they've found?"

Travis was starting to dread the things the bard and the lady uncovered. However, he slipped from Patch's back, then took Tira from Grace's outstretched arms and set the girl on the ground as Grace hopped down. They followed after Falken, along with Aryn, Lirith, and Beltan. Durge remained astride his charger, gazing into the distance with sober eyes.

"What is it?" Lirith said, eyeing the milky stone that Falken had revealed by parting the weeds.

Travis drew closer. The stone was not natural. It was shaped like a pyramid, reaching about waist high. Although its surface was worn smooth by centuries, he could still make out the intricate patterns carved into its surface.

"It's a *talmaren*," the bard said, squatting down to peer at the stone. "A Way Marker—a relic of the war against the Pale King a thousand years ago."

Aryn's blue eyes went wide, and she took a step back. "A relic? Do you mean like the pylon?"

"No," Melia said. "The *talmareni* had nothing to do with the Pale King. They were placed here by the Tarrasians who fought against Berash. Each one marked a place where a battle was fought and acted as a guide for those who came after."

Beltan gestured to the Way Marker. "So what does it say? I'm afraid my ancient Tarrasian is a little rusty."

Melia knelt and traced slender fingers over the surface of the *talmaren*. "Here fell Galarus of the Golden Horn and Tileros the Silent. Twenty *maltheru* were slain by their arrows before the coming of the *siltheri*."

Travis shook his head. "What are they, Melia? *Maltheru* and *siltheri*, I mean."

The regal woman stood. "*Maltheru* was the Tarrasian word for *feydrim*." She turned her amber gaze on him. "And the *siltheri* were wraithlings."

Travis adjusted his spectacles, and it almost seemed he saw them, like faint ghosts on the side of the nearby hill, two shining warriors, raining arrows down on a roiling horde of gray fur and yellow fangs, until the others drifted over the top of the hill: pale and deathly as frost on steel.

Grace's voice dispelled the vision. "Falken, that symbol on the stone—it looks like the one on your brooch."

Travis looked at the symbol on the *talmaren* to which Grace pointed: a stylized knot with four loops. She was right—the silver brooch that clasped the neck of Falken's cloak bore the same four-looped knot.

The bard touched the silver brooch. "Yes. This is a symbol of Malachor."

Grace frowned. "But I thought you said the Way Marker was a relic of Tarras."

Now Falken laughed, although it was a sad sound somehow. "That's right as well. It was the Empress Elsara of Tarras who founded Malachor, along with King Ulther of Toringarth. And do you see?" He ran a finger over the brooch. "The symbol is not quite the same as on the stone. It is the Star of Toringarth at the center of the knot, not the Sun of Tarras."

Melia let out a sigh. "So many that were so brave perished in the War of the Stones. It was so long ago— sometimes I forget. Yet I must not."

Falken laid a hand on her shoulder, his faded blue eyes filled with concern. Melia reached up and touched his hand, still gazing at the *talmaren*.

Travis scratched his red-gold beard. There was something here—something about this stone—that was important. But what was it? "You were born in the south, weren't you, Melia?"

The lady turned glittering eyes on him. "Yes," she said. "I was."

He scratched some more, then glanced at the bard. "What about you, Falken? Where were you born?"

"Asheron," the bard said, his voice barely above a whisper.

Beltan snorted. "Asheron? I've never heard of it."

Falken looked up, his eyes suddenly flat and hard. "That's because it's gone." He turned his back and marched toward the horses.

Beltan glanced at Melia, his expression wounded. "What did I say?"

Melia patted his hand. "It was nothing you said, dear, really. I'm afraid this sorrow is his own." She started after Falken.

Beltan let out a snort. "Bards."

Lirith laughed. "Well spoken, Sir Knight."

67

The mists crept up from low places and closed in around the riders as evening drew near.

After leaving the *talmaren,* they had given a wide berth to the still-smoking ruins of a group of stone cottages. Travis had lost count of the burnt villages, farms, and hovels they had passed since leaving the temple; each day had brought more than the last. He could only believe that Grace was right, that they were nearing the center of it all.

They stopped to make camp along a line of tall trees that were nothing like any Travis knew; slender branches ended in flat, dark green tufts raised like hands, palms up to the sky. The trees followed the course of a brook that Travis guessed, by the polished stones, was usually brisk and full to the bank, but which was now little more than a trickle oozing over slimy rocks. They scraped what they could from brackish puddles and tried not to notice the bitter tang as they drank.

"How much farther is it to Spardis?" Travis heard Melia ask as he walked back toward the others with another half-full water flask. The regal woman knelt before a fire, alongside Aryn, as the two prepared a meal from what scant foodstuffs they had managed to discover in the saddlebags.

"We've been making good time these last days." The bard paused in the act of shaving his chin and cheeks with a razor-sharp knife—a feat also performed regularly by Beltan and Durge, and which Travis had never dared to attempt for fear of immediate death. "If we set out before dawn, we should make it to the castle before sunset tomorrow."

Beltan let out a snort and looked up from the mail

shirt across his lap, which he was polishing with a rag. "If this fog gets any thicker, we're not going anywhere, except maybe off the edge of a cliff in the gloom."

Durge gave the blond man an approving nod. "Well spoken, Sir Knight."

Beltan blinked, then shook his head and bent back over his armor.

Travis set the water flask beside Melia. "Here's the last of that puddle."

"Thank you, dear. I'll use it in the stew."

"You know, it sort of already *is* stew."

"I see." Melia set the flask down a safe distance from the pot.

As Travis turned away, he caught a glimmer of blue. Aryn. The young woman had been looking at him. Across the camp, Grace and Lirith sat with Tira. Grace smiled at him, and even Tira wriggled small fingers in his direction, but Lirith did not look up as she combed the girl's red hair.

Earlier that day, Travis had finally had a chance to talk to Grace. Alone. And now he knew why Aryn and Lirith had kept their distance from him ever since their conversation with the dragon.

It's the Witches, Travis. One of their tasks is to watch for the one called Runebreaker.

To watch for me, isn't that what you mean, Grace?

Picking up another flask, he headed for the line of trees, deciding to give the brook another try.

"Do you need some help, Travis?"

He looked back at the blond knight and smiled. "Thanks, Beltan. I think I can manage."

Travis continued on toward the brook. At least Beltan had not turned away from him. Or Grace, or Durge.

But maybe they should, Travis.

His smile faded, and a tightness constricted his chest. Maybe Aryn and Lirith were the smart ones, the ones who knew to avoid a monster when they saw one.

When he reached the brook, he set the flask on a boulder, then hopped to the other bank. It had been a long day of bouncing in the saddle, and he had yet to relieve himself since they had stopped. He slipped through the line of trees, and tendrils of fog wove themselves behind him.

Travis skidded down a slope—the loose rocks slick with moisture—then jerked to a halt at the bottom. Several stones rolled past him and went spinning into the mist. It was long seconds before he heard them strike far below him.

"I guess Beltan wasn't kidding about cliffs in the fog."

He reminded himself to warn the others of the precipice in case they ventured this way, then struggled with his hose and tunic. Add pants with zipper flies to the list of things he missed. Once finished, he cinched up the too-large clothes, then turned to start back up the slippery incline.

He had gone only a few steps when the lumpy outline of a tree stump loomed in the fog before him. Except Travis didn't remember seeing any trees as he descended the slope. With a shrug, he started around the obstacle. Then a stray breath of wind stirred the mist, and Travis lurched to a halt.

"Hello, Master Wilder," the stump said in a bright, bubbling voice. "It's so very good to see you again."

It took several thuds of Travis's heart before he recognized the man—and not stump—who stood before him. "Master Eriaun!"

The short man took a step toward Travis. "How kind of you to remember me."

Travis swallowed a metallic lump in his throat. There was something wrong about this. Master Eriaun had vanished from the tower after the failed attempt to execute Travis. Why had he suddenly appeared here and now?

"What is it, Master Wilder? Are you not pleased to see an old friend?"

Travis had no idea what to say. It was Master Eriaun, yes, but he no longer seemed the plump, kindly runespeaker Travis remembered. Instead he was leaner, his cheeks sunken, as if some wasting disease had consumed his flesh. His gray robe was smeared with dirt, its hem ragged from trailing the ground, and his eyes were glittering pits in his face.

Eriaun moved forward once more, and this time Travis took an involuntary step back, toward the edge of the precipice hidden in the mist behind him. Eriaun frowned.

"Really, Master Wilder. I should think you would show me more gratitude. Do you not remember who it was that spoke runes over you when you were ill?" He grinned: a sickly expression. "Well, do not worry. I shall remind you, then." He reached out with soiled hands.

Travis froze. He saw again the hands reaching out of the darkness of his delirium, and heard the voice hissing a single word. Yes, Eriaun had spoken runes over him. But not runes of healing. *Krond.* . . .

"It was you! You gave me the fever in the Gray Tower."

Eriaun bared his teeth. "Yes! I spoke the rune of fire over you, again and again."

Travis fought for understanding. "But why?"

"Why else?" The runespeaker's voice became a hiss. "I could not let you help the Runespeakers find a way to harm the *krondrim*. That is why my master sought me out at the Gray Tower, why he made me kneel before him and vow to serve. To watch for you. And to kill you when you came."

Travis's jaw worked, but he could make no sound.

"Only you would not burn. Instead you resisted

the rune of fire like none I have ever seen. But I have been following you, yes, and I have found you." Eriaun's hands turned into fists, and he thrust them over his head. "And now you will burn!"

Travis heard the sizzling first. Then, one by one, they appeared from the mist: three slender, sooty forms outlined in crimson light. Despite the wave of heat that rolled over him, Travis broke out in a chill sweat. He stumbled another step back down the slope. Stones clattered as they rolled away from his boots—then became silent as they tumbled into space. With slow, weaving motions, the Burnt Ones approached.

Eriaun's grin broadened. "My master has grown interested in you, Master Wilder. He is curious about your talent with the Great Stones, and he thinks you might be made to help him. But I know he is wrong in this. I know that you are dangerous." He stretched out a hand. "And that you must—"

"Travis?"

A tall figure, dim in the mist, appeared at the top of the slope, and a clear tenor called out again.

"Travis, are you down there?"

Eriaun changed the motion of his hand into a sharp jerk, and the *krondrim* turned and shambled up the slope. Fear filled Travis's lungs like the mist.

"Beltan! Get out of here!"

His cry came too late. The Burnt Ones clambered toward the knight, leaving molten footprints behind them. Eyes wide, Beltan jerked his sword from its sheath just as the first of the *krondrim* drew close. Metal clanged off obsidian flesh. The Burnt One fell, rolled halfway down the slope—then staggered back to its feet and started up again.

The other two *krondrim* had reached the knight, but there wasn't enough time for him to recover from his first swing. Instead he twisted awkwardly, took his sword in two hands, and with a roar used the flat of the blade to batter both of the fiery creatures back. They fell, sliding down the incline, leaving trails of hot, glowing rock. Then, like the first, they lurched to their feet and started back toward the knight.

Travis's heart ceased to beat. Beltan was hunched over his sword now, the tip of it planted in the ground. Pain wracked his face, and he clutched his side with a hand.

Eriaun let out a wheedling laugh. "Your friend is valiant, Master Wilder, but nobility is simply not good enough. The Burnt Ones will make ashes of him, and I shall do the same to you." Eriaun's fingers splayed apart. *"Krond."*

Instantly the air around Travis became an oven. He had only a second, perhaps less, to respond. He lifted a hand and spat out a word in reply. *"Reth!"*

He felt the magic of Eriaun's rune turn and rush away from him. Then, as if striking a wall, the magic stopped—and began to move again toward Travis. Sweat poured down his face, and his body went rigid. It was slower this time, but he could not stop it: The heat rose within him.

Eriaun's lips peeled back from his teeth. "You see, Master Wilder? My master has made me strong. The runes I speak are not so easily broken now."

Travis clenched his jaw as he fought to stave off Eriaun's magic, but his hold was slipping. The air crackled around him, and the hairs on his arms shriveled and curled.

"Get back!"

Motion was impossible, but at the shout Travis managed to shift his eyes. On the slope above, Beltan swung his sword with one hand while gripping his side with the other. This time the *krondrim* dodged the clumsy blow. Beltan staggered. Then the Burnt Ones reached for him with dark hands.

Fury roared through Travis. No, he would not watch a friend burn, not again. He opened his mouth, and this time when he spoke it was not just with his voice, but with Jack Graystone's, and with a hundred other voices all speaking through him in a single, thundering chorus.

"RETH!"

Power hotter than any fire coursed through Travis. The wall of Eriaun's magic shattered like spun glass, and the runespeaker's eyes flew wide.

"But my master . . ."

The words were lost as Eriaun burst into flame. With a shriek the runespeaker threw himself at Travis, scrabbling with burning hands. Travis stepped aside. Eriaun stumbled forward, over the edge of the precipice. Like a blazing comet, he plunged into the twilight below. Then both fire and scream were extinguished.

Travis turned and ran up the slope toward Beltan, then halted in mid-stride. The Burnt Ones pulled their hands back from the knight. As one, they curled their bodies into balls and flung themselves down the incline. They bounced over the precipice, following their master into the depths below.

"Travis . . ."

He looked up to see Beltan stagger toward him. But the knight shouldn't be moving, not now. Travis ran to him. He started to reach out to help his friend—

—then pulled his hand back. Even in the gloom Travis could see the ripples of heat distortion rising from his own body. The heat of Eriaun's rune, and that of the rune of breaking Travis had spoken, still radiated from him.

"Travis, are you all right?"

Was he? He didn't know, but he nodded all the same. "I'm fine, Beltan."

Despite the gloom, Beltan's green eyes shone, and while pain registered on his broad visage, there was something else: an intensity Travis couldn't quite name.

"I came when you didn't return after a time. But if I had known what was happening I would have come sooner. By Vathris, I . . . I should have . . ."

Beltan shook his head, and Travis tried to speak, but the heat in him fused muscle to bone.

"I'll never leave you again, Travis. By my blood, I swear it." The pain vanished from Beltan's face, replaced by calm. "I never thought I could tell you this, that you were as far above me as the sun, but now I know that Melia was right, that I have to say it. Because ever since that day I first saw you in the ruins of Kelcior, I . . ."

The roar of fire filled Travis's skull, drowning out Beltan's words. What was the knight saying? Travis couldn't hear. Then Beltan reached for him, and horror filled Travis's chest. If the knight touched him now, before he had had a chance to cool, Travis knew Beltan would burn.

"Get away from me!"

Travis didn't mean the words to be a shout, but it was all that could get past the roaring inside him.

Beltan froze. His face went white, and the light vanished from his eyes, but he did not pull back.

Travis was shaking now. "I said get away from me!"

Now Beltan snatched his hand back, and his eyes became dull and flat. The din of the fire was beginning to recede. Travis could just make out Beltan's softly spoken words.

"I see now. It was wrong of me to burden you like this, Goodman Travis. I am so sorry. You must forget I ever said these things."

That he ever said what things? Travis didn't understand, but something had happened—something terrible. Beltan's cheerful face was now as lifeless as stone. He opened his mouth, but Beltan had already turned away, and before Travis could speak another voice called out from above.

"Travis! Beltan! By the gods, what's happened?"

A figure stepped from a bank of mist. Falken. More shadows appeared behind him. The others were there as well.

Beltan staggered, gripping his side. "Ask Travis."

Grace and Lirith rushed to the blond knight, and he slumped against them.

Travis shook his head, wishing he understood. But he was cooling—the sweat no longer rose like steam from his skin. He could talk to Beltan later. Licking parched lips, he started up the slope to tell the others about Eriaun.

68.

Grace only half heard Travis's story as she examined him, making certain he had not been injured in the struggle with Eriaun and the *krondrim*. His tunic was singed in places, and he had lost much of the hair on his arms, but as she ran her fingers over him experience and instinct told her that he was all right. She gave Travis a nod of reassurance, then moved to the tall, fair-haired knight who sat on the bank of the tree-lined brook.

"Beltan?"

He had been hunched over, but now he looked up at her and grinned. "Grace."

As bright as his smile was, she could see right through it. *He's in agony. That's why he's sitting here, away from the others. He can't stand, and he doesn't want them to see.*

She knelt beside him. "Here, let me."

At first he resisted, holding his arm in close to protect his left side, then she gave him a stern look, and he let her pull his arm away. With practiced motions she reached under his tunic and probed with cool fingers. Beltan sucked in a hissing breath, his body rigid. She kept examining. The wound hadn't reopened, but she would have given her little finger for a portable X-ray so she could see if there had been tearing internally.

But there is a way you can see, Grace.

Before she lost her nerve, she reached out with the Touch. As she had at Falanor green and the bridge over the Dimduorn, she avoided her own thread, instead grasping the shining golden strand she knew to be Beltan's. Quickly she probed the weakness in his abdomen. Yes, there had been a small amount of internal bleeding, but the flow had already ceased. He was out of danger. She started to release his thread—

—and saw the shadow just on the edge of vision. Fear clenched her heart. Had she grasped her own thread by mistake? But no, the shadow was smaller and fainter than the one she knew to be her own, and it was not to her thread that it was attached. It was attached to Beltan's. She peered closer. Something moved in the heart of the shadow: two bloody hands slipping from the hilt of a dagger.

"Grace?"

The thread slipped through her fingers. She blinked, mundane vision returning.

Beltan raised an eyebrow. "What is it, Grace?"

She pulled down his tunic. "Your muscles are still weak where they were torn by the *feydrim*. That means you could easily injure them again. I think you'll be all right this time, but that might not be the case if you do this again. I know it's not easy in your line of work, but I need you to be careful."

"I'm sorry, Grace."

"Apology accepted." She brushed his white-blond hair back from his high forehead. "You've got to take care of yourself, Beltan of Calavan. I need you here. We all do."

An odd light crept into his eyes. His gaze moved

past her and, it seemed, toward Travis. "Really, my lady?" His voice was soft. "Is that truly so?"

Grace stared. Something else was causing the knight pain, beyond the old wound in his side. Only what? "Beltan," she said on a hunch. "When I gazed into your wound, I saw something else. It was an image of two hands. They were covered with blood, and they were just letting go of a knife."

Beltan frowned. "That's strange. I wonder why you would see that."

"What is it?"

He shrugged. "It's an old dream I used to have sometimes. But if it means anything, I never knew what it was. And I haven't had the dream in a long time."

She started to ask more questions, but he spoke first.

"We should go, Grace. The others are heading back."

She stood, then reached down a hand to help him. Beltan hesitated, then clasped her hand. Pain lined his face, and she supposed she was pulling on a good hundred kilos of knight, but together they got him to his feet.

When Grace and Beltan reached the camp, they found the others standing in a half circle, staring with jaws open. Grace blinked, then she saw the reason and stared herself. An elderly man in a snowy white robe sat beside the campfire they had built, fixing himself a cup of *maddok*.

Durge drew his greatsword from the harness on his back. At the ringing noise, the old man looked up, his eyes golden beneath shaggy white eyebrows.

"Well, that's hardly necessary, young man," he said in a gentle voice. "There's plenty in the pot for everyone."

Durge halted in mid-stride, an expression of shock

on his face, although whether it was from the audacity of the intruder, or from being called *young man*, Grace wasn't sure. Before she could wonder more, a small form in blue rushed forward.

"Tome!"

The old man rose spryly to his feet just in time to have Melia throw herself into his arms.

"Dear child, how good it is to see you again, and so soon."

Now it was Grace's turn to gape. She had never thought she would ever hear anyone call Melia *child*. But at that moment the regal woman *did* seem childlike, small and slender, held tight in the grip of the old man who, now that he stood, was every bit as tall and straight as Beltan.

"Come on, everyone," Falken said with a laugh. "This is our old friend we told you about. Make that our *very* old friend."

The stranger—the one called Tome—looked up and fixed the bard with his brilliant gold eyes. "And a fine one you are to talk about age, Falken of Malachor!"

Grace wasn't certain exactly how it happened, but minutes later they all sat around the fire, laughing and drinking from wooden cups Tome handed them, and which Grace was not altogether certain contained just *maddok*. Like the drink, Grace suspected there was more to Tome than first met the eye. He was old, certainly. Deep lines etched his face, and his beard—as pure white as his robe—tumbled over his chest, while his bald pate was polished smooth.

However, Grace guessed Tome's wrinkles were the result of mirth as much as wisdom, and bright gold rings dangled from each of his ears. Aryn clapped her hands together and giggled—a rare gift these days—as the old man handed her a cup, and Tira almost immediately set up camp in his lap.

Of them all, only Beltan seemed unaffected by

Tome's joyous demeanor, for the knight hunched on the edge of the firelight and sipped quietly from his cup. It seemed Beltan's eyes moved once toward Travis and lingered there. Had something happened between them in the battle with the *krondrim*—something Travis hadn't told them about? Before Grace could wonder more, she felt a cup pressed into her hand.

"Drink up, Your Radiance," Tome said, eyes shining. He refilled the cups of Lirith and Aryn, who sat beside Grace. "And you as well, Daughters of Sia."

Grace took a sip from her cup. "Who is Sia?" she said without really thinking about it. Maybe it was just that she had heard the word spoken so many times—by Lirith, by Melia, and even by the dragon.

Tome grinned, displaying the most beautiful teeth Grace had ever seen. "Who is Sia you ask? Now that, dear child, is a good question. Oft I've wondered the same myself. Perhaps Lady Melia would care to answer?"

Melia crossed her arms. "I should think not!"

The regal lady's cheeks were bright with color, and she listed noticeably to one side. Had Grace not known better, she might have thought the lady to be drunk.

Falken peered at Lirith over the rim of his cup. "And should not Grace and Aryn's teacher in these matters answer the question? Indeed, I'm surprised she has not already."

Startled, Grace glanced at Lirith, and Aryn did the same. The Tolorian woman nodded, then set down her cup. The laughter quieted as all leaned close to listen to her.

"Sia is called by many names in many places, but all of them mean one thing: the Goddess. From Sia springs the Weirding, the web that weaves all life together." With a finger, Lirith traced a circle in the dirt. "It was Sia who gave birth to the world. And who *is* the world, for all of Eldh is her body."

Travis scratched his scruffy chin. "But I thought the Worldsmith forged the world when he spoke the First Rune." He glanced at Falken. "At least, that was how I heard it."

"So the Runespeakers believe," Lirith said, her voice cool. "But there are other tales of the beginning of Eldh than those told by the men of the Gray Tower."

Aryn brushed the circle with a finger. "But if it's from Sia that the Weirding comes, why haven't you spoken of her before?"

Lirith seemed to choose her words with great care. "There are those among the Witches who would rather not speak the name Sia these days."

"Why?" Grace said, startled.

Lirith shrugged. "Some associate Sia with the old days, and the workings of hags and hedgewives."

Now Grace understood. "So Sia conjures an image the Witches would rather forget, is that what you're saying?"

Lirith's silence was answer enough. Grace opened her mouth to ask another question, but Melia spoke first, and any traces of intoxication Grace might have detected a minute ago were nowhere to be seen.

"I hate to break up this interesting conversation about theology, but we do have some important matters to discuss. Such as why you are here, Tome." She cast her amber gaze toward the old man. "I thought we were supposed to meet you in Spardis."

At once all traces of merriment fled the circle. Grace set down her cup, and all watched Tome.

The old man looked at Melia. "We were. But when I reached Spardis and you weren't there yet, I thought I'd come meet you instead. You see, I've learned something about the one who has stolen Krondisar."

500 • MARK ANTHONY

Falken nodded. "As have we. We went to the temple in the Fal Erenn. You were right—the Stone was stolen from there. And it was Dakarreth who did it."

Sorrow flickered across Tome's visage, then as quickly it vanished, replaced by a surprising new expression: anger. "So, that is who has done this. But I am not surprised, especially given what I have learned."

"But what is it, Tome?" Melia laid her hand on his. "You must tell us."

The old man sighed. "I know now why he stole Krondisar. He seeks to use it, to be transformed."

These words sent a chill through Grace. "Transformed," she murmured. "But into what?"

Tome turned his golden eyes on her.

"A god," he said.

69.

"Long ago, thirteen of the Nindari took bodies of unliving flesh to walk upon the face of Eldh in service to Berash, the Pale King, as his Necromancers."

Travis watched as Melia spoke in a quiet voice. He felt Grace's hand on his, and he squeezed back. All of them had gathered close around the fire to listen to the bard, the lady, and the golden-eyed stranger speak.

Falken held out his gloved hand and watched the flames through the screen of his fingers. "It seems Dakarreth has grown weary of the flesh, and now he wants to go back to being one of the Nindari."

"No, not just one of the New Gods," Tome said. "Before he became a Dark One, Dakarreth was neither greatest nor least among the Nindari. But now he seeks to return greater than when he left, and rule over all the New Gods."

Melia clenched small hands into fists. "But he can't do that."

"I'm afraid he can, dear one." Tome laid wrinkled hands atop Melia's and with gentle strength smoothed her fingers out.

"But I don't understand," Grace said. "Why didn't the New Gods do anything to stop the ones . . . the ones who became Necromancers?"

"Because it was done in secret, child," Tome said in a heavy voice. "And when the dread deed was discovered by the Nindari, it was already far too late to do anything."

"But they *did* do something," Falken said to Grace. "As thirteen took bodies to serve the Pale King, so nine others forsook their celestial homes and took shape so they could walk upon the face of Eldh and work against the Necromancers."

Falken's words ignited a spark in Travis's chest. "So there's hope then. Maybe we can find some of these nine Nindari—maybe they can stop Dakarreth."

Melia gazed up at the star-strewn sky. "No, Travis, there will be no more help from the Nine. So many of them are gone now." She breathed a sigh. "So many . . ."

Travis shook his head. "But where did they go?"

It was Tome who answered. "Some sank deep into the soil, some faded onto the wind, and some became as foam on the sea to melt away. It is wearying, Goodman Travis—wearying in a way you cannot imagine—for a god to walk the world as one undying and yet not truly living. After the War of the Stones, when all thought the Necromancers were no more, most of the Nine gave up their burdens and passed from the world."

"You mean they became gods again?" Aryn said, her voice quavering.

"No, child. There was never any going back to

what was, for either the Thirteen or the Nine. Those who vanished are lost to us forever."

Travis shuddered. Tome said he couldn't imagine the sorrow of a god, and maybe the old man was right. But he could imagine giving up everything he had ever loved *because* he loved it. That was what the Nine had done for Eldh, wasn't it?

"So why has he not done it, then?" Durge said.

"What's that, young man?" Tome peered at Durge over the fire.

The craggy-faced Embarran winced, then recovered. "If Dakarreth stole the Stone of Fire that he might use it to become a god, why has he not done so already?"

Tome snapped his fingers. "Good question, young man. And the answer is the reason we sit here now, speaking as we do, rather than toiling beneath sun and whip to raise high a temple to the great god Dakarreth. The Stone of Fire has the power to transform one into that which one chooses. But only for one who knows the key. Sooner or later, all others will be destroyed."

Melia's eyes fluttered open. "Of course," she said, the sorrow gone from her voice. "He lacks the key to Krondisar. And without it he cannot become what he seeks."

Tome nodded. "That is why the *krondrim* are flawed as they are, and why so many perish before completing the transformation Dakarreth has chosen for them. Without the key, Dakarreth cannot truly unlock all the powers of Krondisar."

Lirith glanced at Falken. "Did not the man we saw at the border of Perridon—the Spider—speak of a key?"

The bard returned her gaze. "That's right. He talked about meeting a Burnt One who could still speak, and who claimed to be seeking the key to fire. You have a good memory."

The Tolorian woman nodded, pressing her hands against her knees through the fabric of her riding gown.

"That must be the purpose of the *krondrim*," Beltan said. The blond knight had sat silently on the edge of the circle, but now with stiff motions he drew closer to the others. "Their movements have always been best explained as a kind of search. Now I guess we know what it is they're searching for."

"I believe you are correct, Sir Knight," Tome said. "That is why Dakarreth created the Burning Plague—to create an army of slaves to seek and find the key to Krondisar."

Travis licked his lips. "There was another who talked about a key."

All eyes turned toward him. Travis took a breath, then he spoke of the words the man in black—the runelord Mindroth—had uttered in the Mine Shaft.

Yes, it is you to whom I must give the key. . . .

He finished to silence and the crackling of flames.

At last Tome spoke. "And did he give it to you?"

"What?"

"The key. Did Mindroth give it to you?"

Travis hunched down. "No. All he said was, 'Beware—it will consume you.' Then . . . then he burned."

A wind blew out of the night, stirring the fire, and sending crimson sparks up into the sky to wink among the stars.

Falken leaned back from the fire. "Well, I think we know what we need to do now. We've got to keep Dakarreth from finding the key to Krondisar."

"But how will we find him in time?" Melia said.

Tome spoke in a low voice. "You will find him in the Keep of Fire."

Beltan sat up straight. "The Keep of Fire?"

The old man frowned. "Yes—the place where Dakarreth has hidden Krondisar. I have learned that the Keep lies in the Barrens, to the north and east of Spardis. But there is something else to your question, Sir Knight. What is it?"

Beltan did not answer. Instead, Falken spoke. "It was something the dragon Sfithrisir said."

Travis turned to find Grace already looking at him. She tightened her grip on his hand.

Tome's shaggy eyebrows drew down in a scowl. "And I trust you know to be wary of the wisdom of dragons, Falken."

"But they speak the truth, don't they?" Beltan whispered, almost more to himself than the old man.

"No," Tome said, "the dragons speak *their* truth."

Beltan shook his head, but said nothing more.

"Thank you, Tome," Melia said. Tira had climbed into her lap, and now the lady stroked the girl's hair as Tira stared into the fire. "This knowledge will help us. Although in a way I feel I should have known all of it sooner. Dakarreth was ever cruel and petty, even before the Pale King used the Imsari to bind the Necromancers to him."

Durge frowned. "You speak almost as if you knew him personally, Lady Melia."

Her amber eyes flashed. "I did know him."

Travis wasn't certain how he made the connection. Maybe it was the result of a hundred other clues—things Melia had said and done—that, with this final piece, finally formed a clear and stunning picture: one he never could have expected, and yet which made perfect sense.

"You," he said, staring at Melia across the dancing flames. "You're one of them, aren't you?"

"One of who?" Durge rumbled.

"One of the Nine." Before the others could reply, Travis turned his eyes toward the old man in the white robe. "And you, too. Melia said you were old friends." Mad laughter rose in his throat. "She just didn't say *how* old."

Aryn shook her head. "What are you talking about, Travis?"

"They're gods, Aryn. Or they were. Until they came to Eldh to fight the Necromancers."

The baroness's blue eyes went wide. She looked to Falken. After a long moment he nodded—as did Beltan and Lirith.

"Why, Melia?" Travis choked on the words but got them out anyway. "Why didn't you ever tell us who you were?"

"And have you told me who you really are, dear?"

He pounded a fist against his knee. No, that wasn't good enough. "Falken, why didn't you say something?"

Melia's lips coiled in a smile, although it was a sad expression. "But Falken has his own secrets, dear. After all, I am not the only one who knew Dakarreth."

Travis gaped at the bard. "What does she mean? How could you have known Dakarreth?"

Falken was silent so long Travis thought he would never answer. Then the bard lifted his black-gloved hand. "It was Dakarreth who did this to me."

All gazed at the bard, unable to speak. Falken's voice was as bitter as poison.

"It was as a reward, you see, that he took my hand. And as a reminder. For the part I played unwittingly at his bidding—the hand I had in the death of a kingdom."

"Of what kingdom do you speak, Falken?" Durge said in a soft voice.

The bard clenched his gloved hand into a fist and spoke a single, shattered word. "Malachor."

Melia laid her hand over his fist, her eyes shining with sorrow. "You mustn't blame yourself, dear."

Falken lowered his hand. "No, that's for others to do."

Aryn twisted the fabric of her gown into a knot

with her left hand. "But this can't be. Malachor fell seven centuries ago."

"Yes," Tome said. "It did."

Travis no longer felt shock. "Of course. Falken of Malachor. That was how you introduced yourself to me in the Winter Wood. Which means you're—"

"Seven-hundred-and-forty-two years old," the bard said with a mirthless laugh. "And does it make you feel better to know the number?"

"But how?" Grace said simply.

Falken shrugged. "That was part of Dakarreth's reward for me as well. That I never die, so that I might forever remember what deeds were wrought by the hand I had lost."

Melia circled her arms around the bard, and the two bowed their heads together as Tome watched them, his gold eyes gleaming with tears.

A shard of sorrow pierced Travis's heart . . . then he discarded it. Who were these people—no, these *beings*—to use them all like this? They were worse than Sfithrisir. Like Duratek, the dragon had not concealed what it was from them. Instead Melia and Falken were like the Seekers, revealing only that which would make others do exactly the things they wanted.

Grace gazed at him with startled eyes. "Travis, what is it?"

He leaped to his feet, glaring at the bard and the amber-eyed lady, his voice a snarl. "So, what other secrets have you hidden from us?"

Melia looked up, her lips pressed together in a thin line. Then she bowed her head again, leaning against Falken, and spoke in a voice that was filled, not with sadness or anger, but simply weariness.

"Leave us alone, Travis. Please. Just leave us alone."

Like water from a broken flask, the anger poured out of him, leaving him hollow and brittle. He sank back to the ground and stared at the pale faces of the others. Then a hand touched his, and he looked up into green-gold eyes.

"It's all right, Travis," Grace said quietly. "It's still Melia and Falken."

I know, he wanted to say to her. *But is it still me?*

Instead he lay down, rested his head in her lap, and wept.

70.

From Shandis's back, Grace surveyed the castle that thrust upward from the misty waters of the lake below.

Well, I guess I made it here after all, Boreas.

She reached inside her cloak and fingered the still-crisp parchment folded inside a pocket. It seemed an age since Boreas had given her the letter of endorsement. On the journey, she had seen things and done things that she had never—could never have—imagined. And she had all but forgotten the mission given to her by King Boreas that summer morning in Calavere, to act as his spy in Castle Spardis. Yet, in the end, their travels had brought her here, right where she was supposed to be, and right on time.

Minus two knights and one boy, Grace.

Her heart stumbled in mid-beat. Had it been worth it? Had this mission been worth the deaths of Kalleth and Meridar? And that of Daynen?

But Grace knew that none of it—their journey, saving Travis, the task Boreas had given her—would be worth anything if they did not find a way to stop Dakarreth from gaining the key to the Stone of Fire. Yet Grace hardly even believed in gods. How was she supposed to fight one?

But you're not going to fight him, Grace. Not you

and not Travis. Falken and Melia are traveling to the Keep of Fire, and they're going to face Dakarreth. Alone.

While Falken and Melia had been adamant about this point when they discussed it that morning, Beltan had spoken with a vehemence Grace had never witnessed before, his voice hard and unmalleable as the sword at his hip.

"You're not going into the Barrens, Grace. And neither is Travis. Do you understand?"

Both stared at the blond knight, too stunned to speak.

Beltan crossed his arms over the broad expanse of his chest. "The dragon said both of you would die if you went to the Keep of Fire. So you're not going. Instead you're staying in Spardis where I can keep watch over you."

Grace knew she shouldn't speak the words, but they escaped her all the same. "And what of Lady Melia?"

Beltan's green eyes hardened, but Melia stepped forward, laying a slender hand on his arm.

"I have released Sir Beltan from his duties as my Knight Protector."

The expression on the knight's face gave way to shock as he looked at Melia.

"For the moment," she said crisply, meeting his eyes. Then she regarded Grace again. "It is best that Falken and I make this journey ourselves, dear. We will be traveling to places where . . . mortals cannot tread. All of you can remain safely in Spardis until we return."

If you return, Grace added to herself, but she didn't speak the words. For if Melia and Falken failed, it didn't matter what any of them did. The fire would find them all.

Now, from the back of his jet stallion, Falken pointed toward the castle. "Shall we?"

Aryn clutched her cloak around her shoulders. "Yes, let's. It will be good to get out of this chill and damp."

Grace huddled inside her own cloak. More than once she had been tempted to fling the garment from the back of her horse as they rode across the ever-hotter expanses of Perridon. However, that afternoon as they drew near the castle, the temperature plunged, and moisture beaded like fine pearls on every surface. This was Perridon as Grace had imagined it: shrouded in cool fog and mystery.

Durge led the way down the slope, and the others followed. Even were it not for the shifting fog, Grace knew it would be no easy feat to count the towers of Spardis. Great and small, fat and slender, soaring and squat: They crowded on the island in the middle of the dull silver lake.

As they rode, Grace guided Shandis toward Melia's pale mare. There was something she wanted to know.

"Where did he go, Melia? Tome, I mean."

Melia kept her gaze on the castle ahead. "He had other things to attend to, dear. And this is not a task for one such as Tome. He was ever the gentlest of our kind."

Grace shivered, and not only from the mist. *Our kind. One of the Nine, she means.* She stared at the regal lady, then her eyes moved to the bard who rode nearby. Knowing the truth about Melia and Falken had changed everything. They were immortal—Grace could never forget that. Yet it changed nothing as well. Just because Grace knew something about them she hadn't before, it didn't mean the two were any different. If the knowledge had changed anyone, it was Grace.

They reached the causeway that spanned the flat surface of the lake, then guided their horses onto it, hooves clopping against stone. The fog closed in, concealing the water, and Grace had the odd sensation that they were crossing a bridge over a sea of clouds. Then the fog parted, and an expanse of ironbound wood loomed before them.

Lirith glanced at Falken. "Is it usual for the gates to be closed by day?"

"In Spardis it is," the bard said with a laugh. "Suspicion is the rule, not the exception."

Durge glowered at the closed gates. "And how are we to gain entry?"

"We knock," Melia said. She dismounted and glided toward the gate.

Falken, Grace, and Aryn followed after Melia while the others remained with the horses. However, knocking was not necessary, for a small grille opened in the gate as they drew near.

"Begone!" a voice rumbled. "You are not welcome here!"

Falken gave Melia a wolfish grin. "I like it here. They seem friendly."

"So I noticed," she said.

They stopped before the gate. Through the small opening, Grace glimpsed a steel helmet and a pair of decidedly unfriendly eyes.

"I am Falken Blackhand," the bard said. "With me is the Lady Melia, Her Highness Aryn, Baroness of Elsandry, and Her Radiance Grace, Duchess of Beckett. We beg hospitality of the king."

The eyes widened at the bard's words, then grew hard again. "I cannot grant your request, Lord Falken. There is no king in Perridon, and the regent has ordered the gates of the castle be sealed as a ward against plague. You must go."

Grace had to admit, it was a reasonable order—self-imposed quarantine to avoid contagion. Still, they had to get into the castle. She reached into her cloak and pulled out the folded parchment.

"I have a letter of endorsement from King Boreas. He has asked that you—"

"I do not serve King Boreas," the voice behind the gate said, angrier now. "I have told you—the regent has forbidden any to enter Spardis until his return. Now go."

Grace opened her mouth, but Melia drifted past her. Her amber eyes glowed beneath half-closed lids. "But the regent is expecting us," she said in a soothing voice.

A pause, then the voice spoke from behind the door—duller now. "The regent is expecting you. . . ."

"We are his guests," Melia said.

"Yes, you are his guests. . . ."

"Good," Melia said. "Now, you must open the gates to us, lest the regent be displeased with you."

Terror flooded the eyes beneath the helmet. "No! The regent must not be displeased!"

The small opening snapped shut, then there was a grinding noise, and a larger portal set into the gates opened. The bard motioned to the others, who followed after with the horses.

Falken leaned close to Melia as they stepped through the doorway. "I knew you wouldn't be able to resist tampering with him."

"I didn't tamper," she said. "I merely nudged him toward the only logical conclusion."

"Nudge. Tamper. I don't see the difference."

"The difference is that I got us in, and you didn't."

Before Falken could reply, Melia proceeded through the gate, chin high.

The guard—clad in armor of some dark, polished metal—appeared before them. He gave a precise bow. "You may leave the horses here—I assure you your steeds will be well taken care of. Now, if you will follow, I will take you to the great hall and the chamberlain at once."

"Of course you will, dear," Melia said.

If the guard chose the most direct route to the great

hall in his urgency, Grace wouldn't have known it. This seemed more maze than castle, and the mist didn't help. She quickly lost all sense of direction as they wove among the towers, passed through narrow archways, and crossed slender bridges.

Melia groaned as they walked. "The Perridoners have to make everything complicated, don't they?"

Falken shrugged. "I think it's something in the water."

At last the guard pushed open a set of double doors, and they entered a space that looked much like the great hall of Calavere. Rushes covered the floor, and high, tapestry-draped walls rose to smoke-blackened beams. At the far end of the hall was a dais, atop which was an ornately carved chair, empty at the moment. However, another chair had been set on the lowest step of the dais, and this was occupied by a small, sunken-chested man whose eyes—small and darting in his pockmarked face—reminded Grace of the pet ferret a medical student had once brought to the hospital only to lose it in the ventilation system.

The guard presented them, and at first the chamberlain—whose name was Lord Siferd—was enraged that they had been allowed into the castle. However, after a brief conversation with Melia, Siferd's attitude improved remarkably.

"You must forgive me," he said, quivering before Melia. "I had no idea I had been brought such exalted guests. Be assured those responsible will be punished. Severely." Siferd cast a withering glance at the guard, whose eyes bulged.

"Not too severely," Melia said, laying a gentle hand on the chamberlain's arm.

His head bobbed. "Of course, my lady."

Melia's smile was more than a little smug.

Grace approached the chamberlain. She might as well not waste any time getting started. "Lord Siferd, we were told the regent is away."

"Yes, my lady, it's true. I doubt you are aware, but there have been rumors of plague in some of the more remote regions of the Dominion. The regent has ridden forth to see what he might do for the people." He clasped a hand to his concave chest. "Such a brave and kindly man he is."

"I'm sure," Grace said. "But in the meantime, might we see Queen Inara?"

Siferd sighed. "Alas, no. The queen is in seclusion while she mourns the loss of her husband, King Persard."

Grace chewed her lip. That was bad news. She had wanted to speak to the queen. Young though she was, Grace knew Inara might have insights into the political situation here.

"What of Duke Falderan or Lord Sul?" she said. "Might I see one of them?"

"Once more, I fear I must disappoint you, my lady. After the king's death, Lord Sul departed for his home in the north of Perridon. And while Duke Falderan is in residence here at Spardis, he fell gravely ill this spring and is receiving no visitors."

Grace couldn't suppress a frown. Why was everyone she wanted to talk with unavailable? But then, she should have known Inara would still be in mourning. It had been less than two months since her husband's death. And it was logical that Lord Sul had returned to his home; no doubt the new regent had counselors of his own. As for Falderan falling ill— Grace of all people knew the high likelihood of catching a disease on this world. There was the Burning Plague, after all.

Except, from what she had seen—and from the guard's words at the gate—it was clear that the Burning Plague had not yet reached Spardis. But that was strange, for all the evidence had pointed to Spardis as the epicenter of the pandemic.

Grace let out a breath. King Boreas had told her to

expect mysteries in Castle Spardis, and she had found them. At least she wouldn't want for things to do once Melia and Falken left.

Siferd clapped his hands, turning from Grace to regard the others. "Well, if there are no more questions, I shall have rooms prepared for you—the finest in all of Spardis." He bowed to Melia repeatedly, then scurried from the great hall.

Falken glanced at the amber-eyed lady. "You know, you really have to teach me that trick sometime."

"Not on your life," Melia said.

71.

"You have to admit," Grace said to Travis, glancing back at the bard and the amber-eyed lady across the great hall, "former goddesses and immortal bards do have their uses. I think the poor chamberlain's feet were hardly touching the floor when he left to go find rooms for us."

Travis smiled at Grace—he appreciated what she was trying to do—but he wasn't certain he was ready to joke about it. Not just yet, anyway. His smile dissipated.

She hesitated, then touched his shoulder. "We're the ones who are different you know, not them. They didn't change just by telling us who they really are."

"I know, Grace." He looked down at his hands. "Believe me, I know. I just need a little time to get used to it, that's all."

She folded her arms over her chest and turned away. "I suppose it's easier for me, really. In a way, everyone's like a stranger to me. Maybe that makes it harder to be surprised by anything I learn about other people."

A needle pricked Travis's heart. He took a step toward her. "Am I a stranger to you, Grace?"

She nodded, her back still turned to him. "But I love you, Travis."

He opened his mouth, but before he could speak the words he wanted more than anything to say—

I love you, too, Grace.

—she walked away across the great hall, toward Lirith and Ayrn, who sat on a bench with Tira.

Travis sighed, then turned and moved to the saddlebags heaped in a corner. Durge and Beltan had left to make certain the horses had been properly stabled. He supposed he could be useful by organizing the group's possessions. He knelt to begin sorting through the foodstuffs—then snatched his hand back too late to avoid a swipe of four needle-sharp claws.

"I really don't know what you have against me," he said in a sulky voice, clutching his wounded hand.

The black kitten licked its whiskers and returned to the nap it had been taking in one of the saddlebags. Travis edged away from the creature. As he moved, a slender shape caught his eye. He stood up, gripping the runestaff All-master Oragien had given him.

The staff was still wrapped tightly in felt—Travis had not uncovered it on the journey. There hadn't been much time for study, he told himself, although he knew that wasn't the true reason he hadn't examined it. Even now he could feel it—muted through the thick felt, but unmistakable—like a faint vibration resonating along the shaft. Power.

Just what you need, Travis. Another way to hurt people.

He started to set the runestaff back down.

"Are you ever going to uncover it?" a voice said behind him.

He turned, clutching the staff. "Melia. I didn't hear you coming."

"Of course not, dear." The lady glided closer. "You

can't keep it hidden forever, you know. Someday you'll have to bring it into the light and see what has been given you."

He tightened his fingers around the staff. "I didn't ask for it, Melia. I didn't want it."

"And does that make a difference?"

She was right, of course. He ran his fingers over the felt, wondering what secrets would be revealed when he removed it.

"I'm so sorry we didn't tell you sooner, dear."

He looked up, and his heart caught in his throat. It seemed impossible that one such as she should weep for him, but now tears shone in her eyes. Suddenly his earlier anger seemed selfish and stupid.

"But you did, Melia. You did tell me. And that's all that counts."

"No, we should have told you before we did. I see now how it wounded you that we didn't." A sad smile touched her lips. "I suppose we thought we were protecting you."

He almost laughed. Wasn't that why he kept his own power under wraps, just like the runestaff? To protect people? Yes, Melia and Falken had lied. Just like Deirdre and the Seekers had. But at least none of them had used the truth to harm. Like the dragon did. Like Duratek. And which of them was Travis like? Melia said he couldn't keep things hidden forever. But if he let his power into the light and used it— knowing as he did that it could hurt others—how was he any less a monster than Sfithrisir?

An icy blade pierced the fog that clouded his mind, bringing with it clear understanding. Yes, there was another way after all. . . .

A shadow touched Melia's brow. "Travis, your face—what's wrong?"

He was spared having to speak a lie of his own, for at that moment Beltan and Durge burst through the doors of the great hall, their mail shirts chiming in chorus.

Falken stepped toward them. "What is it? Is something wrong with the horses?"

Beltan snorted. "No, despite Durge's predictions, they're just fine. It's the queen."

Grace stood. "The queen? You mean Inara?"

"We glimpsed her a moment ago," Durge said. "She was walking across the inner bailey with her ladies-in-waiting."

In three long strides, Beltan covered the distance to a shuttered window. "If I've got any sense of direction left at all after mucking around this rattrap of a castle, I think we'll be able to see her from here. If any of you want to get a look at her, that is."

Together they clustered around the window. Travis peered over the heads of the others, into the narrow courtyard below. At first all he could see was a lone peasant hauling a cart of peat across the cobbles. Then a slight figure veiled in black drifted into view, her head bowed. Three woman followed behind, one of them carrying a wriggling bundle wrapped in white.

"That must be her son, Perseth," Falken said.

Aryn sighed. "She looks so sad. Do you suppose she really loved King Persard after all?"

Durge let out a rumbling breath. "It is impossible that one so fair in the spring of life could truly love a man well into his winter."

"No, I can believe it," Lirith said quietly. "The heart is a mysterious artifact."

Durge did not look at the witch but only stared out the window.

Grace shook her head. "I wish we could talk to her. There's so much I need to ask her about the—*Tira!*"

As Grace spoke, the barefoot girl had clambered past her, hopping onto the low windowsill. Evading

Grace's grasping hands, Tira slipped through the window and onto the ledge beyond. The sound of Grace's shout echoed off stone walls. Below, the queen came to a halt, then turned her veiled face upward.

Tira grinned and waved at her.

The ladies-in-waiting stared up in round-mouthed shock. Queen Inara hesitated, then lifted her hand in a tentative wave. Grace finally got her hands around the elusive girl and hauled her back in through the window. Below, the queen and her entourage continued on their way, passing out of sight.

Beltan closed the shutters as they stepped away from the window. Grace hugged Tira to her chest.

"Don't ever do that again," she said, her cheeks flushed. "Do you understand me?"

Tira did not struggle. Instead she shut her eyes and leaned her scarred face against Grace's breast.

"Is something amiss, my lords, my ladies?"

They looked up to see Lord Siferd walking across the great hall. Behind him came a servingman bearing a tray of pewter goblets.

Melia drifted forward. "No, my lord. All is well."

The chamberlain beamed and bowed low. "Your rooms are nearly ready, fair lady. I beg your patience for just a short time more. Please, refresh yourself while you wait."

The chamberlain scurried from the hall again, and the servant approached. Each of them took a cup of pale wine from the tray. Travis sighed as he drank. He was thirsty, and the wine was crisp, cool, and just slightly sweet.

Beltan grunted as he set his cup back down. "It's not ale, but I could get used to it." He picked up two more goblets as the servingman stared with wide eyes.

Most of them sat as they waited for the chamberlain's return, while a few wandered the great hall or explored side doors that opened on small antechambers. Travis sat on a bench, staring into his wine cup. Could he really do what he intended? But there was no other way to be sure he would never accidentally hurt someone he cared about.

"What lies through that door, Travis?"

He glanced up. Melia approached the doorway next to the bench where he sat.

He shrugged. "I don't know. I haven't looked."

Melia tried the knob, and the door swung open. Her eyes glinted. "Well, I've always held that if the door's not locked then it isn't snooping."

Travis grinned at her. He couldn't argue with that. She opened the door and passed into the room beyond. Sighing, Travis bent back over his wine.

A gasp drifted through the open doorway, followed by a soft but clear voice.

"Oh, dear!"

A moment later came a soft thump followed by the clang of metal against stone.

Shock jerked Travis to his feet. He stared at the doorway, then dashed toward it. Beltan was already ahead of him. The two men came to a halt in a small room. Light from a high window illuminated scant objects: a chair, a table, and a marble bust on a pedestal that depicted a handsome man. However, none of those things held Travis's eyes. He gazed down, and the blood drained from his heart.

A small figure in blue lay on the floor in a puddle of spilled wine. The goblet had rolled from her limp hand, and her eyes were shut in her ashen face.

"No!" Beltan's cry echoed off stone. He fell to his knees beside the small, still form as the others rushed into the room.

"What is it?" Falken said from the doorway.

Travis turned around—he felt as brittle as glass—and met the bard's eyes. "It's Melia," he said.

72

At dawn two days later they gathered beneath the shadows of many towers in the castle's lower bailey. Grace clutched her cloak around her shoulders. After the sweltering heat of the journey east, she had yet to grow used to the chill that permeated the stones of Spardis.

Falken started to mount his black horse, then paused and regarded Grace with haunted blue eyes.

"You'll take good care of her, won't you, Grace?"

She spoke in a voice made steady and reassuring by years of practice. "I'll do everything I can, Falken."

He nodded, then swung up into the saddle.

"Are you prepared, my lady?" Durge said from his vantage astride Blackalock.

Lirith adjusted her riding gown over the withers of her palfrey, then nodded. "I am ready."

Grace tried to swallow the lump in her throat but failed. She was the only one who had come to the outer bailey to see the three off on their journey. Beltan could not be parted from Melia's bedside. Travis had stayed with the knight, and Aryn was looking after Tira. Grace knew she should have stayed as well, but she couldn't let her friends leave without saying good-bye. Not when she knew that, if they indeed reached their destination, they might never return again.

Besides, she had instructed Travis to come find her if there was any change in Melia's condition. Not that she expected any change. She still had no idea of the cause—no one had seen Melia fall, and there was no visible sign of any illness or trauma—but Melia had slipped into a deep coma.

Falken had wanted to go alone on this journey, of

course. Until last night he had been adamant that only he venture into the Barrens, to find the Keep of Fire, and to wrest Krondisar from the Necromancer before it was too late.

"I'm the only one who knows Dakarreth and the things he can do," he said, pacing like a caged wolf in the chamber adjacent to where they had laid the small woman's unconscious form. "Besides, you heard Sfithrisir. If either Travis or Grace goes to the Keep of Fire, they'll die there."

Lirith stepped toward him, her dark eyes intent. "The dragon spoke nothing of my going to the Keep of Fire."

"Nor of me," Durge said in a solemn voice.

Falken had opened his mouth, but at last all his arguments had been spent. Instead he had nodded, then turned away.

A wind sprang up, stirring the mist and catching Durge's charcoal-gray cloak. "We should be going," the knight said. "If we linger in the courtyard too long, the chamberlain is likely to see us preparing to depart."

Melia had worked her trick almost too well on the chamberlain. Lord Siferd was now convinced they were important guests and friends of the regent, and no doubt he would protest any of them leaving the castle before the regent's return.

"Will we be able to get by the guards at the gate?" Lirith said, glancing at the bard.

Now the old wolfish grin cut across Falken's haggard mien. "We'll find a way."

"Farewell, my lady," Durge said to Grace, bowing low in the saddle. "It has ever been my honor to serve you."

Lirith cast one of her mysterious smiles at Grace. "I'll miss you, sister."

Grace nodded. An ache welled up in her chest. There was so much she wanted to say—that she loved them all, that she wanted them to take care of themselves, and that she was so terribly afraid they would never come back. But the mist seemed to creep into her lungs, constricting them, and all she could say in a soft voice was, "Good-bye."

The three wheeled their horses around and rode across the bailey. After a moment the fog closed behind them, and they were gone. Grace gazed into the mist, then sighed, turned, and headed back into the castle.

It took her longer than she had intended to return to their chambers. However, in Castle Spardis—she had discovered over the last two days—the shortest distance between two points was nothing even close to resembling a straight line. She passed through archways to nowhere, walked down corridors that led her in circles, and climbed stairways that ended in blank walls.

In a way getting lost was welcome, for it gave her time to think—something she had not had in great quantities since leaving Calavere. Falken, Durge, and Lirith had their mission, and Grace had hers. And it wasn't simply determining the political situation in Spardis.

Once again, in her mind, she went over every aspect of Melia's condition she had been able to assess. Melia's breath rate and pulse were depressed, and she exhibited no pain response. However, her pupils still responded to light, and there was no sign of reflexive contraction in her extremities. That was good—it meant there wasn't brain damage. If brain damage was even something one like Melia could suffer from.

And that was part of the problem. Melia was not mortal. Grace had no idea what effect that had on her physiology—if the lady even *had* a physiology. However, Grace had no choice but to treat her as she would anyone, and so far there was nothing that indicated a diagnosis.

She had examined the room where Melia fell, but she had found nothing of interest—some furniture, a tapestry, and a marble bust of a man. That was all. Beltan had suggested the wine might have been the cause, but all of them had drunk of the same wine, and Lord Siferd was the last person in the castle who would have wanted to poison Melia. Besides, Lirith had examined the residue in the wine goblet with the Touch, and she had detected no trace of toxin.

Before Grace found any answers, she found their room. With a breath she opened the door and stepped through. Travis looked up from the chair in which he had been slumping.

"Well," she said, "they're gone."

He nodded, his gray eyes dim behind his spectacles.

Grace glanced at the door that led to Melia's chamber. "How is she?"

"The same. Beltan's with her. He still won't sleep. I think he's waiting until he collapses on top of her. But Aryn and Tira are resting in the other room."

"You should get some rest yourself. You look awful."

He grinned up at her. "Thanks."

"Don't mention it."

Travis lay down on a cot. Grace set his spectacles on a table and covered him with a blanket. Then she rose and started to turn away.

"Do you think they'll do it?" His voice was low and hoarse. "Get the Stone of Fire from Dakarreth."

Grace turned around. His eyes were shut.

"I don't know," she said. "Yes, I believe so. I think maybe I have to."

Travis did not open his eyes, but he nodded. Grace watched him until his breathing grew deep and even—it took a minute, perhaps less—then she moved across the room and slipped quietly through the door, into the corridor beyond.

Now what?

She sighed. There was nothing more she could do to help Melia. She supposed she might as well work on her other mission, the one given her by Boreas, although it hardly seemed important. If Falken failed, then who ruled what Dominion would be moot. Dakarreth would rule them all. But if she really believed the bard was going to succeed, then it *was* important to find out who this new regent was, and whether he had Queen Inara's and Prince Perseth's best interests in mind.

Renewed purpose brought energy to Grace's limbs. She started down the corridor.

Five missteps, a half-dozen questions asked of servants, and thirty minutes later, she found herself in front of a gilded door in the castle's north wing. Exactly *which* north wing it was she couldn't say, for Spardis seemed to have three of them. As she approached the door, two guards in black polished armor intercepted her, crossing spears to bar the way.

"No one is to disturb Queen Inara," one of them growled.

Grace took a quick step back to avoid having her nose sliced off. "Then could I please send a message to her?"

"The queen is taking no messages during her seclusion."

She lifted a hand to her chest. "By whose orders?"

"By command of the regent. If you wish to send a message to the queen, you may petition the regent when he returns."

Grace ducked her head, then turned and walked down the corridor before she got a spear stuck in her. She hadn't thought she would be able to get in to see the queen, but the attempt had been interesting. If Inara really was in seclusion, shouldn't the prohibition against communication have been her own?

Not if it's a forced seclusion. You have to admit,

it's a convenient way to keep her out of the picture. If she breaks the mourning, she looks callous. So she has no choice but to stay in her room and watch the regent rule things for her.

She was jumping to conclusions, of course. For all Grace knew this regent had Inara's complete support. If only there was someone else she could talk to. But maybe there was. . . .

It was afternoon before Grace finally found the room she was looking for. She spoke to a dozen servants, but as soon as she said who she sought, each cast a startled look over his or her shoulder and scurried away. Finally she found a boy carrying a bucket of refuse who, in exchange for a silver coin, was willing to talk.

"My grandmum is watching him," the boy said. "You'll find his room in the east wing."

"*Which* east wing?" Grace said with a sigh.

A grin split his scabby face. "Why, there's only one, my lady." Then he had scampered down the hall.

Surprisingly, the boy's words had proved accurate. Grace hesitated, then knocked on the door.

"Come in," a cracked voice spoke from the other side.

Grace opened the door and stepped through, then nearly fell back against the stench. She lifted a hand to her mouth, steeled herself, and moved farther into the dim chamber.

So this is what happens to sick dukes in Spardis.

There was little more to the room besides a cot and a chair. On the cot, propped up with ragged pillows, was a middle-aged man in a filthy bedshirt. His hair was greasy and unkempt and his cheeks unshaven. He stared with blank eyes while spittle rolled down his chin. In the chair sat an old woman who looked little cleaner than the man. She leaped to her feet when she saw Grace.

"My lady!" she said with a clumsy curtsy.

Grace moved closer to the bed. The scent of feces was strong. When had his sheets been last changed? She studied the man's unseeing eyes, then looked at the old woman. "Is this Duke Falderan?"

"Aye, it is." The woman pawed at her snarled hair, utterly failing to smooth it down. "I've been set here to care for him, I have."

Grace clenched her teeth. What use was there chastising the old woman? She knew nothing about caring for the infirm, that was clear. No, it was the one who had sent her here who deserved Grace's wrath.

She knelt beside the bed and snapped her fingers in front of Falderan's eyes. No blink response. Then she noticed the bandage on the side of his head, dark with old blood. She looked up at the woman. "How long has he been like this?"

A shrug. "Since I came to him, my lady. Over a moon it's been now."

"Do you know the nature of his illness?"

The woman let out a harsh cackle. "A disagreement with the regent, that's what his illness is, my lady. He took a tumble on the steps, but not without help, I'd say."

Grace rose. There was nothing she could do for Falderan.

"You think the regent had this done?" she said.

Now the old woman's eyes went wide. She backed up against the wall. "Oh, bless me! Are you a spy then, my lady? But it was only a jest. Yes, a jest. I love the regent, I do. Gods be with him." Tears streamed down her dirty face. "Bless me, oh, gods bless me."

"It's all right," Grace said. "Really." She reached out a hand, but the old woman howled as if stuck with a knife, cringing and sniveling in the corner, snot running from her nose. Before she made things worse Grace left the chamber, shutting the door behind her.

Outside, she drew in deep breaths, trying to clear the stench from her lungs, but the reek of death followed her all the way back to her room.

73.

Travis moved down the corridor, glancing left and right, wondering if anyone had seen him.

What do you think, Travis? This is Spardis. Probably two dozen people have noticed you in the last minute.

But he was not concerned about any of the scheming residents of the castle spying on him. It was the eyes of his friends he was trying to avoid. He didn't want any of them to ask him where he was going. He didn't want to lie to them. And he didn't want to wound them with the truth.

You've got to get away from the others, Travis—before you hurt one of them—and this is your last, best chance. Beltan's not going to leave Melia, not while she's sick. And Grace has a mission here she's got to finish. With what she found out about Duke Falderan the other day, it looks like there's plenty for her to investigate here.

As for Aryn and Tira—Travis knew they would stay wherever Grace was. He gripped the felt-wrapped runestaff in one hand, shifted the bag he had tossed over his shoulder with the other, and kept walking.

He had nearly blown it all that morning. He had taken breakfast with Grace, Aryn, and Tira in their chamber, and gazing on their faces—for what he knew was likely the last time—had conjured bitter tears.

"What's wrong, Travis?" Aryn had said, touching his arm lightly with her left hand.

"I've just got something in my eye," he had said—the lie had come easily—then turned away.

After that he looked for Beltan—not to say fare-well, he couldn't do that—but just to see the knight one last time. Of them all, Travis had thought most of Beltan since his decision to leave. He wasn't entirely certain why; maybe it was just that Beltan was his Knight Protector. Regardless, Travis wondered if he would ever again feel as safe as he did when Beltan was close. But now it was his turn to be the protector. After all, how long would Beltan be safe if Travis remained?

The knight had actually left Melia's bedside that morning—to stretch his legs, he had told Aryn, al-though the baroness believed that Beltan had gone to find a shrine of Vathrìs where he might pray. Travis had searched for an hour, then had finally seen the knight heading away from him down a corridor.

"Beltan!" he had called out.

By the way the knight had hesitated, missing a beat in his stride, Travis knew he had heard. Then the knight continued on without turning, disappearing around a corridor.

Travis's heart sank in his chest. It was clear Beltan had been avoiding him ever since their struggle with Eriaun and the *krondrim*. Had he done something to offend the knight?

He didn't know. Maybe, in the end, Beltan did think of him as a monster, and not a man. Either way, it was for the best, for it made escape easier. Al-though, at that moment, Travis suspected he would have given anything to see one of Beltan's brilliant smiles one more time.

Instead he retrieved his things from the alcove where he had hidden them earlier, then headed down the passageway with quick steps. He had to make sure he was outside the castle walls before the others found out he was gone.

Ducking through an archway, he stepped onto a cobbled street crowded with people. He fell in with the crowd, walking in the direction of two soaring spires that he knew flanked the castle's gates. Beyond them was—what?

Travis sighed. He supposed he would find out when he got there. But maybe he already knew. Even now he could feel it on his heels, following him like a shadow. Power.

Go, Runebreaker! Go destroy the world by saving it!

No—that was why he was leaving, going as far away from anyone as he could. Travis clenched his hand around the runestaff and quickened his pace.

The movement of the crowd slowed. Ahead, Travis caught a glimpse of a cart of turnips that had spilled across the street. A flock of goats milled around it while a barefoot boy with a willow switch tried in vain to gather them together. Travis groaned. He didn't need a delay just then. Searching, he spied an archway that opened onto a side lane. He jostled his way between angry people, then stepped through the arch.

After the bustle of the main street, the lane was dim and quiet. The walls leaned toward each other above, nearly shutting out the sky. Travis started into a trot.

After a few minutes, he began to wonder if this detour had been such a good idea. At first he had been able to see the tops of the towers that marked the castle's gate. Then the lane turned, and the towers were lost to sight. Again the narrow way twisted, and again, until Travis wasn't certain if he was going away from the center of the castle or toward it. Here and there bridges arched overhead, but it had been some time since he had seen an opening that led out of the lane, and there was no end to the way in sight.

"Are you lost, friend?"

Travis came to a skidding halt. He jerked his head from side to side, but all he saw were blank stone walls.

"No, friend. Over here."

He spun around and watched a man step away from a patch of wall that he had stared at seconds ago. How had he not seen the other before? Then he noticed the man's cloak: The fabric was the exact same gray as all the walls in Spardis.

The man was young—younger than Travis's thirty-one years, that was certain—slightly built and with a face that was more pretty than handsome. A pointed blond beard adorned his chin, and his eyes were a blue-gray so pale they seemed silver. He held up a hand covered by a pearl-gray glove.

"Hail to the queen. May her secrets never be spoken."

Travis blinked. "Excuse me?"

The man frowned. He hesitated, then made a complicated motion with the fingers of his left hand. Travis shook his head. What was the other doing?

It happened so fast he didn't have time to react. The man stepped forward and pressed the tip of a small, sharp dagger to the underside of Travis's jaw.

"Who are you?"

"I'm Travis Wilder," he said, too shocked to answer with anything but the truth.

The other's eyes narrowed. "Where did you get the cloak?"

"What?"

"The cloak!" The man flicked Travis's mistcloak.

Travis swallowed. "Falken gave it to me."

For the first time, the other seemed to hesitate. "Falken? You mean Falken Blackhand?"

Travis started to nod, then sucked in a breath as the knife pricked his skin. "Yes."

The stranger studied him, then in one smooth motion lowered the dagger and stepped back. "I see in your eyes that you speak the truth. You must forgive me. So many of my order are dead now. I feared you stole the cloak from one who had fallen."

Travis rubbed his throat. "Your order?"

The stranger said nothing. Travis lowered his hand, then he remembered the man they had encountered at the border of Perridon, the man with the Burning Plague—who had worn a gray mistcloak just like Travis's.

"You're a Spider!" he said.

The man raised a slender eyebrow. "I would be within the rights granted me by the monarchy of Perridon to kill you for that knowledge."

For a reason he couldn't name, Travis felt suddenly bold. "So why don't you?"

The man bent and slipped the dagger into his boot. "There has been enough death in this castle of late."

"What do you mean? Has the plague reached the castle?"

"No. Not yet, at least. We know it's coming, but that's all. Some of the Spiders ventured from Spardis to investigate. None of them have returned." The man turned his silvery eyes on Travis. "And they won't, will they?"

Travis shook his head.

"I thought as much."

"I saw one of them," Travis said. "At the border."

"And did he have it?"

Travis hesitated, then gave a shallow nod. The Spider turned his head away. He was silent. Finally he turned back.

"So you came here with Falken Blackhand's party."

"That's right."

The Spider gave a rueful smile. "There was a time not long ago when I would not have had to ask for that information, but I fear we have been . . . disenfranchised. It has made our work a bit more difficult."

He held out a hand. "Would you take me to see Falken? I would speak with him."

"I'm afraid he left a few days ago."

The Spider winced. "And that I did not know either. Well, it's no matter. You should go as well, you know."

"I was just on my way out of the castle."

The Spider laughed. "Not by this route, you weren't."

Travis sighed. "I suppose I'm lost."

"Yes, I suppose so. Come, I'll take you to the gates. Or at least most of the way, for it would not do if I were seen. Consider it a favor to Falken Blackhand, for the aid he gave us in times past."

Without further words, the Spider started down the lane. Travis stared, then jerked into a run before the other was lost to sight. He followed as the Spider moved through a dizzying series of twists and turns. Just when Travis was certain the other was just as lost as he was, they rounded a corner and, through an archway a dozen paces ahead, Travis saw a flat expanse of cobbles and a pair of high gates.

The Spider touched his arm. "Give the guard with the eye patch a gold coin and he'll let you out. Do you have a gold coin?"

Travis nodded. He had a little Eldhish money Beltan had given him. "Thanks," he said.

The Spider smiled, his teeth dark with decay. "Don't mention it."

Travis was almost sorry to say good-bye. He didn't even know the Spider's name, but he found that he liked the man.

"I hope you find a way to help your queen."

The Spider pressed his lips together, then nodded. Travis turned and started toward the archway.

High and clear, trumpets blared.

A hand clamped on Travis's shoulder, jerking him back. He stared into the Spider's inscrutable face.

"What is it?"

The Spider shook his head. "You're too late, friend."

"What?"

"The regent returns."

The Spider pointed toward the castle gates. Travis stared through the archway. Even as he watched the gates swung inward and a man on a prancing white horse rode through, followed by a dozen knights on glossy black chargers. At this distance it was hard to get a clear look at the man on the white horse, but he sat tall and proud in the saddle. His golden hair streamed behind him, as did his cloak of the same color. Ruby light glinted off his brow.

Travis turned back toward the Spider. "Who is that?"

"That, friend, is Regent Darrek. I heard this morning that, once he returned to Spardis, the gates would be sealed, and no one would be allowed to enter or leave for fear of plague. I'm afraid you're not going anywhere."

Fear pierced Travis, colder and sharper than the Spider's dagger. "No!"

"It's true, friend. Just trying to get past the gates now will land you in the dungeon."

Travis started to protest, then stopped. He wasn't sure how, but he knew the other was telling the truth. Turning, he watched the man in gold ride by.

"Here he comes," the Spider said in a poisonous voice. "Just what the people want. A strong leader for dark times."

Travis shuddered. "You sound as if you hate him."

"I do, Travis Wilder. And for good reason. You see, it is he who keeps us from our queen. And it is he who ordered the execution of all members of my order."

Fear gave way to astonishment as Travis stared at the Spider. The man gave a bitter smile.

"Good luck, friend. And take my advice—don't wear that cloak of yours where the regent can see it."

The Spider lifted an arm, and gray fabric fluttered before Travis's eyes. Travis blinked, and by the time his vision cleared the Spider was gone.

Travis knew better than to try looking for the spy. Instead he took off his cloak, wadded it into a tight ball, and stepped through the archway. He let his eyes linger on the gates. Then he sighed and started back toward his chamber, his shadow stretching out before him.

74.

Lirith pressed her body harder against the rough sandstone wall behind her as another streak of hot, yellow energy annealed the metallic sky.

Get ahold of yourself, sister. It's only a lightning show, nothing more. You ran out in the rain as a girl to watch noisier storms than this.

However, this was not southern Toloria, where warm showers gently washed the green hillsides while the scent of flowers rose on the air. Nor was it the noise of the storm that drove needles into her skull until she knew she must scream. Thunder would have been a comfort. Instead the lightning whispered across the sky like serpents, the only sound the hiss of wind-driven sand as it scoured stone, flesh, and nerves alike.

She clamped her eyes shut and searched with her mind again, but it was no use. If there was any trace of the Weirding—any trace of *life*—left in this place, then it was beyond her to detect. The area was called the Barrens for a reason.

After three days of riding across empty grasslands, they had come upon the edge of a stark, broken plain just before sunset last night. Lightning had flickered in the distance, illuminating sharp heaps of slag thrust up from the ground and the edges of chasms. It struck Lirith like a wall: the sensation of death.

She had gasped. "What is this place, Falken?"

It was Durge who answered in his somber voice. "It is the Barrens, my lady."

Falken gazed out over the badlands. "This was the place where, long before people came into this world, the Gordrim and the Eldhari—the Dragons and the Old Gods—made war upon each other. The Dragons sought to tear the world down, and the Old Gods to build it back up."

"So who won?" Durge said.

A sigh escaped Lirith's lips. "It looks like no one did."

Falken had cast her a piercing glance, then guided his stallion down a treacherous slope and into the Barrens. Lirith and Durge had followed after.

For what seemed like hours they had picked their way across a shattered land where no rain fell, where no water flowed, and where no life had grown in eons. To Lirith—used to the constant presence of the Weirding all around, encapsulating her like a warm, golden cloak—it was like being shut inside a stifling sarcophagus carved of stone.

Then, finally, they had seen it illuminated in a flash of lightning: massive columns carved from the face of a cliff, and beyond them darkness. Neither Lirith nor Durge had needed Falken to tell them this was the place they had come seeking. The Keep of Fire.

"But why is it so dark?" Durge had said. "I see no guards upon the steps. Should not there be defenses to prevent others from entering?"

Falken had shaken his head. "Dakarreth doesn't need guards. He has . . . his own defenses."

Together they had ridden over the last expanse of cracked stone toward the fortress.

Now Lirith shuddered as another bolt of lightning snaked across the sky. Her view of the world was blocked as a figure stepped down into the hollow where they had sought scant shelter from the storm, and where Falken had told them to wait. She looked up into grim brown eyes.

"Any sign of him?"

The Embarran shook his head, and sand fell from his hair. His mustaches were white with dust.

Lirith forced her mind to calm, letting the panic drain from her like water. "But it's only been an hour since he went in, hasn't it?"

It was so hard to tell what time it was. Sunset yesterday had been the last time they had glimpsed the sun. There had been no dawn. Night was the same as day in this place.

"Nay, my lady," Durge said, squatting beneath the rock overhang to get out of the worst of the blast. "It has been four hours at the least by my count."

Her fingers scrabbled against sandstone, trying to dig in. She made her hands unclench. "Well," she said in her most calm voice, "that means he'll likely return soon."

"If you wish, my lady."

Softly spoken as they were, Durge's words slapped her like the wind. She turned her face away. Falken had gone alone into the fortress of the Necromancer, and they had known better than to argue with the bard on this.

"You are here only for one reason," Falken had said. "To ride back and warn the others if I fail. If Melia wakes, there is yet a chance of defeating Dakarreth. If I do not return after a day, you are to leave. And you are not to enter the fortress yourselves on any condition. Do you understand?"

Lirith had never seen the bard like this before—his

face was as hard as the wind-blasted rocks. She was not one who frightened easily, but at that moment she had feared Falken. Both she and Durge had nodded. Then, without another word, the bard had left them, ascended thirteen stone steps, and disappeared between two gigantic columns into blackness beyond.

Durge sat on the dusty ground. "I will go back to watch for him, my lady. I just need to . . . to rest for a moment."

Lirith studied the knight. The lines in his haggard face were caked with dust, and his shoulders slumped beneath the weight of his mail shirt. How long had it been since he had slept?

How long has it been since any of you slept, sister?

Nor were they likely to. Not there, and not then. But of them all Durge had rested the least on the journey, always watching over them, keeping alert for danger.

Lirith moved deeper beneath the overhang, to the horses who stamped and snorted. She pulled a flask from her pack, then returned to Durge. They each drank a scant sip of water—the flask was less than half-full—then sat in silence, listening for the sound of approaching feet.

"Do you think what it said is true, my lady?"

She looked up.

"The dragon," he said. "Do you think Falken is right, that it spoke truth?"

Lirith thought of the ancient creature and its soft, poisonous words.

Here are two Daughters of Sia, both doomed to betray their sisters and their mistress.

And what had the dragon spoken about Durge?

Strong as stone, you present yourself, Sir Knight, and yet your heart is tender and weak with thoughts of another, is that not so? If only you were young and handsome enough to deserve her.

They were bitter words. Was it thinking of them that made the knight's shoulders droop so?

Lirith gathered her thoughts. "I believe the dragon spoke *a* truth. A truth it wishes to come to pass, and which it seeks to shape. But there are many truths, Durge. After all, Sfithrisir said that Travis and Grace would die if they came to the Keep of Fire. Yet they are not here, are they?"

Durge grunted, but his brown eyes were distant. Lirith sighed. She wished there was something she could do to ease the kindly knight's troubles. If only she could Touch the Weirding, she could have taken a bit of its warmth and life and granted it to the man.

But there *was* life in this place. There was herself, and she could give the knight a small amount of the Weirding that flowed through her. It wouldn't be much—she was weary as well—but it might be enough to help the knight weather the storm: that outside, and that within.

Without asking, she reached out and placed her hand atop his. She shut her eyes, and she could see them both shining against the emptiness all around. With a thought she spun a slender thread from the web of her own life, then reached out and brought the strand in contact with Durge.

There was a flash in her mind as their threads connected. Too bright. Tensing, Lirith tried to pull back—she had not meant the Touch to bring them so close. But the power of his life drew her in faster than she had thought. She should have known it would happen—that with no other threads along the Weirding to pull at her the connection would be deep and immediate. But she was so tired herself.

She could feel Durge's astonishment as life coursed back and forth between them. Lirith tried to close off the ebb, but she was too slow. Images and thoughts sped back along the thread of the Weirding toward her: memories that were not her own.

She saw Durge as a very young man, no more than nineteen, clad only in breeches beside a silver lake, homely in his hawk-nosed way, but grinning, his hair long and flowing, and his chest and arms already hard with muscle as he swung his greatsword: a knight freshly born.

The image melted and re-formed. Now Durge fought in a bloody battle, wielding his greatsword with deadly force, still grinning as men fell before him.

Again the images changed. This time Durge was a little older—in his twenties now. In his arms, he caught a pretty, slender young woman with large brown eyes. He swung her around, and both laughed. Then there was a small form in her arms. A child. Durge bent down to kiss the baby.

Mist passed before the vision, and when it cleared again Durge was alone. He knelt on the ground, head bowed, before two freshly turned graves: one large, one small.

Now the images came faster. More battles, but the grin was gone now, and Durge's face old, harder, grimmer. Everything was one endless river of gray and red. Then, just as Lirith managed to turn away, she caught one shining glimpse of color: again it was a pretty young woman. Only this time her eyes were not brown, but sapphire-blue.

Lirith's eyes snapped open, and she fell back, away from Durge. The knight lifted a hand to his brow, staring at her. On his face was a look of horror.

"What . . . what have you done to me, my lady?"

She shook her head. *I'm sorry*, she wanted to say. *I'm so sorry, Durge. I didn't mean for this to happen.* But when she opened her mouth, she spoke other words.

"It's Aryn, isn't it? She's the one the dragon was talking about. You love her, Durge—don't you?"

Now the fear left Durge's face, replaced by a look

so stern he seemed carved of stone. He scrambled forward and gripped her shoulders. Hard.

"You must never tell her, my lady." His words stung like the windblown sand. "You must swear to me. Now, and by all that you hold sacred." He shook her with terrible strength. "You must never tell her what you know!"

Dread at what she had done paralyzed Lirith. She could only stare at his shattered face.

"Say it!"

A moan of pain escaped her. "By Sia, I swear it!"

Durge let go. His face was weary and ashamed. He turned away from her and clutched his hands together. "Forgive me, my lady. Please forgive me. I did not mean to hurt you."

Nor I you, she tried to say, but she was sobbing. What had she done to him with her foolishness? She had taken what was private and hidden and had stolen it from him. With a trembling hand, she started to reach toward his broad back.

She halted at the grinding of boots against stone. Both she and Durge looked up to see a dark figure above them.

"Falken!" Durge sprang to his feet.

The knight grabbed the bard as he staggered, then helped him sit on the ground. Lirith crouched beside Falken and held the flask to his lips. The bard drank a little, choked, then drank some more.

He pushed the flask away. "Thank you, Lirith. I . . . I will be all right."

She studied him, not at all convinced of his words. Even without the mask of dust his face was pale and drawn. Shadows lingered in his eyes.

"What is it, Falken?" Durge said. "Did you find Dakarreth?"

Falken shook his head. "He's not here."

Lirith could only stare.

"I don't understand," Durge said.

The bard gripped his hands together but could not stop their trembling. "He's not in the fortress. Dakarreth. I searched everywhere, but it's empty. By the look of things he left months ago. And he took Krondisar with him."

At last Lirith found her voice. "But if Dakarreth's not here, then where is he?"

Falken turned his head and gazed with haunted blue eyes—back in the direction from which they had come. Lirith went rigid as Durge looked at her. She opened her mouth, but any words she might have said were lost as the wind rose to a keening howl.

75.

"I am greatly pleased all of you could join me at table tonight."

Grace gazed at the tall, broad-shouldered man who stood at the head of the long table in Spardis's great hall. *And if we had not, would you have had all of us put to death, my lord?*

She clutched her wineglass. That wasn't fair. Even if what the Spider had told Travis the other day was true—that this man, Lord Darrek, Regent to Prince Perseth, had ordered the murder of all Persard's personal spies—it was still only one side of the story. And as Grace had learned, in politics there were always two sides. Or three or four.

The regent raised his glass. "We are fortunate to have so many remarkable guests in our keep. In the name of the prince, I welcome you all."

Grace raised her glass and studied the regent over the rim. At least Darrek paid lip service to Prince Perseth. Yet how long would that last? How long would it be before the regent ceased to make commands in the prince's name, finding it more convenient to make them in his own?

Darrek drank, and Grace could not help but watch him. She could see each well-defined muscle move beneath the tanned skin of his throat. Darrek was the most handsome man Grace had ever seen. His body was perfectly proportioned, his fingers long and well formed, and the fine, strong features of his clean-shaven face were utterly symmetrical. His eyes and flowing hair were both as tawny as a lion's. Only the regent's lips seemed at odds with his manliness, for they were soft, full, and sensual. Yet it was that incongruity which made the whole so compelling.

Grace's glance flickered across the table, to Aryn and Beltan. Both stared at the head of the table. So she was not the only one who found it difficult not to look at the regent. She had wondered how it was *this* man who had bested all schemes to come to power in the turmoil following Persard's death. But maybe she had all the evidence she needed. Who—man or woman—could resist the regent's sheer physical power?

But there has to be more to it than that, Grace. Pretty only gets you so far. You've got to be smart, strong, and fast to beat out twenty other plotting nobles. And ruthless.

So perhaps she knew more about Lord Darrek than she had thought. Except whether he was sincere in his desire to rule in Prince Perseth's name, and with Queen Inara's blessing, until the boy reached the age of ascension.

The regent sat and smiled, displaying a set of teeth that seemed more numerous than the typical human complement of thirty-two. "I am looking forward to being entertained by tales of your journeys, and what brings each of you to Spardis."

Grace looked again at Beltan and Aryn, hoping the

panic wasn't completely apparent on her face. Beltan caught her gaze and made a small flick of his hand to either side of him. Grace forced herself to breathe. The knight was right. They were not the only guests who had been invited to sup with the regent. Sitting around them were traveling earls, countesses, and even a wealthy merchant or two—including one who had come from the Free Cities far to the south of Toloria.

All of the regent's guests—aside from Beltan, Aryn, and Grace—talked, laughed, and drank. Perhaps none of them had seen the results of the Burning Plague on the road to Castle Spardis. Or perhaps they were used to seeing peasants drop dead and had simply ridden on past. And there was no sign of plague in Spardis. Nor would there be, now that Darrek had sealed the castle's gates.

Grace froze in her chair as a thought occurred to her. When Falken, Durge, and Lirith returned, how would they get back into the castle?

That's assuming they come back at all, Grace.

She lifted her glass and drained the contents, hoping the wine would restore the color she felt drain from her face. Aryn cast her a concerned glance. She shook her head. It would have to wait until later, until they were alone. Then she could tell the others about her fears.

"I see an empty glass." The regent snapped his fingers at a passing servingman. "More wine for the fair lady with the green eyes." He smiled at Grace, and this time the expression pierced her heart. "You have extraordinary eyes, my lady. I've never seen anything like them. They're not simply green are they, but gold as well?"

Grace clutched the now full glass, trying not to slosh the contents over the rim. She groped for something to say. "Will the queen be attending supper tonight?" Even as she spoke the words, she winced. What was she thinking?

Darrek's visage grew solemn—although not angry. "The queen is taking supper in her room this evening, my lady. As she has each evening of her mourning."

Sympathetic murmurs rose around the table.

Grace licked her lips. She was in this deep and the water hadn't scalded her yet—she might as well jump all the way in.

"And what of Lord Siferd?"

Darrek's smile returned. "Look—the roast swan has arrived."

Grace sighed, glad to have the attention turned away from her. But she noticed that Darrek had not answered her question. What *had* happened to Lord Siferd? She had not seen the chamberlain since just after the regent's return.

Grace gagged as a burnt smell reached her nostrils. Her stomach turned as she watched servants place several platters on the table, each bearing an entire swan cooked in its feathers. She tried not to think of the burnt husks she had seen in each of the villages destroyed by *krondrim*.

"Some swan, my lady?" a servant spoke beside her.

She clenched her teeth and tried not to vomit as the servingman placed several pieces of dripping, half-cooked meat on the trencher in front of her. More trays of food were brought in: steamed puddings, spiced breads, roasts representing an array of species both mammalian and avian, and confections of fruit and cream. Grace was able to chew on a small amount of bread and was grateful no one made notice of her lack of appetite.

After the meal was well under way, a pair of servants carried another tray toward the table, draped in a white cloth. By the way they bent under the burden it was heavy.

Darrek's eyes shone. "I have been waiting for this."

While the men still supported the tray, Darrek rose and plucked away the concealing cloth. On the tray was not another dish, but instead the head of a man.

For a terrible moment Grace thought it to be the head of someone who had displeased the regent, and by the gasps around her she was not the only one with this thought. Then she blinked and saw the head was carved of marble. It was an exquisite likeness. She glanced at Darrek, then at the bust. Save for the paleness of the marble, the two were identical.

The regent spread his arms. "What think you, everyone?"

Nods and murmurs of approval went all around the table.

"It's beautiful," Grace said, although she hadn't meant to speak the words, for they weren't meant entirely as a compliment. Now that she looked at the bust it seemed familiar. But where had she seen it before?

Darrek bowed in her direction. "Thank you, my lady."

The regent's cheeks were flushed, which Grace found odd. Then she saw his gaze linger on the bust, and she understood.

It's vanity, Grace. That's the problem with pretty people—they have to keep being told they're beautiful or else they'll start to doubt it, along with everything they are.

"Your Highness, were there not some other members of your party?" Darrek said as he sat down, directing this question not to Grace but to Aryn.

"One is weary from the long journey here, Lord Regent," Aryn said. "She rests in our rooms, and another stays with her." True nobility paid off—Grace doubted she could ever sound that assured and gracious.

Earlier that day, when they received the unexpected dinner invitation, Beltan had insisted that he stay with Melia while the others attend. However, Travis had told the knight to go, that he would stay with Melia and Tira.

"As far as I can tell, there's only one still-conscious adult in this group who isn't a noble." Travis had raised a hand. "By the way, that would be me."

Travis had won out, and Beltan had gone to dinner.

Darrek spoke again to Aryn. "I have not had a chance to meet the knight who sits beside you, my lady. Is he your husband?"

"No, my lord. This is my cousin, Lord Beltan of Calavan."

"I see." Darrek's gaze moved to Beltan. "Am I mistaken in thinking you a warrior, sir? And a follower of Vathris?"

Grace could see the muscles of Beltan's jaw tense. "I am both, my lord."

Darrek coiled his fingers loosely around his wineglass. "You know, I could use a bold warrior such as yourself, Lord Beltan." His gaze flickered up and down Beltan, and color sprang to the knight's cheeks.

Grace almost laughed and clutched the edge of the table instead. *At least now you know, if nothing else, Darrek has good taste in men.*

"Now, tell me, what has brought you all to Perridon?"

Grace was stunned to see that Darrek's gaze had returned to her. She fumbled for words. Something told her she really didn't want to say she had come here to spy.

"King Boreas has heard word of the troubles in Perridon, my lord," she said, surprised and a little pleased at how quickly the words came to her lips. "He sent me to ask you if there was any aid he might send to Spardis."

The regent nodded. "That is most kindly of your

king, my lady. But I have recently returned from a tour of the Dominion, and matters are well under control. You may give your liege my thanks, but no aid is necessary." He ran his fingers lightly over the golden fabric of his tunic. "Now tell me, is this not the finest cloth of gold you have ever seen, my lady?"

Grace stared. She opened her mouth, knowing she had to say something, anything.

A flash of crimson caught her eye, and she turned to see a small form dash toward her. She opened her arms barely in time to catch the girl's thin body.

"Tira! What are you doing here?"

The girl looked up at her with tranquil eyes.

"What is this . . . this *thing*?" The regent had stood, and his face was ashen as he pointed a finger at Tira. The other guests stared at the girl, mouths open. "Get it out of here at once!"

Servants rushed forward. Grace stood, clutching Tira away from them. Of course—children weren't allowed at the table with the lord. And Tira's face was frightening to most people in this world.

"Forgive us, my lord," Grace said. "I do not know how she came here. We will take our leave at once, if you will."

She glanced at Aryn and Beltan. The two were already on their feet.

The regent sat, his visage composed again. "No, you must forgive me, my lady. I was merely startled, that is all. I saw a number of such children on my recent journey. Please, go if you wish."

"Thank you, my lord."

Holding Tira, Grace hurried from the great hall, Beltan and Aryn on her heels.

"What was that all about?" Beltan said when the doors closed behind them.

Aryn clutched her left arm around herself. "I don't know, but I'm glad to be gone from there. Darrek has the queerest face. It's so lovely to gaze upon, but the more you look at it, the more you realize it's utterly empty."

Only as Aryn said this did Grace realize the baroness was right. She tightened her hold on Tira. "Let's get back to the rooms."

They had nearly reached their chambers when they turned a corner and ran into Travis.

He staggered back, grabbing his spectacles to keep them from flying off his face. "Tira! There you are!"

Grace set the girl on the floor. "Travis, how did she get away from you?"

"I don't know. One minute she was right there, and the next she—" His eyes went wide. "But you have to come. Quickly."

Beltan stepped forward. "What is it?"

"It's Melia." Travis drew in a breath. "She's awake."

Moments later they burst through the door of their chamber.

"How?" Grace said between gasps for breath.

"I don't know," Travis said. "Not really, anyway. I found some old *alasai* leaves in one of the saddlebags, and I thought she might like the smell of them—you know, that it might remind her of her home. So I crushed some into a bowl of hot water and set it by her."

Grace nodded—it was logical. Smell was the most evocative of the senses. Sometimes a smell strongly associated with old and fond memories could induce consciousness in one who had been unresponsive.

"Melia!" Beltan called, pushing through the door into the side chamber.

"I can hear you quite well, Beltan," a crisp voice said. "You needn't bellow like a mad bull."

All of them skidded to a halt in front of Melia's bed. The small woman sat up against the pillows, her skin pallid but her eyes clear and bright.

The knight knelt beside the bed and took her hand. "Melia, are you all right?"

Her gaze softened. "Yes, Beltan. I am now. I had finished my healing, but it was so difficult to wake up. The scent of the green scepter helped enormously." She glanced at Travis. "Thank you for that, dear."

He only nodded.

Tira escaped Grace's grasp and climbed onto the bed beside Melia. She leaned her head against the lady's shoulder.

"Tira," Grace said, "you should leave Melia alone."

"No, she's fine," Melia said, stroking the girl's fiery hair. "But there are matters we must discuss. Important matters. Tell me, how long have I been ill?"

"It has been over a week," Aryn said.

Melia stiffened. "Over a week?" A sigh escaped her. "But you are still here—that means there is yet hope."

Beltan frowned. "What are you talking about, Melia? What made you ill?"

"Do you remember seeing a bust of a man in the room near the great hall?"

Grace slapped a hand to her forehead. "Of course—that's where I saw it before. It's a likeness of the new regent. We just returned from having supper with him."

Melia sat up straight. "You had dinner with him?" Her eyes narrowed to glowing slits. "But he was ever skillful at the art of dissembling."

Beltan glowered at her. "I don't understand. Who are you talking about?"

A black, fluffy form jumped onto the bed. Melia stroked the kitten's soft fur. "It was the bust of the regent that caused my sickness. I was foolish to touch it, but how could I have known what lay embedded within it? A grain of Krondisar. And the magic of the Imsari has ever disagreed with me. If only I could have told you then."

Grace felt like she was drowning. "Told us what?"

"That the regent is Dakarreth." Melia's eyes glinted. "You just had supper with a Necromancer, dear."

76.

"Spider!" Travis peered into the shadows and fog that filled the lane and called out again as loud as he dared. "Spider, where are you?"

Travis shivered inside his mistcloak. He was certain if anyone could help them now, it was the Spider. And they *did* need help. But how was he supposed to find someone who had perfected the art of not being found?

He searched the gloom. This was the place where he had encountered the Spider before, wasn't it? However, the more he looked, the less he was sure. Everything was transmuted in the fog; stone melted away, soft as mist, molding itself into unfamiliar shapes.

Travis sighed. It was time to return to the others—if he could find his way back, that was. They would just have to come up with a plan on their own. According to Melia, they had only hours, perhaps less, before Dakarreth sensed her awakened presence in the castle and was on to them. Holding his mistcloak around him, Travis turned to head back the way he had come—

—and smacked face first into a wall hidden by the fog.

"Now that," a sibilant voice spoke behind him, "had to hurt."

Travis snatched his hand from his head and spun around. A slender man wearing a gray cloak stepped from the fog, and Travis forgot his throbbing skull.

"Spider!"

Silver eyes gleamed in the faint moonlight that seeped through the mist above. "What is this, Travis Wilder? Why are you not in your room where you should be? You place yourself at great risk in trying to find me. 'Spider' is hardly a popular word to call out in Spardis these days."

Travis stepped toward the other. "I'm glad I found you."

A soft, mirthful laugh. "You did not find me, Travis Wilder. I found you. And by the look of it, it's a good thing I did. Or do you enjoy trying to walk through solid stone?"

There was no time for this—it didn't matter who had found whom. "You've got to come with me."

"And why is that, Travis Wilder?"

Now it was Travis's turn to laugh. "We need your help saving the world."

The Spider raised a single, golden eyebrow.

Minutes later—far fewer than Travis would have thought possible—they stepped into Melia's chamber. The others looked up, surprise on their faces. Beltan's hand slipped to the hilt of his sword.

The Spider grinned at Travis. "Your friends don't exactly seem happy to see me."

Despite his thumping heart, Travis returned the grin. "They just haven't gotten to know you yet like I have."

Melia sat on the edge of the bed, dressed in her usual blue kirtle now, and gave her blue-black hair a final twist, binding it neatly into a single coil. "Is this your little friend who you thought might help us, dear?"

Travis nodded. "Everyone, this is . . ." But he couldn't just call the man *Spider.*

The slender man bowed before Melia. "My name is Aldeth, Great Lady. I am at your service."

Melia's eyes glowed as she let the Spider kiss her hand. "You're awfully polite for a spy and assassin."

"Excellence in all things, my lady. That's my philosophy."

"You're right, Travis," Melia said. "He does grow on you rather quickly."

"So now what do we do?" Grace said. She sat on a chair, Tira on her lap, and the black kitten on the girl's.

Aldeth stroked his pointed blond beard. "May I suggest you begin by listening to the message I have for you?"

A shadow touched Melia's brow. "A message? From whom?"

"Falken Blackhand."

The Spider had their undivided attention.

"I met Falken earlier this evening just outside the walls of the castle. He and his two companions were unable to enter Spardis because of the regent's order."

"Wait a minute," Beltan said, glowering at the spy. "If the castle gates are sealed, how did you get out to talk to Falken?"

"And then back in to speak to us?" Aryn added.

"There are other ways in and out of Spardis besides the gates."

"The message, Aldeth," Melia said. "Please."

Aldeth turned toward her. "Falken and the others have just returned from a long journey. Into the Barrens, I believe, although why they would venture there I have no idea." He cocked his head. "But I suppose you do. At any rate, Falken's message was this: *The Keep of Fire is empty. The Stone has moved west. Spardis is not safe.*"

Melia pressed her hands against the fabric of her dress. "Falken's message comes a bit late. I'm afraid we already know these things. It is here, in Spardis."

Aldeth frowned. "What is here?"

Travis opened his mouth, but before he could answer, a portion of the room's wall swung out with a *whoosh* of dusty air, revealing a dim opening beyond. Two figures draped all in black stepped from shadow into light.

Shock paralyzed Travis, but Beltan moved with a speed that seemed impossible. The knight drew his sword and leaped in front of the opening, his blade before him.

"If you want to come closer," Beltan said between clenched teeth, "you'll have to pull yourself along this sword to do it."

The figure hesitated, then lifted small hands to push back a veil of black lace.

Beltan's sword dropped. Travis stared, shock renewed, at the young woman—no, the girl, really—who stood before them.

Aldeth rushed forward, then dropped to one knee and bowed his head before the young woman in black. "My queen! You have placed yourself in grave peril by coming here!"

She directed large brown eyes toward Beltan. "So it would seem."

Beltan's fair cheeks brightened. "Please forgive me, Your Majesty."

"Nay, good knight. You should be commended for your swiftness of action. Although I find them remarkably convenient, that is the disadvantage of secret doors—it's quite impossible to step through one without startling those on the other side."

The queen spoke in the high, clear voice of a child, but there was a keen edge to her words that hinted at an adult intellect. Then again, Travis had a feeling

Inara had had to grow up fast in this castle in order to keep her head.

He remembered himself as the others bowed before the queen and followed suit. Inara nodded, indicating that they could rise. The second figure stepped out of the doorway: a serving maiden barely older than the queen, her round face frightened.

"My queen," Aldeth said, "what are you doing here?"

"I might ask the same of you."

The Spider took a step back. "I can explain."

The queen smiled—a pretty expression that was not altogether comforting. "And you shall, my Aldeth."

Melia glided closer to the young queen. "We heard it spoken you were in seclusion, Your Majesty."

"Many things are spoken about me, Lady Melia. Few of them are to be believed. I yet mourn my husband, that is so. But I am secluded only as a prisoner is secluded in a dungeon."

Grace gestured to the secret door. "Not quite, Your Majesty."

Inara smiled again. "A queen—even one who is not allowed to rule in her son's name—is not without resources. But I am not the only one in peril here. That is why I have come."

"What is it, Your Majesty?" Melia said.

"A messenger arrived for Regent Darrek shortly after supper. I was not able to see who it was, for he was clad all in a robe—and a filthy one at that. Nor did I hear what they spoke of. But afterward the regent was angry, and he gave orders to his guards—orders to search the castle, to find a woman with golden eyes and black hair, and to bring her to him."

Beltan gripped his sword. "How long, Your Majesty?"

Inara shook her head. "I cannot say. The castle is large, and they did not begin with this wing. But there are many guards, and they are moving swiftly. You have a quarter hour. A half hour at most."

Melia's eyes glinted. "And why are you warning me, Your Majesty? What if the regent seeks me because I am perilous?"

"I imagine you are perilous indeed, Lady Melia. I have heard some stories of you. But I know that Regent Darrek is more dangerous yet, to me and to my son." A shudder coursed through Inara, and suddenly she seemed more girl than queen. "I don't know why, not entirely, but he's horrible. That man has no soul."

Travis almost laughed. "You know more than you think, Your Majesty."

Both Inara and Aldeth looked up with questioning eyes.

"Now it is time for us to tell you something," Melia said.

By the time the lady finished speaking a few minutes later, both Aldeth and Queen Inara sat on the bed, and the serving maid crouched in a corner, hands clutched to her ears. Aldeth's silvery eyes were wide, but Inara stood, her tiny hands clenched into fists.

"I knew there was something queer about Darrek—or Dakarreth, as you call him. He has a power over others, a way of making them do as he wishes with a look. A lord with no heritage who came to Spardis should have ended up in the moat with a knife in his back after a day or two. Instead, in a matter of weeks, he gained the regency." She looked at Melia. "Thank you, Great Lady. At least I know I am not mad now. Or a complete fool."

Despite her young age, Travis knew this was the woman who should rule Perridon until Perseth was old enough to be king. And maybe for longer. He glanced at Grace. She nodded—she had reached the same conclusion.

"So now what?" Beltan said. "We've only got a few more minutes until they get here."

Melia folded her arms. "We have to find where he's hidden the Stone of Fire."

"Is this Stone something precious?" Inara said.

Travis squeezed his right hand shut. "You might say that, Your Majesty."

Inara moved to the window and opened the shutters. "There, the mist is clearing now—do you see it? The slender tower with two horns at its summit. All but Dakarreth are forbidden to enter that tower, and he goes there often late at night."

"That's got to be it," Grace said.

In moments they had sketched out a plan, although to call it desperate was far too generous. Aryn would accompany the queen back to her chamber—the serving maid was quite beyond use at the moment—in case Dakarreth came looking for Inara. In such an event, Aryn and Inara were to delay him in any way possible without putting themselves at risk.

Beltan's task was to follow a map drawn by Aldeth to a hidden portal in the castle's south wall, at the level of the lake. He was to unlock the door and wait for Falken, Lirith, and Durge to arrive there by boat—for Aldeth had made a plan earlier to meet the bard and his companions there at moonset. Aldeth had another task now. He was to show Melia the way to Dakarreth's tower. And Travis was coming with them.

"Only you can touch the Stone, dear," Melia said. "You saw what a small grain flecked from its surface did to me."

Beltan started toward the door, then hesitated. "And what of Grace?"

"I'm going with Melia and Travis."

Melia arched an eyebrow. "And Tira, dear?"

Grace gripped the girl's shoulders.

"She can't stay here alone," Travis said.

Melia nodded, and Grace sighed.

Beltan moved to the secret passage. "Let's go then."

With his left hand Travis gripped the runestaff Oragien had given him. He had no idea how to use it—or if it did anything at all—but if nothing else it would keep him from falling down. He glanced at Beltan, to wish him luck, but the knight turned his back and disappeared into the gloom of the passageway. Aryn and the queen followed, propelling the weeping serving maid between them.

Aldeth glanced at Melia. "Ready, my lady?"

"Lead the way," she said.

Travis wasn't certain, but he thought he heard the echo of booted feet in the corridor outside Melia's chamber. Then Aldeth pulled the secret door shut behind them, and they were in darkness.

Light flared. Aldeth held a candle in a tin lantern. "This way," he said.

Melia followed the Spider, Grace and Tira behind her, while Travis brought up the rear. Sooner than Travis had expected they came to a halt. The passage ended in a door of thick wood planks bound with rusted iron bands.

Aldeth shut the lantern, dimming the light. "This door leads into the regent's tower." He tried the handle, but the door did not budge. "It's locked. It will take me a few minutes to open it." He pulled a thin wire from a pocket.

Travis stepped forward. "No, let me try."

Before Aldeth could protest, Travis laid a hand on the door and whispered a word. *"Urath."*

There was a faint *snick*, and the door swung open. Beyond was darkness.

Aldeth shot him an impressed look. "There is more to you than meets the eye, Travis Wilder."

Melia patted Travis's scruffy cheek. "So we've learned."

"Come on," Grace said, moving through the door with Tira in tow. The others followed up a spiral staircase.

"Is he here, Melia?" Travis whispered after a few steps.

"I don't sense him within. But there's something . . . wrong here all the same."

That goes without saying, Travis nearly muttered, but he bit his tongue as they ascended through shadow and silence.

"We are near the top now, I think," Aldeth whispered, as they stopped before another door.

Travis ground his teeth together. As they climbed, a wave of dread had risen inside him with every step, and now it threatened to crest. *We should have been stopped by now. If this is where he's keeping the Stone, where are his defenses?*

"There's no use waiting," Melia said.

Travis reached for the door, but when Aldeth pushed against the wood it opened. Together they stepped into the circular space beyond.

Aldeth was right. This was the highest chamber in the tower. Through narrow windows he glimpsed the castle all around. Torches burned in iron sconces, obviating the need for Aldeth's lantern. Travis took a staggering step forward. The wave of dread broke, filling him with watery fear.

"There's nothing here," he said.

The others gathered to either side of him, staring as he did at the empty room. They had come here for nothing.

"No," Grace said. "Look."

Travis followed her gaze. On the farside of the chamber, something hung on the wall. It looked like a bundle of rags. He approached with the others. Then, when they reached the center of the room, they stopped. Bile rose in Travis's throat, and he gripped the runestaff. It wasn't a bundle of rags. Rather it was a man nailed to the stone wall with iron spikes, his face twisted into a wide-eyed mask of horror and death.

Grace clutched Tira, trying to turn the girl away from the grisly sight.

Aldeth swore. "Lord Siferd!"

Only as the Spider said this did Travis realize it was indeed the chamberlain crucified to the wall.

Melia's eyes shone with sorrow. "It seems this is what happens to those who displease Dakarreth."

"As you will all soon discover for yourselves, Great Lady," a voice as harsh as smoke said behind them.

They turned to see a man in a dirty robe the color of ashes step through the door. The scent of rot rose on the air. Aldeth drew the dagger from his boot, but Melia held him back with a hand. She stepped forward.

"Who are you? I demand you reveal yourself."

A cackling laugh. "As you wish, Great Lady."

The man lifted hands that were oozing and twisted, then pushed back the hood of his robe. Two words escaped Travis like a gasp of pain.

"Master Eriaun!"

The runespeaker grinned, teeth white in the blackened ruin of his face. "It's so good to see you again, Master Wilder."

77.

Beltan moved deeper into steam-filled catacombs, his bare feet silent on slick tiles.

By Vathris, you had better be sure of what you're doing, Beltan of Calavan. You had better be sure.

But it was far too late to question his decision. Beltan moved past pools of hot water fed by ceramic pipes. Water dripped from arches that spanned over-head. The baths of Spardis had been fashioned centuries ago in emulation of the old Tarrasian style. A series of rectangular pools allowed the bather to grow used to immersion in increasingly hot water. Blue mosaic dolphins swam beneath the water, and green tile waves flowed on the walls.

It had been easy to discover where to find the regent—too easy for Beltan's liking. After asking only a few questions, a servingman had taken him to the entrance of the baths. He had feared guards would prevent his entering. However, on stepping into the moist-aired antechamber, he had found only a pair of naked boys, perfumed oil in their dark hair, gold rings adorning their wrists, ankles, throats.

Without words, the boys had taken Beltan's sword, then had undressed him with deft movements. In return they had given him a short linen kilt to wrap around his waist. The boys had watched in silence as he took a dagger from his folded tunic and slipped it beneath the kilt. They had gazed with placid brown eyes as he stepped through an archway into the baths beyond.

Now, as he walked, he could feel the blade, hot against his skin. He touched it beneath the fabric of the kilt, making sure it was still hidden and secure. Sweat beaded on his skin, and he pushed wet hair back from his brow.

"Where are you, Dakarreth?" His whisper merged with the hiss of vapor. "Where are you?"

His eyes slid across a mosaic of brown-skinned men in a boat spearing black seals in azure water. Had the moon set yet? Had Falken, Durge, and Lirith reached the hidden door in their own boat? Perhaps, but there was no way to be sure of the time.

Earlier, he had found the door that the Spider Aldeth had described. He had opened it to find the misty waters of the lake lapping beyond. For a time he had peered into the gloom, waiting for the bard and the others to arrive. But waiting was not something Beltan was good at. He took a piece of charcoal from a burnt torch and, on the back of the map Aldeth had drawn, he had written the best letters he could manage:

Melia, Travis, Grace in tower of two horns. Seek Stone of Fire. Join them there.

Beltan

He had left the note wedged in the door, then had gone to find the regent. Melia and Travis needed time to find the Stone of Fire, and he was going to make sure they had it. Maybe it would be the last act of service he would ever do for them—he knew he was no match for a former god—but what better way for a Knight Protector to die than in the course of duty?

Besides, it wasn't as if Melia needed him. Beltan had always known it—that as a former goddess herself she was as far above him as the moon in the sky. But for his sake, out of kindness, or perhaps out of pity, she had accepted his pledge. And even though he knew better, he had let himself believe that he truly had the power to protect her.

Of course, Melia was not his only ward. *And Travis needs you even less than she does, Beltan. You're worse than an idiot because you asked for something you already knew you couldn't have. You might have been content with his friendship, but you had to go and muck even that up.*

He could still see the horror in Travis's eyes that moment beside the chasm, after they had defeated Eriaun and the *krondrim*, when Beltan had reached for Travis and had told him the truth in his heart.

Get away from me!

And what had he been thinking? Obviously Travis hadn't heard the call of the bull, not like Beltan—and like so many who found their way to Vathris's inner-most circles—who had known at a young age that his was a destiny not shared by most men.

A sound echoed off the tiles all around: the splashing of water. Beltan came to a halt, his hand pressing against the knife beneath the kilt. He peered ahead, but the steam rolled thickly on the air.

"Is someone there?" he called, his voice echoing.

Silence, then the sound of water again, followed by a voice as burnished as gold. "Come nearer."

Despite the warmth and sweat, Beltan shivered. Then he stepped between two columns. The vapor swirled, parting before him. He stood on the edge of a grotto, at the edge of what was certainly the last and hottest of the pools. Crisp curls rose from the surface of the water like steam from a cup of freshly brewed *maddok*.

A man stood in the pool, immersed to the neck, his face turned away. Beltan could see only his tawny hair; the bubbling water obscured all else. The knight opened his mouth, but the other spoke first.

"I knew you would come to me, Sir Beltan. I knew it when I saw your eyes upon me at table this evening, try as you did to conceal your glances from me. But you cannot hide from fate. You see, we are meant to be together, you and I."

Beltan fought for something to say, but speech escaped him. If he had expected any words from the other, certainly it had not been these. A heat rose in him with the steam. He stepped to the edge of the pool and gazed down. Beltan did not need to test the water to know it would scald the flesh from his bones if he were to set foot in it.

The man in the pool turned and ascended tiled steps, rising from the water. Beltan stared, unable to move.

While he had been beautiful at supper in the great hall, Dakarreth's appearance then had been but the barest shadow of what it was now. His golden skin glowed from the heat of the pool, and his eyes were molten. Water beaded on his oiled body, and his naked flesh was smooth and hairless, revealing each line and muscle beneath. In every way his proportions were those of an ancient hero hewn from marble: shoulders broad, waist slender, phallus thick and jutting.

Beltan's knees became jelly, and he fought the desire to fall to the tiles and prostrate himself there. Dakarreth looked like a god.

By Vathris, he is a god, Beltan. Or he was, at any rate. And he seeks to become one again.

And why shouldn't he? Seeing Dakarreth now in his naked splendor, it seemed ridiculous that others should not worship him, and Beltan among them.

No, that's not why you came here. Beltan clenched his jaw and locked his knees. No matter what, he would stand.

Dakarreth ascended the last step from the water. A towel rested on a bench, but he did not pick it up. Instead, moisture evaporated from his skin in visible coils of steam.

"Your companions seek to destroy me, Sir Beltan." Even speaking terrible words, his voice was rich and compelling. "But they cannot be allowed to succeed. You know that, of course. And nor will they, for I have sent a slave to deal with them."

So, you can't do your own dirty work? Beltan tried to say, but once again his lips would not form words.

"I spoke truth earlier," Dakarreth said, his molten eyes gleaming. "I do need a warrior to stand beside me, to smite down all who would oppose me that I might shine all the brighter. And I would have you for that warrior. Your face and body are crude, of course, if not unmanly in their way. But that is of little concern. I can mold flesh like clay, into any shape I please. But there is a fire in you that is not so easily found or created. That is what I require." He reached out his hand. "Come with me, Sir Beltan. I can create a new body to house the fire of your spirit, one that is both beautiful and immortal."

Bile rose in Beltan's throat. *You can burn me, you mean.*

He wanted to flee this place, but as he had vowed he forced himself to stand. Any time he might buy for the others was worth it, whatever the cost. At last he managed to speak. "Show me."

Dakarreth's smile deepened, an expression of deep and endless mystery. He drew close. Maybe the Necromancer's body was not truly alive, but all the same a clean, sharp smell rose from him along with waves of heat.

Dakarreth ran his fingers lightly over Beltan's chest and stomach, then he leaned close, encircling the knight with powerful arms. Through the kilt, Beltan felt Dakarreth's hardness press against him, and he felt himself stir in answer. Dakarreth's lips touched his own, hot and stinging with salt, and a moan rose from deep within Beltan. He did not want this.

No, that wasn't true. He *did* want it. It had been so long—so many cold, lonely, and bloody years—since he had given himself to another. Perhaps this was what he truly needed. Not death, but release. With fierce strength he returned Dakarreth's embrace.

Dakarreth pulled back. "Yes, Sir Beltan! It has been too long since I have known the pleasure of mortal flesh given to me willingly."

Beltan was a strong man, but he could not resist as Dakarreth pushed him downward, bent him back, and laid him upon the marble bench: a sacrificial calf on a temple altar. The stone was hot and slick against Beltan's back.

Dakarreth leaned over him, pressing his fingers

into the flesh of Beltan's chest, digging in toward his heart. There was pain. Much pain.

"Now, Sir Beltan," Dakarreth said, his perfect face a mask of rapture, "be transformed!"

Beltan grasped the pain, held it, and let it clear his mind of the heat and torpor. Dakarreth was a god, yes, and beautiful. But he was evil, and Beltan would never serve him. In a single movement, Beltan reached into his kilt, pulled out the dagger, and drove the blade deep into Dakarreth's shoulder.

Dakarreth's eyes flew wide. With a cry he stumbled back. Beltan sat up, grinning. So gods could be harmed after all.

But he's not a god, Beltan. Not yet. That's why there's still a chance.

His grin crumbled as Dakarreth's molten eyes turned on him, shriveling his soul to nothing.

"You have betrayed me!" With his right hand, Dakarreth reached up and pulled the knife from his shoulder. Blood gushed forth. He cast the dagger aside, then brushed his fingers across the wound. The river of blood slowed, then reversed, flowing back into the wound. When Dakarreth lowered his hand, all traces of both blood and wound were gone. His flesh was golden and perfect again.

Beltan gripped the marble bench, knowing the end had come. At least, if nothing else, he had gone out fighting.

Dakarreth's voice was a venomous hiss. "I should have known you would turn against me. But then, you are skilled at treachery, are you not, Beltan son of Beldreas?"

A new dread filled Beltan. "What do you mean?"

Dakarreth drew near. His face was still beautiful, but it was terrible to gaze upon now: the face of a wrathful god. "You yet quest for your father's murderer, is that not so, Sir Beltan? Yes, you seek the one who slew your father, old, strong King Beldreas—the one who stuck a knife in his back like a coward and ran. Is that not so?" Dakarreth knelt before the bench. "Consider your quest ended."

"You!" Beltan said, gasping in the wet air like a drowning man. "It was you who killed my father!"

The Necromancer laughed. His fingers moved across Beltan's chest in a mockery of a caress.

"No, my good knight. It was not I who slew Beldreas. It was you."

This was madness. Beltan didn't want to listen. He turned his head, but he could not close his ears. Dakarreth's fingers found the ragged scar on Beltan's left side—the barely healed wound he had received from the *feydrim* at the Rune Gate—and danced along it.

"When the Pale King awoke," the Necromancer said softly, "he bid me to sow strife in the Dominions, a task I willingly accepted. And it was so simple. A few whispers in your dreams over a few nights, that is all it took. But then, the mortal mind is so easily shaped."

Beltan tried to move, but his body was stone. "No," he said in a ragged whisper.

"But you know it is true, Sir Beltan. Have you not seen it in your dreams? Who else could get so close to Beldreas without arousing the old king's guard but his own bastard son?"

Dakarreth's fingers pressed against the scar, and pain coursed through Beltan's body along with terrible and perfect understanding. A vision flashed before his eyes, one he had seen in countless dreams: a hand slipping away from the hilt of a bloody knife. His own hand.

"No!"

Dakarreth's laughter filled his skull. "Yes, Sir Beltan. See the fruit of your treachery. Watch yourself as you murder your own father."

Beltan screamed. Like knives of steel, the Necromancer's fingers dug into his scar, ripping the wound open again as blood and memories spilled forth.

78.

Grace stared, unable to move, as Master Eriaun lurched into the high tower chamber. The runespeaker's hands were black and curled inward like claws, and cooked bits of flesh peeled from the blistered, oozing mask of his face.

What had happened to Eriaun? Was it the Burning Plague? No, his eyes were not black and empty, but instead brown and blazing with mad light. It had been fire—the fire of the rune Travis had turned on him. But his body should have been dead. It *smelled* dead. How then was he alive?

"My master was right," Eriaun said in a pleasant tone that was all the more unnerving. "He suspected you would be up to some bit of foolishness, Lady Melia. And here you are, right on cue."

The lady's amber eyes flashed. "It is Dakarreth who is the fool. Even as a god, he was a petty and sniveling brat. I see little has changed in two thousand years."

A shock jolted Grace. Maybe she had the answer to the question of Eriaun's condition after all. Was not his master a Necromancer—a death wizard? She clutched Tira's shoulders. How could they kill someone who wasn't even alive?

Eriaun flicked a finger, and the door swung shut behind him. There was a grinding sound as the lock turned. "There," the runespeaker said, his ragged lips slurring the words, "now we will not be disturbed."

Travis stepped forward, past Melia and Aldeth, gripping the runestaff. His face was hard in a way

Grace had never seen before, his gray eyes solemn behind his spectacles. He looked strong. No, that wasn't it.

He looks noble, Grace.

"I stopped you once, Eriaun. *We* stopped you. And we can do it again."

"Can you, runelord? Can you really?" Eriaun lumbered closer. "Burning has made me so much stronger. It is the nature of fire, you see, to sublimate that which is soft and frail, and to temper and purify what remains. I do not think you will find me so easily dismissed this time."

Motion caught Grace's eye, then she quickly forced her gaze away, so as not to betray him. While Eriaun spoke, his eyes fixed on Travis, Aldeth had backed away and circled around. Even then the Spider approached Eriaun from behind, his boots silent against the floor. From a fold of his gray cloak, he drew a slim stiletto. In a motion too fast to be anything but a blur, he brought the dagger down and drove it into the base of Eriaun's neck. Grace could hear the wet sound as metal parted flesh and sank deep into the runespeaker's body.

Eriaun's eyes flew wide, and he stiffened. Was that it, then? Did even this thing need a spine connected to a brain in order to function?

No. A shriek emanated from Eriaun's open mouth, shrill and inhuman as a siren. It seemed impossible his shriveled hands could move so quickly, but in one motion he grabbed the stiletto, pulled it from his neck in a gush of black blood, then turned and drove it into the center of Aldeth's chest. Aldeth's mouth opened in an expression of astonishment. His eyes fluttered, and he stumbled backward against a wall.

"Oh," he said softly.

The Spider slid down to the floor, then his eyes shut as he slumped forward and was still.

Grace pushed Tira behind her and started to move

toward Aldeth—she had to help the Spider, to see if he yet lived—then stopped at a look from Eriaun.

"No more tricks, my pets," he hissed. "If you submit to me now, perhaps I will show you mercy."

Melia raised her arms. "We shall never submit to the likes of you, corpse." A blue corona ignited around her, dancing along the outlines of her slender body.

"Oh, I think you shall, Great Lady."

From a pocket of his filthy robe, Eriaun drew out an object. Crimson light welled between his clenched fingers. Melia gasped, and the blue corona surrounding her flickered. She took a step back as both Grace and Travis gaped at her.

Eriaun's ragged lips pulled back in a grin. "What's the matter, Great Lady? Is something amiss?"

The corona dimmed and vanished. Melia lifted a hand to her throat. "What . . . what is that thing?"

"You mean this?"

Eriaun unfolded his fingers, revealing an orb of clear crystal on his palm. At the center of the orb shone a hot spark of light, so bright Grace had to avert her eyes or be blinded. Melia cried out softly and stumbled back.

"Does it bother you, Great Lady?" Eriaun laughed. "But then, the Great Stones ever disagreed with you and your kind, did they not? So weak all of you were."

Grace spoke despite her fear. "Is that . . . Krondisar?"

Again Eriaun laughed, a wet sound. "No, my pet. It is merely a single grain of the Great Stone, removed by my master, and bound within this sphere. A gift, it was—a bit of light to comfort me in dark times."

He lifted the orb high. Melia staggered and sank to her knees, her hands clutched to her head.

Grace's body went rigid. *Do something, Grace. Touch the Weirding and do something.*

But how could she? The shadow that lurked between her and the web of the Weirding was more horrible to her than even Eriaun. She clutched Tira and did not move. Eriaun lurched toward Melia, gripping the orb before him. The lady moaned.

Travis interposed himself between Eriaun and Melia. "Leave her alone."

"Get out of my way!" the runespeaker snarled.

He thrust the orb toward Travis, but Travis didn't flinch.

"Move, runelord, or I will burn you with runes!" Eriaun stretched out his other charred hand.

Travis bowed his head over his staff, and panic shredded Grace's heart. Was he just going to let Eriaun kill him? Then a queer smile touched his lips, and he nodded, as one who was listening.

"No, Master Eriaun," he said, lifting his head. "It's time you finished what you began."

Before the runespeaker could react, Travis lifted the runestaff and touched the tip to the orb in Eriaun's outstretched hand. The staff flared blue, then Travis turned and cast it aside even as it burst apart in a spray of splinters. Grace turned her head from the blast, then looked back.

Eriaun stood unharmed, and he laughed. "Poor runelord. Your staff is no match for the—"

His words faltered as, with a crystalline sound, the orb cracked in half on his hand. Free of its prison, the crimson spark contained within danced on his palm.

"It's so beautiful!" Eriaun whispered.

Then his words became a scream as the spark expanded into a miniature sun. The runespeaker stiffened, his body becoming a pillar of flame. Grace turned away, shielding Tira with her body. Heat roasted her back—

—then was gone.

The echo of Eriaun's shriek faded into silence. Slowly, Grace turned around. Travis helped Melia to her feet. The lady was pale, and she still held a hand to her brow, but the pain was gone from her expression. Of Eriaun and the orb there was no trace save a scorch mark on the stone floor.

Grace shook her head. "What happened to the shard of Krondisar?"

"It is gone," Melia said. "Consumed with Eriaun, I believe."

A motionless figure caught Grace's eyes. She left Tira, dashed across the chamber, and knelt beside Aldeth's fallen form. Two fingers pressed to his neck revealed that he lived—his pulse was faint but steady. The stiletto had fallen from his chest, and she probed the wound with precise motions. It was not deep. His sternum had deflected the worst of the blow, and while he had lost some blood, the flow had nearly stopped.

She jerked her head up at a pounding from the other side of the door.

"Stand back," Travis said. "I'll bind it shut."

Grace closed her eyes, then opened them again. For a fleeting moment she had glimpsed them before she had had to let go of the Touch—three shining forms in the web of the Weirding.

"No," she said, standing. "Open it."

She met Travis's eyes. He nodded, then moved to the door.

"*Urath,*" he spoke, and the door swung inward. Grace breathed a sigh as three familiar figures stepped through.

Melia rushed forward. "Falken!"

The bard caught the lady in a fierce embrace. Grace gasped as she found Lirith's arms around her, and while she wasn't certain, she thought she even saw a momentary grin cross Durge's face as he gripped Travis's arms. Then they gathered in a circle in the center of the chamber, Tira at the middle.

"Where's Beltan?" Travis said.

Falken shook his head. "I don't know. He left a message for us, telling us where to find you. I thought he'd be here."

Grace clenched her jaw. This was bad news—she was certain of it. But they had other matters to discuss. In quick words they explained what had happened in the days since Falken, Durge, and Lirith had left Spardis.

Anger and sorrow shone in Falken's eyes as he held Melia tight. "I nearly lost you."

She leaned her head against his chest. "Never, dearest one. It was for you that I came back."

Lirith returned from the edge of the chamber. Grace saw that Aldeth now lay peacefully on his cloak.

"He sleeps now," the witch said. "I do not believe he will die."

Grace met Lirith's mysterious brown eyes. *Thank you*. She wasn't certain whether she spoke the words or not, but Lirith nodded all the same.

"Now what do we do?" Durge said in his rumbling voice. "We have not yet found the Stone."

"It's not here," Grace said.

"No. There's one place it still might be."

They turned toward Travis. He had opened a narrow side door she had not seen before. Behind was the beginning of a flight of steps.

Minutes later they stood at the very summit of the tower, on a circular stone platform bounded only by a low wall. The fog had cleared, and now stars shimmered in the dark net of the sky above, bright in the absence of the moon. To the south, a crimson spark pulsed above the horizon: the red star. Light shone in the east. Dawn was approaching.

Melia turned around, then glanced at Travis. "It's not here, either, is it? The Stone."

He sighed, then shook his head. Falken clenched a fist and let out an oath.

Grace gazed at the others. They had come so far—they couldn't simply give up. "We'll think of something. It's got to be in the castle somewhere."

"Are you truly so certain of that, Your Radiance?"

As one they turned to watch a figure step from the head of the stairs onto the platform. He was tall and beautiful, clad in a loose-fitting tunic of gold. Tawny hair tumbled over broad shoulders. He smiled, and fire ignited in his golden eyes.

Melia trembled as she spoke the word. "Dakarreth!"

He nodded to the lady—a mocking gesture. "Dear Melia. It has been some time, hasn't it? An eon? Or is it two?"

Her eyes narrowed. "Either way, it's not been long enough, Dakarreth."

He pressed his hand to his chest in a feigned expression of dismay. "Dear sister, that is hardly a proper greeting for your brother."

"You are not my brother, Dakarreth."

Falken gripped Melia's shoulder, holding her back. Durge started to reach for his greatsword, but Dakarreth glanced at the knight, and the Embarran froze in mid-action.

"No, Sir Knight. Do not even think to harm me. Nor you, Daughter of Sia." Now he turned his gold eyes on Lirith, knotting her fingers even as they wove together in a spell.

Grace stared at her friends. Both knight and witch were as motionless as statues. Were they dead? Rich laughter sounded. She looked up to see Dakarreth regard her.

"No, Your Radiance. They are not dead. None of you need die—not if you kneel before me now and accept me as your one true god."

Melia's small hands were fists. "Never!"

Dakarreth shook his head. "Never is a long time, dearest. Especially for one such as you."

Tira stepped from behind Grace, and Grace was too slow in snatching the girl back. Dakarreth whirled around as if someone had struck him. Now his beautiful face was twisted by hate.

"What is this? You've brought that hideous little . . . thing with you." He pointed at Tira. "Get her away from me!"

Falken's eyes were unreadable. "Why, Dakarreth? She's just a child."

"Just a child?" Again the Necromancer laughed. "Oh, no, my pathetic bard, she is much more than just a child. By Mindroth's hand she was chosen, by his will she came to him, and by the Stone of Fire she was marked. Her presence tainted the temple—*my* temple. But I drove them both away and took Krondisar before Mindroth could finish his foul work with her." He spun toward Grace. "Now get her away from me, or your friends die, just like the big, stupid knight."

Dakarreth clenched a fist, and both Lirith's and Durge's eyes bulged as their bodies stiffened. Grace snaked out her hands, grasped Tira, and pulled the girl back, holding her tight.

Travis took a step forward, his expression unreadable behind his spectacles. "Beltan? Are you talking about Beltan?"

Dakarreth gave a dismissive flick of a hand. "Yes, I believe that was his name. Not that names matter to the dead. Was he your friend? You might be interested to know that, big as he was, he was a good screamer."

Travis staggered. Falken started to reach for him, to pull him back, but the bard halted at a glare from Dakarreth.

"No, keep away from him." The Necromancer drew close to Travis, his golden eyes intent. "It is you, is it not? The one Eriaun spoke of—the one who touches Great Stones, and who spoke to Mindroth ere he finally burned."

Grace could see the sweat bead on Travis's brow.

"Yes, it is you," Dakarreth whispered. "It is you who holds the key to Krondisar. Mindroth fled before I could wrest it from him, but you will tell me now—you dare not resist."

The cords on Travis's neck strained against the skin as he clenched his jaw, but he said nothing.

"Where have you hidden it, Dakarreth?" Melia said, her voice thin but angry. "Where is the Stone of Fire?"

"Why, don't you know? It's been right above you all this time, Melia dearest."

Dakarreth stretched his arms wide and turned his face up. Grace followed his gaze to the pulsing crimson spark in the southern sky. The red star flared, then began to grow, its fiery light expanding to fill a quadrant of the sky. Crimson light danced across the upturned faces of the others as the star grew.

No, Grace, you're wrong. It's not getting larger. It's coming closer.

Like a meteor it plunged toward them, so brilliant she knew it would burn them all. Then, at the last moment, it slowed, and the spikes of fire contracted into a small, shining sphere. The red star drifted down among them, then came to a rest on the outstretched hand of Dakarreth. But it wasn't a star at all. It was a stone. *The* Stone.

Krondisar.

Melia let out a wordless gasp of agony and slumped to her knees. The rest of them stared at the Stone of Fire resting on Dakarreth's upturned palm as its bloody light illuminated his beautiful, terrible visage.

Out of the corner of her eye, Grace saw the light of dawn brighten on the horizon. But it was far too early for the sun, and it wasn't dawn at all. The light came from every direction now, red and flickering. The land burned. Then she saw them: dark, slender shapes moving against the rising flames. Hundreds of them.

Thousands. The light closed around the castle. All the world was on fire.

Dakarreth bent his face toward Travis, baring pointed teeth in a lurid smile. "Now give me the key, runelord, or watch all of your friends die."

79.

The air sizzled around Travis. He was aware of his companions standing motionless behind him, and of the wall of fire that encircled the castle. Somewhere people were screaming. But these things registered only passingly on him. The Stone filled his gaze with its fiery beauty. He could think of nothing else but how good it would be to take the Stone, to hold it in his hand, and to feel its warmth against his flesh. On reflex, he began to reach for it.

Dakarreth jerked Krondisar back, closing his hand around it. Crimson light welled through his fingers like blood. "Do not even think to take the Stone of Fire, runelord. None of you have the power to wrest it from me—not Falken or Melia, and certainly not you. So much of its power is mine now, far more than any of you can imagine. I need only Mindroth's key to unlock its final mysteries. Now give it to me!"

Travis tried to moisten his lips with his tongue, but it was like dragging sandpaper across them. It was so hard to speak. "I don't know . . . the key."

"You lie!" Inhuman fury honed the perfect features of Dakarreth's visage to razored edges. "Mindroth gave the key to you. How could he not? You are his kind after all, runelord. Now, for your lie, you shall watch me destroy one of your precious friends. Shall I begin with the sly witch? Or perhaps the doughty knight?"

The Necromancer glanced at Durge. The Embarran's eyes strained in their sockets as he rose onto his toes.

Travis held out a hand. "No, don't! Please!"

"Will you give me the key?"

Durge's face darkened, and his eyes fluttered.

Travis nodded. "I will give it to you."

The Necromancer smiled. "Good, runelord. Very good. I knew you were not entirely a fool."

He flicked a finger, and both Durge and Lirith went limp, falling to the floor. Falken started to move toward them, but a look from Dakarreth kept the bard in place, next to Melia, who still slumped on her knees. However, both the knight and the witch were moving. They were alive.

But how long would any of them stay living once Dakarreth realized Travis didn't really know the key? He had bought them a few seconds, nothing more.

Dakarreth drew near, his face mere inches from Travis's own. "Now, give it to me, runelord."

Travis opened his mouth to speak.

Travis!

He froze at the sound of the voice speaking in his mind. It was not Jack Graystone.

Travis, can you hear me?

Grace? Is that you?

Yes.

But I thought you couldn't use the Touch.

I can't. Not for long at least. There's . . . there's a . . .

But she didn't need to speak. He could see it there, just past the green-gold light of her presence: a monstrous, hulking shadow. It laughed with a door mouth, baring broken-glass teeth, hungry to rend apart her light. In that moment, Travis gained a shard of understanding.

Oh, Grace. . . .

No, Travis. There's no time. You've got to listen—I think I understand.

Understand what?

Why Dakarreth hasn't been able to become a god yet. It was hard—he's not alive, not really—but I think I just got a glimpse of his mind. It's the same reason Tome gave for why the krondrim *are so flawed. He's not letting the transformation be completed. He's afraid of it.*

Afraid? Afraid of what?

Of burning.

He stared, trying to understand.

Travis. I—

The green-gold light vanished from his mind.

Grace!

But she was already gone. Out of the corner of his eye he saw her form slump to the floor. Only a heartbeat had passed, but already time had stretched too thin. Dakarreth waited for an answer. But what should he say?

Beware—it will consume you.

Once again the rasping voice whispered in his mind. Only this time Travis finally understood. Grace was right—the transformation had to be completed. Mindroth's words weren't a warning; they were instructions. That was the key.

Travis knew what he had to do. He gazed into Dakarreth's impossible golden eyes. Then he reached out and laid his hand atop the Necromancer's. He could feel the heat of the Stone through Dakarreth's unliving flesh.

"What do you think you're doing, runelord?"

Travis tightened his grip around both hand and Stone. He felt the first hot pricks of pain.

"I'm giving you what you want, Dakarreth," he said through clenched teeth. "The key to transformation."

Dakarreth's eyes flared. "Get away from me!"

The Necromancer started to pull his hand back, then Travis whispered the word. *"Krond."*

The Stone heeded the call. Blazing light welled forth, conjuring a sphere of fire that surrounded Travis and Dakarreth. Travis heard screams—his friends—but the sounds were lost in the roar of the flames.

"What have you done?" the Necromancer shrieked.

He started to let go of the Stone, shifting it to Travis's hand.

"Don't do it, Dakarreth!" Travis shouted above the voice of the fire. "Don't let go—not if you want to be a god. That's the key. You've got to let it burn you."

Anger blazed again in Dakarreth's molten eyes. He gripped Krondisar. "I am not afraid, runelord. It is you who will let go in fear!"

The two clutched the Stone, and fire coursed through them. Dakarreth's gold tunic vanished in a puff of flame. Travis felt his own clothes burn away. Dakarreth's long tresses flared and were gone, and Travis's hair curled and became ashes, until his body was as smooth as the Necromancer's.

The pain crested into agony, except now the pain came from within Travis, not from without. He saw Dakarreth writhing before him.

Travis's words were a scream. "Don't resist the fire, Dakarreth! That's why it hurts. You've got to give yourself to it—let it burn everything away!"

Dakarreth threw his head back and roared above the fire. "I *will* be a god!"

The Stone grew brighter yet, its light like burning blood. Travis watched his arm blacken and wither, but he did not let go of the Stone. Before him, Dakarreth shone brighter and more golden than ever.

Now Dakarreth gazed at Travis, grinning. "Yes. . . ."

Travis felt his flesh peeling off bone. Was this it,

then? Was this when the Necromancer became a god and destroyed them all? Laughing, Dakarreth tightened his grip on the Stone—

—and his fingers shriveled under the heat. His muscular arm followed, withering to a stick, then the smooth skin of his chest turned black and cracked.

The Necromancer's exultant expression crumbled. "No!"

Fire charred Dakarreth's legs to stumps, and his beautiful face bubbled and melted. Travis could feel his own body doing the same—burning away—but still he did not let go of the Stone.

"Do it, Dakarreth," Travis said as his lips were seared away from his teeth. "Become a god!"

They locked eyes, gripping the Stone between them. Then fire transmuted the fury in Dakarreth's eyes into horror. A shriek burst with tongues of flame from the Necromancer's mouth.

"The pain!"

Then Dakarreth let go of the Stone.

The blackened husk of the Necromancer's body fell back, then vanished beyond the boundaries of the sphere. Within, the flames tossed Travis like molten waves. It was too late to think of letting go of the Stone. His arm had been charred to nothing. Travis felt his flesh, his bones—everything he was and ever had been—burn away.

Tome had said Krondisar possessed the power to transform those who had the key. But if that was so, what would he become? Anything at all? Then, with his last, flickering thoughts, Travis understood. Deirdre's words, spoken what seemed so long ago in the Mine Shaft, whispered once more in his mind.

In the end, we must each choose what we become.

Travis pictured Dakarreth, who had wished to be a god. And he thought of the dragon, who was a monster. Then one last image came to him, of a tall man with fair hair and a smile like the new light of dawn.

Travis made his choice. He was neither god nor monster; he was simply a man. The last shreds of his being burned away, and there was only . . .

. . . light.

Travis blinked. The light came closer: soft, blue, and cool.

A coppery voice spoke. "Does he . . . ?"

"Yes," a smokier voice said as gentle fingers touched his throat. "He lives."

"He's shivering," another voice—this one deep and musical—said.

Only as this voice spoke did Travis realize he was terribly cold. A cloak was draped over his body. The cloth hurt—it felt coarse and rough against his soft, naked skin—but he clutched it around himself anyway.

"Travis?"

Hands helped him sit up.

"Travis, can you hear me?"

A face came into focus before him, and he smiled. "Grace."

She smiled back, then threw her arms around him. "I thought we had lost you."

"I think maybe you did," he murmured, then returned her embrace with strong, new arms.

Falken and Durge were there then, and they lifted him to his feet. The bard grinned. "You needed a shave, Travis, but this is taking things to extremes."

Travis ran a hand over his bald head and the smooth line of his jaw. Everything—hair, beard, eyebrows—was gone. Only his spectacles, along with the rune of hope and the pouch with the silver half-coin, had somehow survived the flames. Everywhere Travis's skin was as pink and fresh as that of a newborn baby. But maybe, in some ways, he *was* a baby. He took a step forward, certain he had never walked on these legs before.

He looked down and saw a charred, vaguely human husk. Smoke still rose from the twisted form.

"You were right, Grace. Dakarreth was afraid of becoming what he really wanted—afraid of being transformed. In the end, he turned away from the fire."

"But you didn't, Travis. You weren't afraid."

Except I was, Grace. I was so incredibly afraid. I just didn't let go. However, he only smiled.

Falken helped Melia approach with halting steps. The lady gazed at the remains of the Necromancer. Tears streamed down her cheeks, but she said nothing.

"What of the *krondrim*?" Lirith said, rubbing her throat as she approached the tower wall.

Durge peered into the gloom. "The fires are burning out now. I think perhaps they fell when their master did."

Falken nodded. "You're right, Durge. It was through Dakarreth that the Burning Plague came. When he ceased, so did the *krondrim*."

Travis sighed. A breeze caressed his face, and he turned to the east. Light glowed on the horizon, warm and golden. Dawn. True dawn.

A small form moved past Grace, padding on bare feet to stand before Travis. The wind blew fiery hair from her face. He smiled, gazing down into placid eyes: one beautiful, the other drooping beneath a half-melted lid.

Tira held out her small hands. "Krondisar," she said.

Startled, Travis glanced at Grace. Her own eyes were wide. He looked at Melia and Falken, but they stared at the child as well. Kneeling, he gazed again into Tira's serene face. He held out his hand, and only then did he see that he still gripped Krondisar. One by one he uncurled his fingers. The Stone of Fire gleamed dully on the palm of his hand, quiescent now.

Grace started forward. "Tira—no!"

The girl laughed, then reached out and picked up the Stone in both her small hands.

It did not burn her. Instead, Krondisar pulsed with ruby light. As Travis had seen once before, a shimmering corona danced along the outlines of Tira's body, as red as the Stone. Only this time he knew all of them could see it.

Durge gripped Grace's arm, holding her back. "No, my lady. You must not touch her."

Grace nodded, and when Durge released her she did not move, but she gazed at Tira, her face stricken.

Tira smiled up at Travis, then she turned toward Grace. "Krondisar," she said again. A light throbbed beneath her shift, in the center of her chest, in time with the pulsing of the Stone. Then the light expanded, until Tira's entire body shone.

Lirith gasped. "What's happening to her?"

"I'm not sure," Falken said.

"I am," Melia said. The lady stepped forward, stronger now that the Stone was no longer being wielded against her. She knelt before the child. "Welcome, sister."

Tira pressed a small hand to Melia's cheek. Then the girl's feet left stone as she rose into the air.

"No!" Grace cried, reaching upward.

However, she was far too slow. Tira's tiny body shone brightly until they could no longer see the girl, only a bright spark of light. The spark soared skyward, faster and faster, until it reached the other stars shimmering in the predawn sky—then hung there among them. The new star glimmered gently, as clear as a ruby in the eastern sky.

"Behold," Melia said softly, "a goddess is born."

80

Grace watched fire break over the horizon as a new dawn came to Eldh. A fresh morning wind blew over the lake, whisking away the dark smoke of night.

"Who was she?" Lirith said, gazing at the ruby star that hung low in the sky.

Falken stood beside the witch. "I'm not sure we'll ever know. I think she really was just a girl—probably from a village in western Perridon—until she stumbled upon the valley of the temple somehow and found Mindroth."

"No," Melia said quietly. "It was Mindroth who found her, and who led her to the temple. That much I was able to glimpse. And it was for this reason that he raised her there, to make her a goddess, that she might protect Krondisar. Except Dakarreth came before her transformation could be completed."

Falken laid a hand on her shoulder. "It's been completed now, Melia."

The lady sighed, only it was not a sound of sadness, but rather of mystery. She turned her amber gaze to the sky. "I hope we'll be able to learn more of you soon, little sister."

Durge cleared his throat. "Now that Krondisar is a star again, will the Burning Plague return?"

Melia shook her head. "No, dear. The plague is over. On this world. And on the other."

She glanced at Travis, and he nodded, his gray eyes thoughtful behind his spectacles.

The wind dried the tears on Grace's cheeks, but it could not blow away the hurt in her heart. "I'll miss her," she whispered.

Just above the horizon, the ruby star of the east faded and was lost in the gold light of the fresh-born day. But it would be there again that night, and the next, and every night after. And each time Grace gazed at the star, she would remember.

Lirith wrapped slender arms around her shoulders, and Durge stepped near.

"You always have us, my lady," the Embarran said in his rumbling voice.

Despite her tears, Grace could only smile. "Yes, I suppose I do."

She leaned against Lirith, then reached out to grip Durge's hand, drawing him in close. However, as she did, Lirith pulled away, turning her back. Durge stared at the witch, his brown eyes intent. What was wrong? Had something passed between the two on their journey into the Barrens?

A high, clear voice drove the thought from Grace's mind.

"I see that Dakarreth is no more."

They turned to see a slight form in black step from the top of the stairway and approach. Falken bowed low and Melia curtsied, then the others remembered themselves and did the same.

"Rise," Queen Inara said. "The saviors of the Dominion need not bow before me."

Grace straightened, then gazed at the queen of Perridon. Inara had removed her black veil, and now her pale hair tumbled free around the oval of her childlike face.

Inara nodded in response to Grace's look. "Yes, I have removed my veil. The time for mourning is over. Now is the time for healing Perridon in the name of my son."

Despite the softness of Queen Inara's visage, her eyes glinted with a keen wisdom beyond her years. Grace knew the young woman would face many intrigues and perils as she worked to cement her son's claim to the throne of Perridon. All the same, she knew that Inara would succeed.

The queen gazed at the shriveled husk that had once housed Dakarreth's fire. "I see that much has happened." Her gaze rose to Melia and Falken. "More perhaps than I can fathom. But that must wait until later. You must come with me now."

Travis stepped forward. "What is it, Your Majesty?"

But Grace already knew what Inara would say, and by his face Travis did as well.

"We have found your companion, Sir Beltan," the queen said. "He is not . . . well. The Lady Aryn is with him. If you wish to speak to him, I suggest you come quickly."

Grace knew well the meaning of those words. Beltan was dying. She met Inara's eyes. "Take us, Your Majesty."

Minutes later they stepped into the warm, steam-filled catacombs of Spardis's baths. Grace breathed in moist, soothing air. Then the steam parted before them, and for a moment her breath ceased.

Beltan seemed almost peaceful as he lay on his back on the marble bench, his face turned to one side, his eyes shut. He was naked save for a short kilt around his waist. One arm draped to the floor, while the other was folded over his chest. It almost seemed he was sleeping. However, the illusion was shattered by the river of crimson that flowed from his side, over the bench, and onto the mosaic floor.

Melia gasped, and Falken held her tight as they approached.

Aryn was kneeling beside the knight. As they drew near she looked up, her face wet not only with the steam. "I tried, Grace. I tried so hard. But I just can't do it, I can't bind his thread to the Weirding. Not like . . ."

The baroness clamped her mouth shut, but Grace knew what the young woman had been about to say.

Not like you could, Grace.

Weeping openly, Aryn leaned on the bench, bowing her head over Beltan's. Lirith glanced at Durge, but the knight only stared forward. The witch shook her head, then moved to Aryn and helped the young woman gain her feet and move away.

Grace knew Travis was looking at her, but she didn't return his gaze. He didn't know—he *couldn't* know what he was about to ask her to do. Or did he? In that fleeting moment when she was able to speak to him across the Weirding, to tell him what she had glimpsed of Dakarreth, his presence had been right there with her . . . as had the shadow.

"Please, Grace," he said simply. "Heal him."

But I can't! she wanted to scream at him. *Don't you understand? I killed Garf, and I'll kill Beltan, too. Damn you, I can't do it!*

Instead she met his eyes and nodded. "I'll try."

Grace knew all of them were watching her as she moved to the bench, but she let them fade away into the steam. It was only she and Beltan.

Quickly she assessed his condition. He was breathing and his airway was clear. However, his pulse was weak and rapid. Tachycardia. The old wound in his side had been opened again: a gash eight inches long that pierced the peritoneum. She could close the wound, but he was in shock, and the blood loss was profound. His organs could already be shutting down. She needed to get him on a respirator, to get him stabilized so they could operate, and . . .

And what? This wasn't Denver Memorial, and the nearest intensive care unit was precisely a world away. There were no crash carts here, no respirators, and no means of artificial life support.

Except that wasn't true, and she knew it.

Connect him to your own thread, Grace. That's all you have to do—that will give you the time you need to take him somewhere you can repair the damage.

But she couldn't, and she knew that as well. To

connect herself to the Weirding was to go back through shadow. And doing that was to surrender herself unto it.

"I can't do it," she whispered.

Travis met her eyes. "I know, Grace." His voice was low, for their ears only. "I saw it when you spoke to me. I saw the shadow of the orphanage. And I'm so sorry. I'm so sorry for what they did to you there. But don't you see, Grace? If you don't do this, it means they've won."

Her heart fell to dust in her chest. "I think they did win, Travis."

He took her hands in his own. "No, I won't believe that, Grace. Not when I know how much life there is in you—not when I've seen it myself. You can still beat them."

Grace wanted to scream, or to wail, or to fall into his embrace. However, she could only kneel stiffly on the hard floor and stare at him.

Travis drew a deep breath, then he spoke in a voice both gentle and unrelenting. "Melia told me that you can't keep your power hidden forever. She was right. And this is your power, Grace—the thing you can't hide from. It's like the Stone. You've got to let it burn you to get past it."

His words made her feel like vomiting. "But if I do that, I'll lose myself."

To her shock, Travis smiled. "No, Grace. That's when you'll find yourself."

Grace shut her eyes, and for a moment she remembered a sun-drenched garden.

I don't think I could do it, she had said.

The old woman, her skin as thin and delicate as the petals of a flower, had smiled.

Yes you could, sweet. You just have to decide to give yourself up for another—to sacrifice everything with abandon.

Grace opened her eyes. "Help me."

Travis grinned at her.

She took his hand and laid it over Beltan's wound, then pressed her hand on top. Taking a breath, she shut her eyes, and in an instant she saw it: the shimmering threads that bound all of them together. Quickly she found Beltan's thread. It was dim and so terribly slender. Once again she saw the shadow attached to it; the blot seemed larger, and closer, but she couldn't think about that. There wasn't much time.

She found Travis's thread, strong and bright, and tried to connect Beltan's to it. Both slipped through her glowing fingers. It wouldn't work—she couldn't connect them, not directly. First she had to bind them to a common thread. Even as she thought this, it shone before her: the green-gold strand of her own life. She hesitated, then she reached out and grasped it.

The shadow was there, shocking in its speed and monstrous size. Burnt doors flapped like wings, and broken windows stared like blind, accusing eyes. Her thread led directly toward the heart of the darkness.

This time Grace did not pull away. Instead, she followed her strand into the shadow. Memories flew through the darkness like pale owls, calling for her. Hands reached out, grasping her, holding her down. Something pressed against her face, soft yet cruel, smothering her. She shuddered as cold air touched naked flesh. First came sick pressure, then—in one stabbing jolt—pain: bright and shattering. Somewhere a door opened, and in that moment Grace remembered. Truly remembered.

The flood of memories nearly drowned her. There would be no denying them now that she had finally let herself remember—no ignoring her own wounds. But they could wait a little while more. She turned her back on the shadow.

The blot passed behind her—although it was not

gone, it would never really be gone now—and she passed into light. Again she saw Beltan's thread: the barest wisp of gossamer. She caught it in one hand, then found Travis's thread with the other. Then she brought them both close to her, and with a smile—

It's so simple, Doctor.

—she bound both strands to her own.

Grace's, Travis's, and Beltan's eyes all flew open at once.

A gasping breath rushed into Beltan's lungs, and he started to sit up. Travis caught his shoulders, supporting him, as Grace pressed him back down.

"Am I . . . alive?" the knight said in a hoarse voice.

Grace smiled and nodded as her tears fell upon his chest. "You stupid dope. You said you were going to take better care of yourself. You said you were sorry."

Despite the pain in his green eyes, Beltan grinned. "Just because I'm sorry doesn't mean I won't do it again."

Melia drew close, her amber eyes shining. "Is he healed?"

Grace sighed, then looked up at the lady and shook her head. "I've bought us some time, Melia. That's all. We've got to get him somewhere I can operate."

But where in a medieval castle could she do that?

"Travis. . . ."

Beltan's eyes were hazed again as he spoke. Travis eased him back down on the bench and leaned over.

"What is it, Beltan?"

The knight's voice was fainter now. "I don't think I've got much longer. So I just wanted to tell you something. I just wanted to tell you that I'm not sorry after all."

Travis shook his head. "I don't understand, Beltan. Not sorry for what?"

"For this."

The knight lifted his head and touched his blood-stained lips to Travis's own. Then Beltan fell back to the bench, and his eyes fluttered shut. Travis looked up, his gray eyes wide, his lips flecked with red.

Melia clasped a hand to her throat. "Is he . . . ?"

"No," Grace said. "He's not dead. But he will be soon if I don't do something. Only I don't have the tools here." She shook her head. "I need medicine now, not magic."

Travis gazed down at the unconscious knight. "I understand, Grace. Why he was so upset when I told him to get away from me after we fought Eriaun that first time. I was so hot—it was dangerous for him to touch me. And the roaring. I couldn't hear what he was saying. . . ."

Grace remembered the conversation between Beltan and Melia she had once overheard. "He loves you, Travis. That was what he was trying to tell you. He loves you more than his own life."

Travis looked up at Melia, and the lady nodded.

"Do you love him as well, dear?" she said softly. "*Can* you love him?"

Travis gazed again at the fallen knight. "I don't know. Yes, I think. Maybe—I'm not sure. But I've got to find out. You've got to save him, Grace."

She sighed. "If I could get him back to Denver Memorial, I could do it."

Melia glided closer. "Remember, dear. There is a way."

Both Grace and Travis stared at the regal woman, then they locked eyes.

Scant minutes later they were ready. Grace stood with Travis beside Beltan. They had wrapped the knight in Falken's cloak, and Travis wore Beltan's clothes, which Aryn had found at the entrance to the baths.

"You remember what to do?" Falken said, his faded blue eyes solemn.

Grace glanced at Travis, and he nodded.

"We'll both picture the hospital," she said.

Melia clasped her hands together. "Do be careful, dears."

Grace gripped the silver half-coin—the one Brother Cy had given her what seemed an age ago. Travis held the other half of the coin. Grace hoped the coin would indeed take them to Denver Memorial. She wasn't sure they would have much time once they got to Earth, that her magic would sustain Beltan for long. As they readied themselves for the journey, Travis had told her that runes did work on Earth, but they were not as strong as on Eldh. Would it be the same for the Weirding?

"May Sia watch over you," Lirith said.

The witch stood beside Aryn, holding the young woman's left hand in her own.

"We'll miss you," the baroness said, her blue eyes bright with sorrow.

Durge stood to one side. He had been silent as they readied themselves, and now Grace saw why. A tear rolled down one of his weathered cheeks.

She reached a hand toward him. "Oh, Durge. . . ."

"Come back to us, my lady," he said, a trembling note in his somber voice. "Whenever you may."

"We've got to go, Grace."

She met Travis's eyes. "Let's do it."

"You know," he said softly, "the dragon was wrong. Spardis was the Keep of Fire after all. But we didn't die here."

Grace sensed the shadow that lurked just behind her, never to be shut away again, and she laid a hand atop Travis's own, feeling his new, pink skin.

"No, the dragon was right," she murmured. "We did."

Travis said nothing. Instead he faced her, Beltan on the bench between them. Each rested one hand on the knight's chest, then with the others brought the two halves of the coin together.

"Let's go home, Grace."

And all shadows were banished as the world filled with silver light.

———

Here ends *The Keep of Fire*,
Book Two of *The Last Rune*.
The journeys of Travis, Grace,
and their companions will continue in
Book Three, *The Dark Remains*.

ABOUT THE AUTHOR

MARK ANTHONY learned to love both books and mountains during childhood summers spent in a Colorado ghost town. Later he was trained as a paleoanthropologist but along the way grew interested in a different sort of human evolution—the symbolic progress reflected in myth and the literature of the fantastic. He undertook this project to explore the idea that reason and wonder need not exist in conflict. Mark Anthony lives and writes in Colorado, where he is currently at work on *The Dark Remains,* the third book of *The Last Rune.* Fans of *The Last Rune* can visit the website at http://www.thelastrune.com.

Be sure not to miss

THE DARK REMAINS

the epic third novel of

THE LAST RUNE

by Mark Anthony

Travis Wilder and Grace Beckett have returned to modern Earth on a mission of mercy: to get medical help for the severely wounded Beltan, a knight from the otherworld of Eldh. But as Beltan lies unconscious in the ICU of a Denver hospital, a shadowy organization plots to kidnap him for use in its cruel experiments, while sinister forces of dark magic cross the boundary from Eldh in a murderous search for Travis and Grace.

Meanwhile, in Eldh itself, a young baroness, her witch companion, and their mortal and immortal friends journey to a dying city to confront a nameless evil that has begun to annihilate the gods.

Somehow Travis and Grace must save Beltan and themselves, and then make their way back to Eldh, for only in this realm of gods and monsters, myth and runecraft, can they hope to defeat a demonic enemy that can shatter time, devour space, and turn existence into nothingness.

On Sale in March 2001

wherever Bantam Spectra Books are sold.